FOR YOU, THE
A SPECIAL INV

<u>Come journey with</u>
<u>wildest frontiers of the heart</u>...

Diamond
Wildflower
Romance

<u>A breathtaking new line of</u>
<u>searing romance novels</u>

...where destiny meets desire
in the untamed fury of the
American West.

...where passionate men
and women dare to embrace their
boldest dreams.

...where the heated rapture
of love runs free and wild
as the wind!

She begged him to take her . . .

"Please take me. I'm afraid you won't come back," she whispered.

He stared into her tear-filled eyes and groaned as he watched her tongue come out to moisten her lower lip.

"Please take . . ."

Nick felt himself wavering. No. She couldn't go and that was that. Somehow he had to shut her up. He bent his head; his mouth, hard and commanding, fastened on hers. His lips stole her breath, swallowing her words.

She whimpered and sagged against him, her lips soft and sweet as honey.

In spite of his intentions, his kiss changed, exploding into a sensuous, passionate demand. He slid his hands down her body, caressing, exploring her velvety softness. . . . He shuddered, his passion rising to a white-hot flame.

COLORADO TEMPEST

MARY LOU RICH

DIAMOND BOOKS, NEW YORK

This book is a Diamond original edition, and has never been previously published.

COLORADO TEMPEST

A Diamond Book / published by arrangement with the author

PRINTING HISTORY
Diamond edition / October 1992

ISBN: 1-55773-799-1

Diamond Books are published by The Berkley Publishing Group, 200 Madison Avenue, New York, New York 10016. The name ''DIAMOND'' and its logo are trademarks belonging to Charter Communications, Inc.

PRINTED IN THE UNITED STATES OF AMERICA

10 9 8 7 6 5 4 3 2 1

This book is dedicated to

My husband, RAYMOND RICH,
my own very special hero

My grandson Jonathan O'Shell,
for being so patient

My critics and friends, Vella, Tallie, Joyce, Terry, Liz
and Sue, for the encouragement when I needed it and the
prods that kept me going. Thank you.

Oh! How many torments lie in the small circle of a wedding ring.
   —Colley Cibber, *Double Gallant,* Act I, Scene 2

COLORADO TEMPEST

CHAPTER

* 1 *

Canyon Springs, Colorado
August 1866

A LONG, SLENDER FINGER OF SUNLIGHT REACHED
out and jabbed Samantha Storm's aching eyes. She moaned
and turned her face away from the invading beam. Shivering
in the early-morning cold, she tugged at the blanket and
snuggled closer to the warmth at her side. "Umm," she murmured sleepily. Childlike, she nuzzled the smooth, hard
surface beneath her cheek, burrowing her face into the pliant
pillow. She frowned, rubbing her chin against the object.
*Why, it feels almost like a shoulder. A shoulder? Don't be
ridiculous. It can't be. I must be dreaming.* Intent on getting
a few more hours of sleep, she pushed the thought out of her
mind.

A soft masculine snore tickled the hair next to her ear.

Jerking her eyes open, Samantha gasped. It couldn't be.
She blinked in disbelief. But it was. Beside her, a bewhis-
kered, dark-haired man slept. Lips parted slightly, he snored
with obvious contentment.

Samantha bolted upright, staring at her slumbering companion. Eyes wide with fear, she opened her mouth to scream, but only a tiny squeak slid past her lips. She scooted away, feeling the edge of the bed an instant before she tumbled off onto the floor. Dusty, cold, rough wood met her bare buttocks. Bare? She looked down. Sunlight illuminated her totally naked body. ''Oh no!''

She sprang to her feet and grabbed her head with both hands. The room tilted crazily. She reached for the wall to steady herself. *Oh, my head hurts, and why am I so dizzy? And where are my clothes?* She peered through the gloom, searching for her black dress. It was nowhere in sight. In fact, she didn't see any of her belongings . . . anywhere. Looking for some way to save her modesty, she spied a gray wool blanket . . . draped over the man.

Snatching the end of the coverlet, she jerked it free and flung it around her shoulders. It scratched and smelled of mildew and old dust. Wrinkling her nose in distaste, she glanced toward the bed. She sucked in her breath, her eyes feeling too big for her face.

The lean, bronzed figure on the bed wore nothing more than a disturbed frown.

''Merciful heavens!'' Samantha clamped her hand over her mouth and stepped backward, coming to a stop with her bottom against the rough log wall.

The man shifted slightly, moving toward the warm spot she had vacated. He muttered, then exhaled with a loud snore.

She watched him, not daring to move, not daring to breathe, making sure he was still asleep. When the snores followed one upon another, she released a ragged sigh.

Frantically, she scrutinized the other side of the dank

one-room cabin, squinting to pierce the gloom. An ugly, black potbellied stove hulked in one corner; a rickety hand-hewn plank table and two chairs occupied the other. *Where am I? And how did I come to be here*—naked—*with him?* She raised her trembling hand to her brow. *My head hurts too bad to think.* She licked her dry lips. *My tongue tastes awful, and my mouth feels like I've been chewing cotton.*

Peering back at the bed, she studied the man's face. *Who is he? And how on earth did I come to be in his bed?* She had never been in bed with a man before in her life. She knew she would have remembered that. She'd never seen him before; she was sure of it.

Black hair, thick and wildly tousled, framed lean features that looked harsh even in sleep. Long, sooty lashes lay against deeply bronzed cheeks.

The new growth of a stiff dark beard shadowed the lower half of his face. Wide, powerful shoulders gleamed like polished mahogany against the worn feather tick. A fine sprinkling of silky black hairs darkened a chest that rose and fell steadily with his even breathing. Tight muscles rippled down the hard plane of his stomach to the prominent evidence of his gender.

Oh my! Heat flushed her cheeks. She looked away, searching the cabin for something to cover him. Not a single scrap of cloth, not even a gunnysack, lay anywhere in sight. She turned back.

He moved.

She froze in place. *What if he wakes up?* A chill ran along her backbone. She trembled at the thought. *I must get out of here!* Watching him, she edged toward the door.

He moaned and turned over, presenting her with his bare backside. A deep snore told her he was still asleep.

Faint with relief, Samantha took another cautious step backward. She groped behind her, closing her searching hand over the doorknob, then carefully turned and gave a slight pull. The rough-plank door careened inward with a loud screech. Samantha gasped, her gaze flying to the man.

He didn't move.

Her knees weak, she edged through the opening. When her feet finally touched the splintery plank porch, she reached out and slowly eased the door shut.

Trembling, she sagged against the wall and breathed a prayer of thankfulness. *Now to get away from this place.*

Clutching the blanket around her, she fled into the yard, paying scant notice to the sharp stones piercing her bare feet. She spun around, scrutinizing the surrounding area. No sign of habitation anywhere . . . except for the isolated shack, and by its state of disrepair it appeared to have been deserted for some time.

A cold wind whistled around the dwelling, rattling shingles on the dilapidated roof. A last weather-beaten shutter swung crazily by one hinge, struggling to detach itself and join others decaying on the pine-needled ground. Lofty pines moaned and swayed in a taunting dance. Snowcapped peaks loomed cold and inhospitable in the distance.

Samantha shivered and drew the blanket closer, feeling small and vulnerable in this savage, hostile land. Fighting back hysteria, she scanned the area again, more slowly this time. Hope leaped in her breast when she spied a narrow, rocky path leading off through the brush. She hurriedly followed the trail to its end—a broken rail fence encircling . . .

an empty corral. She bit her fist, choking back a sob. *No horse? Then how did I—did we—get here?*

Panic gripped her. She raced back toward the cabin, frantically searching the brush. "There must be a horse," she cried. But there was no sign of life, just a few scattered pines and some scrub brush butted against a steep forested hillside.

Halting, she planted her feet firmly on a mound of soft earth. She took a deep breath, forcing her racing heart to calm. "Damn." She stomped her foot stubbornly. "There *has* to be a horse."

Tiny shards of pain shot through her feet and legs. She stared down. "Ow!" A horde of red ants nettled her limbs. "Damn it!" She jumped back and dropped the blanket. Bending forward, she hysterically stamped her feet and viciously slapped at her tender flesh. "Damn! *Damn!*" With the last of the insects dispatched, she grabbed the blanket and flipped it angrily. Wrapping it tightly around her, she charged back to the front of the cabin.

Distraught, she slumped down beside a tree stump. The seriousness of her plight shook her all over again. She was naked, trapped in this horrible place, completely at the mercy of a strange man sleeping just a few yards away. *Dear God, what am I going to do?* Rubbing her stinging legs, she gave in to a torrent of hot tears. *What's happened to me? How did I get into this mess?* She drew her knees to her chest and hugged them close. A swirl of leaves blew around her. Her thoughts cascading like the stream from her eyes, she searched her memory for an explanation.

Was it only two months ago that she'd left school and returned home? June, and now it was almost September. Two months—it seemed like a lifetime.

She clenched her teeth. Two months of hell, with her dreams shattering like glass around her. She knew that the events of this time would always haunt her: her father's sudden death; the argument with her stepmother, Lucinda, and Lucinda's son, Matthew; and her own alleged illness. She trembled, remembering how they'd drugged her in order to force her to marry Matthew. The night of her escape—the night she had killed him—flashed into memory. Shuddering, she brought her hands to her eyes, trying to push the gruesome scene from her mind.

She raised her head. The law would be after her now. Visions of her face on wanted posters flashed before her. The law? Her eyes widened. Was the man inside a sheriff? Impossible. If he was, she'd have found herself in irons and on her way to jail, not naked in his bed and miles from nowhere. She rubbed her aching temples. *Why can't I remember?*

I was on my way to Billy's and . . . I do remember something. The stagecoach. She stared at chips of pine cones littering the ground. She'd been sick. She'd gotten off the stage and left in a wagon with a blond cowboy. Puzzled, she looked around. But where was he? Where was the wagon? Had he brought her here? She shook her head.

She sighed, frowning. The only thing she vaguely remembered was a strange dream. Candlelight. She'd been standing in candlelight and apparently not feeling very well. She'd leaned against a tall man for support. A funny little man spoke to her in a strange language. Someone had asked her name. A very strange dream indeed . . . but wait, there was something else—

A squirrel scolded angrily from a pine tree. Samantha jumped in fear but found she was still alone. She tightened her hands into fists of frustration and pressed them to her temples. *What was it I was about to remember?* It seemed important, but try as she might, the memory eluded her.

The wind whistled around her, irritating the bites on her legs. She lowered her hands, trying to close the gaps in the fabric and draw the tattered wool blanket over the wounds. It wouldn't reach. There wasn't enough of it. She shivered in the growing chill of the high, thin air.

Another blast of wind made her glance toward the cabin. She hesitated for a moment, then stood up. Pulling the blanket closer, she reeled forward. The shack swam dizzily before her eyes. A thousand devils pounded her head with every step. She was so thirsty—and she was freezing. Grabbing a porch post for support, she looked around for a well. *It must be in back.* She closed her eyes. *I don't recall seeing one, and I don't feel like hunting for it.*

Reluctantly she climbed the steps to the rickety front porch and crossed the splintery planks to the door. She reached out and closed her hand over the knob. With a gasp she jerked it back, shaking her head. *What am I thinking of? I can't go back in there.*

Stifling a sob, she found a place on the porch partially out of the wind and slumped to the floor, resting her back against the building. A tortoiseshell comb fell from her hair and slithered down the blanket. She retrieved it, then reached up and removed the rest of the pins. She shook her head, letting her waist-length hair tumble around her. It was a deep red gold, an unusual color she'd been told she'd inherited from her grandmother, a Spanish Gypsy. Samantha combed the heavy locks with her fingers and angrily twisted them into a tight knot on top of her head. She'd

wished she'd inherited something else from her ancestress—
the ability to see into the future.

The fierce wind edged its way under the ragged blanket,
prickling her flesh with icy fingers. Shivering, she pulled
the cover closer and stared again at the door. The picture of
the man stretched out on the bed flashed to mind, and a
different kind of tremor clawed up her spine. She didn't
know him. She didn't know where she was or how she got
here. But one thing was certain; she couldn't stay out in the
cold. She stood up and took a hesitant step forward. Taking
a deep breath, she closed her trembling hand around the
doorknob of the ramshackle building.

Nick McBride shuddered, turning away from the bright
midday sun streaming through the open window. "Awww!"
He raised a shaking hand and massaged his aching temples.
It didn't help. *I really must have tied one on last night.*

He eased one eye open and squinted at the shadowy
interior of the one-room shack. He glanced around, confused. He wasn't at the ranch, and he damn sure wasn't at
the Cheyenne camp. A grin tugged at the corner of his
mouth. Probably a good thing, too. His uncle Two Feathers
would have roasted him in that sweat lodge until he looked
like an overcooked side of beef. To Two Feathers everything Nick did was a personal insult to the tribe. Nick
sighed, thinking he'd had enough lectures on the evils of
alcohol to last a lifetime.

He opened the other eye, his gaze landing on a rough,
hand-hewn log table and two rickety chairs. Across from
those squatted a dirty potbellied stove. His brow creased
into a bewildered frown. *Well, if I'm not home, and I'm not
at the village, then where the hell am I?*

Nick shut his eyes and tried to think. He scratched his chin, where a heavy growth of whiskers told him that whatever'd happened had been at least two days ago. He kind of remembered having an argument with someone. But that wasn't unusual. Seemed like he was always arguing and fighting about something these days. Didn't even need an excuse anymore.

He ran his hand over his eyes as though to wipe away the fog clouding his mind. His thoughts drifted back to the ranch, his rumbling stomach reminding him of the argument he and Jake'd had at breakfast. He groaned, remembering his grandfather's words.

His face purple with rage, Jake had shaken his head, making his thick mane of silver hair stand on end. He'd looked like a grizzled old lion. "You boys got to stop this hell-raisin' and settle down," he'd shouted at Nick and Jeff, Nick's younger cousin. The old man had slammed his fist down on the table, rattling the dishes. "Yessir, I've had enough of it. It's high time you both got married!"

Jake'd shaken a finger at him. "Find some *goood* woman and settle down. I want to see some littl'uns around here before I reach the great divide." Jake'd taken a deep breath, picking up steam. "Nick, forget about Amanda. She's married, and good riddance, if you ask me. Never did care much for her, too narrow between the eyes," he'd muttered.

Lying in the bed, Nick's gaze idly traced the cobwebs across the cabin's ceiling. "Narrow between the eyes." Jake had talked about her like she was a damned horse. The hurt still too raw to ignore, Nick'd slammed the coffee cup down and stomped out the door.

Jake, his voice like a buzz saw, had chewed the air behind

him. "And do somethin' about that wild horse. He's been in that corral a month."

Looking around the strange shack, Nick snorted in disgust. *I'm glad Jake can't see me now, lying here buck naked. I don't even know where I am, and the horse is* still *in the damned corral.* "Owww!" Nick sat up and grabbed his aching head. Muttering, he peered through the gloom around him. "How in the hell did I get in such a mess? And where's my clothes? Can't even find my hat." He fell back, watching the feathers from holes in the worn feather tick float around him. He frowned, trying to retrace his movements of the last few days.

He'd ridden into Canyon Springs to get a hackamore for the horse. Jeff had followed with the wagon to get supplies. That's when Nick had seen Amanda and her new husband. His eyes narrowed as the anger surged back to confront him. That's when he'd gone to Molly's saloon to get a drink and cool off.

Nick absently flexed his fingers and winced at the pain. He rubbed his skinned, swollen knuckles, vaguely recalling the fight with a couple of cowhands. After Molly had thrown him out of the saloon, Jeff had helped him across the street to Ma Greene's Eatery.

He remembered eating a big steak and Jeff talking about the new saloon singer arriving on the stage, and about how it'd serve Jake and Amanda right if Nick married her.

"Married!" He bolted upright in the rustic bed. "God, no!" He peered through the gloom, searching the corners. "Whew!" *Jeff and his harebrained ideas. But what the hell am I doin' here stark naked? I couldn't have ridden out of town like this.* He shook his head. *Must be another of Jeff's pranks. Probably waiting for me to make a bigger fool out of myself.* He scowled. *Sometimes he's downright peculiar. But, damn it anyhow, this time he's gone too far.*

A sound on the porch outside penetrated Nick's thoughts. *Jeff! I'll just play possum, then I'll get even.* A vengeful smile on his face, he curled up, his backside to the door . . . and waited.

CHAPTER

* 2 *

FAKING A FAINT SNORE, NICK HEARD THE DOOR
open and close. Light footsteps crept softly across the floor,
paused, then took a step closer. Something gently bumped
the bed. He heard a sharp intake of breath.

His body uncoiled like a too tight spring. In one motion
he whirled over, grabbed his quarry, threw him on the bed,
and pounced on top of him. He doubled his right hand into
a fist. His left closed on his victim's throat. ''Now you'll get
it!'' He looked down. . . . It wasn't Jeff!

''Hellfire! A *woman*!'' Nick gaped into blazing green
eyes. A mad, *naked*, redheaded woman.

''Get off me, you snake!'' she screamed. She reached out
a slender hand and snatched at the end of a ragged blanket
lying on the bed.

Amazed, Nick jumped to the edge of the mattress.
Suddenly noticing his own bare state, he grabbed the other
end of the same bedcover.

The girl scrambled to her knees, trying to hold the blanket
up in front of her. ''Get away from me,'' she screamed,
tugging for control of the ragged covering.

12

"Well now, miss. I just cain't hardly do that—unless you want me to sit here in my altogether," Nick argued. He peered around him. "Damn, wish I had my hat."

Her green eyes narrowed. "Who are you? What am I doing here? And what have you done with my clothes?" she demanded, tossing her head to shake a lock of red-gold hair out of her eyes.

Fascinated, Nick watched a tortoiseshell hairpin, loosened by her movement, snake its way down her neck and come to rest on the rosy crest of her breast. In wonder he raised his hand as if to retrieve it.

"Don't you dare!"

Catching himself, he jerked his hand back.

She yanked at the blanket, her red hair tumbling wildly around her body. "Answer me, damn it!"

Nick grinned and shook his head. "I don't know. I can't remember." She reminded him of a kitten he'd found once, small and full of fight. He swore that if she'd been standing, she would have stomped her foot. He kept a tight hold on his end of the blanket while she tugged away at the other, making a flurry of feathers drift up from the ragged mattress.

One floated to a stop on her nose and she stuck out her lower lip to blow it away. Again she jerked at the tattered quilt. Another cloud of white rose and fell around them.

Nick chuckled, observing the feathers. "Looks like we're sittin' in a nest." *I can't believe I'm here with a girl, naked to my toes, fighting over a blanket.* When the image crossed his mind, he laughed.

Arching her eyebrows, the girl pulled away from him. "You must be demented."

"Sorry. Guess I've been around Jeff too long."

She stared at him, recognition dawning in her eyes. "Jeff?" She looked thoughtful for a moment, then shocked, then outraged. "Jeff McBride. Now I remember. *He's* the blond cowboy who took me off the stage."

Nick groaned. He couldn't remember a thing, but if *she* remembered his cousin, Nick knew he was in deep trouble. "Are you one of Molly's girls?" he asked hopefully. Damn. He wished he knew what happened.

"I don't know any Molly," she said, her eyes flashing. "Where am I? He said he was taking me to the ranch. Where is he? And where is my dress?"

Nick slid his legs over the edge of the bed and slowly stood up, keeping his end of the blanket covering his private parts. He held on to the rustic bedpost. His head felt like an overripe melon ready to burst. "Whew."

"Don't come any closer," she warned, her body tense.

"Calm down, little lady. I won't hurt you. I just need to see if I can find our clothes," Nick said slowly, softly, like he would to a skittish colt.

"Don't bother," she said. "I've already looked."

"Are you sure?"

"Of course I'm sure." She tossed her head. "Surely you don't think I'm running around like this because I like it!"

I like the way you're dressed just fine, Nick thought, giving her a lecherous smile.

When she glared at him, Nick chuckled and looked thoughtfully down at the mattress ticking. It was so full of holes it would probably fall apart if he tried to wrap it around him; besides, the way those feathers clung, he'd never get it emptied. He sighed. It'd be bad enough going back to the ranch naked. But he sure as hell didn't intend to show up lookin' like he'd slept in a chicken coop with feathers stickin' out all over him.

"Well, I'm gonna look again," Nick said. He yanked at the blanket, intending to take it with him.

"No, you don't!" she spat, digging her nails into his arm.

He jerked back, scowling down at the scratches she'd inflicted. "Sooner try to take a bone from a bobcat," he muttered. "Aw, hell! Keep the damned thing." Disgusted, he threw the blanket at her and stood up. Ignoring her shocked gasp, he stomped off across the room. *Who does she think she's foolin'? She's a saloon girl. She ain't seein' nothin' she ain't seen before.*

He searched every corner, hoping she had overlooked something. High on a shelf, he spotted a dusty, red clump. He took it down and shook it out. It was a pair of moth-eaten wool long johns. He measured them to his long frame. They barely covered his knees. *They'll have to do.* He turned his back to the girl and slipped them on.

He tugged the front together over his middle, but the back of them hung open, baring his bottom. The buttons were long gone, and it gapped open at the most awkward spots. *Hell, may as well run around naked.* He tore two narrow strips from the ragged sleeves and twisted them, then he used his finger to poke holes in the rear flap where the buttons used to be. Threading the strips through both sets of holes, he tied the rear end shut. He did the same with the lower front. But he could do nothing about the fact that the long johns were four sizes too small . . . or the large moth holes. *Shit. If I'm not a sight.* A nervous giggle drew his attention to the bed.

The girl sat wrapped in the blanket, one hand over her mouth, obviously enjoying his discomfort.

"What the hell is so damned funny?" he asked.

"Not a thing," she gasped. She clamped her mouth even tighter to smother her laughter.

He flushed crimson. *Damn woman, she's worse than Jeff.* Trying to silence her with an ineffective glare, he swung toward the door, catching his big toe on the leg of a chair. "Ow!" He grabbed his throbbing foot and hopped in circles. "Damnit!" He straightened, trying to regain his dignity, and hobbled out the door, slamming it on the choked laughter echoing behind him.

Ears burning, Nick tiptoed across the yard, cursing Jeff, women, and the sharp rocks beneath his tender feet. He paused to pick a sticker out of his foot and tried to get his bearings. "I've been wearing boots too long," he muttered, recalling boyhood years at the Cheyenne camp when he ran barefoot over all kinds of rough ground. He was glad Two Feathers couldn't see him. He'd never live this down.

He stared at the cabin, the way it leaned toward the north, and the steep hillside behind. It seemed familiar. He'd been here before, a long time ago. This was the line shack where that crazy old hermit used to live. The old man died two years ago last spring. It didn't look like anybody'd been here since.

He limped down the path to the corral. No sign of his horse, but surely Jeff wouldn't take it, too. *The spring.* If Scout was anywhere, he'd be there. He hobbled down an overgrown path, cursing the burrs. Nearing the spring, he whistled. Nick sighed, relieved when the pinto nickered and came out of the brush toward him. "Howdy, Scout." After giving the gelding a pat, he walked to a steep bluff, emerald with mosses and cascading fern falls.

Nick stuck his head under the trickling stream, letting the

ice-cold water clear his mind, then drank deep and long, savoring the sweet liquid.

Feeling better, he stood up and brushed his straight, black hair out of his eyes. He searched the brush for his gear. "Damn." No saddle, no bridle. He'd have to ride bareback. Taking hold of its mane, he leaped onto the mustang and headed back down the path.

He guided the horse over to the ramshackle corral, leaned out, and retrieved a length of rope dangling from a post. While he sat on the horse's back, fashioning a makeshift hackamore, he decided on a course of action.

He figured he was roughly ten miles from Canyon Springs. But he wasn't about to go there dressed—or undressed—like he was. He'd go straight to the ranch, murder Jeff, and . . . "Oh hell. What am I gonna do about her?"

He threw a disgusted glance toward the cabin. Well, she couldn't go with him. He only had one horse. Besides, she wouldn't be able to travel naked like that. He'd build a fire, make her as comfortable as he could, then leave. He rubbed his chin. She wouldn't like him going off without her. In fact she'd probably have a ring-tailed fit, but she'd be all right, he reasoned. The only problem was, he was a hard day's ride from the ranch, and she'd be alone here during that time. He frowned, then brightened. He wouldn't be gone that long. The horse was sturdy, and if he rode all night, he'd be able to send somebody back for her first thing in the morning. They could take her to Molly's, and he could forget the whole thing. His plan firmly outlined in his mind, he rode back to the shack.

When he entered the cabin, his arms loaded with wood, he heard a muffled curse coming from the area of the bed.

Turning in surprise, he saw the girl, one small fist full of feathers she'd ripped from the ticking, her eyes red and angry with tears.

"What in heck is the matter with you?" he asked.

"I—hic—th-ought you had left me," she whispered in her low husky voice.

"I wouldn't go without telling you first," he said. "I'll build a fire so you can get warm." He bent in front of the stove and made a spark under the wood with some flint rock he'd found on the table. He knelt there, staring at the flames until the fire was blazing. A small scraping noise made him turn to see the girl dragging one of the broken-down chairs across the room.

She placed it close to the stove. Perching gingerly on the edge of the seat, she gathered the blanket tightly around her. Her green eyes big in her small, white face, she stared intently at him.

Watching her, Nick shook his head. *She's gonna scream, holler, and have a wall-eyed fit when I tell her—I know that for a fact. Well, better get it over with.* He stood up and took a deep breath. "We can't stay here with no food or clothes. I've found my horse, so I'm gonna leave you here and head for the ranch. You've got a fire and enough wood so you'll be all right. I'll have to ride all night, but I'll send someone back for you in the morning." He'd run out of air and the last words came out as a hoarse whisper.

She flung herself at him. He staggered, amazed when her bare arms crept up to clutch desperately at his shoulders. He swallowed, noticing all but one end of the blanket had slipped unheeded to the floor, leaving her shapely backside bare to his gaze.

"Oh, please. You can't leave me here in this awful place. You have to take me with you," she sobbed.

Stunned by her reaction, Nick stared at her. Her eyebrows arched like the wings of a bird above long dark lashes spiked with her tears. She peered imploringly up at him. Her eyes, earlier the color of new spring grass, were now the deep emerald green of a bottomless pool. Hypnotized, he felt drawn into them. He gasped, drowning as the water closed over him.

A smudge of dirt dampened by her tears ran down one pale cheek. Helplessly, he reached down with a shaking finger and gently wiped away the spot. *Damn, I didn't think she'd cry.* Her skin, the color of cream, was like satin to his touch. Her nose, small and straight, sniffed above a trembling mouth. Full lips, red as an apple, tempted him to take a bite. "I can't take you," he croaked, hearing his voice crack like a green kid's. "I don't have a saddle, and you can't ride like that," he said, trying to reason with her. Just the thought of holding this naked armful next to him all the way to the ranch made him weak in the knees.

She clung to him, sobs shaking her body.

He raised his hand to pat her head, to comfort her like he would a child . . . but this was no child—this was all woman. His hand, clumsy in the attempt, brushed the one remaining tortoiseshell pin confining her hair. Pictures flashed through his mind, recalling the flight of the earlier pin. The image of its final resting place on the pink tip of her breast jolted through him like a lightning bolt. He grew warm and powerful against her stomach. Damn it, he couldn't let her rule him. Tears or not, she couldn't go. He gritted his teeth, struggling to regain control of his overheated body.

Jerking his hand away from her head, he hit the comb. It spun to the floor. He sucked in his breath, watching her untethered hair fall around her face. A heavy strand of silken red gold slid across his hand, caressing it. The rest tumbled in a shimmering cascade to her firm rounded hips. Lord, he hadn't bargained on this!

Her quivering fingers branded the back of his neck, sending rivers of fire down his spine. He trembled like an unbroken colt. The rosy tip of one of her full white breasts poked through a gaping hole in his wool underwear, searing his bare skin. Nick swayed, his breath coming thick and fast.

"Please take me. I'm afraid you won't come back," she whispered.

He stared into her tear-filled eyes and groaned as he watched her tongue come out to moisten her lower lip.

"Please take . . ."

Nick felt himself wavering. No. She couldn't go and that was that. Somehow he had to shut her up. He bent his head; his mouth, hard and commanding, fastened on hers. His lips stole her breath, swallowing her words.

She whimpered and sagged against him, her lips soft and sweet as honey.

In spite of his intentions, his kiss changed, exploding into a sensuous, passionate demand. He slid his hands down her body, caressing, exploring her velvety softness with his callused palms. He cupped her buttocks, pulling her fiercely, impatiently against his throbbing body.

Her lashes fluttered; her lips opened slightly, releasing a faint gasp.

He shuddered, his passion rising to a white-hot flame. He tangled his fingers in her hair, holding her immobile while his tongue plundered her mouth, tasting her sweet nectar.

The blood roared in his ears, desire blocking out all reason in his need to possess her. A deep, gnawing pain tore at his vitals. Ablaze with hunger, he lifted her, capturing her thighs between his. He trailed a hand down her flat stomach to stroke her silken golden triangle.

She trembled against his searching fingers.

He drew in a ragged breath, shaking with eager excitement. He had never wanted a woman so badly in his life. He released her love-swollen lips and reached down, sliding one arm under her long, shapely legs. Still bent, he turned toward the bed.

Her eyes flew open. She stiffened. "Nooo!" Jerking loose, she gave him a shove.

Nick's mouth dropped open. He rocked on his heels, clawing desperately at the air. But it was no use. He reeled backward, picking up speed. "Ohhhh—shit!" He jolted to a stop—his rear planted firmly on the hot wood stove. "Yeow!" he bellowed. He bolted upright, both hands clasping his branded backside. The cabin air filled with the odor of burned wool and singed flesh. Aghast, he gaped at her. "Damnit woman! What did you do that for?"

Eyes wide, she crouched naked on the floor behind the chair. She reached out one slender white arm and snatched at the edge of the blanket that lay just out of her reach. Finally grasping the edge with the tips of her fingers, she slowly eased it toward her.

Rubbing his sizzled bottom, Nick took a step forward, catching part of the tattered covering under his foot.

"Don't you touch me!" she screamed. Unable to retrieve the blanket, she wrapped her arms around her legs and pulled them close to her body.

Frowning, he took another step.

She looked up at him and raised a shaking hand. "Please, don't," she sobbed.

"Calm down, missy. I'd sooner tangle with a catamount." That was the truth, he thought ruefully. She sure knew how to cool a man off. Hell, he'd bet he had blisters. He gingerly crossed the floor and knelt beside her. She trembled when he reached out and gently touched a blotch on her leg. "What's this?"

She jerked her leg back, away from his hand. "I stepped in an anthill."

"Do they hurt?" he asked.

"Of course they hurt," she cried. "And they itch."

Nick closed his eyes. Gritting his teeth, he shook his head. *Damnation!* Now he'd have to take her with him. He couldn't leave her here like that. Those spots were swollen and hot. It'd be just like her to get blood poisoning. Sighing with disgust, he reached down and picked up the ragged blanket. "Stand up," he gold her.

"I will not," she said, holding her legs even tighter.

"Oh hell!" He shook the bedraggled cover at her. "I ain't gonna *rape* you."

Her green eyes flashing, she reached up and snatched the blanket from his hand. "Oh really? It certainly appeared that way to me."

"Believe me, lady. I don't want to even get near you," he roared.

"Ha! Then what was I doing in your bed this morning?" she asked. Glaring at him, she wrapped the coverlet tightly around her.

He stopped, dumbfounded. He couldn't answer. Hell, he didn't know she'd been in his bed. Too damn bad he couldn't remember. He turned to her again, explaining, slowly and distinctly saying each word. "I only want to measure the blanket on you so I can make a hole for your head to go through. There is no saddle. We have to ride bareback. If you're going with me, it needs to be longer in back so you'll have something to sit on."

"Oh," she said, getting to her feet. "Well, you don't need to talk to me like I'm simple." Raising her small chin, she turned her bare backside to him and haughtily dropped the blanket.

"Of all the contrary females, you'd take the prize," Nick bellowed, reaching down to snatch up the ragged cover. Clenching his teeth, he held it to her rigid body. He measured her slender neck. His hands shook with rage. It was all he could do to keep from strangling her.

CHAPTER

* 3 *

"OW!" SAMANTHA CRIED, HER BACKSIDE SLAM-ming against the backbone of the horse. "You didn't have to throw me on."

"How else did you intend to get there—fly?" he growled back, picking up the reins.

"Insufferable beast," she muttered, glaring down at the back of his head. Gripping a handful of mane, she fumed as he led the pinto down the path past the ramshackle corral.

Entering a patch of deep shade, he stopped the horse and came back to her side. "I expect you need a drink."

She nodded, watching him.

"Well, you'll have to settle for water," he said dryly. He raised his hands and fastened them around her waist, carefully lifting her down beside him. He stared at her with mocking, light gray eyes, then turned and pointed the way toward a steep bank of dripping, ice-coated fern.

Samantha hesitated, completely unnerved by the gentleness of his touch, especially since she'd expected to be yanked off the same way he'd thrown her on. Eyeing him warily, she walked toward the spring. She cupped her hands and brought the water to her mouth, drinking her fill. She splashed her face and hands and the hot bites on her legs. Shivering from the cold, she turned to see Nick watching.

"Come here a minute," he said, patting a large rock.

"Why?" she said, staying where she was.

"I want to put a mud poultice on your legs. It will draw the poison and help the itching."

While not fully trusting his motives, she took a seat on the boulder and watched him scoop up a handful of the thick goo. He knelt in front of her and lifted her leg, cupping her heel in one hand. With the other he smoothed the mud over the swollen blotches ending just above the knee.

Samantha swallowed, trying not to remember the caressing touch of his palm against her skin when he'd almost seduced her in the cabin. She jumped when he lowered her leg and lifted the other to begin the same ministrations.

"Did I hurt you?"

"No," she said, glancing into quicksilver eyes that sent her pulses racing. When he grinned, she quickly shifted her gaze, attempting to focus her attention on the treetops, on anything but the dark head bent so close to hers.

Finally, he finished and grasped her hands, pulling her to her feet. "Is that better?" he asked, without releasing her.

She nodded, trying in vain to stay the tremors running through her body.

"You're freezing," he said softly. Releasing her hands, he lapped the sides of the poncho more securely around her to protect her from the frigid wind.

Just when Samantha was afraid she might swoon, he turned and walked to the spring and washed his hands. Taking the time to get her emotions under control, she chided herself for being so foolish. Heavens, she'd acted like a silly schoolgirl mooning over the first man to kiss her. But she couldn't stop the lurch her heart gave when she looked up to find him by her side. Once again the strong hands closed around her waist and lifted her gently astride the docile pinto. Feeling the closeness of the masculine body settling himself behind her didn't help either.

The afternoon sun cast deep shadows on the land when Nick turned the horse off the rutted wagon road and followed a narrow trail down the mountain. Sitting astride in front of him, Samantha tried to suppress a shiver when the cold wind flapped the ends of the poncho against her bare thighs, but her chattering teeth gave her away.

"Scoot back and I'll try to keep you warm," he said.

She straightened, shaking her head. Another gust hit her. She hugged her arms against her as another chill racked her frame.

"Muley-headed female," he muttered. He wrapped his arms around her, pulling her back against his muscular chest.

She stiffened, then reluctantly relaxed, allowing her frozen body to siphon warmth from him while he shielded her from the cold. Just beginning to get warm, Samantha realized another problem. The rocking motion of the horse made her short, scratchy garment itch steadily up her backside. Mortified, she twisted, trying to tug the reluctant cover back under her. But her motions made matters worse. She felt her naked bottom rub the front of the man's thin wool underwear.

"Now what's the matter?" he asked with a sigh.

"It's the blanket. I need to fix it," she whispered.

"Oh," he said, pulling the pinto to a stop.

She leaned forward on the horse's neck, reached behind her, and grabbed the ends of the wayward poncho. She hastily tucked it under her. Trying to sit more firmly on the horse's back, she tightened her legs against its sides, hoping she could hold the crawling cover in place. To her dismay, before long she again felt the bare back of the animal under her naked hips. Too embarrassed to have him stop the horse again, she clenched her teeth and rode in painful silence. Finally, when the torture was more than she could bear, she again leaned forward and attempted to stuff it back under her.

He muttered, shifting his body stiffly away from hers.

Uneasy, she felt the tenseness build between them. Well, there was nothing she could do about it. *Damn, there it goes again! The blamed thing seems alive.* Flustered, she squirmed, trying to rearrange it—for what seemed like the fiftieth time.

The tall man gritted his teeth and groaned like he was in pain.

Uneasy, she turned her head and peered up at him.

Eyes dark as a storm cloud scowled ferociously down at her. "Woman, would you sit still?"

"I can't help it. The blanket won't stay put," she said. "I don't know what you're so mad about. It's *my* backside that's uncovered," she muttered. She tried to wrap the sides of the garment around her legs, but it wouldn't reach. The bites on her legs itched unbearably, and she reached down to scratch them. *Oh no! There it goes again!*

"Shit!" the man cursed, yanking the horse up.

"What's the matter?" she asked.

"Not a damn thing."

"Then why are we stopping?"

"I . . . the horse needs to cool off," he said.

Puzzled, she looked down at the horse. Leaning forward she ran her hand down his satiny neck. "He looks just fine to me. He isn't even breathing hard."

The man muttered something under his breath.

"Were you talking to me?" she asked. "I didn't hear you."

"Good," he said, taking a deep breath. "Maybe you'd like to get down and stretch your legs."

She smiled and shook her head. "I'm just fine."

"Well, I'm not," he said, sliding off the horse's back.

She watched his tall figure disappear into a grove of white-barked aspens. *He must be awfully warm-blooded,* she thought. *He doesn't appear to feel the cold.* Why, she'd even noticed beads of perspiration on his forehead. Her eyes widened. "Merciful heavens!" she gasped, suddenly realizing she was the cause.

She looked at the ground. Maybe she should get down, too. She sure wasn't as comfortable as she'd tried to make him believe. Stiff and sore, groaning in pain, she slid to the ground.

Giving the pinto a pat, she picked up the rope and led him toward a small grassy ravine next to the road. She loved horses. Being raised around them, she'd ridden before she could walk. She rested her head against his neck, breathing in the warm, musky aroma. The smell brought back pleasant memories of her early childhood.

The gelding, wanting attention, nuzzled her gently. She rubbed his velvet nose and scratched behind his ears. The animal wasn't anything like the proud Arabians they'd raised at Storm Haven. He was about the same size, but stouter, stronger, and more even-tempered. Nick had told her the horse was a mustang, an offspring of the breed left behind by early Spanish explorers.

While the horse grazed Samantha examined her surroundings, noticing the terrain had changed from the rocky barrens of the higher reaches to softer, greener slopes of dark, dense forests. Bright splotches of autumn orange and gold from oaks and aspens dotted the hillsides and canyons. Boulders, some large as houses, littered the red, dusty ground. She inhaled, breathing in air both ice cold and sharp with pine pitch. Even though it was breathtakingly beautiful, she thought the country was too lonely and wild for her.

A sudden gust of wind set the trees aflutter. It moaned like a lost soul through the tops of the pines. Uneasy, she moved closer to the horse. She looked for her companion, but he was nowhere in sight.

Nick McBride had to be the strangest man she'd ever met, although she hadn't met many, having been at school for so long. Sometimes he was almost stiffly polite and at others insufferably rude. Definitely a man of contradictions. Her hands fingered the short length of rope he'd tied around her waist, and she remembered the concern on his face when he'd lapped the blanket sides to protect her from the cold.

He wouldn't talk about himself, but he seemed very curious about her. So far she'd managed to evade his questions. She didn't intend to tell him anything until she found out what was going on. She had the oddest feeling he thought she was someone else. He'd mentioned someone named Molly, and a saloon . . . what this had to do with her, she couldn't imagine.

She recalled his cousin Jeff mentioning that he had come to take a redhead off the stage. She'd been sick and thirsty and he'd given her something in a bottle, spirits, amber-colored, that had burned her throat and taken her breath away. But that was all she remembered. Apparently Jeff had taken her to the cabin. Why he left her with Nick she didn't know, as Nick'd seemed surprised she was there. If they were kidnapping her, it couldn't have been for ransom. They didn't even know who she was. And why had Jeff taken their clothes and the saddle gear? It was all a mystery.

After she decided the two cowboys weren't from Billy's ranch, she thought they might be acting as agents for Lucinda. But she was sure her disguise as a widow in mourning had been effective, at least until the last stage stop—when she had lost her heavy veil to the whirlwind. She bit her lip, worried that someone would be hunting for her; either a sheriff, or worse . . . someone seeking vengeance for Matthew's death. She shuddered. She hadn't intended to kill him, but she wasn't sorry he was dead.

Whoever he was, she felt safer with Nick than she had at Storm Haven. If he intended to harm her, he would have done it when she'd pushed him and he'd landed on the stove. He'd been furious, but he hadn't hurt her.

He claimed he didn't remember how they came to be at the cabin, and incredible as it seemed, she believed him. She was sure the mystery had something to do with his cousin. When she'd mentioned Jeff's name, Nick'd glared at her so fiercely she'd been afraid to ask again. Even though he'd almost seduced her in the cabin, she didn't think he would force her against her will. She sighed, finding her situation most peculiar.

The horse jerked his head up, bringing Samantha out of her thoughts. Startled, she whirled to see Nick behind her, an odd look on his face.

''We'd better go. We need to travel as long as the light

holds.'' He picked up the reins and led the horse back to the narrow road. Grabbing the gelding's mane, he swung himself aboard and slid forward on the pinto's back.

"Where am I going to sit?" Samantha asked. Before, she'd been helped on first and had sat where he was now.

"I think it will be safer if you ride behind me," he said. "Take my hand and I'll help you up."

Samantha held out her hand, her brow creasing into a frown when he lifted her onto the horse. "Safer? Are we in danger?" she asked, peering anxiously around.

Not answering, he nudged the horse into a fast walk.

The country did look wild . . . untamed. Glad of his company, she put her arms around his waist to hold on. She marveled at the ripple of his muscles beneath her hands and drew comfort from his strength. Noticing the way he blocked the wind, she leaned against him, savoring his body heat. Well, she couldn't see much, but at least she was warmer.

She studied the back of his head. Black hair, straight and shiny as a raven's wing, hung low on his neck. Broad shoulders tapered to a narrow waist and lean hips. Riding close to him, she felt the taut muscles in his long legs moving easily with the horse. He rode like he'd been born in the saddle. *Nick McBride, desperado or gentleman, whoever you are, I could be in worse hands.*

Her hands flat against his ribs, she felt the hair on his chest where the underwear didn't cover it. Unconsciously, she trailed her fingers through it. It was smooth, silky, the skin underneath firm and warm.

Nick gasped, sucking in his breath.

What am I doing? Horrified, she jerked her hand back. The blanket, coming undone with the sudden movement, slapped her bare backside. She tilted toward him, raising her bottom to tuck the garment under once more.

He muttered and kicked the horse, startling the mustang into a bone-jarring trot.

Samantha leaned forward and locked her hands around his waist to keep from falling. The rough pace rubbed the gray blanket against her breasts, making the nipples stand out in rigid peaks. The sensitive tips pressed against the large moth holes of his garment, and even through the poncho she could feel the heat of his bare skin. She gasped, her thoughts racing back to the passionate embrace in the cabin.

Her breath came faster as another kind of warmth spread through her. His touch had kindled a fire in her very being, making her respond to his kisses with a passion she hadn't known she'd possessed. The power this man had over her wildly excited . . . and *frightened* her. Her heart raced just thinking about it. Thank goodness he'd pulled her hair when he bent to pick her up back at the cabin. The pain brought her back to her senses. A few minutes more and she couldn't have stopped him . . . nor would she have wanted to. These feelings were new, unfamiliar. She wasn't sure she could cope with them.

She peered up at the side of his face, at the long, lean jaw. He wasn't the handsomest man she'd ever seen, especially with the growth of beard. He reminded her of a panther she'd seen once in the bayou. He seemed wild, barely civilized, as if at any time he could revert back to something savage, primitive. Except for a few scars on his chest, his skin was smooth and tanned to a deep copper. In fact, he was tan all over. Her face grew warm when she remembered how he'd looked in bed when she had stolen the blanket. He was certainly very male.

He looked around at her, arching his eyebrows in a silent question.

Her cheeks flamed even hotter when her eyes met his. A slow knowing smile crossed his face, increasing her discomposure. Mortified, she tucked her head down. *Good heavens! It's almost as if he can read my thoughts.*

Chuckling, he turned his attention back to the horse.

Those eyes of his, a strange, deep gray, like flint, cut through you when he was angry, but shone quicksilver when he laughed. She would have to be on her guard against this man. He was a puzzle . . . and dangerous.

Oh, drat that blanket! The horse's back prickled her bare underside. Gritting her teeth in exasperation, she leaned against Nick once again to fix the straying garment. She detected the rapid beating of his heart as it drummed against her breast. Struggling to stay on the horse, she almost had the cover secure when Nick uttered a muffled curse and yanked the mustang to a stop. Off balance, she clutched at him to keep from tumbling off.

"We'll stop here for the night," he said gruffly.

Regaining her seat, she looked around, confused by his statement. "You said we were going to ride until dark."

"Damn it, woman, do you have to argue about everything? It's dark enough!" he hissed through clenched teeth. Throwing his leg over the horse's neck, he dropped the halter rope and jumped to the ground.

She jerked toward him, pain shooting through her head. "Ow!"

"What's wrong with you now?"

"My hair's caught in your underwear." Bending from

where she sat on the horse, she tugged frantically at the long wayward lock. The threadbare long johns stretched precariously from Nick's body. Samantha, afraid his underwear would part long before her hair did, released her hold. She stared down helplessly at him.

"Oh shit!" He glanced backward, tracing the strand of hair to where it was knotted in one of the rag fasteners on his rear flap. He reached up and lifted her down beside him, then turned his attention to the ensnared curl.

Her hair twisted and tangled like a silken snake in his unsteady grasp. She heard him take a deep breath, then another. He worked frantically, trying to get free. The more he tried, the more tangled it became. Finally, he threw up his hands and gave her a desperate look.

"Maybe if we untied it," Samantha suggested, motioning to the rag that held the garment together.

"Well, I can't do it," he said. His hands shook like he had the ague. She saw him clench them at his sides.

"Let me try." She slipped her fingers under the knot, touching his bare skin. He jumped, his muscles tensing as he pulled away from contact with her hand.

"Are my hands cold?" she asked.

"Yes—no!" He looked skyward and said something she didn't understand.

"What?" she asked.

"Nothing," he muttered, and closed his eyes.

She reached her other hand under the twist, attempting to hold the material steady when he squirmed away from the touch of her fingers. "You'll have to stand still," she said, plucking at the gnarled mass. But it was no use. They were shackled firmly together by the entangled coil.

"I'm afraid I can't undo it either." She sighed.

"Hellfire!" Nick groaned, grunting under his breath.

Mystified, Samantha peered up at him. "What kind of language is that?"

"Cheyenne," he said, gritting his teeth. "I'm an Indian, in case you haven't noticed."

"Oh, that's why you're so dark all over." The heat rushed to Samantha's cheeks, realizing too late what she had said. She clamped her hand over her mouth, covering it against any other telltale utterances. Fearful, she peeped up into his dusky face. What she'd heard about Indians certainly wasn't reassuring.

He smiled wickedly down at her. "Don't worry, I'm not going to scalp you, kitten. Just cut off a little of your hair. Bend down," he ordered.

Not going to scalp me? That thought had never occurred to her. Alarmed, her heart racing, she pulled away from him, until the tangled mass brought her up short.

"I only want to get a sharp rock to cut your hair. Besides," he said, grinning, "I'm only half-Indian and I try not to scare children."

She didn't know why he thought that the fact he was only half-Indian would reassure her. Doubtful, trying to calm her racing heart, she bent down so he could find a sharp rock.

Finding one that would suit his purpose, he straightened and pulled her toward him.

When the rest of his remark registered, Samantha glanced up into his lidded gray eyes and drew herself up to her full five feet four inches. "I am not a child. I'm eighteen," she said. "Almost."

"Lord, you're even younger than I thought." He took the rock and whacked at her hair, severing it more than a foot above the tangle. "Coup," he said, fingering the coiling lock dangling from his hip.

"Coup?" she asked. "What's that?"

"Indians count coup when they take a scalp. It's a kind of trophy."

"You didn't scalp me. You only cut off a lock of my hair. And you didn't need to remove so much," she protested, watching him wind the long curl around his hand.

Giving her a fierce look, he raised the sharp rock and took a menacing step toward her.

She backed away, her eyes widening in alarm.

He laughed and tossed the rock away. "Don't worry, baby. I won't hurt you."

"I'm not a baby," she said, stomping her foot. Placing her hands on her hips, she eyed him up and down. "Just how old are you . . . *Grandpa*?"

"Twenty-six and gettin' older by the minute." He sighed. "We'd better get settled." He pointed. "There's a creek over there, if you want to get a drink and freshen up. I'll get a fire started." Taking the horse's halter, he walked toward a small clearing surrounded by huge boulders and tall pines.

Samantha went in the direction he'd pointed and found a rushing stream bubbling musically among the rocks. Kneeling down, she cupped her hands and lifted the ice-cold water to her face, finding it sweet and refreshing. She swallowed it greedily. Her thirst satisfied, she washed her grimy face and hands and wiped them on the blanket. Gritting her teeth, she eased her bare feet into the creek and splashed the frigid liquid onto the ant bites. It cooled the heat and stilled the itching. She stepped back to dry ground and dried her feet with a clump of grass. Wincing, she ran her fingers through her tousled hair, trying to bring some semblance of order since the pins had fallen out long ago. Feeling better, she straightened her blanket and followed the trail to camp.

She saw Nick tossing wood onto a small blaze. When she approached, he glanced up and motioned to a flat rock bench he had fashioned. "Sit here by the fire and get warm. I'll be back in a minute."

Samantha watched him walk away, marveling at the way he moved so silently with the grace of a dancer. *An Indian, hmm.* She stared after him thoughtfully. Sitting on the seat he had made for her, she held out her hands to the fire, grateful for both the bench and the warmth.

A short time later he returned carrying two plump fish and some sturdy green sticks. Fascinated, she watched him hammer two of the forked sticks upright on the outer edge of the fire. He threaded the cleaned fish on a third one and placed it across the forks of the other two.

"How did you catch the fish?" she asked amazed, knowing he didn't have a pole or line.

"I just tickled them," he said.

"Tickled them?" she repeated doubtfully.

"Yes. You just reach down next to the bank, and when the fish swim up, you tickle them. They like it so much, you can just pick them out of the water." He flashed her an engaging grin.

She smiled back, not sure whether to believe him or not.

The fish bubbled and broiled over the open flame, sending a heavenly aroma into the air. Samantha inhaled and rubbed her rumbling stomach in anticipation of the feast. It had been a long time since her last meal.

When the fish were done, Nick deftly removed them from

the stick. He split one open, pulled out the bones, and placed the succulent chunks of meat on a clean flat stone. He picked it up and handed it to her.

"Thank you," Samantha said, taking her rustic meal. She picked up a portion of the pink flesh between her fingers and popped it into her mouth. "Um, it tastes wonderful. I've never eaten out like this before, except at picnics or barbecues, and I never attended many of those."

"This is the way the Cheyenne cook trout," Nick said.

She ate every tiny morsel then licked the savory juice off her fingertips. She flushed, raising her lashes to see Nick watching her.

"You must have been hungry," he said, gathering up the bones. He grinned when she nodded. He walked a short distance from camp and knelt. After scooping out a hole, he buried the bony remains under a mound of dirt.

Samantha glanced up at the fast-darkening sky. She walked once again to the stream and washed the remnants of the meal from her face and hands. After a quick trip to the bushes, she hurried back to camp.

Welcoming the fire's warmth, she sat on the rock bench and held out her icy hands. She heard Nick busy doing something in the brush a short distance away. When the sun slipped quickly down behind the canyon wall, darkness fell like a heavy velvet curtain, cloaking the area around them.

Whistling softly, Nick joined her at the fireside. "Where are you from?" he asked.

She frowned. "Uh, back east."

"Where back east?"

"Several different places," she said, trying to evade his questions without being rude.

"What's your name?"

Not wanting to tell him, Samantha glanced up. "Oh, look at that," she said, pointing to a falling star. "They look so close, you could almost reach out and touch them."

"That's because the air is so clear," he said. "There's another one."

They watched until after a while, feeling warm and sleepy, she yawned. "What do we do now?" she asked.

"We go to bed." He stood up, pointing toward a pile of pine boughs he'd arranged back from the fire.

"Oh." She looked at the narrow mattress. So that's what he'd been doing in the brush. She smiled, grateful that he'd thought of her comfort. "But where are you going to sleep?"

"There, with you," he said matter-of-factly. "It will be freezing cold tonight. Since there isn't enough downed wood to keep the fire going, we will have to share the blanket and our body heat."

Samantha stared at him. He couldn't be serious. Getting up, she wrapped the covering tightly around her. "What blanket are you referring to?" There was only one that she knew of and she was *wearing* it.

"That one," he answered, motioning to the one she hugged to her.

"Not on your life." Giving her head a toss, she whirled on her heel and stomped away. "Humph!" She should have known he wasn't thinking of *her* comfort. She peered around the area, spying a small cleared area between two rocks a short distance away. *That place is as good as any,* she thought. After kicking away a few small stones, she lay down, curling on her side. She squirmed, trying to get comfortable on the cold, hard ground. *Ouch. I've seen softer rocks,* she thought. She lifted her head, hearing the man call out something. "What?" she asked.

"I said, watch out for snakes."

"Hmmph," she muttered. "The only snake around here is the one by the fire. Wonder if he thinks *that* will get my blanket." She pulled the cover tighter. "I haven't seen a snake since I've been here; probably all froze to death." She curled into a ball and attempted to warm as much of herself as possible with the inadequate blanket. Trying to ignore the increasing cold, she sighed and closed her eyes.

Something stirred at the edge of the rocks.

What was that? Her eyes flew open. She lay motionless . . . holding her breath . . . listening. *There it is again.*

Something moved, slowly, rustling along the ground just a few feet from her.

She bolted upright, squinting into the dark. *Oh Lord. What if he* wasn't *joking?* Crouching on her knees, she heard it again, closer this time. *Well, I'm not going to stay around and find out.* Scrambling to her feet, she dashed back into camp, colliding with Nick in her haste.

"Whoa! Where are you going in such a hurry?" he asked, grabbing her by the shoulders.

"S-s-snakes!" she said, pointing a shaking finger back toward her bedsite.

"Oh?" He arched his brows. "Well, I'm going to bed. See you in the morning." He sauntered off into the night.

She sniffed, ignoring him. She stalked to the fire and sat down on the ground. "I'll spend the night right here," she said, tucking the blanket around her. Staring into the fire, she inhaled the pitchy fragrance of the burning pine wood. The flames danced and twisted, changing the colors of the smoldering coals from orange to red to violet. She curled next to the embers and watched a shooting star scatter diamond dust across the sky. Samantha, warm and comfortable, felt her eyelids begin to droop. "I'll be just fine here. I don't need Nick McBride . . . or his tree bed."

Starting as a low moan and increasing to a wavering crescendo, a long eerie howl rent the night air.

Samantha screamed and leaped from her place by the fire. The fine hairs rose on the back of her neck. Her eyes wide with terror, she searched the darkness, but the pine-bough bed was empty. *Where was he?* "Mr. McBride? Nick?"

"I'm over here," he answered from the edge of the trees.

She clasped her hand over her heart, relief flooding her. Giving the bushes a fearful glance, she sprinted toward his tall figure. "Did you hear it?" she asked, breathlessly clutching his sleeve. She stared in horror at the blackness of the surrounding night, expecting to see some ferocious beast leap out of the brush.

The sound came again, long and quavering on the night wind, louder and nearer this time. Others, more distant answered it.

"What is it?" she asked, moving without hesitation into Nick's open arms. Strong and safe, they closed around her and pulled her tightly to his bare chest. His skin felt warm and comforting against her cheek, and the even beat of his heart echoed against her ear.

He raised his hand and gently stroked her hair, soothing her like he would a child. "It's only a wolf, calling to the pack."

"Wolves? Pack? Merciful heavens? What kind of horrible place is this?" she cried, shivering against him.

Nick drew her even closer. He bent, brushing the top of her head with a gentle kiss.

She raised her lashes. Quicksilver eyes, bright as the night stars, stared into hers. She shivered again, but this time it was not from fear.

Lowering his head, he kissed her forehead, then each eyelid. His whiskers caressed her cheek. After a faint touch at the end of her nose, his warm mouth moved down to claim her trembling lips.

Her heart leaped at his touch and her lips throbbed against his. Suddenly more afraid of her emotions than of the beasts, she pulled back. "Nick?"

"Hmm?" He dreamily gazed into her eyes. He sighed. "Don't worry, little one. You're safe." Carefully, gently, he bent and lifted her into his arms.

She snuggled against him, her arms around his neck, her head on his shoulder. Feeling protected, warm, and happy, she made no protest when he carried her through the darkness toward the fragrant pine bed.

CHAPTER

* 4 *

THE LONE WOLF HOWLED, CALLING FORLORNLY to the pack. The sound rose in a mournful crescendo, trailing to die on the cold night wind.

Carrying the girl through the darkness, Nick felt her shudder. Her trembling hand tightened on his neck. He crushed a twinge of guilt, remembering the trick he'd played on her. *Damn it, she was too stubborn for her own good. She would have frozen to death over there all by herself.*

A suppressed smile twitching the corners of his mouth, he recalled the lessons he'd learned during his childhood at the Cheyenne village. He still made a pretty convincing wolf, if he did say so himself. Sheer luck made the pack answer his call. Feeling ornery, he'd made up the part about the snake. He'd almost laughed out loud seeing her face when she'd run back into camp. She'd probably heard a mouse, or at worst a raccoon. He hugged her closer, feeling sorry for scaring her like that. She felt so small and light in his arms.

Unable to help himself, he bent his head and kissed the top of her tousled head. Somehow she seemed innocent, vulnerable. The longer he was around her, the more uncertain he became that she really could be Molly's new singer . . . if she was, she was also a damn good actress.

Unanswered questions hummed in his head. *What happened at the cabin? Did I make love to her? She'd said she had woke up in my bed. Damn! Why can't I remember?*

He stopped in his tracks when even worse answers hit him. Maybe she was innocent . . . somebody's daughter, or sister . . . or wife? Beads of perspiration popped out on his forehead in spite of the cold. He shuddered. Hellfire! He'd be lucky if he didn't get hung or shot full of holes over this mess.

"Nick? What's wrong? Are the wolves here?" she asked, her voice quavering, her eyes wide and fearful.

Feeling lower than a snake's belly, he answered, "No, kitten, it's all right. I'll take care of you." His mouth formed a grim line. *That* was a promise he intended to keep.

Reaching the pine pallet, he knelt and lowered the girl. His hands shaking, he removed the rope belt from her waist and laid it aside. He swallowed, slowly lifting the poncho over her head, releasing the sweet woman smell of her. His heart walloped his chest like a sledgehammer. He tried to turn away—to concentrate on untangling the ragged blanket, but found he couldn't move.

Her eyes big, she stared up at him. Her hair, shimmering like a silken waterfall, tumbled around her body, curling around the tip of one naked breast.

Damn, why did she have to look so trusting? His throat squeezed shut. He fought for air. He'd had lots of women— pretty women—come running to be in his bed, but none of them had ever affected—or confused—him like this. He didn't like the feeling either. Before, if he'd wanted to make love to a woman, he made love to her. He'd never had any complaints yet. But the other women hadn't looked so damned innocent either.

The full autumn moon tangled in the treetops, kissing her all over with falling silver beams, clothing her whole body in a shining radiance. Nick gaped in openmouthed wonder. *Lord, she looks like an angel.*

Trembling beneath his gaze, she drew back from him and crossed her arms over her bare breasts.

Battling his lecherous body, Nick snatched up the blanket and spread it lengthwise, quickly wrapping it around her. Shaken to his core, he understood what Adam went through in the Garden of Eden. Poor fool, he hadn't had a chance.

With a shaky sigh he stretched out beside her, trying to get his mind off the tempting curves that tensed at the nearness of his body. He cursed himself for his lust, thinking he was no better than a rutting bull. He'd promised to protect her . . . but he knew the only thing she was in danger from—was him.

When exhaustion overcame her fear, she slumped against him and drifted off to sleep. He pulled her closer, making sure she was covered by the skimpy blanket. She sighed, cuddling next to him like a drowsy kitten. Satisfied she was warm enough, he stared up at the night sky and reflected on the uselessness of his life. It was well past midnight when he finally felt the pull of sleep.

Nick struggled, being drawn into, ensnared, in a silken net of red-gold hair. Like a fly in a spiderweb, he fought to be free. But instead he found himself bound tighter and tighter by a bewitching temptress who coaxed and teased him ever closer. Unable to resist the temptation, he reached out and drew her to him by the golden strands. His chest branded by the heat of her naked body, he kissed her full red lips, savoring their forbidden sweetness.

She taunted him with eyes like pools of emerald water. Twining her arms around his neck, she pressed against him, inviting his caress. Pale twin globes swelled beneath his questing hands, their buds rising firm and hot under his fingertips. He bent his head, his lips brushing each peak, his tongue lapping at the quivering tips, until she moaned with desire. He blazed a molten trail down her belly, discovering every satiny inch of her pliant flesh.

When his mouth again traveled up to cover her own, she kissed him hungrily, wantonly, her passion matching his own. She twisted and turned, arching her body in a frenzy to meet his. His fingers sought her pulsing velvet passage. Pulling at the silken curls, he massaged the satin hill until she was warm and moist where he touched her.

His gut tightened into a knot, fiery and churning. When he raised himself above her, she held up her arms in protest, crying out at his desertion. Swiftly, he reached down to where he throbbed against her flat stomach and freed himself from the constricting bonds of his clothing.

She moaned as he covered her again, spreading her creamy thighs, his fingers opening her molten core. Like a lance, he drove straight and true through a satin curtain to the very heart of her. She uttered one surprised, strangled cry before he covered her mouth with his own. She struggled frantically, becoming the captive. She lay impaled beneath him, her arms fluttering like the wings of a trapped bird.

Motionless on top of her writhing body, he pillaged her mouth with his tongue. Slowly, he began to move in her, deliberately coaxing her with knowing hands, until her arms ceased to push against his chest and crept up to wind themselves around his neck. He plunged in her, thrusting upward, faster and faster until she raised herself to meet his onslaught. A whirlwind of emotion stormed his body. His loins churned, building to a thundering peak, before he erupted in an all-consuming blaze. With a fierce wild cry of victory he possessed her, claimed her, made her his own.

Nick woke bathed in sweat. Hot with desire, he throbbed with urgency against the confining underwear. In the faint pink light of dawn, his gaze took in the sleeping female shape beside him. *Damnation, it was a dream! And here I am hard as a fence post.* Still dazed by his fantasy, he stared at her, reliving the illusion.

The girl slept on her side, facing him. Her cheek rested on one slender arm stretched over her head. Her other arm lay over his chest, her fingers gently curved on the side of his neck. A shining curtain of firelit hair spread around her, grazing the side of his face. The gray blanket covered only her backside, leaving the rest of her pale and naked to his view.

The satin globe of one breast rested warm and full on the leathery surface of his open palm. He cupped his hand under it, brushing the delicate pink bud with his thumb. He sucked in his breath, watching its pebbled surface grow taut and eager. She tossed her head and moaned, her sooty lashes fluttering on ivory cheeks.

He studied her face for a moment, then leaned forward and gently kissed the pout from her mouth. She sighed, moistening her lips with her small pink tongue.

He traced the outline of her jaw with his fingertip, following the dimple in her chin to her full red lips. When she frowned and her mouth opened slightly, he kissed her again, slowly, teasingly, his tongue darting in and out. He pulled her closer, enveloping her against his tense body, his kiss becoming more urgent. He massaged her soft curves persuasively, roaming her breasts, her hips, her thighs, until her body sprang taut, responding to his every touch.

Startled green eyes flew open to stare into his.

Kissing her again, he murmured close to one small ear while he hypnotized her with his eyes. "Come on, kitten, relax. You'll enjoy it." His mouth nuzzled hers again, coaxing her into submission.

Her eyes narrowed. Uttering a snarl of pure rage, she raised her head and fastened flashing white teeth on his lower lip.

"Yeow!" Pain tore through him. He yanked his head back, ripping free from the snapping female. He licked his lips, tasting a salty, metallic tang. His face contorted, his body aching, he reached for her, determined to finish what he'd begun. "Damn you woma—"

Her clenched fist struck with the speed of a rattler.

Flustered, he scrambled to his knees over her. His hands flew to cover his injured eye.

Quicker than hot grease on a griddle, she slid from beneath him. Still on her back, she raised one foot and gave a powerful kick. "Get off me, you stinking goat!"

He rolled away from her, holding his groin. He gagged, black swells of nausea riding through his body. "Damned little bitch!" He struggled to his feet. Shaking a fist in blind fury, he staggered toward her.

"Randy bastard!" she hissed through clenched teeth. Her green eyes flashing, she stood at the edge of the pine bed, glaring at him. "You'd seduce your own mother."

He stalked toward her. "Well, you sure as hell *ain't my mother!*" He took another step, opening and closing his fists. Seduce her? Hell, the way she'd kissed him back, she practically seduced him! Another wave of pain shot through his lower region. He fell to his knees. *Oh God, she's ruined me for life.*

She faced him, bare to her toes, her face prim as a schoolmarm's.

"What you need is a good spanking!" he roared.

"You touch me, and you'll wish you hadn't!" She bent to the ground and scooped up a rock in each hand.

"You wouldn't dare!" he snarled, getting to his feet.

Holding a stone big as his palm, she drew her hand back, "Oh, wouldn't I?"

He ducked, feeling a whiff of air as the missile flew past his ear. "Ha! You missed," he taunted. He straightened only to see her let fly with another before he could move.

"I don't think so."

The rock thumped him soundly, bounding off his skull. Shards of pain splintered through his head making it ring. "Now you've done it," he bellowed. Nostrils flaring, reason gone, he charged forward.

Before he could reach her, she bent and snatched up the rope and ragged blanket. After giving him one last scathing glance, she spun on her heel and darted off into the woods as nimbly as a startled doe.

Groaning, Nick clutched his sore head where a knot already swelled under his hands. "Damn, I ain't never seen such carryings-on over a few kisses." His lower region in agony, he staggered toward the stream to doctor his wounds and clear his mind in the frigid water.

He knelt at the creekside and scooped up the icy liquid.

Parting his hair, he touched the growing lump. Something warm and sticky oozed over his hand. "Blood!" He gingerly traced the gash with his fingers. Bleeding like hell, but it didn't seem too deep. He'd had worse given to him . . . but not by a woman! "Damn your ornery hide!" he called, scowling in the direction of her retreat. *Can't imagine why I ever thought she was innocent . . . or helpless. She cusses like a muleskinner and is meaner than a rabid dog.*

He splashed the cold water on his head until the bleeding stopped, then did the same to his split lip. "Ow, that hurts—but looks like I won't bleed to death," he muttered, no longer seeing the pink stain in his palm.

Raising his hand, he cautiously poked at the flesh around his injured eye. "Damn, it's already swelling shut." He picked up a chilled rock from the stream bed and pressed it against the puffy skin. When the stone lost its frigid edge, he replaced it with another until he could feel the outline of his cheekbone beneath his fingers.

How could she have managed to do this to him? An itty-bitty thing like her, whipping him like a dog? And after all he'd done for her, too. *Little hellcat!* Groaning, Nick struggled to his feet. He stared back toward camp, uneasy despite his anger. *Where in the heck did she go?* Not that he was worried—anything she came up against was bound to get the worst end of the deal. But she didn't know the country. *She'll probably get lost . . . or get herself hurt.* He thought about the ant bites. Her legs were still hot and swollen. She'd get sick and die out here, and it would all be his fault. "Shit! Damned woman!"

His emotions torn, he stomped back to camp and whistled up the horse. When he eased the halter over the pinto's head, the gelding raised its velvet-brown eyes and gave him a reproachful look. "Aww, Scout, not you too?"

The mustang nudged him, then pranced about, eager to be on its way. "All right, let's go see if we can find the little wildcat," he muttered. Grasping the animal's mane, he eased himself carefully onto its back and turned his mount in the direction she had taken. Bending low over the pinto's neck, he searched for signs of her, hoping she'd have sense enough to stay on the main trail.

He rode slowly, scanning the ground. Nothing. He frowned. Pulling the horse to a stop, he spotted the imprint of one small bare heel in the dust. Sighing in relief and giving thanks for his Indian upbringing, he watched for any other telltale tracks. She'd kept to the edge of the trail, hiding her footprints among the leaves and pine needles. *Foxy little devil. Wonder where she learned that?* He kicked the horse to a faster gait, muffling the hoofbeats in the thick ground covering. He caught a quick movement from the corner of his eye. Glancing up, he saw her dart off the road and into the brush.

"All right, missy, go ahead and hide," he said softly. Slowing Scout to a lazy walk, he slouched on the pinto's back and began to whistle, like he hadn't a care in the world. *Damn, my lip hurts.* Continuing his tune, he neared the place where he'd last seen her, careful to keep his eyes on the road ahead. She'd have to come to him. He knew if he chased her, she'd just run again.

Nonchalant, gazing at the soft, puffy clouds overhead, he ambled past her. From the edge of his sight he saw her white face peeping out from behind a tree. After he was some distance down the road, he leaned forward and patted the horse's neck, sneaking a peek under his arm. His lips twisted in a satisfied smirk when he saw her reaction.

Once again dressed in the gray blanket, she stood in the middle of the road, legs apart, hands on her hips, watching him disappear from sight. He could almost feel her fury when she stomped one foot, making a puff of dust.

"Wait," she demanded.

Nick pretended he didn't hear. He clucked to Scout, urging him into a trot. *It won't hurt her none to worry and wonder for a while. Serves her right.* Besides, right now he didn't trust himself to have her riding that close to him. He might just be tempted to wring her neck. He'd mosey along and let her hoof it for a spell. She wouldn't get too far from the road, and walking a few miles might get some of the contrariness out of her. A smile of sweet revenge stretched across his face. He grimaced when the effort pulled his split lip.

A while later he pulled Scout to a stop where a tall snag leaned over the trail. Nick lifted his head and sniffed the air. He smiled. Yep, there it was. The unmistakable smell of sulfur mixed with the road dust and tangy pine. Reining the gelding off the road, Nick pointed him down a faint path overgrown with red-berried elder and thickets of choke-cherry. He made his way through the brilliant red foliage, entered a grassy clearing, and stopped. Mineral water bubbled noisily over a large moss-covered boulder, cascading into a deep, green pool.

Leaving Scout free to graze, Nick bent and untied the string fastenings on the front of his wool underwear. He stepped out of them and kicked the garment to one side. *If I ever get my own clothes back, I'll freeze to death before I ever wear another pair of them blamed things.* Scratching his various itches, he glared at the tattered suit, half expecting to see it crawl off on its own. When it didn't, he kicked it into a shallow puddle. After scrubbing it clean, he draped it over a large, sun-warmed rock to dry.

He walked to the end of a jutting fallen log and plunged into the small lake. It was bottomless and . . . *cold*! Sputtering, he rose to the surface. He swam and cavorted like an otter, allowing the healing waters to soothe his harassed body. His skin chilled and dotted with gooseflesh, he reluctantly climbed out and sprawled on a flat slab of granite.

Numb with cold, he climbed back into the still-damp wool long johns, appreciating the garment's warmth in spite of his earlier declaration. As he thought of the girl a lopsided grin crossed his face. He held up his arm and sniffed at the sleeve. "Well, I may be randy, but at least now I don't *smell* like a billy goat." Brushing his hair out of his eyes, he went to find Scout.

In a much better mood Nick rode back to the dusty red road. Spotting the girl sitting on a rock by the side of the trail, he turned the horse toward her dejected figure.

She glowered at him, her face streaked with mud and tears. She bent toward the foot she held in her lap.

"What's the matter?" he asked.

"Not that it's any of your business, but I stepped on a sharp rock," she said. "At least I think it was a rock."

Well, the walk hadn't improved her disposition any, Nick thought. He slid off the horse and ambled toward her.

"You're all wet," she said, eyeing his clinging garments. She wrinkled her nose. "What's that smell?"

"I went swimmin'."

"You left me and went swimming?"

"That's right, that's just what I did. Felt mighty good, too," he drawled, feeling self-righteous. *If she wants my help this time, by damn, she's going to have to ask for it.*

She let go of her foot and wiped her hand on the blanket, smearing a dark red stain across the faded gray surface. Her foot oozed scarlet from a deep gash.

Something bunched in Nick's middle. He bent toward her. "Damn it, your foot's bleedin'."

"Don't you think I know it? I'm not stupid."

"You were stupid enough to step on the rock." He knelt beside her and reached for her foot.

She jerked it away. "I don't need your help."

"Like hell you don't," he snapped.

She glared at him, both hands covering her bleeding foot, her mouth shut tight in a pout.

Fury shaking his body, he turned toward the mustang. "Of all the damn muley-headed females I've met, you're the worst!" He ran his hand through his hair and stomped back toward her. "Are you going to let me see your foot or not? If not, missy, you're on your own, and I'm gettin' the hell out of here!"

Dust-covered and bedraggled, she sat mute and defiant.

Infuriated when she didn't give in, Nick spun on his heel and leaped onto the horse. Gritting his teeth, he cursed her under his breath, his anger surging when she didn't say a word. He nudged the horse in the ribs . . . one hundred yards . . . two hundred yards . . . three hundred yards. Silence. *Now what the hell am I going to do? I can't beg her to let me help.* Cursing himself for seven kinds of fool, he lifted the reins, ready to turn the gelding, when he heard her.

"Wait."

"For what?" he said, looking at her over his shoulder.

"All right, you can look at my foot," she muttered.

"Well, whoop-de-do. Don't know if I care to."

"All right!" she shouted. "I need your help!"

"That's better." He wheeled the horse. Dismounting again, Nick gave an exasperated sigh and strolled toward her. He knelt and picked up the small foot, and gently examined the gash. It was deep and full of dirt, but at least the bleeding had slowed. "This will have to be washed out," he said, frowning.

Bending over, he scooped her up in his arms. His mouth tightened when she held herself rigidly away from him. Cursing, he tossed her onto the horse. Stonily silent, he picked up the halter and led Scout back toward the snag.

From her perch on the horse's back, Samantha glared down at the top of Nick's head. Her injured foot throbbed, but the pain did nothing to detract her anger. *Damn him for being an insensitive beast. Making me practically beg for his help.* Hot tears burned her eyelids. She stubbornly blinked them back, determined not to let them fall. She wouldn't give him the satisfaction of seeing her cry.

How could I ever have been attracted to him? It's apparent there's only one thing he's interested in . . . bedding me! She clenched her teeth. *How dare he treat me like a loose woman!* Her cheeks flushed with mortification as she remembered the way he'd kissed her. *The lecherous lout*! Last night, when she'd heard the snakes and wolves, she couldn't believe she'd run to him for protection. Heavens, she'd have been safer with the wolves! *The conceited ass! He seemed to think I should be thrilled to have him maul me. Well, I showed him a thing or two.* She sniffed. Good thing she'd remembered the stable master's lessons in self-defense.

Realizing she would never be able to outrun him, she knew enough to stay away while he was really angry. But judging by the look of him, she didn't think he would be giving her any more trouble. A satisfied smirk crossed her face when she noted the egg-sized lump on his head, the discolored eye, and the swollen lip. Served him right! And that kick had cooled his lust in a hurry. She noticed he still wasn't walking straight. Well, it was no more than he deserved for bullying a defenseless woman.

She frowned when he turned off the main road and followed a dim trail through the brush. "Stop!" she demanded. "Where are you taking me?"

Nick, his eyes like shards of dark granite, glared back at her. "Do you want me to take care of your foot or not?"

"Yes, but—"

"Then shut up and let me do it!" He jerked the horse's rope and stomped on down the path.

Samantha chewed nervously on her lower lip, uneasy at this turn of events. He could take her off in the brush and leave her—or even murder her. He seemed angry enough.

A peculiar smell made her sniff the air. They entered a clearing, and the sound of water drew her attention to a deep green pool. Relief flooded her. He only wants to wash my foot, she reasoned. But as she watched him her apprehension returned. Savage and tall, his figure still rigid with anger, he stalked toward the pond. She sucked in her breath. *Maybe he intends to drown me instead.*

He stopped the horse close to the edge and came back to stand below her. "Do you want my help?" he asked gruffly.

Still wary, she watched his eyes, trying to read his intentions. She found no comfort in what she saw in the slate-gray depths. "I'll get down by myself," she said, jumping down on her uninjured foot.

"Sit on that rock and soak your foot," he said. "After-ward I'll bandage it."

Samantha remained where she was until Nick walked away, then hobbled painfully to the pond. "Phew, it smells foul."

"It's a mineral spring. Would you hurry up?" he called out. "I'd like to get home sometime tonight."

"Well, I certainly wouldn't want to slow you down," she snapped, gingerly forcing her foot into the water. "Oh, it's so cold!" she cried, wincing as the frigid liquid entered the open wound. Gritting her teeth, she kicked her foot back and forth in the pond. The water splashing on the red dust made her legs look like they were bleeding, too. She washed them and her face as best she could, and soaked her foot until the cut grew numb and her teeth chattered with the cold. Miserable, she couldn't hold back a sob.

"Quit blubbering and wash it out," Nick said impatiently, walking back toward her.

"I'm not blubbering," she said. Trying to stop her tears, she drew her foot from the water. Clenching her teeth against the pain, she dug at the gash with her fingernail. Finally, when it looked like all the sand was out of it, she swished her foot one more time and examined the cut again.

"Here, let me see it," he said, kneeling beside her.

Holding it up, she sighed with relief when he nodded his head. Ripping a large strip of cloth from the leg of his union suit, he wrapped her injured foot and tied a knot to hold the bandage secure. When he finished, he turned without a word and whistled for the horse. He threw his leg over the mustang's back. Wincing, he slid forward. He glowered down at her. "Try not to have any more *accidents*. I'd like to get home with some of me covered."

"You act like I did it on purpose."

"I wouldn't put it past you. Now get on the damned horse!" he thundered, his eyes like jagged flint.

She grasped his extended hand and clamped her mouth shut to keep from crying out when he yanked her up behind him. "You don't have to break my arm," she complained peevishly.

"Just shut up, woman. You've tried my patience enough."

"Yes, master!"

"Not another damned word!"

Seething, Samantha rode in silence. Vowing to get even, she sat rigidly behind him. Her eyes drilled him full of holes. *Someday, Mr. McBride,* she promised silently. *Someday . . . soon.*

CHAPTER

* 5 *

AS THEY LEFT THE POND TURNOFF THE DUSTY
road meandered through tall pines and wound steadily
downhill, but Samantha scarcely noticed the changing
landscape. Her angry thoughts were filled with Nick Mc-
Bride. She hated being dependent on him, but she had no
choice. She couldn't survive in this wild country on her
own. The cut on her foot reminded her of that, throbbing
incessantly with every step of the horse.

It was his fault, she fumed. If she hadn't been running
from him, she wouldn't have stepped on the rock. Now he
was in a hurry to get to the ranch—well, she couldn't *wait*
to get there. His cousin—Jeff—had some explaining to do.
He'd also better have her clothing, or what she had given
Nick would only be a taste of what she'd have in store for
him.

After she got her answers, and a bath, and her own
clothes, she couldn't get far enough away from them. If the
two McBrides she'd met were any sample, the whole family
must be a bunch of raving lunatics.

She shifted her weight, agony tearing through her inner

thighs, rubbed raw from the constant friction on the horse's back. Gritting her teeth, she forced herself into a mindless state where there was no pain, only numbness. It was the only way she could endure.

A shadow on her face brought her out of her misery to notice they had entered a canyon. She gazed in wonder at the stark beauty surrounding her. Solid rock walls streaked in vermilions, creams, and mauves rose sharply upward on both sides to a cloudless, cornflower-blue sky. At the bottom of the gorge, a thin strip of grass and green willows edged the banks of a narrow stream that slid over flat layers of water-carved sandstone. The sun, shining through a crest of tall pines on the ridge, cast long, purple fingers of shadow on the trail. Samantha rubbed her arms, enjoying a sudden warmth. "Why, it's almost hot," she said, finding it hard to believe only a short time ago she'd been freezing.

"The steep walls of the ravine block the wind," Nick said, reining the pinto to one side of the dusty road. "We'll get a drink of water and rest the horse for a while." He slid off and removed the halter.

Samantha noticed he hadn't even offered to help her down. *Who needs you, anyway?* she thought. Before she could dismount, the pinto shook his head and trotted after his master. Caught by surprise, she slipped sideways. Lunging forward on the animal's neck, she grabbed for a handful of mane, but it was no use. By the time she passed Nick, she was falling. She felt his hands close securely around her and lift her to the ground. "Thank—" she began. Ignoring her, he turned and walked away. "Fine," she muttered. Damning the perverseness of men, she hobbled to the stream.

The crystal-clear water rolled in shining sheets over

smooth striped rocks. She knelt, cupping her hands, and lifted the sweet cold liquid to her lips. She splashed her arms and washed her face, removing as much of the trail dust as she could. Exhausted but refreshed, she lay back on a flat slab of rock, and enjoyed the scenery.

On a limb over her head, an agitated blue jay noisily scolded the horse nibbling grass beneath its perch. The raucous call echoed off the steep canyon walls. Scout ignored the bird's outburst and continued feeding, stomping his feet occasionally against the buzzing flies.

The musical water and the warm sun on her body soothed her troubled spirit. Content and warm, she closed her eyes. But her dreams were confused—violent. She was glad when Nick's hand upon her shoulder shook her back into reality.

She awoke with her head pounding, her mouth parched, and her skin pink and hot to the touch. Sharp pain shot through her foot with each beat of her heart. Her stomach rumbled, reminding her she'd had nothing to eat since the fish last night.

"Get up and get a drink. We're leaving," he said.

She sat up, her head whirling. Nausea rolled in her empty middle. "I don't feel like going anywhere. My head hurts. I'm hot and I'm hungry."

"Well, I don't feel too pert myself," he snapped. "Either you hurry up and get on the horse or you stay here."

Holding out her hand, Samantha glared up at him, waiting for him to help her.

His eyes icy, he turned and marched off with the halter swinging from his shoulder. He whistled for the mustang.

She narrowed her eyes. "Bossy! I'll teach you," she said. Struggling to her feet, she ambled slowly to the stream, knelt and drank at her leisure. Trailing her hand in the ripples, she cast a furtive glance over her shoulder. Instead of waiting, as she'd expected, he was already some distance down the road. "Damn him! He really would leave me!" she cried. Mentally sending him to perdition, she hobbled after the horse. "Wait."

Nick reined the mustang in. He extended his hand without even looking at her and yanked her up behind him.

Outraged tears stung Samantha's eyes and flowed down her hot cheeks. *He is just plain mean. I can't wait to be on my way. If I never see him again, it will be too soon.*

Nick felt the fury steaming from the redhead's body as she sat rigidly behind him. It did nothing to cool his own rage. *What does she think I am, her maid or somethin'? Nobody tells me what to do—let alone a minx like her. Hellfire!* He was one mass of pain from the lump on his head, to his blistered bottom to his raw bare feet, and she complained she was hot and hungry! *Well, in a few hours we'll be at the ranch, and she can eat a whole damn cow if she takes a notion.*

He couldn't wait to get rid of her. And the first thing he intended to do after they got there was turn her ornery carcass over to Jeff. A sardonic smile twisted the corner of Nick's mouth as he imagined the result of that meeting. Well, Jeff deserved whatever happened to him. Secondly, he planned to take a bath, eat a steak, go to bed, and sleep for a week. He made a note never to go near Molly's Saloon again, at least not as long as *she* was there. That little spitfire was enough to make a man swear off women for good.

He scowled, knowing the ribbing he'd take when the hands saw him ride in wearing the tattered underwear, besides being black and blue from head to foot. He'd never live this mess down. Cowboys loved to gossip worse than a bunch of old women. It'd be all over the territory in nothing flat. Nick shook his head. He'd have to change his name or leave the country.

Another thought occurred to him and his mood brightened. Maybe, if he waited until after dark, they could sneak into the ranch yard unnoticed. Nobody had seen him so far. He'd kept to the back trails, except for crossing the road that led back to Canyon Springs. He'd held his breath, knowing she'd want him to take her straight into town. But she hadn't even noticed—must have been asleep or something. He frowned. Up ahead they'd *have* to take the main road for a spell. There wasn't any other way to get to the ranch.

He glanced down at the sunbaked trail and caught a glimpse of her bare leg, straddling the horse just behind his. She'd sure gotten sunburned, falling asleep like that. He'd intended to warn her, but she'd been so sassy he hadn't bothered. He didn't know she'd burned that quick.

Nick closed his good eye to the glare of the sun off the sandstone. *Damn, my head hurts.* In the canyon he'd gone upstream where she couldn't see him and pressed more cold rocks to his injured eye. It hadn't done much good. He shook his head in disgust, recalling his reflection in the water. The eye, black and purple, had swelled almost shut—and his lip looked like he'd been stung by a bee. Lord, he'd *have* to go in after dark. After he'd gotten rid of her, he'd tell anybody who dared ask that he'd been drunk and fallen off his horse or something. He sure wasn't about to tell them he'd gotten beaten up by a woman!

The canyon opened abruptly onto a brushy plain dotted with a few rocky hills along the roadway. Nick slowed Scout, watching the junction of the main road ahead. Clear so far. Good. Now if he could get another five miles without being seen, he'd take the back trail on home.

"I'm so thirsty," she whispered.

"Well, you'll have to wait. The nearest water is about eight miles ahead," Nick told her. Damn, what did he say that for? He had no intention of staying on the main road that long. But if he didn't, there wasn't any water until they reached the ranch. Well, he'd almost have to go there now. Besides, his own mouth felt like he'd been chewing cotton, and a cool drink would be mighty welcome. He could taste it already. He nudged the horse into a smooth gait that ate up the miles.

A while later, knowing the water hole lay just around the bend, Nick slowed the sweating pinto. He approached cautiously, noting with relief that there was no one in sight.

Scout, apparently smelling the water, quickened his pace, not stopping until he stood in the shade of a willow with his nose submerged in the creek.

"Looks like you weren't the only thirsty one," Nick said, jumping off the animal. He placed his hands around the redhead's waist. Marveling at the way his fingers spanned her middle, he lifted her down beside him. "You're a mess," he said, shaking his head.

Her hair hung limply in weed-tangled knots around her sun-blistered face. Streaks of dried mud and tears ran in jagged lines from her green eyes to a spot even with her red nose. She gave him a scathing glance and hobbled upstream to kneel by the water.

After Nick walked downtrail and relieved himself behind a clump of bushes, he came back to where she sat leaning against a willow trunk. Her damp hair curled around her face where she'd washed the grime and tears away. She didn't say a word when he walked on upstream.

Finding a shady spot, Nick satisfied his thirst, then splashed water over his head and face. Shielding his eyes, he squinted at the long tree shadows cast by the afternoon sun. He judged the time to be around four o'clock. He knew they should make it to the ranch before dark.

He shifted his gaze, his brow creasing. The girl drooped against the base of the tree, weariness etched in every curve of her body. He'd better get her moving. She looked done in for sure. Nick picked up the horse's rope and led him to a stop beside the woman. He knew the sooner he got her to the ranch, the better off she'd be. He frowned when she didn't move, didn't look up, as if she didn't know he was there. "It's time to go," he said, worry nagging at him.

She raised her head as if surprised to see him. "What?"

"Get up. Let's go," he repeated. He slid an arm around her waist and helped her to her feet. Her legs buckled. He caught her, slipping a hand under her right knee, and lifted her over the horse's head. Mounting, he gathered her against his chest and cradled her crosswise in front of him.

She stiffened, trying to hold herself erect. Then, apparently overcome by exhaustion, she slumped against him.

His attention on the girl, Nick guided the horse onto the roadway, not realizing they had company until they came nose to nose with a wagon. He looked up. His mood plummeted. *Oh hell! Alice and Fred Posley.*

The wagon's occupants, a heavyset man in faded overalls and a thin, pointy-nosed woman in gingham and a sunbonnet, craned their necks. "Why, Nicholas McBride, is that you? Whatever do you have on?" Alice chirped.

Her husband reined the wagon closer, trying to get a

better look. "Fred, he's practically naked and look at his face," she said, peering at Nick from under the rim of her bonnet. "Who's that woman with you?" She leaned closer.

Nick felt the girl stir in his arms. Green eyes opened; she peeped up at him. Seeing his discomposure, a vengeful smile crossed her face. "Nicky, darling, aren't you going to introduce me to your friends?" she asked.

"Shut up," he whispered, his face growing hot. *Just what I need, the worst busybodies in the territory.*

The girl lifted a hand to touch his swollen eye and turned a serious face to the curious couple. "Just a lover's spat. Wasn't it, dear?" She caressed his cheek.

Gritting his teeth against her touch, Nick glared down into the merciless green pools of her eyes. He couldn't strangle her here in front of two witnesses, much as he'd like to. Nodding stiffly to the pair, Nick kicked his startled horse into a gallop. The wind brushed his flaming face. He peered back over his shoulder and saw the couple standing on the wagon seat, stretching their necks to get a better view. "Shit!" And he'd worried about the cowhands seeing him. He groaned. He'd never be able to show his face again.

The girl's body quivered against his. Alarmed, he looked down. She was laughing.

Her eyes met his. She crinkled her sunburned face in a slow, wide grin, obviously delighted to see his embarrassment. "Serves you right, Nicky darlin'," she drawled.

"Woman, if you live long enough to get to the ranch, it'll be a miracle," he growled.

"Why didn't you introduce me?" she teased.

"For one thing, I don't know your name," he hissed. "And for another, I don't want to know it either." Hearing another giggle, he gave her the look that set most of his enemies shivering in their boots. It had no effect on her. The tears of mirth running down her cheeks made his own face even warmer. "Damned woman!" What'd he ever done to deserve this?

He rode in furious silence with the girl, done in by her fit of laughter, asleep in front of him. As she cuddled next to him the heat of her body seared his bare skin. He hoped it was only sunburn and not a fever or something worse.

He turned off the main road and before long saw the cross timbers that marked the eastern boundary of the JMB Ranch. A smile of relief crossed his face when he passed beneath the weathered wooden sign he and Jeff had carved so long go. *Just two miles now, thank God!* He pulled the weary horse to a walk, noticing the white rings of sweat and lather on his neck. "Just a little further, Scout."

At the sound of Nick's voice the horse's ears pricked up, and he walked a little faster, recognizing the road home.

Riding into the ranch yard, Nick groaned. He'd hoped to make it into the house without being seen, but his grandfather sat in a rocking chair on the porch.

The old man ambled to his feet and shook back his mane of white hair. Scowling, he removed the pipe clenched between his teeth. "Nick, where in hell have you been?" he boomed out, hobbling down the porch steps to meet them. "Jeff came home two nights ago, drunker'n sin, carryin' your clothes. He had a passel of female clothes, too. Probably stole 'em off'n a clothesline somewheres. Couldn't get nothin' out of him, just giggled and shut his mouth tighter'n a tick on a dog's back."

Jake took another step. "What have you got there?" He raised a gnarled fist and rubbed at his eyes as if he couldn't believe what he saw. "By gad, that's a woman!" The old man's shocked gaze met Nick's. "What in the world's she got on? Wh—"

"I'll tell you all about it later," Nick interrupted, definitely not in the mood to explain. He gritted his teeth, seeing one of the hands peek curiously from the door of the bunkhouse. *So much for trying to sneak in,* he thought. "Where's Jeff?" He looked around for his cousin. He'd seen Jeff's horse, still saddled, tied by the corral.

"He's in the house." Jake turned toward the building. "Jefferson, git out here!" he bellowed.

The girl stirred in Nick's arms. "Where are we? Why are you shouting?"

"Wake up. We're at the ranch," Nick said.

Rubbing her eyes, she pulled away from him and looked anxiously around her. "We made it?" she asked, as if unable to comprehend what he had said.

Nick didn't answer, but handed her down to his grandfather until he could dismount. After sliding off his horse, he lifted her from Jake's arms and stood her on her feet. She swayed, and he took hold of her arm to steady her. The front door creaked open. Nick glanced up to see his cousin standing on the porch.

Jeff stuffed his hands in his pockets and gaped at Nick and the girl. "Hello, Nick." He giggled nervously and shifted from one foot to another. Blue eyes widening, he leaned forward and removed one hand to point at Nick's battered face. "What happened to you?"

Nick gingerly touched his split lip. Fuming, he thought of his eye, the lump on his head, and his bruised and scorched lower region. Narrowing his eyes, he stalked toward Jeff, who stood there grinning like an opossum. "Nothing compared to what's going to happen to you."

The grin left Jeff's face. He backed toward the door, but found it shut. He edged sideways, inching his way toward the porch rail.

"Oh, no you don't," Nick snarled. Releasing the girl's arm, he leaped onto the porch. His body tensed, ready for battle. He curled his hand into a fist and drew back.

Jeff cowered against the building, his face as white as his sun-bleached hair. He raised his arms, attempting to protect his face.

Nick threw a right, the blow striking hard and fast.

Jeff bounced off the wall, blood spurting from his lip. He jerked at his shirtfront, tearing the pocket. A folded paper fell to the porch floor. "Nick, wait."

But Nick, not in the mood to wait for anything, doubled his fist and struck again. He felt the flesh under Jeff's eye give beneath the impact.

"Ow! Nick, wait, I can explai—"

Too furious to listen, Nick grabbed Jeff's shirtfront and drew his fist back again.

"No! It can't be! No!"

Nick heard the girl's stricken cry, then a muffled thud.

"Damnit, that's enough!" Jake roared. "Nick, stop it!"

Nick stood, his body shaking, his fist poised.

"Nick, I said stop it!"

Nick unclenched his fist from Jeff's shirt. He slowly dropped his arm. Sighing, he turned to face his grandfather. He sucked in a sharp breath.

The girl lay crumpled on the ground. Jake knelt beside her, cradling her head in his arms.

"What the hell happened?" Nick asked.

Jake glared at him. "She fainted." He raised his hand and brushed the hair back from the girl's face. A thin line of blood oozed from a cut and ran down the side of her head. "Damnation! She's hurt. Must have struck her head on the hitching rail."

Nick leaped off the porch and dropped down beside them. He slid his arm under her and lifted her to his chest. "Open the door," he yelled. "Jeff, get the doc." He glimpsed Jake pick up a paper from the dusty ground and stuff it in his pocket. When the old man moved out of the way, he turned to find Jeff still standing by the open door.

"Damnit, Jeff," the old man roared. "You heard him. Get goin'! The girl needs help."

Jeff jumped over the railing and ran to his horse. Swinging into the saddle, he left in a thick cloud of dust.

Nick rushed inside, lengthening his stride across the living room. Guilt and concern wrinkling his brow, he looked down at the unconscious girl in his arms. *Damn, she might be ornery, but she sure doesn't deserve this.* He took the stairs two at a time and turned toward his bedroom.

Jake puffed behind him, his breath sounding like a leaky bellows. "Rosa! Rosa! Consarn it, woman, where are you?"

"I'm here." The plump, gray-haired housekeeper came out of Nick's bedroom, her arms filled with dirty linen. She stopped, staring at Nick and the girl. "*Madre de Dios,* what has happened?" Not waiting for an answer, she dropped the sheets and ran back into the room ahead of him. At the bed she jerked the blankets down and stepped back, her worried gaze flitting to the girl.

"She fainted and hit her head," Nick said. He bent and placed the girl on the hand-carved Spanish bed. He pulled the fresh linen sheet over her slender frame.

Clucking like a mother hen, Rosa scurried to the washstand and picked up the empty china pitcher. Muttering in Spanish, she bustled out of the room.

Nick fell to his knees beside the bed. Shaken, he reached out to smooth back the tangled red hair from her pale brow. "Kitte—" he started. He pulled back his hand, staring in horror at the bright red stain oozing over his fingers. Aghast, he glanced up at Jake.

His brow knitted into a frown, the old man looked at Nick. "Don't mean nothin'. Scalp wounds always bleed bad."

Carefully parting her hair, Nick saw a thin line of red beads running from her temple to a spot just above her ear. "She must have hit her head pretty hard."

Rosa rushed back into the room, sending water sloshing over the rim of the pitcher she carried. She crossed to the nightstand and poured a small amount into the large china bowl. She pulled a ladder-backed chair up next to the bed and sat down opposite Nick, then dipped a clean cloth into the liquid, squeezed it out, and pressed it to the cut on the girl's pale face. *"Pobrecita."* Her brown eyes snapping, she glared at Nick. "What have you done to this poor child?" She blinked, her eyes widening when she noticed his battered eye and lip—and his lack of clothing. "Were you attacked by *banditos*?"

"No." Nick sighed. "Only Jeff."

"Glory be!" Jake yelled from across the room. The elder man let out a whoop and slapped his knee. "Glorrry be!"

Nick, irritated at the interruption, turned in exasperation to his grandfather.

Jake stood by the window, his head bent, intently reading a crumpled piece of paper he held in his hand.

"What's that you've got?" Nick asked.

Jake's eyes, bright with unshed tears, gazed into Nick's. "You finally did it! Congratulations, boy!"

"Congratulations? For what?" Frowning, Nick rose and walked to the old man's side. He took the paper from his hand and laid it on the desk, smoothing it out with his palm, curious to see what had the old man in such a state.

Nick struggled to read the fancy gold letters that twisted and turned across the page. The words leaped up at him, wrapping around his consciousness. "No!" he gasped. He recoiled from the paper like he would from a striking rattler. He felt the blood rush from his face. He clutched the desk for support, staring in horror at his grandfather. "I'm married?"

Jake beamed with confused happiness. A wide grin split his weathered face. "You sure are. Yessir, boy, you've finally done it!"

"I'm married!" Nick croaked. Wide-eyed, he stared at the figure on the bed. "To *her*? God help me!"

CHAPTER

6

JEFF PULLED ON THE BUCKSKIN'S REINS, SLOW-
ing the heaving animal to a walk. He couldn't afford to have
the horse quit on him now. The vision of the unconscious
redhead flashed through his mind. Samantha needed his
help.

A muscle jumped in his clenched jaw. *Damn, of all the
things to have happen.* Out of the corner of his eye he'd seen
her pick up the paper when it blew off the porch. Next thing
he knew she'd dropped like a stone. Hell, she probably
didn't remember anything after all that whiskey. It appeared
to have been quite a shock finding out she was married. And
then to find out she'd married someone like Nick . . . He
shook his head, remembering his cousin's rage. Nick's
behaving like a wild man hadn't helped any either.

Nick scared most people anyway. They seemed to think
he was going to scalp them or something any minute. A
shiver crawled up Jeff's backbone as he recalled the wild,
savage look in Nick's eyes. That cold, flat look of death that
made people walk softly, then step quickly away.

He'd seen it only once before, aimed at a cowhand when

Nick caught him mistreating the wild red horse. He knew for a fact that if Nick'd been wearing his gun, the man would be resting under a tombstone right now.

Jeff lifted a trembling hand and wiped away the blood trickling from his split lip. He'd never expected to see Nick that mad at him. But then he'd never gone that far before. *It must have been the whiskey.* He'd only intended it to be a joke, but things sure got out of hand. "What's Nick going to do to me after he sees that paper?" Jeff groaned. Nick married? He'd never seen anybody as bit shy as his cousin. "He *is* gonna kill me."

His thoughts went to the girl. Poor Samantha. What was going to happen to her? Shame swept over Jeff, recalling the way she'd looked, her hair all tangled and matted with sticks and leaves. Sunburned and wrapped in an old, ragged, dirty blanket. And now she was hurt and it was all his fault.

Damn it, me and my big idea. He rolled his eyes toward heaven. "Lord, if you let me get out of this, I promise I'll never pull another prank as long as I live." When the horse snorted and pricked up his ears, Jeff sighed. "I really mean it, Buck." He nudged him into a mile-eating gallop.

"Why in hell did I get so drunk? How did things get so confused?" The soft drumming of Buck's hooves in the thick dust took Jeff back to the events in the cabin.

He'd thought it would be a good joke, both on Jake and Nick. He and Nick had decided they would take Molly's new saloon singer off the stage before she got to town and offer her twenty dollars to pretend to be married to Nick. Being drunk, they thought when Jake discovered Nick hadn't really married a saloon girl, he'd be so relieved he'd forget about getting them married. Jeff sighed. It probably would have worked out if that old priest hadn't shown up in the stable and begged Jeff to help him get to Santa Fe. It was too much temptation. He groaned, remembering how he'd ended up promising the padre one of the team if he'd perform a marriage for him. After he'd left the priest at the cabin, he'd gone to fetch the girl.

Jeff frowned. He never did understand why she'd been wearing that ugly old black dress. Maybe she didn't want to get her fancy things dirty. She had sure been glad to see him, almost like she'd been expecting him or something. She hadn't been feeling too good either. She'd been real dizzy and thirsty. Not having any water, he'd offered her his bottle. He grinned, remembering the way she'd polished it off and started in on a second. When they'd reached the cabin, she'd staggered off and gone to sleep under a tree.

Nick had been in worse shape yet. He'd fallen in the dirt trying to get off his horse.

Jeff remembered he himself had been drunker than sin, and he'd been the soberest one there, except for the padre. After the wedding Nick passed out on the bed and the girl ran outside. Jeff had found her sick and out cold in the ash bin. Heck, he couldn't leave her there in those wet, stinking clothes. That's why he'd undressed her and put her on the bed.

It hadn't seemed quite fair for Nick to be lying there with his clothes on, especially it being his honeymoon. Since Nick wasn't in any shape to do it himself, Jeff had undressed him and rolled him over next to the girl and covered them both with a blanket. With the priest in a hurry to get to town, Jeff'd gathered up the clothes and the saddle gear and thrown the whole works in the wagon, intending to come back the next day.

When they reached Canyon Springs, he'd kept his word and gave the padre one of the team. Then he went to

Molly's, picked up another bottle, and went back to the wagon. He didn't remember starting for the ranch . . . or reaching it. Jake had found him curled up asleep in the wagon bed the next morning.

Jeff shook his head—that had been yesterday. He'd woken up so hung over and sick he'd been unable to think of what he'd done . . . let alone the consequences—until today. When he'd opened the front door and seen Nick sitting there on his horse, he'd wanted to run.

Remembering his cousin's battered face, Jeff wondered what'd he'd tangled with. Nick had sure been mad, but he hadn't mentioned what'd happened at the cabin. Jeff had the uneasy feeling Nick didn't remember, or he would have said something. Jeff rubbed his aching jaw. Still, Nick was mad enough to kill him not knowing. Cold sweat sluiced like ice water down Jeff's spine. "Sooner or later he is gonna find that paper and read it," he said with a shiver. "And I don't want to be anywhere around when he does."

Jeff thundered into Canyon Springs, stirring up a cloud of choking dust. He slid the weary horse to a stop in front of the doctor's office and raced inside. Finding the waiting room empty, he charged forward and opened the door bearing the sign KEEP OUT.

Dr. Henry Johnson, bending over the examining table, turned, scowling at the intrusion. "What in the world's wrong with you, Jeff? Can't you read? I'm busy."

"Sorry, Doc, but you're needed in a hurry at the ranch."

"Go get the buggy, then sit down or go over to Molly's. I'll be through here in a minute." He turned to the fat backside of the man lying on the table and raised a scalpel above a boil.

"Can't you lock that door, Doc?" the patient complained. "Half the town's been in here since I dropped my pants."

"Sorry, Reverend," Jeff said gleefully. He slowly backed out and closed the door. Stifling a laugh, he thought of the man on the table. The Reverend Herman Wilkes was always preaching at him and Nick, condemning them to hellfire and damnation. The reverend wore *pink* underdrawers. "Old Holy Herman" wouldn't be looking down his nose at him anymore. A wide grin on his face, he walked out of the office and onto the board sidewalk.

The grin disappeared as he looked down the street toward the saloon. He had to tell Molly her new singer was hurt and out at the ranch. But he sure wasn't about to tell her Nick'd married the girl or anything else. He sucked in his breath, thinking of the mess he'd caused. A tug on his sleeve made him look down.

A small, dirty-faced boy of about seven stood next to the buckskin horse, holding the bridle. Blue eyes, bright and hopeful under a thatch of red hair, peered up at him. "Can I water your horse, Jeff?"

"Sure thing, Tommy. And would you tell Mort over at the livery to hitch Doc's buggy?"

The youngster nodded eagerly. "Shore thing."

Jeff flipped a coin toward the snaggletoothed sprout. He watched the boy for a minute, then crossed the street and pushed through the batwing doors and entered the saloon.

Molly, sitting at the bar, looked up. "Hello, Jeff." Her eyes widened. "What horse stomped on you?"

He ambled over to join her. "A stud named Nick."

Molly chuckled. "Sit down here and have a beer. You're just in time to hear our new singer."

Jeff caught the beer Joe slid his way and took a sip. He began, "That's what I came to tell you, Molly, she's—"

"'Buffalo gals—'" rang out a coarse voice.

Jeff stopped and turned toward the stage. His mouth open, he stared at the hard, painted face of a woman about thirty. Orange hair bouncing, she pranced about the stage, flipping her skirts over ample hips in time to the bawdy song she bellowed.

"That's your singer?" he gasped, getting to his feet.

"Yeah, she finally made it. She missed the stagecoach and hitched a ride on a wagon with a whiskey drummer." Molly grimaced when the woman hit a sour note. "I'm only going to let her stay long enough to get a stake, then I'll get rid of her. She's driving all the customers away."

Jeff swayed and fell back onto the bar stool. "Give me a whiskey," he croaked. Good Lord, if that was the singer, who was the girl he'd taken off the stage? The one he'd left at the cabin . . . *the one who was now married to Nick?*

Nick and his grandfather stared at each other in confusion. Nick examined the document, hoping to find something wrong with it. But it looked real, too real.

"Nick, what's wrong with you? Did you marry the girl, or didn't you?"

Nick saw that in his excitement, Jake's pipe had fallen out of his mouth and lay unnoticed on the floor. A faint curl of fragrant smoke rose from the bowl. He bent to pick the pipe up. Straightening, he handed it to the older man. "I don't know. I was drunk," he answered, still stunned. "But I sure as hell aim to find out."

Nick knew he had to get out of here. He had to think. Before his grandfather could ask any more questions, he snatched some clothes off a peg and grabbed up his boots on his way out the door. His mind in a turmoil, he hurried down the stairs and headed toward the back of the house.

Years ago when Jake laid out the house, he'd built an L-shaped room over a natural hot spring, rocking up an area about three feet deep for bathing with a spillway and ditch at one end to carry off the overflow. Large shuttered windows opened to let in summer breezes and closed to form a steam room in the winter. The ranch never ran short of hot water, but drinking water had to be brought down in barrels from a mountain spring.

Anxious to get back to the girl, Nick washed hurriedly instead of lazing in the pool like he usually did. ''Samantha.'' Her name rolled off his tongue. At least that's what it said on the marriage license. He groaned, vaguely recalling the foolish bet he'd made with Jeff. He scowled. Damn it, he wasn't supposed to really get married. But the paper seemed real. He bent his head forward and held it between his palms. Lord, looked like he'd done it after all. He still couldn't believe it. Naw, it just had to be one of Jeff's jokes, but Jeff hadn't been laughing. He'd looked worried . . . and scared.

Nick climbed out of the pool, dried himself, and slipped into a pair of soft cotton underdrawers, then pulled on black whipcord pants that hugged his lean body. He sighed. Damn, it was good to wear something that covered him, something that didn't itch, something he didn't hang out of in all the wrong places. He sat down on a rustic wooden bench, put on his socks, and tugged on the black high-topped boots, savoring the feel of soft leather against his sore feet. He shrugged on the silky black shirt, fastened the pearl buttons, and tucked the tail into his pants.

Rubbing his bearded chin, he peered at his face in the mirror. No, he was too worried about the girl to take the time to shave now. Giving the discarded long johns a kick, he saw a flame of red gold jump in the light. He smiled. "Coup," he said, remembering. Removing the curl, he wound it about his finger then placed the coil in his left shirt pocket. Throwing the underwear in a corner, he left the room and headed for the stairs.

Nick opened the bedroom door and quietly eased his way into the room. Light filtered through the lace curtains, casting soft shadows on his grandfather and Rosa sitting at the bedside. Nick stepped closer and looked down at the woman on the bed. His heart thudded heavily in his chest. She was still unconscious. He raised his eyes to meet his grandfather's.

Jake shook his head. Showing every day of his almost seventy years, he slowly got up from his chair and hobbled toward the window. He parted the curtains to peer down into the ranch yard below. He raised a gnarled, callused hand and wiped hastily at his eyes.

Nick turned away, knowing his grandfather, with his gruff exterior, would not welcome any witnesses to what he would consider a weakness. He sat down in the vacated chair, despair surrounding him. His gaze traveled over the figure lying on his massive hand-carved bed.

She looked so little, so frail. Her lips were bloodless in a face white as the china pitcher on the washstand. A wet cloth lay neatly folded on her forehead above long, sooty lashes. Damp wisps of red-gold hair curled softly about her small face.

Guilt and shame flooded him. He looked at Rosa. While

she would never say anything, condemnation was plainly written in her expressive brown eyes.

She murmured her prayers, her plump work-worn hands reverently fingering the jet beads of her rosary, counting them off one by one. When she'd finished, she placed the beads on the coverlet and picked up Samantha's pale, blue-veined hand, massaging it between her two brown ones.

"Hasn't she moved at all?" he whispered.

Rosa slowly shook her head. "No, and it is not good that she has not opened her eyes." She patted the girl's hand and covered it with the quilt. She removed the cloth from her head and rinsed it in a basin of cool water on the bedside table.

Nick studied Samantha's temple, relieved that the gash wasn't as bad as it had first appeared. It had closed, but the deep purple bruise under it frightened him. He watched Rosa squeeze the water out of the rag and refold it before placing it on her patient's forehead.

Nick ran his hand through his still-damp hair. Never had he felt so helpless. What if she never woke up? What if she died? The thought was more than he could stand.

He jerked to his feet and joined Jake at the window, staring down at the empty road. "Where in the hell is the doctor?" he said, more to himself than to Jake or Rosa. He yanked the curtain aside, squinting at the countryside, hoping his keen eyes could see something his grandfather had missed. Nothing. He paced back to the bed. Damnit, he had to do something. He couldn't just stand here, but what could he do? He prowled the distance between the bed and the window.

"Nick, come here," Jake called out. "Look over there."

Nick rushed to the window and focused on the direction Jake was pointing.

"Is it the doctor or a twister?"

Through the dust Nick faintly made out a buggy racing toward the ranch house. "It's the doctor. He's here," he said, turning to the housekeeper.

Tears ran in rivulets down Rosa's fat brown cheeks. She made the sign of the cross and kissed the crucifix of her rosary, giving thanks for an answered prayer.

Nick silently joined her as he raced from the room. He leaped down the stairs to open the massive oak paneled door, and waited impatiently for the carriage to careen to a stop in front of the porch.

A small, spritely man, gray with dust, jumped down and hurriedly slapped at his clothes with his hat. He grabbed his black bag and turned sharp, blue eyes toward Nick. "Where's my patient?" he said gruffly.

Calling to a ranch hand to take care of the winded horse, Nick ushered the doctor into the house and gestured toward the staircase. "Upstairs, Doc. She fainted and hit her head. She's still out."

The doctor snapped his head around. "It's a her?" His brow pleated into deep furrows, he squinted up at Nick. "First, I'll need to wash up."

Jake called from the front of the stairs, "Right this way, Doc." He showed the physician to the washroom.

Taking the stairs two at a time, Nick hurried into the bedroom to wait with Rosa. Seconds later the doctor arrived and shooed him from the room. Reluctantly, Nick went down the stairs and joined his grandfather.

The old man stood in front of the fireplace, staring at something on the mantel. He reached out a rough hand and gently picked up a small picture of a young woman. The hair on the back of his wrist shone the same shade of silver as the frame, which was timeworn and burnished by the years. His eyes sad and faraway, he lifted a gnarled finger to touch the girl's smiling face. "Your grandma at sixteen. That girl upstairs kinda reminds me of her, except your grandma's hair was the color of a ripe chestnut. She was little and pretty as a newborn filly. Her laugh sounded like little bells blowin' in the wind. I thanked God every day of her life and cursed the day He took her from me."

Nick stared at the flames, remembering how Jake had changed when she died of pneumonia. How all the joy had gone from him, leaving him an embittered, broken man.

"That's what I wanted for you and Jeff. That's why I told you to get married. The love of a good woman can bring you paradise on earth." He raised a shaking hand to cover his eyes. "But now, because of my meddlin', that poor child lies up there unconscious. God forgive me, for I'll never forgive myself."

The break in his grandfather's voice pierced Nick's heart. He swallowed, placing a hand on the bent elderly shoulder. "Jake, it wasn't none of your doin'. It was all my fault." Sick with self-disgust, he told Jake what he remembered of the previous days' events.

When he'd finished, his grandfather sat down heavily on the large leather couch in front of the fireplace. His eyes wide, he stared at Nick, as if he couldn't comprehend what he was hearing.

Nick lowered his lean frame into an adjacent chair and put his head in his hands. "I'm sorry as anything that she's hurt. I'd give anything for it not to have happened. But there's one more thing—" He raised his eyes to look at

Jake. "She's not a good woman. She's a dance-hall singer, a whore from Molly's Saloon."

When he heard the front door close softly, Nick turned to see Jeff standing there.

A dazed look on his bruised face, Jeff walked slowly into the room. He stopped, then took a deep breath. "But Nick, she's not. I just came from Canyon Springs. Molly's singer was there, at the saloon. That girl I took off the stage, she ain't one of Molly's girls. That Samantha Storm—the girl you married—I don't have no idea who she is."

CHAPTER

* 7 *

JEFF LEANED BACK IN HIS CHAIR AND SHOT A cautious look at Nick. "That's all I remember," he said softly.

"That's enough," Nick said, staring at his cousin for a moment. He bent forward, propped his elbows on his knees, and cradled his head in his hands. It was worse than he could have imagined, but knowing Jeff as he did, it all now made sense—the marriage, the girl naked in his bed, all of their clothes missing . . . and everything after that.

His thoughts went to the girl and the way she'd reacted to him. No wonder she'd acted so strange. She probably thought he was crazy with him trying to seduce her at every turn, thinking she was a saloon girl. She'd said she didn't know any Molly, but he hadn't believed her. But that still didn't tell him who she was . . . or why she went with Jeff in the first place. "Damn. Damn!" The more he thought about it, the madder he got. "Of all the damned stupid stunts you've pulled, this is the worst." Straightening, he glared at Jeff. "I ought to pound you good."

"You already did," Jeff said, ducking his battered head.

His busted mouth drooped at the corners, while his sorrowful blue eyes peeped woefully through slits of purplish flesh.

"Hell." Nick sighed in disgust, thinking Jeff reminded him of a whipped puppy.

"Settle down, Nick. Jeff wasn't the only fool involved in this mess." Jake ran his fingers through his mane of gray hair. "The problem is, what are we going to do now?"

"For one thing you could quit shouting at each other," said a voice behind them. "The lady needs some peace and quiet, not that she's likely to get it around here."

Nick jumped to his feet and strode across the room to meet the silver-haired physician. "Doc, how is she?"

Dr. Johnson cocked his head and looked up at Nick. "Right now, she's pretty sick. She seems to have a concussion, a cut foot, bites all over her legs, is sunburned, and otherwise just plain exhausted. If I could move her to town, I would. But in her condition she's better off here. Besides, I know I can depend on Rosa to watch over her." He placed his bag on an end table and crossed to the fireplace. He held out his slender, well-formed hands, rubbing them together to warm them by the fragrant pine fire.

"Is she going to be all right?" Nick asked, his throat tight. She had to be.

The doctor straightened and raised a finger to rub the side of his nose. "Yes, I think so," he said, squinting over gold-frame glasses at Nick. "I left some medicine for Rosa to give her when she wakes up."

"When's that going to be?" Nick asked. It seemed to him she'd been unconscious for way too long.

"I have no way of knowing, Nick, but I hope later this evening." The old man hesitated, then lifted a finger to lecture him. "You have to remember, she's had a bad bump on her head, and she's got a slight fever. She may not be herself at first."

"What can we do, Hank?" Jake asked his old friend.

"Just keep these two wild men away from her. Keep them quiet if you have to gag them." The doc scowled, motioning to Nick and Jeff. "I don't want her upset."

"Then we'd better not remind her she got drunk and married Nick," Jeff muttered.

Dr. Johnson looked shocked. "Good grief, I hope not. Do you want to kill her?" He raised a questioning eyebrow at Jake.

Jake sighed and shook his head.

The physician picked up his bag. He turned to give them one last look. "Lord help her."

Jake followed his friend toward the doorway. "I'll have one of the hands hitch up a fresh horse to your buggy. I could send yours into town tomorrow."

"Don't bother. I'll be out here anyway, Jake. I have to check on my patient."

When the door closed, silencing the rest of their conversation, Nick left his spot by the fireplace and strode toward the stairs.

"Nick?" Jeff started. "Don't—"

Nick faced him, daring him to say anything more.

Jeff, apparently thinking he'd already said enough, shrugged his shoulders and turned back to the fire.

"I *am* going up and nobody's going to stop me," Nick said softly. "After all, thanks to you, she is my wife."

When he entered the room, Rosa raised a finger to her lips and patted the chair next to hers, motioning for him to sit. "How is she?" he asked.

"Doc put ointment on her legs and cleaned and bandaged her foot. He thinks they will be all right. It's her head that worries him."

Nick gazed at the slender figure on the bed. Samantha, his wife. Wife. It sounded so strange. *Kitten, what will I do with you?* he wondered. He looked at the white bandage wrapping the cut above her ear. "She didn't have to be sewed up, did she?" he asked anxiously. The thought of a needle piercing her delicate flesh horrified him.

Rosa patted his hand, "No, no."

"I'm glad of that." He leaned back in his chair, studying his room, from the carved Spanish bed and dresser to the brightly woven Indian rugs on the polished wood floor. One whitewashed wall held the shiny pelt of a large black bear, along with pegs for guns, knives, and other belongings. The cured hide of a bull elk spread across another wall. An oak desk took up the far corner, with shelves hung above for his books. A comfortable leather chair sat in front of the desk and a matching one in front of the fireplace. It was a man's room, smelling of leather and tobacco, totally masculine, except for the lace curtains at the windows.

He switched his gaze to the girl lying on the bed. So feminine, so delicate—so out of place. She didn't fit— not into his room, nor into his life. He frowned. Well, she was here and he'd married her. Fit or not, until she got well, there wasn't a whole hell of a lot he could do about it.

"Oh my." Rosa sighed wearily. She lifted a hand and rubbed her temples.

Nick cursed himself for not noticing how tired the old lady was. Leaning forward, he placed a hand on her shoulder.

"Why don't you go get some rest? I'll stay with her for a while."

The gray-haired housekeeper peered up, doubt written across her face. "You'll call me if anything happens?"

"I'll call you. Now go." Getting to his feet, he placed a hand under her elbow and helped her to stand. He walked her to the door and planted a kiss on her soft, lined cheek. "Go now. She'll be fine."

She hesitated for a moment, patted his hand, then walked slowly toward the stairway and her room below.

Nick scowled. The way everybody acted, you'd think he was going to go into some kind of fit or something. Too restless to settle anywhere, he went to the window. Pulling aside the curtain, he stared out into the starlit night sky. So much had happened in such a short time. So many lives had changed. Noticing the room had lost some of its warmth, he turned to see the fire had burned down to glowing embers.

He quietly crossed the room. Crouching by the hearth, he added some good-sized logs to the coals. The fire cracked and popped, sending a fragment shower of sparks into the room. He watched the dancing flames for a while, then yawning, settled in the chair Rosa had vacated and pondered the uncertainty of his life.

He nodded. His chin hit his chest, jerking him awake. *Damn, I must have dozed off.* He bent toward the girl, making sure she was still covered. She lay just as he'd last seen her. She hadn't moved. Asleep, she looked like a child, so different from the little hellcat who'd been with him at the cabin. He frowned. Who was she? He knew nothing about her but her name—Samantha Jade Storm—and she hadn't told him that. She hadn't told him anything at all.

Why? What was she hiding? He had so many questions, but they'd have to wait until she was better.

He picked up her hand and cradled it in his own, tracing the fine blue veins with his fingertip. It was so small compared with his . . . and so hot! He leaned forward and touched his palm to her forehead. *Damn, she's burning up!* He jumped to his feet and hurried to the washstand. He picked up the pitcher, intending to pour water into the bowl. *It's empty.* Carrying the china container, he rushed toward the doorway. When he turned the knob and opened the door, he met Rosa on her way in to check on her patient.

"What's wrong, Nick?" Her eyes narrowed in suspicion.

"I didn't do anything," he protested. "She's got a bad fever. What do we do?"

She rushed past him to the bedside. She placed her hand on the small forehead. *"Madre de Dios,"* she gasped. "She's like fire." She whirled on him. "Go to the storehouse and get some ice. Tell Jake and Jeff to bring up the big washtub. They'll need to fill it with water. Hurry!"

Nick raced down the hall. Opening a door, he stuck his head in and shouted, "Jeff, get up! I need your help!" Not waiting for an answer, he dashed back into the corridor.

"What's all the racket?" Jake growled. He came out of his bedroom barefoot, pulling on his pants.

"It's Samantha—high fever," Nick said breathlessly. "Rosa said to get the washtub and fill it with water. I've got to get ice," he called back, running down the steps. By the time he reached the front door, he heard his kin coming down the landing.

Nick ran to a sturdy log structure built into the side of a hill. He slid the bolt on the heavy plank door and pulled it open. He pushed back the sawdust that covered the ice. The moonlight, filtering into the building, showed only a few chunks left. He hoped it would be enough. Scooping up a large block, he wrapped it in a burlap bag. He shoved the door shut and hurried back toward the house.

Nick leaped past his grandfather and Jeff waiting in the hall and carried the ice into the room.

Rosa, busy stripping the nightclothes from the girl, turned toward him. "Help me lift her into the tub, Nick."

Nick placed his arms under the girl's burning body and eased her gently into the water. He felt her give a slight quiver when the cold liquid rose over her simmering skin.

Rosa, her sleeves rolled up, slid her arms into the tub, supporting her patient. "Break the ice into pieces and put it into the water around her," she instructed.

After placing the bag on the hearth, Nick walked to the wall and removed a hefty hunting knife from a peg. He chipped the ice and placed the chunks in the water around the girl. "Is that enough?" he asked, his eyes on Rosa.

One arm holding Samantha, the other grasping the wet washcloth, Rosa nodded. "Go now; I have work to do."

Go? Sit in the hall and wait? Not knowing how she was? His eyes narrowed with resolve. "I'm not leaving. You need help, and after all I am married to her."

Rosa arched an eyebrow and handed him a washrag.

Nick took the cloth and began applying it to Samantha's feverish body, bathing her until the icy water became tepid and her skin cool. "I think she's better," he said. He lifted a wet hank of hair from her shoulder. It was matted and stained with blood. "Do you think . . . ?" he asked, lifting his eyes to meet Rosa's.

"If we don't get the bandage wet," she said, "it would

be good." Together they washed her hair until it was squeaky clean. When they'd finished, Rosa wrapped a dry towel around Samantha's head and Nick lifted her from the tub. He looked down. It was like holding a feather.

Samantha, her fever gone, trembled with cold.

Trying to warm her with his body, he cuddled her closer, ignoring the cold water saturating his clothing.

"Nicky? Are you going to stand there all night?"

Nick glanced up, surprised. The housekeeper waited by the bed, holding towels and a dry nightgown.

Nick flashed her a sheepish grin and strode to the bed. Placing Samantha on a blanket, he lifted a towel and helped Rosa dry her shivering body. Her skin, smooth and silky, was like satin under his callused palm.

After she was dry, Rosa replaced the wet cloth around her hair with a dry one. She shook out one of her own nightgowns and slipped it over the girl's head. Lost in the abundant folds, Samantha appeared more delicate than ever. "Hold her, Nick, while I put fresh linen on the bed."

Nick bent and lifted Samantha into his arms, the nightgown billowing around her. He drew her close and felt her heart throb against his, beating in time, the two merging into one. It was strange . . . wild . . . wonderful.

Her head lay against his shoulder. Thick sooty lashes closed against ivory cheeks. Anguish and remorse tore at him. "Oh kitten, I'm so sorry." He bent his head and gently brushed her forehead with his lips.

Samantha's eyelids quivered at the sound of his voice. Sighing, she nuzzled her head against his chest.

"You can put her down now, Nicky," Rosa said softly.

"Did you hear her? I think she's waking up," he said, his heart leaping with hope.

Rosa peeped over his arms at her, then slowly shook her head. She turned down the blankets and stood waiting.

Sighing, Nick reluctantly placed Samantha on the mattress. He tucked the covers around her, waiting, watching her eyes, but she had drifted back into a deep sleep.

Rosa touched his growth of beard. ''Why don't you go shave? If she does wake, you don't want her to see you like this. I'll wait with her until you get back,''she said, settling her ample frame into the bedside chair.

Nick rubbed his scratchy face. Damn, he'd forgotten. He'd better get rid of the whiskers. Rosa wasn't about to let him back in until he did. He opened the door and stepped out into the hall, stumbling over his grandfather and Jeff, who sat on the floor outside the door.

''Well, how is she?'' Jake asked impatiently.

''The fever's down now,'' Nick called back. ''And I think she's going to wake up.''

''Where are you going?'' Jeff asked.

''Oh, I've got to go shave.''

''Shave?'' Jeff asked. ''At three o'clock in the morning?''

Smiling broadly, Nick continued down the stairs, whistling as he neared the bottom.

''I don't think she's the only one with a fever,'' Jeff called. ''Jake, you'd better check on him too.''

Nick heard Jake chuckle, then tell Jeff to go on to bed.

The house was quiet when Nick reentered the room. ''Any change?'' he whispered.

''She's sleeping quietly and the fever is staying down.''

Nick gazed fondly at the short, round housekeeper and stuck his chin out for her approval.

Rosa raised her hand and patted his cheek. "Better, *hijo*," she said tenderly.

She'd called him son, and she'd been like a mother to him since his grandma died. He put his arm around her shoulder and gave it a squeeze. "No sense in both of us staying up all night. Why don't you go on to bed? I'll call you if there is any change."

Rosa nodded and squeezed his hand. Stifling a yawn, she placed a hairbrush on the washstand and went out the door.

Nick sat down in the vacated chair and stared at the small figure in the bed. Samantha's hair spread above her head, a glorious, shimmering red fan against the white linen sheets. He picked up the brush and carefully drew it through the silken strands, reveling in the feel of the long locks against his fingers. He brushed her hair until it was dry. Afraid he would disturb her by continuing, he reluctantly put the hairbrush back on the table.

Leaning forward to pull his chair closer to the bed, he noticed a matching ringlet lying on the floor near his boot. Dismayed, he bent to pick it up, feeling the softness against his palm. *The doctor must have cut it away from the gash on her head.* He carefully wound the hair around his finger and then placed the flat, shining coil inside his shirt pocket with the other curl he'd severed when she'd tangled her hair in his long john's. He rested his elbows on the bed and propped his chin with his hands. He watched her sleep, confused and uncertain for the first time in his life. She was his wife. His mate. He'd always been alone, except for Jake and Jeff.

When he was five, his dad, Jim, and his mother, Little Fawn, died in a wagon accident. He'd stayed with Jake and his grandma, spending summers with his mother's people.

He'd lived with the Cheyenne, but he'd been half-white, and in the white man's world, he'd been half-Indian. He'd always felt torn between the two races, never really belonging to either one. Not that he hadn't been loved; he had. But for him loneliness had been a way of life.

What would she do when she woke up? Would she remember she was married to him? God knows he was no prize. He'd always been wild and rowdy, and he'd earned that reputation. He was proud of his Indian blood, proud to be the grandson of Chief White Eagle, but the townspeople treated him like a leper, calling him a dirty savage. When he was little, the names had hurt. After he was older, he got even by being meaner and tougher than they were. He'd had to, to survive.

Thinking about it brought back the bitterness and anger. Not that he hadn't bedded his share of women, but they had been mostly whores, except for Amanda. He hadn't been the first, even though she'd claimed he was. He'd always felt, for her, anybody would have served the purpose. She'd refused to marry him because of his mixed blood.

He picked up Samantha's hand and traced her lifeline with his finger. His grandfather's words came back to him: "pretty as a newborn filly." Now he understood why Jake acted the way he did. The old man only wanted him to be happy.

But he'd always been wild, free, and he'd liked it. Responsible for no one, answering to no one, doing what he wanted, when he wanted. Now everything had changed. He was married. A sense of being trapped washed over him, of being ensnared by a slip of a girl with red-gold hair. A deep frown wrinkled his brow. He'd planned to settle down eventually, but not now, not yet.

But as he watched her a vision floated through his mind, of his ranch on the mesa, Samantha by his side, a passel of copper-haired kids running around. Cold winter nights with them all tucked into their beds. He and his wife, sitting by the fireplace, him holding her, getting lost in her emerald-green eyes, making love by the firelight. He leaned close to the bed, burying his face in her hair, inhaling her sweet fragrance. He traced the delicate line of her chin with his finger. His wife.

"Wonder how you'll feel being married to a half-breed." Afraid he already knew, he felt a pang of fear pierce his heart, shattering his dream. She had fainted when she read the paper. He knew some white women married Indians, but most didn't unless they wanted to be disowned by their own kind.

Another thought occurred to him, sinking him lower still. *Maybe she is engaged, or maybe she is married already.* With her being so pretty, it was more than likely that there was a man somewhere. Another vision flashed into mind, of some other man putting his hands on her body, making love to her. He clenched his teeth, jealousy gnawing at his vitals. He wasn't sure he wanted her, but he wasn't sure he didn't either. One thing he knew, he didn't want anybody else to have her. "I'll kill the man that dares to touch her."

Hearing his voice, she stirred in her sleep, murmuring something, seeming distressed. Nick leaned closer, straining to hear.

"Matthew," she breathed.

Nick's heart thudded painfully, hearing her call the name of another man.

"No! Run, Katie." She twisted, writhing on the bed. "Matthew! I—can't—breathe," she gasped.

Nick leaped to his feet and bent over the bed. He jerked the sheets lower to see if there was anything tight around her neck, but there was nothing. "She's dreaming."

"Katie, help—Matthew's—going—kill me."

The terror in her voice was so real, so immediate. A helpless rage filled him, knowing he couldn't vanquish the foe tormenting her. He sat down on the bed and lifted her into his arms. He held her close. "Shh, Samantha, it's all right. You're safe. No one is going to hurt you. I'll never let anyone hurt you."

She opened heavy-lidded eyes and gazed into his. "My love," she whispered. She raised her hand and touched his cheek.

Nick's heart leaped. She had called him her love.

Her eyes closed. "My love, mu—go—Billy."

Billy? . . . Her love? . . . Billy? Nick reeled, his bittersweet vision vanishing into the night, mocking him. Still he cradled her in his arms, soothing her, protecting her from the demon of her dreams. Finally, when she was quiet, he laid her back onto the bed and tucked the covers around her. An indescribable sadness enveloped him, and he felt alone as he never had before.

Nick turned from the bed and walked slowly to the desk. He removed a cigar, clipped the end, and placed the butt in his mouth. His hand shaking, he fished a match from his shirt pocket. He watched the flame, then touched it to the tobacco, puffing until the cigar glowed red at the end.

He walked to the window and sat on the sill, opening the casement enough to allow the smoke to drift into the bleak remains of the night. His course was clear. He had to find the man she called out for in her dream, the man she had called her love . . . the man she'd called Billy.

From the distant hills a plaintive wail rose, wavering and dying on the cold night wind. Nick raised his eyes, his heart echoing the cry—the mournful, lonesome howl of a lobo wolf.

CHAPTER

* 8 *

WEARY TO HIS BONES, NICK DRAINED THE LAST of his coffee and pushed his chair back from the breakfast table. Getting to his feet, he stretched his arms over his head and smothered a yawn. "I just want to check on Samantha again, then I'll be ready to go," he said to his grandfather.

Jake puffed on his pipe, sending a wreath of fragrant smoke around his white hair. His brow pleating in a frown, he shook his head. "It ain't necessary, Nick. Why don't you stay home and get some sleep?" He pointed across the table. "Jeff and I can handle the herd."

Nick shook his head. "You need all the help you can get to flush those cattle out and bring them down." He didn't add that he'd rather be busy—it'd give him less time to think. He knew even if he did stay home, sleep, if it did come, would only bring tormenting dreams of what might have been. He knew what he had to do and no amount of wishful thinking could change it. He left the room and went up the stairs.

When he opened the bedroom door, the early-morning

sky outside was alight with the sunrise. Slender, rosy beams crept across the floor toward the sleeping girl. He bent over the bed and placed his palm on her pale cheek. It was cool to his touch, and the swelling on her temple had gone down, but she still hadn't opened her eyes.

The door behind him opened and shut. Rosa bustled in carrying a pitcher of steaming water. "Don't worry, Nicky. She'll be all right," she whispered.

He lifted Samantha's slender hand and encased it in his own. "I hope so," he said.

Rosa stepped to his side and put a hand on his arm. "Your saddlebags are packed and in the hall downstairs. I'll take good care of your little one until you get back," she reassured him softly.

"I know you will, Rosa." Nick brushed a stray curl away from Samantha's face, his hand lingering on her hair. Stifling an impulse to kiss her good-bye, he abruptly turned away from the bed and strode out of the room. He hadn't told anyone about the nightmare Samantha had had last night—or the names she'd called in her sleep. That was something he had to handle on his own. His mind troubled, he picked up his saddle pack and walked out to join Jeff and his grandfather.

Jeff, his eyes full of mischief, handed Nick the reins of a mouse-colored horse.

Aware that Scout needed rest, Nick sighed, took the reins, and climbed into the saddle. The grulla dun arched its back. It was the only horse on the ranch that had to be bucked out every time it was ridden. Grateful he didn't have a hangover, he let it sunfish a time or two then settled it down to a steady lope.

Because of dry conditions in the valley, the cattle had stayed on the alpine meadows longer than usual. Due to the scanty hay crop, Nick knew most of the steers would have to go. He'd contracted an order for beef with Colonel Carson, the commander at Fort Garland. The cows with calves had been driven to the lower pastures, but the majority of the herd, the steers and yearlings grazing on the high reaches, were the most difficult to find.

When they reached the foothills, Jeff helped move the chuck wagon to the high pasture and set up camp while Jake and Nick organized the roundup. Jake split the hands into groups to comb the lower breaks. Nick and two punchers took the trail to the high country.

Nick, on the dun, led the way up the ridge, his keen eyes searching the brush-covered draws and thickets that provided perfect cover for the cattle.

The horse snorted, puffing streams of breath out in the early-morning air. Frost crunched under his dancing feet. The buffalo grass, gray sage, and mesquite sparkled as if covered in diamond dust.

Nick sucked in the crisp, cold air, using the bite of it to clear his mind. When the dun tossed its head and pranced, Nick grinned, knowing before the day was over the horse would be too tired to do much more than walk.

He noticed it was a lot colder now than it had been last month when he'd cut out fifty head and delivered them to the Cheyenne, an old custom between Jake and Chief White Eagle dating back to that first winter when Jake, his grandma Martha, and the two boys had little except the clothes on their backs and a few head of cattle. Caught in a blizzard while hunting, Jake would have frozen if White

Eagle's band of starving Cheyenne hadn't found him. They didn't kill him, but instead took him back to the ranch. Figuring he owed the Indians his life and the lives of his family, Jake cut out a dozen head for payment. Every fall since then, he sent cattle up to the Cheyenne winter camp above High Mesa.

In spite of the cold, sweat drenched Nick's shirt as he rode from one brushy draw to another, flushing out a few cattle and bunching them in groups. About halfway through, he removed his hat and wiped his forehead with his neckerchief. Puzzled, he studied the small herd. He turned to the freckle-faced man riding up behind him. "Danny, are you sure there aren't more of them up there?"

"Shore seems like there ought to be, but there ain't," the hand answered. "Slim ain't finding many either," he said, motioning to a cowboy so skinny he wouldn't make a shadow standing sideways.

Nick frowned. They hadn't found any carcasses, so wolves and such hadn't been bothering them. "Take this bunch back, and I'll check farther up." Leaving the hands, Nick rode into increasingly rugged terrain.

Discovering a faint trail, he dismounted and took a closer look. Senses alert, he climbed back on his horse and followed a trail just wide enough for the horse until he came to a rock slide. "Damn it, so that's what happened to them." The cattle had gotten in here and couldn't get out.

He dismounted and climbed over the rocks, following the trail into a wide box canyon. He skirted the area, keeping close to the scant brush, trying to get a head count. He found forty steers in one group and about twenty or so yearlings. Squatting on his heels, he moved slowly, trying not to get their attention. He knew that to a man on foot the wild cattle could be more dangerous than a grizzly bear.

The wary cattle were lean and hungry, but they were still alive, which told him they'd found water somewhere. He edged around the side of the draw until he came to another pile of rocks with a small pool at the foot. The slide had uncovered a spring. He grinned, feeling a rush of excitement. In this country water was more precious than gold. Tracing the stream to its source, he entered a small U-shaped area where water trickled out of the cliff. He bent, filling his hands with the cool liquid. Intent on getting a drink, he had buried his face in his palms when a noise behind him sent a chill creeping up his spine. He turned.

There, pawing the ground, stood the biggest, meanest-looking bull he'd ever seen. The animal snorted, staring at Nick with small, red eyes, then lowered his head and shook long, wickedly curved horns.

Glancing around, Nick found himself trapped. "Haa," he yelled, waving his hat, hoping to scare the animal away.

The bull took the noise as a challenge. He charged.

Nick, intending to throw himself to one side, stepped on a stone slick with mud. He crashed to the ground. Unable to escape, he brought his hands over his head, shielding his face from the sharp horns. The bony spikes sliced his flesh. Pain ripped through his arm. Nick cried out as eighteen hundred pounds of fury trampled his body.

Bellowing, the animal backed off, ready to charge again.

Every breath a torment, Nick scrambled to his feet. He groped at his side and removed his long-bladed knife. He crouched, legs apart, waiting for his chance. When the bull made another pass, Nick dodged aside, driving the blade up to its hilt in the animal's thick neck.

Tossing his head, the bull roared, splattering Nick with blood and foam. He lowered his horns.

Exhausted, Nick held the knife ready, aiming for the beast's heart. This time he dare not miss. He hadn't the strength to try again. Reeling from pain, he waited. The ground shook under the charging bull's weight. Using both hands, Nick drove the knife deep into the wide chest. A spurt of crimson covered his arms and hands.

The bull dropped to his knees, his nostrils blowing blood. He rolled to his side and was still.

Retrieving his knife, Nick cautiously made his way out of the canyon and climbed on his horse. Giving the dun his head, he fought the darkness and made his way back to camp.

Samantha twisted and turned, surrounded by nightmarish faces and troubled visions. She choked, drowning in a sea of red. She opened her mouth to scream, but uttered not a sound, enveloped in a smothering silence until a far-distant sound penetrated the quiet. The high-pitched scream of a horse in pain.

Another picture flashed through her mind, of a white horse, his proud neck bowed, his satin sides slashed with ribbons of dripping blood. A blond man raised a whip, again and again. Red foam dripped from the lash.

"No!" she cried, battling her way to her feet. She had to stop him. She threw back the covers and slid her feet over the edge of the bed. The struggle to her feet set the room to spinning. She grabbed the bedpost, tangling her legs in a voluminous mass of white.

Fighting nausea, she dragged her leaden feet through the bedroom to the hallway. Stumbling to the staircase, she clung to the railing and forced her trembling legs down the steps. She made her way across a huge area, her eyes fixed on a heavy-oak paneled door. She tugged it open.

The vision wavered. Miragelike green pastures shimmered and danced. She staggered across the wide veranda and into the parklike yard. Low white, red-roofed barns surrounded by miles of white fences loomed before her. She had to reach the stables. She had to stop Matthew. A blast of cold wind sucked her breath away and whipped her nightgown around her legs. She fought to stay upright. Sharp rocks pressed against a tender spot on her foot, but she paid them little heed. She leaned into the wind until, weak and trembling with exertion, she reached the white-fenced enclosure. Her head swimming, she held on to the rails and pulled herself through the fence.

"Stop it! No!" she called. "Stop!" She lurched toward the man and the white stallion, Cloud, that she'd raised from a colt. She swayed, her legs unable to hold her. Ears ringing, she crashed to the ground. The sky whirled above her, carrying the dream and the memory away. When the ground steadied, she raised herself on her elbow. The corral bars swam dizzily before her. Dust and grit flew into her eyes.

A horse squealed in fury.

She blinked, horrified to see a huge copper horse above her. He danced, screaming in nervous agitation. *He'll trample me.* Mustering her strength, she rolled away. Struggling to her knees, she grasped the pole corral bars and pulled herself to her feet.

Suddenly aware of her surroundings, she stared around her, unable to comprehend what she was seeing. A cluster of barns, sheds, and corrals—all made of logs?

Agony shot through her head, and she raised her hands to

clutch her temples. "Oh," she cried, staggering from the pain. She tumbled backward. Her shoulder crashed into the horse's legs.

He reared, pawing the sky over her head.

She knew she had to move, to get out of his way, but her exhausted limbs refused to obey. Strength drained, she closed her eyes, waiting for the sharp hooves to end her life.

Thundering hoofbeats and shouts came dimly to her ears. Strong arms closed about her, snatching her to safety against a firm, muscular chest. The smell of woodsmoke, leather, and tobacco engulfed her. Dazed, she looked up to see a man, his bronzed face contorted with fury.

He stared down at her, his dark eyes narrowed to slits. The breeze caught long, blue-black hair, draping strands of it across his chiseled features. "Are you all right?" he asked harshly. When she nodded, he carried her to the corral gate and shifted her to the arms of a grizzled, gray-haired man.

The old man gave her a comforting smile, then shifted his attention to something behind her. Twisting to see, Samantha wished she hadn't.

His eyes white with terror, the stallion screamed, thrashing the air bare inches from the man.

Lithe and lean, his large frame padded with sleek, powerful muscles, the dark man eased forward. When the horse charged, he rolled away. His breath coming in labored gulps, his face twisting with pain, he slowly got to his feet. He raised his eyes to the blowing horse. "Easy. Easy, boy," he crooned.

Her mouth dry, she watched him walk toward the stallion. Talking softly, he inched his hand toward the hackamore. Holding the animal steady, he stroked the satiny neck until the big sorrel quieted.

With a sad smile the man turned and limped toward them. Dirt covered the harsh planes of his copper face, and his eyes, intense and piercing, fastened on hers. "Are you sure you're all right?" he asked softly.

She nodded, sucking in her breath, drawn into their shining quicksilver depths. Her pulse quickened, sending her heart fluttering against her rib cage.

"We'd best get the two of you to the house," the elderly man said, breaking the spell. He shifted her in his arms and took a limping step toward the log ranch house.

The dark man brushed the dirt from his shirt and stepped forward. "I'll carry her," he said.

The old man shook his head. "You can hardly walk yourself," he argued. "Besides, she's such a little mite, I can manage."

The tall man stood quietly, his arms extended, waiting.

"Oh, all right," the elder grumbled, relinquishing her.

Transferred into the dark man's arms and cradled against his chest, Samantha felt awed by his strength. Firm cords of muscle ran down from his neck into broad shoulders. Whipcordlike arms held her gently while large hands with slender fingers supported her weight. She looked up into his face. A breeze lifted a lock of his long hair, brushing it across her forehead. Even though his features were harsh, his bones were finely sculpted, his skin weathered to a tough, burnished brown. His face was too rugged to be called handsome but striking nevertheless. She could see his pain, but he moved with a smooth pantherlike grace as he followed the silver-haired man toward the house.

The old man hobbled along, pausing only to wave a hand toward a buggy pulling up in front. He muttered to himself, his words drifting back to Samantha. "Damn young fool. He'll probably fall down and drop her in the dirt. But after all, she *is* his wife."

Overhearing him, Samantha opened her mouth in shock. *Wife?* She stared up at her rescuer. *But I don't know him. . . . I don't know any of them.*

When they reached the house, a frantic, heavyset woman waiting on the porch ushered them inside. Her plump brow crinkled with concern, she patted Samantha's hand. "Oh, my poor little one, what has happened to you?" she cried. Lifting her skirts, she scurried behind them.

The tall man carried Samantha upstairs. Turning into a large bedroom, he bent and placed her on the bed. He gently lifted the covers over her.

She lay back against the pillows, her heart hammering. She frowned. *I don't know this place.* Afraid, confused, she looked about the room. "Where am I?" She shifted her gaze from Nick to the gray-haired woman, then to the two men standing to one side. "Who are you?"

Another man, slender and gray-haired, entered the room. He carried a small black bag. "Young lady, the important thing right now is how are *you?*" He turned, pointing a finger in the direction of the dark man, the elder man, and the blond that had been by the corral. "Rosa, shoo them out so I can examine my patient."

When the door closed, he turned to her with a smile. "I'm Dr. Henry Johnson. I've been taking care of you since your accident. You fell and hit your head. Gave us all quite a scare."

"I don't remember," Samantha said. She received a thorough examination from the physician and found she instantly liked and trusted both him and Rosa, the Spanish housekeeper, who clucked over her like a mother hen. When they asked why she'd gone into the corral, she couldn't give them an answer. She had no idea.

The doctor checked her head and rebandaged her foot. She sat there during the whole process in a state of bewilderment. "How did I get hurt? I don't remember cutting my foot . . . or hitting my head." She saw Rosa give a questioning look to the doctor.

He patted her hand. "Don't worry. Things might be confused for a while. Just relax, rest, and try to sleep," he said. "I'll bet Rosa can round up something to tempt your appetite, too. Looks like you could use some meat on your bones." He closed the bag and got to his feet. "I'll be back to see you tomorrow."

He turned to Rosa before going out the door. "Try to keep things calm around here, if that's possible. I'll see to Nick. Jake said a cow stomped on him."

When he'd left, Samantha looked up at the housekeeper. "Rosa, who is Nick?"

The woman beamed a smile at her. "Why, little one, have you forgotten that, too? Nick is your husband."

The room whirled before Samantha's eyes. "Husband?" It was true. *Why can't I remember?* She raised a hand and covered her eyes . . . nothing. She remembered waking to find herself in a corral with a wild horse—before that her life was a complete blank.

The doctor examined Nick's chest, poking at the bruises where the bull's hooves had struck him. "This is going to be pretty sore for a while. That mossy horn cracked a couple of

your ribs,'' he said, wrapping Nick's chest tightly with
bandages. He opened a bottle of antiseptic and dabbed it on
the cuts on Nick's arm and hands. ''I don't know why I just
don't set up shop out here. You McBrides keep me here
most of the time anyhow.''

''Oww! Damn it, Doc, don't you have something that
burns a little more?'' Nick complained, wincing.

The physician grinned slyly. ''As a matter of fact I do,
but I didn't know you wanted that.''

Nick raised his head to meet the doctor's blue eyes.
''Doc, are you sure Samantha is all right?''

''She's confused, but so would anybody be that stayed
around here very long. Right now she's having a problem
with her memory. I am a little concerned about that.''

''What do you mean?'' Nick asked. ''What can't she
remember?''

''She can't recollect anything that happened before she
woke up in the corral this morning.'' He dabbed at the last
of Nick's injuries then straightened and closed his bag.

''She will remember, though. It will come back to her,
won't it?''

''Probably.''

''Probably? You're not sure?''

''Nick, she hit her head—hard. I've never seen it, but I've
heard of things like this happening. Sometimes they remember, at least some things, and sometimes they don't remember anything that happened before the accident.''

Nick felt like somebody had just hit him in the stomach.
''Can't we do anything to help her?''

''Yes, you can. Try to keep the usual mayhem around
here to a minimum. She needs peace and rest, and some of

Rosa's cooking.'' The doctor started to leave the room, then turned back. ''Nick, are you really married to the girl?''

''Yes, Doc; at least I think so.''

The physician arched his brows, peering at Nick over the rim of his glasses. ''You think so? Don't you know?''

Nick sighed. ''Well, I'm really not sure. Things were sort of confused that night.''

Dr. Johnson shook his gray head. ''I don't know why that doesn't surprise me.'' He rolled his eyes toward the ceiling. Muttering to himself, he went out the door.

Nick washed and changed clothes, then hurried upstairs. He eased the door open and peeked in, but Samantha was asleep.

Rosa put a finger to her lips and heaved herself to her feet. She motioned for him to sit down in the chair. ''I'm going downstairs and fix supper,'' she whispered. She patted his shoulder and left the room.

Perching on the edge of the chair, Nick picked up Samantha's hand and brushed it with his lips. Nick's gut wrenched, shaken by what could have happened to her. Why had she gone to the corral? Another mystery. He kissed her palm gently and held it against his cheek, misery washing over him at the part he'd played in her suffering. ''Oh kitten, I wish you'd wake up and throw something at me.''

''Now, why would I want to do that?'' a soft voice asked.

Nick gazed into eyes the color of new spring grass. ''I didn't mean to wake you,'' he said. ''How are you feeling?''

''Better than you look.'' Lifting her hand from his, she raised it to brush a lock of hair from his eyes. ''How are you? The doctor said a cow stomped on you.''

Nick sucked in a pain-filled breath. He wouldn't care if he was dying, just to have her touch him like that. "Oh, I'm all right."

"Rosa said you are my husband," she said, biting her lip. "I don't know what's happened. I can't remember you."

Nick saw her distress. "You hit your head. It's all right, you'll remember." He wasn't about to tell her he didn't remember either. A glad thought occurred to him. If she didn't remember him, then she didn't remember Billy either. He grinned.

"When were we married?" she asked.

"Uh, not long ago. In fact we're still on our honeymoon," he said. At least that was the truth.

She inhaled. "We are?" Her eyes widened. She looked frightened.

Nick shook his head. "Oh hell, me and my big mouth." He patted her hand. "Don't you worry none. I won't act like a husband until you want me to."

She turned pink and ducked her head.

Nick's pulse quickened. She was pretty as a desert sunset when she blushed like that.

The door opened, and Rosa entered the room carrying a tray. "Well, seems you are feeling better, little one." She placed the meal on the bedside table and turned to Nick. "You run along downstairs. Your food is on the table."

He hesitated, hating to leave.

The housekeeper waved a chubby hand at him, shooing him like she would a stray chicken. "Go now. Let the girl eat in peace," she scolded.

He stood there for a minute, then shrugged his shoulders and grinned at Samantha. The smile she gave him in return made his heart leap. Feeling like a silly schoolboy, he blew her a kiss and stepped into the hall. Maybe her losing her memory wasn't such a bad thing after all. He'd just have to see that nobody told her what really happened until he had time to sort everything out.

CHAPTER

9

"NOO!"

The terror-filled cry jolted Nick from a deep slumber. Blinking, he sat up in bed, listening. It came again. *Samantha!* He snatched his pants from the chair by the bed and yanked them up, fastening them as he entered her room. Lengthening his stride, he hurried to the small figure writhing on the bed. He bent toward her, gently shaking her awake. "Samantha. It's Nick. Wake up, honey."

Still captive to her dreams, she jerked away.

When he shook her again, she opened tear-filled green eyes and stared up at him. She shrank back into the covers.

"It's Nick, honey. Remember? Your husband," he said. He watched her tension ease. "You were having a nightmare."

Her face crumpled. She buried her face in her hands; sobs shook her slender frame. "It was so horrible."

He sat on the bed and gathered her into his arms, drawing her tightly against his bare chest. He lifted a hand and stroked her hair. "It's all right. You're safe."

Gradually the arms clinging to him relaxed, and her sobs became quiet sniffles. She fell back to sleep in his arms.

Reluctant to release her, he buried his face in her hair, brushing his lips against the silken strands. He frowned, thinking about the dark dreams that continued to plague her. So far she hadn't remembered the nightmares when she'd awakened. What had happened to her? *Damn, I wish I knew.* He bent his head, rubbing his cheek against her forehead. She looked so little, so fragile. A strong wish to protect her washed over him, along with a feeling of helplessness and confusion.

He'd never felt this way about a woman before. Why was this one different? She'd been conscious a week now and just one look from her made him weak-kneed and tongue-tied. He eased her back into the bed and gently kissed her forehead. Lifting the bedcovers, he fought the urge to join her and hold her in his arms. He sucked in a breath and quickly tucked the quilts around her. *Hell, I'd scare her worse than the nightmares.* Remembering Billy, he scowled into the firelit darkness.

Some marriage he had, all the responsibilities and none of the benefits. He couldn't do a thing about either one until she either regained her memory, or he found the man she called out for in her dreams. He shook his head. Either way he'd lose her. A sharp pain twisted his insides at the thought, and he cursed himself for already caring too much.

Running a hand through his hair, he walked to the fireplace and added more logs to the glowing embers. As he turned to leave the room he caught sight of the black dress lying over the chair. Another mystery. The two ugly mourning dresses were the only ones she had. She needed something pretty. He smiled. *I'll take care of that little detail today.* He paused for a moment, watching her sleep, then padded across the floor, his bare feet making no sound as he closed the door and returned to his own room.

Samantha awakened to a bright sun streaming through the lace-curtained window. She scooted back against the headboard, drawing her knees against her chest. Noticing the fresh supply of logs on the fire, she smiled. *Nick.*

A week ago she'd opened her eyes to find herself a stranger to the ranch, to the room, to the people hovering over her, and to herself. A stranger with no past, a present that frightened her, and a future that loomed vast and uncertain. In that week she had begun to cope, growing to know and care about the McBrides and Rosa, even though she still couldn't remember them.

Bits and pieces of her past sometimes flitted through her mind—a phrase, a face, names—but nothing made any sense. She fingered the crazy quilt on the bed, thinking how it resembled her life. Odd bits and pieces patched together, with no pattern, no design. And the dreams, dark, bloody nightmares that woke her screaming, her body drenched in perspiration, making her wonder if she was better off not remembering.

She closed her eyes and hugged herself, reliving the comforting feel of Nick's arms around her when she'd awakened last night. She couldn't remember the dream, only the horror. He'd held her, soothed her, made her feel safe.

Since she was better, she'd suggested that she move to the extra room, but he wouldn't have it. He'd said he was comfortable there, and he wanted her to have this room.

She took a deep breath, savoring the faint scent of

tobacco, leather, and pine smoke. His room, his smells, they surrounded her, quickening her pulse.

Nick McBride. Her husband. The idea filled her with mixed emotions. Although she didn't remember him, she found him handsome, strong and masculine enough to make any girl's heart race. But at times something about him frightened her. An undercurrent of tightly leased savagery she didn't understand. And other times he could be so gentle.

She sighed, recalling how Nick, battered and bloody, his ribs broken and so tired he could hardly stand, had insisted on being the one to carry her to the house. Even then, his arms seemed familiar, as though she'd been there before.

Rosa told her Nick had stayed by her side when she was so sick and even bathed her when she had a fever. The thought made her blush, even though she knew they were married.

Married. She wished she could remember their wedding . . . and the honeymoon. Considering the last, she smiled. Yes, especially the honeymoon. She grew breathless just thinking about it. She closed her eyes, wondering what it would be like having him make love to her, but her imagination could go no further than a few kisses. *Drat!* Instead of having nightmares, why couldn't she dream about that?

Anxious to see the object of her thoughts, she scrambled out of bed and removed the overlarge nightgown. She lifted her dress and slipped it on, grimacing as she did so. She certainly hoped the stage line found her trunk soon. She couldn't remember, but Nick said she'd lost all her clothes while they were on their honeymoon. She frowned. He didn't explain how she came to have the two black dresses.

She gathered the folds of extra material around her waist, looking at herself in the mirror. They certainly couldn't be hers. Why, they didn't even fit.

She picked up her brush and tried to bring some order to her hair. Unable to do more than remove the tangles, she left it hanging in shining waves to her waist. After straightening the room, she hurried down the stairs.

Entering the dining room, she found Jake and Rosa sitting at the table. "Good morning," she said, smiling.

Rosa beamed a smile at her and went to get another cup.

"Mornin', honey. How are you feeling today?" Jake asked.

"I'm fine." She sat down beside him. "Where's Nick?"

"He and Jeff went to town to pick up supplies." Jake sighed. "Maybe this time they'll make it home with them."

She looked at him, curious to know what he meant, but before she could ask, Rosa bustled back in with a plate of steak, eggs, and biscuits.

"Here's your breakfast, little one. Eat, and then we will find you something else to wear," she said, setting the platter down in front of Samantha.

"Thank you, Rosa. It looks delicious," she said, buttering the flaky bread. "And the other sounds heavenly. I'm so sick of looking like an ugly old hag."

Jake leaned forward and patted her hand. "You could never look like that, darlin', no matter what you put on."

After breakfast she and Rosa cut down one of the woman's dresses so Samantha could have a change of clothes. Since Rosa's wardrobe was either brown or red, and red clashed horribly with Samantha's hair, they decided on an almost new, brown dress too tight for Rosa.

Bending her head above the sturdy fabric, Samantha

busily stitched up the seams, grateful that at last she'd found something she was good at. In the past week she'd discovered that there were many household things she didn't know how to do, such as cooking, baking, and laundry. Under Rosa's instruction she'd learned a great deal.

She smiled. She could even make rose-scented soap now, like the small cake that had been in her things. She sighed, considering her lack of knowledge. Apparently she'd been extremely lazy in her past life, or extremely pampered.

She looked across the table at the gray-haired woman who was busily mending socks. "Rosa, tell me about Nick. What was he like when he was little?"

Rosa looked up and smiled. "You wouldn't believe to see him now, *chica,* but he was very shy and sweet. He used to bring me presents, things he'd found—wildflowers, tiny bird's eggs, shiny rocks." She lowered her lashes, silent for a moment, as if recalling the memories. Opening her eyes, she gazed at Samantha. "He didn't like to be teased and what a temper! And when he was hurt, he'd try to hide it, but you could tell by looking in his eyes."

Samantha remembered how his gray eyes turned dark when he was angry and lit with quicksilver when he laughed.

Rosa frowned, continuing. "I remember once Jeff was invited to a party in town. Nicky did not get an invitation. He'd tried to hide the hurt, encouraging Jeff to go without him. Jeff did go, but came home early with a black eye. I found out later he'd gotten into a fight because someone called Nick a dirty Indian. Jeff never told Nick, but I'm sure he knew anyway."

Samantha blinked back the moisture in her eyes as Rosa

told her about the prejudice the small, orphaned boy had endured. And sometimes, when he let his guard down, she could see the little boy Rosa'd described. Shy, uncertain, and sweet, with a wistful look in his gray eyes that made her long to hold him, comfort him, and kiss away his cares.

After lunch Samantha gathered up her sewing and went upstairs to her room. She finished the hem and hung the dress on a hanger to allow the creases to fall out.

She stretched her arms above her head to remove the kinks from her back, then smothering a yawn, lay down on her bed. She closed her eyes and drifted off to sleep, her thoughts filled with a tall, gray-eyed man.

Sighing, Nick flipped the butt of his cigar into the street and eased away from the post he'd leaned against for the last hour. He eyed the dressmaking establishment across from him, making sure the coast was clear. Crossing the dusty street, he grinned, thinking the place had been busier than a whorehouse on a Saturday night, except it had been full of women, not cowboys. Spying Jeff coming down the street, Nick hurried inside and shoved the door closed behind him. It crashed shut with a bang that rattled the hinges.

A tiny, voluptuous woman parted a curtained doorway, her wide blue eyes searching the room. "*Mon Dieu!* What een zee world ees all that noise?" Spying Nick, her eyes widened even more. "Was that you, monsieur?"

Nick looked around. He was the only one there. "I ain't monsieur. I'm Nick McBride, and I guess it was me making all the racket." He snatched his hat off his head, twisting the brim nervously in his hands. He scanned the room, taking note of all the hats, laces, and feathers of every description. He felt like a fox caught in a henhouse.

"Can I help you, monsieur?"

"Nick, ma'am, the name's Nick." Suddenly doubting the wisdom of his actions, he edged backward to the door.

She gave him a knowing smile and stepped forward. Taking his hat, she placed a hand on his arm and led him through the curtained area into a sitting room. She raised her hand and gently pushed him back into a chair. "I theenk you weel be more comfortable here, no?"

"No, uh, yes." He ran a finger around his neck to loosen his neckerchief, which had suddenly become too tight.

"You have come to buy something for a lady, perhaps?" She poured a cup of steaming liquid and handed it to him.

Nick took the fragile china cup in both hands, afraid he would drop it. He brought it to his lips and took a swallow. God. What was it? He blinked, trying not to gag.

Smiling, she reached out and retrieved the cup from him. "I theenk perhaps monsieur would prefer something else instead of tea." She opened a cupboard door, removed a tall bottle and a crystal shot glass. "Brandy, I theenk."

Nick nodded. He sure as hell needed a real drink. He lifted the glass she'd put in front of him and took a swallow, washing the taste of the tea away.

She refilled his glass. "And now, m—Neek, what can I do for you?"

He took another swallow, feeling a little more at ease. "I need clothes for a woman—my wife—everything, I guess."

"What size ees she?" the woman asked.

"Size? Hell, I don't know." He frowned, eyeing her. "A

little taller than you, and uh—not quite so—uh—'' he spluttered, motioning with his hands.

She flashed him a dimpled grin. ''I theenk I understand,'' she said, opening a tall cupboard.

Sometime later Nick finished off the last of the brandy and eyed the pile of things in front of him. ''Lord, I never knew a woman wore so much stuff,'' he said, laughing. He'd felt awkward and embarrassed at first, especially buying underwear, but after he'd gotten the hang of it, it had been fun.

''Are you sure about the corset, Neeky?''

''I'm sure, Mimi. I don't want my wife laced up in one of those contraptions.''

''And the bustle?'' she asked, waving a thing that looked like a wire nest in front of his nose.

''Nope.'' He liked watching her sashay around the house and didn't want any bustle spoiling his view.

Waiting until the dressmaker left the room, Nick lifted a lacy, green nightie from the pile. It was soft and so sheer he could see his hand right through it. His lips lifted in a wicked smile. He'd like her in that just fine. Dropping the garment on top of the rest, he parted the curtains and went into the front of the shop. ''You're sure you'll have that other stuff before Christmas?''

The woman nodded. ''It weel be ready.''

He fingered the bolt of green China silk. She'd said it was iridescent. He just knew it shimmered and changed color like Samantha's eyes. He'd ordered the dress, black silk stockings, and soft kid slippers for Christmas.

Nick endured Jeff's teasing all the way home, but today nothing could dampen his spirits. Staggering under the stack of parcels, Nick made his way up the stairs. Jake'd told him Samantha was taking a nap. While he hated to wake her, he just couldn't wait for her to see all the things he'd bought. He grinned, thinking the French dressmaker'd talked him out of everything but his skin, but Samantha was worth it. He raised his boot and gave the door a kick.

Samantha, answering his "knock," opened the door, gasping in surprise. "Nick? What on earth?"

He crossed the floor and dumped the packages on the bed. "Just a few things I thought you might need," he said.

"For me?" she asked, her eyes shining. She picked up a large parcel and tore it open, shaking out lengths of bright calico. "Oh, it's beautiful." She held it up to her and twirled toward him. Holding the fabric with one hand, she looped the other around his neck, drawing his head down to give him a happy kiss.

"There's more," he suggested, grinning. He watched her open the rest, enjoying her delight and embarrassment when she came across the filmy underthings. When the bed was piled high with clothes, thread, pins and needles, lengths of fabric, ribbons and laces, and all kinds of gewgaws, she opened the last package, the filmy green nightgown.

Her eyes widening, she carefully unfolded the sheer garment. She ducked her head, blushing the color of a ripe peach. She raised her eyelashes and gave him a shy smile. She left the bed and came toward him, her eyes like deep emerald pools. She slid her arms around his neck. "Oh Nick. Thank you. Thank you," she said with a sob.

Alarmed, Nick held her away, looking at her tears. "Is something wrong? Why are you crying?" he asked, confused.

"Because I'm so happy," she said, smothering his face with kisses.

"Women." He sighed. He'd never understand them, but at a time like this who cared? Smiling, he enclosed her in his arms, then bent his head, fastening his mouth on her soft red lips.

CHAPTER

* 10 *

SAMANTHA LEANED OVER THE CORRAL FENCE
and scratched the sorrel behind his ears. She smiled when he
nickered and moved closer, nudging her with his nose. "Is
this what you're looking for, big fellow? She took a bright
red apple from her apron and held it out to him. He greedily
lapped his lips over it, nuzzling her palm with his velvety
nose. She patted his neck, raising a cloud of dust. "Whew!"
Waving it away, she glanced at the barn. She should find
what she needed in there.

She entered the building and had just begun to search
among the vast array of saddles and tack when she heard
Nick call her name. "I'm in here," she answered.

A tall shadow fell across the doorway. She looked up to
see her husband watching her.

He scratched his head. "What are you looking for?"

"This," she said, holding up a currycomb and brush.

He frowned. "For the sorrel?" When she nodded, his
frown deepened. "Samantha, that horse is wild."

"Pooh. He's such a baby. I intend to ride him someday,"
she said, smiling up at him.

He stepped forward and grabbed her by the shoulders. "Samantha, leave the horse breaking to me. I don't want you to get hurt." He raised his hand and wiped a smudge off her nose. "Besides," he said, grinning, "you probably don't even know how to ride."

She placed her hands on her hips. "I do so. I've been riding since before I could walk."

He gave her a startled look. "How do you know?"

She stopped. How did she know? "I'm—not sure how, but I know it's true."

"Let's find out." Clasping her hand, he led her back to the house, leaving her outside the room. "I'll be back in a minute." He returned, grinning broadly, and thrust a handful of clothes and a pair of boots at her. "Try these on," he said. "They used to be Jeff's."

When he left, she quickly changed into the clothes. Looking at herself in the mirror, she giggled. The skintight pants were a good foot too long and she could barely button the shirt, even though the cuffs hung down over her hands. *Jeff must have been built like a ruler,* she thought.

"Are you ready?" Nick called from the hall. When she opened the door, he burst out laughing. "A bit long, but they never looked that good on Jeff," he said, eyeing her. He rolled up her shirt cuffs, then bent and did the same with the pants. "How about the boots?"

"A little large, but they'll do," she said, laughing.

"So will you," he said softly.

Her heart racing, Samantha waited breathlessly, hoping for a kiss. Instead he mussed her hair.

"Okay, cowgirl. Let's see if you can ride."

Samantha followed him downstairs and out onto the porch. Her heart plummeted. There, saddled and apparently waiting for her, stood the oldest horse she'd ever seen. "Nick?"

He lifted her into the saddle. "I'm not letting you take any chances until I know you can ride. Jeff learned to ride on Daisy when he was a sprout." Still holding the reins, he looked up. "Do you want me to lead her?"

"Of course not," she said indignantly. Taking the reins, she nudged the horse with her heels. She was probably in more danger on this horse than she would be riding the sorrel. Daisy might drop dead and fall on her. When the mare snorted, Samantha, ashamed of her thoughts, patted the grizzled old neck.

"Well, at least you haven't fallen off yet," Nick teased.

"I'd race you, but I'm afraid she isn't up to it." Samantha raised her eyebrows, noticing a basket tied to Nick's saddle horn. "What's that?"

"Well, the weather is so nice, I thought we should enjoy it. I had Rosa pack us a picnic," he said. "That's why I was looking for you earlier."

Samantha, fascinated, watched dents pop in and out of his cheeks. "I didn't know you had dimples." Amazed, she saw him tuck his head down. Her tall, rugged husband was blushing! She giggled. He raised his head and looked at her so intently, she felt her own cheeks flush with warmth. "Where are we going to have this picnic?" she asked shyly.

Shifting his gaze from her, he pointed to a group of golden aspens. "Down there. Next to the creek."

Samantha stood in her stirrups, trying to see. "It's beautiful." A row of tall white stones on a nearby hill caught her eye. "What's that?"

"That's our graveyard. My dad and mother are buried there. If you like, I'll show it to you after we eat."

"Thank you, I would like that." Another cemetery flitted through her memory, like a scene in a kaleidoscopic dream, disappearing as quickly as it had come. She shivered.

"What's wrong?" he asked, frowning.

She gave him a reassuring smile. "Just a flash from my past, but it's gone now." She looked up at his serious face. "Do you think I'll ever remember, Nick?"

"Sure. I know you will," he said, taking her hand.

"I hope so. I would like to remember our courtship and our wedding." She lowered her lashes. "And our honeymoon." She felt his hand tense. Puzzled, she glanced up to see him chewing on his lower lip, a deep frown on his face. "Nick, is anything wrong?"

"Uhh–no, kitten. Everything's just dandy." He patted her hand, then rode ahead, leading the way to the creek.

Samantha followed thoughtfully. He looked like that every time she mentioned their wedding. *Why?*

"Is this all right?" he asked, dismounting.

"Oh, it's perfect," she said, enchanted by the beauty around her. Trees in bright yellows, oranges, and reds encircled a small green meadow. Sparkling sunlit water rippled musically over a clear, pebble-bottomed stream.

He held up his hands to help her down.

"I can manage," she said, regretting the words the minute they left her mouth. A look she could have sworn was disappointment flashed over his face. The same feeling hit her as she realized she'd missed a chance to be in his arms. She sat gazing after him for a moment, admiring the sleek, graceful way he moved. She sighed, watching him spread the blanket, almost wishing he could find other things to do than eat off it. She closed her eyes, imagining herself living her romantic fantasy.

"Samantha? Are you all right?" he asked by her elbow.

She blinked, giving him a startled look. Her heart thudding, she felt herself turning crimson. "Uh—yes," she stammered. "I guess I was daydreaming."

"Oh?" he grinned.

His knowing look rattled her so much she caught her heel in the stirrup in her hurry to dismount. The muscular arms closing around her might have saved her from landing in the dirt, but they did nothing for her composure.

"Careful, cowgirl," he teased, releasing her.

Heading for the blanket, she stumbled over a rock. *Merciful heavens! He must think I'm the clumsiest person alive.* She concentrated on each step until she lowered herself to the ground. *I wonder how I ever made it through my wedding without falling on my face.* Just one look from him and her feet seemed to lose all sense of direction.

When he carried the heavy hamper over, she unpacked a feast of fried chicken, boiled eggs, a small crock of baked beans, a loaf of sourdough bread still warm from the oven, and last of all, a big slab of chocolate cake and a tin jug full of lemonade. Handing him a tin plate and cup and silver-ware, she laughed. "Do you think this is enough?"

He frowned. "I don't know. Maybe it isn't."

Her mouth open, she stared in disbelief. He was serious. Watching him put away most of the meal, she wondered how he ate like that and remained so slim. She feared she'd put Rosa's bulk to shame if she tried it.

After they'd eaten, Nick lay down and soon fell fast asleep, his chest rising and falling with even breathing, his lips opening slightly to emit an occasional soft snore.

Standing over him, she could almost swear she'd seen him like this before. *Of course you have, you imbecile. He is your husband.* The thought sent a thrill up her spine. His face in sleep lost its harshness. He seemed younger, almost like a boy. He must be tired, she thought. Careful not to wake him, she investigated her surroundings.

Walking to where the swift water was several inches deeper, she stretched out on a sun-warmed slab of rock. Hearing a splash, she turned her head to see a small dark gray bird disappear into the stream and bob along under the water, pecking at the bottom. It surfaced and flew up only to repeat the performance farther downstream.

In a nearby fir tree a chattering pine squirrel noisily scolded a trio of Steller's jays who ignored it and continued to pluck scarlet berries from a sprawling elderberry bush. A pair of small violet-winged butterflies fluttered around a scarlet-berried chokecherry. Entranced, Samantha watched until she grew drowsy and closed her eyes.

A while later she awakened to feel something tickling her lip. Her eyes closed, she wrinkled her nose until it quit. The tickling came again, across her forehead and down her nose. She sighed and brushed it away. When it started again, she raised her lashes to see Nick inches away, grinning at her. "You!" she said, laughing.

"What's the matter, Samantha? Ticklish?" He drew the long blade of grass across her upper lip.

Her eyes locked on his, she eased her hand into the frigid water and splashed him with it.

"Now you've done it," he said, reaching out for her.

Dodging his grasp, she darted away, squealing in mock terror when he caught her. His arms closed around her, he rolled to the ground, carrying her with him. Laughing, she twisted away only to find herself captive again.

Straddling her legs, he pinned her arms above her head. "Give up?" he growled.

"Never," she cried.

He released her hands, lowering his fingers to her ribs.

"No! No! Nick, don't you dare!"

"Ah-ha, you *are* ticklish." He dug his fingertips into her sides.

Laughing hysterically, she twisted and turned under him, trying to free herself from his tormenting hands. "All right," she gasped. "You win."

"I win?" A wicked smile crossed his face. "I think the loser should pay a penalty. Don't you?" he drawled.

Her heart racing, Samantha gazed into his eyes. "What penalty?"

"This." His eyes quicksilver, he lowered his mouth to hers.

Surrendering to his kiss, she trembled as a strange quivering fire flowed through her veins, making her breathless with delight. Her heart thumped loudly against her ribs. "Oh Nick." She sighed when he raised his head. Pushing a long lock of hair out of his eyes, she trailed her finger across his forehead and down his nose to his lips.

He opened his mouth, capturing her fingertip between white even teeth. His eyes devilish, he teased it with the tip of his tongue.

Samantha gasped, her eyes widening.

"Witch," he murmured, releasing her finger. Heaving a shuddering sigh, he gave her a quick peck on the nose and pulled her to her feet. "Now, my delightful imp, it's time we headed home."

Watching him walk away, Samantha sighed with disappointment and followed him back to the picnic site.

He gathered up the scant lunch remains and put the utensils in the basket, leaving her to fold up the blanket. Holding it in her arms, she traced the bright Indian designs with her finger. To him it had been just a place to sit and have a picnic. To her it could have had all kinds of intriguing possibilities. "Drat!"

"Come on, slowpoke," he said.

Releasing a wistful sigh, she tossed the blanket to him and climbed on the mare. He deftly tied the bright cover behind his saddle and mounted to join her.

Side by side they rode in companionable silence to the grave sites. His face sober, Nick helped her down from the horse. Taking her hand, he led her to a single headstone engraved "Jim and Fawn McBride." "This is where my folks are buried. They died when the wagon lost its brakes and went over the cliff going back to High Mesa. I would have been with them except that day they'd left me with my grandparents. We buried them side by side."

Samantha remembered the picture she'd seen in his room of a beautiful, dark-skinned woman and a fair-haired man. She could tell they'd been very much in love. "I'm sure they would have wanted it that way," she said softly, blinking back the moisture in her eyes.

Squeezing her hand, he walked to another headstone. The dark moss-encrusted letters read "Martha McBride." "This is where my grandma lies. She died of pneumonia two winters after I came to live with them." He swallowed, picking a faded rose from a rambling bush. "She liked flowers, especially red roses. Had them all around the place, but after she was gone, they all died." Head bowed, eyes closed, he stood silently by the headstone.

Choking back a sob, she bit her lip, feeling his pain.

Blinking his eyes, he walked to another pair of white markers etched with the names "Joseph and Kierstin McBride." "This is Jeff's folks. They died of cholera when Jeff was three. I was ten when he came to live with me and Jake." He pointed to another small group of headstones behind the family's. "The others belong to ranch hands who didn't have any family. We figured they belonged here, too, same as us." He took a couple of steps.

"This spot over here is saved for Jeff and his family, if he ever finds anybody that'll put up with him." He led her to another spot. "This is for me and mine." He grinned. "But since we don't intend to be there for a long time, we don't need to worry about it yet."

He gave her a swat on the bottom. "Race you to the horses," he said, giving her a head start. "Careful you don't fall off."

Samantha, winning easily, sighed, looking at her mare. Narrowing her eyes, she looked at the bay Nick had ridden. *Why not?* Flashing him an impish grin, she scrambled into the saddle.

"Samantha? What are you doing?"

"The loser pays a penalty, remember?" she triumphantly called back. "You lost. That's your penalty." Giving a joyful whoop, she raced around him.

"Samantha, you'll break your neck. Come back here!"

She doubled over with laughter, watching him climb onto the mare. Daisy was so short and Nick so tall, it looked like he should be carrying the horse. She let him tag along behind for a while before she relented and rode back to him. "Will you admit I know how to ride?" she asked.

"Like the wind," he answered.

"Next time will you get me a decent horse and leave poor Daisy out to pasture?"

"I promise," he said, giving her a hopeful look.

"Good," she said, nudging her horse into a run.

"Samantha, come back here this minute. Samantha!" he bellowed. "Do you hear me?"

"See you later, *cowboy,*" she called back, racing for the barn.

CHAPTER

* 11 *

AWAKENED BY THE HOWLING WIND, SAMANTHA
stared at the ceiling, too keyed up to sleep. Glancing toward
the lace-curtained window, she noticed the darkness outside. She eyed the fireplace where a bit of solitary log
remained. A slow smile crept across her face. He'd be in
anytime.

Propping pillows behind her, she sat up, remembering the
fiery kiss they'd shared after the picnic. *Drat.* She was just
beginning to enjoy it when Jake poked his head in and
called them to dinner.

Later she'd watched Nick, hoping for a repeat performance, but every time she caught his eye, he turned away.
She frowned. He'd been like that for two days, ever since
she'd had the nightmare again. She'd awakened in his arms,
but instead of being warm and comforting, he'd been cold
and withdrawn, not at all like himself.

Yesterday, when she'd cornered him and held up her face
for a morning kiss, he'd just mussed her hair. She sighed.
Although she wasn't certain what she wanted him to do, she

certainly didn't want to be treated like a pesky kid sister, or be avoided either.

She drew her brush through her hair, removing the tangles and coaxing soft ringlets around her face. Putting the brush aside, she lifted her hand mirror and eyed her reflection by the faint firelight. After pinching her cheeks and biting her lips to give them more color, she put the mirror on the table. She adjusted the bedcovers, folding them to come just above her waist, allowing her pale skin to glow through the sheer green nightie. An impish smile crossed her face. That should do it.

Hearing footsteps in the hall, she lay back against the pillows, lowering her lashes when the door slowly opened.

His arms loaded with wood, Nick entered the room and padded barefoot across the floor. Dressed only in his breeches, his hair tousled, and needing a shave, he still made her heart pound like a hammer against her ribs.

After lifting the fire screen aside, he placed the logs on the coals and stoked the fire. When the flame steadied, he replaced the screen and walked toward her.

She peeped from beneath her lashes to see him standing a short distance away, his eyes glowing in the same firelight that played across his lean body, accenting the muscles rippling across his bare chest. Her pulse racing, she moaned and shifted slightly, enticing him closer.

A wistful look on his dark face, he gazed down at her. He drew in a ragged breath. He closed his eyes and shook his head, as if to clear it. Heaving a heavy sigh, he slowly bent toward her.

Afire with anticipation, Samantha felt him reach out, lift the covers—and tuck them clear up to her chin. *Drat!* She lifted her lashes, locking her gaze onto startled gray eyes inches above hers. Before he could move, she raised her arms and fastened them around his neck. She drew his dark head down and molded her lips to his in a lingering kiss. "Good morning," she said softly, retaining her hold.

He blinked and swallowed. "Good morning, Samantha. I didn't mean to wake you."

"I know," she said, nuzzling the rapidly beating pulse in his neck. She ran her fingers through his hair, enjoying the thick crisp feel of it. Lacing her fingers together behind his neck, she again brought his head down to hers.

Uttering a groan, he plopped down on the bed. "Oh kitten," he whispered. Stretching out a sinewy arm, he drew her to his naked chest. He murmured softly in her ear, his breath hot upon her face. His gray eyes dark with passion, he bent his head and smothered her with hungry kisses.

She grew so dizzy she could hardly get her breath, but still she longed for more.

He trailed his mouth across her face to nibble at her neck while his hand fumbled with the ties on her nightgown. He slid the garment down, baring her shoulder. His whiskers tickled her skin. "So sweet," he said. His tongue traced the gossamer neckline of the nightie, sending delightful shivers up her spine. When she sighed, he raised his head, once more seeking her lips. Parting them with a gentle insistence, he eased his tongue into her mouth, probing, teasing, urging hers to do the same. Shyly, she entered his moist cavern, tasting, exploring. His tongue wrapped around hers, drawing her further inside, mingling their juices.

His thumbs drew lazy circles around her nipples. His palms encased her breasts. His touch sent a strange, shimmering fire creeping through the nightgown to enter her veins. Reaching down, he drew the sheer garment up over her hips, wanting nothing between them to mar the sensation.

He lifted it further still, finally drawing it over her head. "Oh kitten. You're so warm, so soft," he said, caressing her with quicksilver eyes. He bent his head, planting kisses on her ribs, stroking her bare flesh, searing it beneath his callused palms. His tongue circled her nipples, teasing them into sensitive, quivering peaks.

Her body shook with a half-thrilling, half-frightening tremor as he awakened new passions. Shyly, she traced his ribs and the ropelike muscles on his back with her questing fingertips, yearning to know this man she called husband.

Eyes closed, pulses racing, she pressed against the lips and hands roaming her body, urging him to teach her more. The quivering warmth between her thighs built to a throbbing ache. She drew him closer, sensing only he could end this sweet torment. "My love," she whispered.

He tensed, jerking as if she'd branded him with a hot iron. He stared at her, his face contorted with naked pain. The silver left his eyes, turning them hooded and dark. "Go back to sleep," he said raggedly, getting up from the bed.

"Nick? What's wrong?" she cried after his retreating figure. The slam of the door was her only answer.

Shaking with jealousy and unsatisfied longing, Nick strode back into his room and closed the door. He sat down on the bed, cradling his head in his hands. His mind reeled with her words. *My love! Damn it, why didn't she just call me Billy and be done with it?*

He closed his eyes, trying to blot out the memory of her satiny skin, shining so smooth, so pale beneath the sheer green nightgown. He clenched the rough blankets on his bed, trying to erase the feel of her from his hands.

But it was no use. Her rose fragrance lingered on his skin, filling the air around him. His flesh tingled from her honey-sweet kisses. His hands ached to hold her swelling breasts. His gut twisted and throbbed with need.

He raised his head and stared into the night, anger flooding him, making him want to rip the bewitching garment from her body and take possession of every part of her, to plunge into her, fill her with his seed, and erase every trace of Billy from her mind and body.

He slumped, hopelessness washing over him. He couldn't do it, no matter how much he wanted her. It wasn't her fault. She couldn't even remember. But he did. Her cries in the night for Billy—her love—tormented him. And when he tried to forget, the nightmares, the desperate cries that drew him to her side, gave him a bitter reminder.

He ran a trembling hand through his hair. He needed a drink and a woman. Someone with passion. Someone who could expel the little green-eyed witch from his mind. Nick yanked on his clothes, picked up his boots, and slipped quietly from the house. He threw his gear on Scout and swung into the saddle, heading through the cold, dark of night for Canyon Springs and the Red Dog Saloon.

When Nick neared his destination, a faint hint of dawn lit the sky with a pale, pearllike haze, only hinting at the gold-and-crimson glory to come. The soft plop, plop of Scout's hooves echoed on Canyon Springs' deserted Main Street. At the back of the whorehouse Nick dismounted and looped the pinto's reins over the hitching rail. He climbed the steep stairway and tapped on a familiar window, waiting impatiently until a lamp was lit and a curtain opened.

A busty young blond woman peered through the glass. Recognizing him, she released the latch and swung the window wide. "Nick? Is that you? Come inside out of the cold."

Climbing through the window, he grinned. Sally'd never failed him yet.

Sometime later Nick slipped from under the covers and fumbled for his clothes. He dressed in the darkness to avoid meeting the eyes of the woman in the bed.

"Nicky, don't take it so hard. It happens to all men sooner or later."

"Not to me it don't," he said, fastening his pants.

"You were just too tired and cold, honey. Are you sure you won't come back to bed? It's still early," she said, attempting to smother a yawn.

"No. But you go on back to sleep," he said. By the time he'd pulled on his boots, she was sound asleep. He took some money from his pocket and placed it on her dresser. He shoved his hat low on his head and slunk out of the room, feeling like an impotent rabbit.

Steeped in misery, Nick hardly noticed the morning sunrise or long ride back to the ranch. The night's happenings and Samantha filled his thoughts. *What the hell has she done to me?* Angry and confused, he thought of Sally's luscious, full-bosomed body. It had always satisfied him before. But tonight every time he'd think it was going to work, he'd seen a green-eyed witch with red-gold hair. For the first time in his life he'd been unable to make love to a woman. He felt like he'd been castrated. *It's unnatural, that's what it is.*

Riding into the ranch yard, he unsaddled the pinto and turned him loose. Slinging the saddle over the corral fence, he glanced up toward her window. A familiar warmth rose in his groin, making his pants uncomfortably tight. He was stiff as a damn cattle prod. "Hellfire! Why now?" Cursing his predicament, he turned toward the barn.

Saddling another horse, he headed toward the range, knowing the hands could always use help with the branding.

Returning late, exhausted and dirty, again Nick waited until the last light went out before he entered the house. After hurriedly bathing in the hot spring water, he wrapped a towel around him and slipped upstairs to his room. He lifted the covers to turn back his bed. He wrinkled his nose as a familiar fragrance drifted upward. Bending forward, he gave the freshly changed sheets a suspicious sniff. "Damn it!" Jerking the covers up, he punched his pillow and sprawled on top of the blankets. It was dawn when he finally surrendered to a dreamless sleep.

Samantha lay in her bed, staring at the ceiling. Her fire had burned down to coals, and a fast-growing chill spread through the room. She frowned, wondering what to do about Nick. She hadn't seen him since the other morning when he'd run out of her room. He'd been avoiding her. He probably had a guilty conscience. She'd found the clothes he'd abandoned in the bathroom. They'd reeked of cheap perfume.

Crossing her arms across her chest, she glared at the wall separating their rooms. *How did you like the rosewater I sprinkled in your bed? Maybe it might remind you you've got a wife!* She sighed. If she hadn't seen the paper, she wouldn't have believed it.

Married—even the word sounded foreign to her ears. *I don't feel married*—although she wasn't sure how being married felt—*and* he *surely doesn't act married.*

That was another mystery, the wedding. Every woman wants to remember her wedding, but Nick didn't seem to remember any more about it than she did. *Merciful heavens, you'd think he could remember* something, *unless he was drunk or asleep.* Rose and Jake didn't seem to know anything either. She narrowed her eyes thoughtfully. She had a feeling Jeff knew more than he was telling, but when she tried to question him, he only grinned and looked silly.

Jake and Rosa were such dears. They really made her feel like part of the family. Jeff seemed like a younger brother, even though he was older than she.

Nick's the elusive one—and he's supposed to be my husband. He treats me like a pesky child. For heaven's sake, we're supposed to be newlyweds.

She had to admit she'd been uneasy at first, afraid he might drag her off to his bed. But he'd assured her that he wouldn't ravish her, and he'd kept his word, she thought with disgust. He had certainly kept his word!

The sun lit the sky with a rosy glow, and knowing the household would be stirring, Samantha slid from her bed. A determined glint in her eyes, she went to the closet and removed the new dress she'd made from the fabric Nick'd brought her. She donned her underthings and slipped it on.

She twirled in front of the mirror, admiring the fit. The calico, pale green with tiny yellow-and-white flowers, hugged her waistline and the lace-trimmed neckline dipped low enough to show a hint of bosom. She couldn't wait to see Nick's face when he saw her in it. She twisted her hair into a shining coil on the back of her neck and secured it with her pins, leaving a few ringlets to curl around her face. She anchored a leaf-green bow into place among her coppery tresses. She bit her lips to give them more color. Her eyes gleaming, she admired her reflection in the mirror. "There, try to resist me now, husband dear." She flipped her skirts at the mirror and headed out the door.

She found the men gathered around the breakfast table drinking coffee. She swept into the room. "Good morning."

"'Morning honey," Jake said, beaming her a warm smile. "My, don't we look pretty."

"Just plain be-oo-tiful." Jeff sighed. "Ain't she, Nick?"

Nick glanced up and nodded, "Very pretty." He took another sip of coffee and turned back to Jake. "If all goes well, I should be back in three weeks."

Samantha sighed. *Well, so much for that idea.* Giving her husband a disparaging look, she went into the kitchen to help Rosa. Damn the man. She had the feeling she could run around stark naked, and he still wouldn't notice. *Today he'll be leaving for Fort Garland to deliver the cattle. Three weeks he'll be gone. What in the world will I do for three weeks?* She loaded the platters and carried them to the table, then sat down next to Nick.

The men filled their plates and began to eat, continuing their conversation about the drive and cattle.

Samantha eyed Nick speculatively, watching him wolf down the steak, eggs, and biscuits. *He surely likes to eat. Maybe I can learn to cook.*

When Nick left the table and went upstairs to fetch his knife, Samantha waited until he was out of sight, then followed, hurrying up the stairway. She slipped inside his room and closed the door. She walked toward him.

Nick turned, a trapped look on his face. "Uh, hello, Samantha. What are you doing in here?"

"I came to tell you good-bye," she said softly. *And the only way you're going to get away from me is to jump out the window.* She grinned when he eyed the curtains. "You've avoided me lately, and I want to know why."

Nick took a step backward. "I've been busy. You know, with the cattle and all."

She narrowed her eyes, thinking about the "and all." "You were going to kiss me good-bye, weren't you?" she asked.

"Sure. Why don't you run along downstairs and wait for me? I'll be down directly," he said.

"You act like you're afraid of me. I won't bite, you know." She ran her hands up his shirtfront.

"You have before," he muttered.

Before? Puzzled, but deciding to ignore his remark, she teased the back of his neck with her fingertips. "I think I'll say my good-byes now." She stood on her toes and pressed against him. Cupping the back of his head with her hand, she forced his head down, kissing his neck, his chin, and his cheek before drawing his bottom lip between her lips. Her tongue traced its smooth outline and she teasingly nibbled at it with her teeth. Releasing his bottom lip, she took the top one in its place. She felt a quiver start in his legs. It shook his whole being until he was left trembling in her arms.

Uttering a curse, he groaned and wrapped his arms around her. Lifting her feet from the floor, he wrapped his hand in her hair, bending her backward over his thigh. His eyes dark and angry, he covered her neck and face with savage kisses. He plundered her mouth, lashing her tongue with his own while his hand kneaded her throbbing breasts. He was fierce, wild, wonderful, and Samantha, her emotions in tatters, shook like a fall leaf in the storm of his embrace.

"Nick? You in there?" Jeff called out from the hallway.

"Shit!" Nick set her feet on the floor and sucked in a ragged breath. He bent and gave her one more lingering kiss before he slammed on his hat and went out the door.

Samantha staggered and fell backward onto the edge of Nick's bed. Turning her head, she caught a glimpse of herself in the mirror. "Merciful heavens!" she gasped. Her bow perched askew atop half-undone hair, the front of her dress gaped open, showing a goodly portion of one breast, her cheeks blushed pink, scraped by the roughness of his face, and her lips glowed red and swollen from his fierce kisses. But the most startling part were her eyes. Large and green, they shone bright with wonder and love. She sighed, lowering her lashes, bringing back the passion she'd felt in his arms. "Someday, Mr. McBride, I'll see that you finish what you start," she whispered. "Someday soon, my love."

The bugle sounded reveille in the predawn light, routing the sleeping soldiers from their beds. Nick peered out the window, wondering how a man could stand having someone tell him when to get up, when to eat, what to do, and what time to go to bed. It didn't seem natural, and was damned constricting. He grinned. Worse even than being married.

Married. His thoughts went back to Samantha. He sure missed her, but at least here he didn't have to be on his guard every minute. Lately he'd felt like a mouse being stalked by a hungry cat. She was getting harder and harder to avoid. He'd turn and find those emerald-green eyes watching him, or smell her perfume, or hear her voice, husky and breathless, drawing his nerves taut as a fiddle string.

He groaned, remembering how she'd cornered him the day he'd left. She'd been so sweet, so pretty in her new dress, he'd lost his head. First thing he knew, he was kissing her back. If Jeff hadn't knocked on the door, no telling what would have happened. The little vixen had him so fired up, he'd had some damned uncomfortable riding for a while.

He had mixed feelings now that the cattle were sold and it was time to go home. Securing the money belt inside his shirt, he hid the bulge with the leather vest he'd slipped on over it. When a knock sounded, he buttoned the vest and opened the door to find Danny Delaney, the new foreman, standing there.

"Hi, boss. Since we're all done, me and the boys decided we'd head on back to the ranch," the puncher said.

Nick raised his eyebrows. "Already? I thought you boys would be raisin' hell for a while first."

"Naw. We might stop at Molly's for some beers on the way home." The freckled man straightened. "Since I'm foreman now, I want to keep track of the cattle we've got left."

"Good idea," Nick agreed. What the young man lacked in experience, he made up for in determination. He was right about the cows. With the drought and the number of cattle they'd had to sell, they'd have to nursemaid every cow and calf they had to stay in business. "I'll be leaving in a little bit myself."

"You want us to wait?" Danny asked.

"No. I don't know how long I'll be," Nick said.

The cowboy waved his hand and went to join the other

JMB hands waiting with his horse. He threw his bowed legs over the saddle and left the post in a cloud of dust.

Nick left his room and walked across the compound to the commander's quarters. Removing his hat, he walked past the sentry and entered the office.

The man behind the desk raised his head and smiled. "Ready to go, Nick?"

"Got some unfinished business to take care of first, Kit. Have you ever heard of a family named Storm?"

Colonel Kit Carson rubbed his chin thoughtfully. "Can't say as I have, Nick." Getting up, he walked to the window and stared toward the mountains. "How is White Eagle?"

Nick tensed. "Are you asking as a friend of the Cheyenne, or as an army colonel?" He eyed the man the Indians called Rope Thrower. Although Carson was only five-foot-six, his courage and exploits were well-known among the Indians. He'd even lived with a Cheyenne woman for a while. But he'd also helped separate the Navajo from their lands. And he'd been present in 1865 when the white man persuaded Black Kettle to sign a treaty agreeing to give up all Cheyenne rights in Colorado.

White Eagle and others had not agreed with this. Now, since the treaty, the army considered any Cheyenne north of the Arkansas River a renegade. Nick's mouth tightened. White Eagle, saying he had not signed any paper, would never willingly leave the land of his ancestors.

The colonel turned. "I'm asking as a friend. I wish the old chief well, Nick. There's been too much fighting."

"The last time I saw my grandfather, he was fine," Nick said slowly.

Carson walked back and resumed his seat behind the desk. "About the Storms," he said, easing the tension between them. "You might ask the trader. The nosy old coot either knows or has known everybody in the territory at one time or another." He chuckled. "Getting him to tell you is another thing." He stood and held out his hand. "Goodbye, Nick. This will be the last time I see you. I'm weary of army life. Thinking on retiring, settlin' down a bit."

Nick grasped the colonel's hand. "Good luck, Kit." He grinned. "I might do a bit of settling down myself." A burst of hearty laughter followed Nick out of the room.

Nick headed Scout around the soldiers marching across the parade grounds and then rode through the double log gate. Relieved to be outside the high walls of the fort, he inhaled fresh sage-scented air and urged his horse toward the squat log trading post. Once there, he dismounted and lit a cigar as he waited for a couple of rough, bearded trappers to leave.

Nick crushed the cigar butt under his heel. Taking a deep breath, he ducked under the low opening and walked inside. He blinked, taking a moment to accustom himself to the gloom and the assortment of smells assaulting him. The stench of tallow, jerky, hides, and spicy venison mixed with the odor of sweat, rotgut whiskey, and woodsmoke.

An old man, bent and wizened by the years, peered at him from the other side of a counter made of rough planks. Short and spare, he chewed a large wad of tobacco in his toothless mouth, sending a steady stream of juice flying at one target or another. "What kin I do for ye?" he asked.

"I'm looking for a family named Storm. Colonel Carson said you might know them," Nick said, holding his breath.

"Storm, ye say?" He scratched his bald head, as if bringing the name to mind. "I seem to recollect some Storms up north of here." He hesitated, his pale blue eyes becoming sharp, intense, as if he were remembering something else. "What do ye want with 'em? You got business with them?"

"I'm looking for a man named Billy. He might be kin to them," Nick said, hating to divulge even that much.

"What's yur name? Where do ye come from?"

Nick narrowed his eyes. The old man was as curious as a pet coon in a candy store. "I'm Nick McBride from Canyon Springs way," he said. "Now, about the Storms."

The old codger gave Nick a sly look. "They had some trouble, cain't rightly recall what it was." A stream of amber juice narrowly missed Nick's boot.

"Do you know where up north they lived?" Nick asked. "Or anything about the trouble?"

The man's eyes became wary, evasive. "Nope, 'tweren't none of my business, so I didn't pay no nevermind."

Nick thought it strange that the trader couldn't remember since the old codger had tried to pry information out of him ever since he'd walked through the door. Either the Storms were a secretive bunch, or the storekeeper did know something but wasn't talking. "Do you know anybody else that might know something about the family?"

"Nope." He peered up at Nick. "Sometimes it don't pay to know too much," the old man whispered. Letting out a cackle that raised the hair on the back of Nick's neck, the old codger hobbled away.

Disgusted, Nick left. The trader's last statement haunted him, leaving him more puzzled than ever. What was the mystery about the Storms? And how did it concern Samantha? Damn it, his problem was further from being solved than ever. His only chance had been the names—Storm, and

Billy. He sighed, knowing they were not nearly enough to go on.

Trouble . . . his mouth tightened, remembering the name Matthew. Maybe his last name was Storm. Maybe he was the trouble. He seemed like an unsavory character and certainly no friend of Samantha's. She'd been scared to death of him in her dream. Nick frowned, recalling how she'd clung to him, her slender body shaking in terror. No, whoever Matthew was, he definitely was no friend of hers. Maybe the old man was right; maybe they were better off not knowing.

An icy wind whistled down from the north, reminding him it was November. Soon it would snow. He sighed, knowing his search for Billy would have to wait until spring.

Drawing his jacket closer around him, Nick pointed Scout in the direction of the distant snowcapped hills. A vision of green eyes and red-gold hair flashed into his mind, flushing his body with warmth. Until he found Billy, or Samantha regained her memory, she was still his. He smiled; his spirits lifted. He hoped it would be a long, cold winter.

CHAPTER

* 12 *

SAMANTHA BRUSHED THE SORREL UNTIL HIS SAT-
iny coat glowed under her fingertips. She'd spent a goodly
portion of the last two weeks currying him and talking to
him, having little else to do with Nick gone. "There, you're
beautiful," she said, laying the brush aside.

He nickered and nudged her with his proud head, wanting
more. "You're such a pet." She laughed. "I've spoiled
you, haven't I, pretty boy?" He rubbed his head on her arm
and she kissed his velvety nose.

She sighed, looking toward the hills. The sorrel had
gotten so attached to her, it was beginning to be a problem.
She wanted to saddle the mare and ride out into the hills.
But every time she'd made the attempt, the stud squealed
and stomped and tried to get out of the corral. Afraid he'd
injure himself, she'd given up riding.

She stared toward the mountains, wondering when Nick
was coming home. He'd been gone three weeks now. Danny
and the boys had returned last night. She rubbed the horse's
head thoughtfully. She'd told Nick she planned to ride the
stallion someday. "Why not today?"

She walked to the corral fence and slid through the poles. The horse nickered, apparently distressed at her leaving. "I'll be back. Then we'll see how glad you are to see me." He shook his head up and down. Chuckling, she left him and walked toward the house.

In her room she changed into her split riding skirt and boots. She shrugged into her jacket and picked up her gloves. She glanced into the mirror. "Well, cowgirl, let's see if you can do it." Shoving her hat on her head, she went to the barn to get the saddle and other tack she'd need.

She returned to the corral and slid between the bars. Crooning softly, she slipped the bridle over the sorrel's head. "So far so good." She lifted the saddle and looked at the horse in dismay. He was too tall. There was no way she could lift it onto his back. Sighing, she put the saddle back on the corral fence. She eyed the horse speculatively. *Well, I've ridden bareback before, but not to break a horse.*

She glanced around. No one was in sight. She grinned. If she did make a fool of herself, at least there would be no witnesses. She looked at the animal, her heart pounding. "Are you going to let me ride you?" There was only one way to find out.

She led him close to the fence, and because he was so tall, she climbed to the second rail. Holding the reins, she talked to the horse. "All right now. I hope you'll agree to this." Taking a deep breath, she eased her leg over his back. He spread his legs, but stood perfectly still. When she was seated, he turned his head and nudged her knee, as if to say, "What took you so long?"

Samantha laughed. "You wild thing. Well, let's see what you can do." She made a few turns around the corral, teaching him how to rein. He amazed her with his calm behavior and the quick way he learned.

A short time later she rode him toward the exit. She leaned out and lifted the latch. The gate swung open. Guiding him through, she closed it behind him. "Good boy." She leaned forward and patted his neck. Leaving the ranch yard, she headed him down the road toward the main ranch gate, putting him through his paces.

The horse was fluid motion, and she reveled in the strength and speed beneath her. *What a horse to build a herd with,* she thought. The strong sons and daughters he'd sire would be long-legged and swift as the wind. Wind? "Red Wind. That will be your name," she said.

The miles between the ranch and the gate dissolved under the horse's hooves. Glancing up, Samantha saw a figure on a spotted horse approaching the crossbars marking the ranch entrance. "Nick!" she called. She leaned low on the stallion's neck and raced toward him.

She flashed past him, grinning at the look of horror and disbelief on his face. She wheeled the horse to see that he had turned Scout and was galloping toward her.

"Samantha! Are you all right?" he shouted, pulling the pinto to a stop.

"I'm just dandy. I told you I'd ride him," she said smugly. She leaned forward and stroked the horse's neck. "Isn't he a beauty?"

"I ought to spank you. That's what I ought to do. Damnation! You scared me out of ten years' growth."

"Nicky, darling, I'm glad to see you too," she teased. She locked her gaze on his and grinned. Even though he looked furious, she could also see pride and admiration in his face. "Give me a kiss?" she asked, bending toward him.

"A kiss? I'm gonna give you a paddling."

"You'll have to catch me first." Laughing, she guided the sorrel down to a clearing by the creek, reining the horse to a stop by a grove of aspen.

Nick chased behind her, dismounting when she stopped. He walked around Scout to stand beside her. Although he looked tired and needed a shave, to her he was the handsomest man alive.

"Come here, vixen, and take your punishment," he growled, reaching up for her.

"Yes, my love," she said meekly. Her heart racing, she slid off the sorrel and surrendered to her husband's arms.

Too nervous to concentrate, Samantha closed the book and put it back on the shelf above the desk. She'd been trying to take her mind off the storm, but it was no use. She walked to the window and lifted the edge of the lace drape, watching the last glimpse of twilight vanish under a curtain of black. The wind moaned around the eaves, driving the icy winter rain in a steady tat-tat-tat against the panes.

Lightning cracked the darkness, splitting the heavens and spearing the earth with a white-hot fork. Thunder exploded, rattling the china pitcher and bowl on the nightstand. "Oh!" she gasped. She dropped the curtain and jumped away from the window, clasping her hands over her ears to shut out the sound. The big log house shivered and quaked under the onslaught.

"I think I'd feel safer in bed," she said, eyeing the covers. She ran to the dresser and grabbed her nightgown. Leaving her clothes in a heap on the floor, she yanked the cotton nightie over her head. She glanced uneasily at the window. Hurrying to the fireplace, she placed another log on the glowing coals. A downdraft sent smoke spiraling into the room. Coughing, her eyes stinging, she waved her hand to disperse the enveloping cloud.

Lightning flickered again, briefly illuminating the room, then the corners, with ghostly shadows.

Rubbing her smoke-filled eyes, Samantha darted to her bed and slid beneath the covers, hiding her head under the yellow-and-blue patchwork quilt. She stuffed her fingers into her ears, trying to shut out the angry giant that roared and stomped outside.

She opened her eyes beneath the quilt. ''The angry giant! I remember!'' She closed her eyes, welcoming the vision from her past.

She'd only been four when she'd awakened in the middle of a violent thunderstorm, screaming in terror. Papa'd come into her room and gathered her onto his lap. He'd smoothed her hair and told her not to worry, it was only the giant having a tantrum because he'd lost his ball. He'd said the giant, only four himself, had been playing with the sun. When he'd rolled his fiery ball close to the edge of the earth, it had fallen off, taking the daylight with it. The giant, angry because he could no longer see how to play, cried and yelled and stomped his feet. Her father explained that the rain was the giant's tears, the lightning his cries, and the thunder was the sound he made stomping his feet. He'd assured her the giant would get tired and fall asleep. When he did, there would be no more noise from the thunder and lightning, and the storm would be over.

She'd snuggled on her father's lap, telling him just what the giant was doing by the sounds of the storm outside. Papa had made her laugh with the tale, and she, like the giant, had soon fallen asleep.

Her face wet with tears, Samantha pulled the quilt from over her face. No longer afraid, she rose from the bed and walked to the window, reaching out to pull the curtain aside. She pressed her face against the cold pane, feeling the beat of the rain against the other side of the glass. She closed her eyes, listening to the storm, remembering that night so long ago. "Oh Papa, thank you," she whispered. Smiling, she picked up the silver-framed miniature that had been found in her bag, grateful for the memory of the man, the kindly man that had been her father.

She walked back to the bed and climbed onto the mattress. She pulled her knees up to her chin and wrapped her arms around them, hugging them to her chest. Even though she was no longer as frightened, she felt small and lonely in the big bed. She hugged her knees closer, longing to feel Nick's arms around her.

She sighed in disgust. Except for a few kisses on the day he'd returned from Fort Garland, he'd been like a skittish colt. Drat the man anyhow! How was she ever going to know if she liked being married or not with her *husband* acting like a bashful virgin?

Lightning cracked, rending the air, filling the room with the strong odor of sulfur. The earth trembled under the thunder. She jumped; her eyes widened. *Oh mercy, that was close. If I hadn't remembered the story about the giant, I'd be cowering under the bed by now.*

A soft knock sounded at her door and a voice called, "Samantha? It's Nick. Are you all right, kitten?"

"I'm—" A mischievous grin crossed her face. She reached over to the nightstand next to the bed and stuck her hand into the water pitcher. She brought her fingers out, dripping wet and slapped at her face. She slid back under the quilt. Muffling the laughter in her voice, she called out, "Oh Nick, I'm *sooo* scared."

She listened, her hand clamped over her mouth to smother a giggle. The door opened and closed. Footsteps crossed the floor and stopped by the bed. Her heart raced. The mattress sagged when Nick sat down on the bed beside her.

"Samantha? Honey, it's only a storm," he said, pulling the quilt back to uncover her face. He reached out and brushed her hair from her eyes, touching her seemingly tearstained cheeks. "Oh kitten, you're crying."

Thunder boomed, giving Samantha the excuse she needed. She squealed and threw both arms around his neck, sobbing with histrionic fright.

He patted her awkwardly. "Don't be afraid. It can't hurt you."

Samantha squirmed from beneath the bedcovers until she was cradled in his lap. She snuggled close to his chest, savoring his clean, manly scent. Burying her face in his neck, she wrapped her arms even tighter, feeling the pounding of his heart against her breasts. She smiled when he sucked in a ragged breath.

"Uh, why don't I light the lamp, then maybe you won't be so scared," he suggested, attempting to loosen her grip.

"Oh no, don't leave me. Please, just hold me," she pleaded. His arms gingerly encased her, holding her loosely against him. "Tighter," she begged. "Make me feel safe." He tightened his grip a little, and Samantha, tilting her head, looked up into his face.

His lips were set in a firm line. A muscle jumped in his clenched jaw. His eyes were riveted downward.

Following his gaze, Samantha saw the top buttons of her

nightgown had come undone, exposing the white swell of her breasts. She wriggled in his grasp, noting with satisfaction that she'd managed to undo two more. If she took a deep breath, the dusky pink of one nipple would peek provocatively from the edge of the lace. Watching him, she inhaled . . . deeply.

He gasped. His eyes widened.

"Oh Nick, I feel so safe in your arms." She sighed. She trailed one finger down his cheek, to his jaw, to his neck, then slipped her hand down the front of his shirt, slowly unfastening the buttons. She drew her fingers through his silky chest hair.

He shuddered and shifted his gaze to her face.

She peered up through lowered lashes and opened her mouth, slowly outlining her lips with the tip of her tongue.

His arms tightened around her, and the hardness of his arousal pressed against the thin fabric of her nightgown. Groaning, he slowly bent his head toward her.

Her heart pounding, she parted her lips. She closed her eyes, breathlessly anticipating his kiss.

The bedroom door burst open. "Sammy, I thought you might be afrai—" Jeff called out, poking his blond head inside the room.

Nick jerked back. He stared at her, a shocked look on his face. Lifting her from his lap, he stuffed her back into bed and yanked the quilt up under her chin. He leaped toward the closing door.

Damn! Samantha shook her head in exasperation.

"I guess you're busy. I'll just run along," Jeff said, withdrawing his red face from the room.

Before the door could close, Nick shoved it open. He grabbed his cousin by the arm and jerked him inside.

"Come in, Jeff. Have a seat. Talk to Samantha. She'll be glad to see you. The poor child's been scared to death." He yanked a ladderback chair from in front of the fireplace and plopped it down beside the bed. He pushed Jeff into it.

Jeff's startled eyes met Samantha's.

She glared at him and turned her attention to Nick.

Nick walked to the desk and lit the oil lamp, letting a soft glow invade the room. Flashing what looked to her like a relieved smile, he bolted toward the door.

Samantha sat up in the bed, crossing her arms over her hastily buttoned nightgown. She stared after the swiftly retreating figure of her husband. *Drat, another minute and I would have had him.* Her body ached with unfulfilled longing. The thunder crashed again. She paid it no mind.

"I thought you were afraid of the storm?" Jeff said.

"What?" she asked impatiently.

"The storm—Nick said you were scared to death."

"Well I'm not—but don't tell him."

Jeff's face lit up. Grinning at her, he slapped his knee. "Ho-ho, so that's the way it was, huh? I guess I sure picked the wrong time to barge in."

"Your timing was perfect, as usual." She sighed. "But he probably would have found some other excuse anyhow." She reached over and grabbed the pillow from the very empty side of the bed, punched it, and placed it behind her so she could be more comfortable. She leaned back, clasping her hands in her lap. Her mind troubled, she looked at her cousin-in-law. "What's wrong with me, Jeff? I don't think I'm that ugly. He's my husband and yet he avoids me like I've got warts." She shook her head. "I don't understand. If he doesn't like me, then why did he marry me?"

Jeff frowned, rubbing the side of his nose with one finger.

"I'd say he likes you plenty. I think that the idea of him being married takes some getting used to." A grin split Jeff's face, showing white even teeth. "He shore don't think you're ugly. Why, I catch him watching you all the time when he thinks nobody is looking. You don't make a move without him knowing it." He chuckled. "I think now that he's got you, he don't quite know what to do with you."

"So he doesn't do anything," she said. "Tell me about his boyhood. What was he like?"

"Well, when his folks were killed, he came to live with Jake. I was too little to remember much, but after my ma and pa died with cholorea, I lived here, too. We used to spend summers together with the Cheyenne."

The hours flew by while she and Jeff talked. He told her tales of Nick's boyhood, of life in the Cheyenne village, and of the prejudice shown to Nick all of his life because of his Indian blood. Samantha's heart ached for the little boy, too young to understand the cruelty, or the contempt, of the white townspeople.

Jeff told her of the courage Nick'd shown in the Indian sun dance, an ancient ceremony to honor the buffalo and ensure good health and good hunting. He'd explained that those taking part pierced their skin, inserting into their flesh pieces of bone with long lengths of rawhide attached. The rawhide, stretched tightly from a center pole, held them captive while they danced, prayed, and fasted, enduring the pain to prove their bravery until finally they twisted and turned, tearing themselves loose.

Samantha felt a little faint just hearing about it. She remembered the scars she'd seen on Nick's chest but hadn't the nerve to mention.

Jeff told of the kindness Nick had shown to him after Jeff lost his parents. She knew that even though Jeff took a fiendish joy in bedeviling his older cousin, he also clearly worshiped him.

"Did he ever have a sweetheart?" she asked.

"Nick's had lots of women, but none he really cared about—except Amanda. He went kind of crazy when she married somebody else." He hesitated, giving her a strange look. "That was right before he married you."

"Is she a blonde?" she asked, suddenly recalling the long, blond hair she'd found on Nick's shirt the night he'd come home stinking with perfume.

"Yeah," Jeff said.

"I might have guessed." Samantha's heart twisted, consumed with jealousy, hating the blond witch that Nick'd loved and apparently still sought in the dead of night. "Tell me more," she prompted.

Engrossed in their conversation, they hadn't noticed the lateness of the hour. The wick in the lamp had burned low when a harsh voice interrupted from the doorway.

"Jeff, I didn't tell you to spend the night. The storm's over, so get the hell out and go to bed," Nick said.

Jeff looked at Samantha and gave her a sly wink. Getting to his feet, he bent and gave her a kiss on the cheek. "Give me a hug, then watch his face," he whispered.

Samantha raised her arms and wrapped them around Jeff's neck. Drawing his head down, she gave him a long, lingering kiss—on the lips.

Jeff's eyes widened in surprise. He smiled at her, his cheeks dimpling, his blue eyes dancing. Patting her on the cheek, he cut his eyes toward Nick, who glared at him from the doorway. "Good night, sweetie. See you in the mornin'," he drawled. Sauntering past his cousin, he paused to grin at Samantha before whistling his way out of the room.

Samantha watched Nick, noting his reaction.

He stood rigid with anger, fists clenched at his sides, glaring tight-lipped down the hall after his cousin.

He's jealous. A smile crossed her face. "Aren't you going to kiss me good night, too, Nicky?" she called softly.

He turned toward the bed.

She raised her arms over her head, stretching, pulling the soft fabric tight against the outline of her full breasts. Managing to unfasten the buttons of her nightgown again while Nick had watched the departure of his cousin, she took a deep breath, feeling the white globes creep up. They nudged the deep V-shaped opening, pushing to be free.

Noticing, he gasped and raised his eyes to hers, the gray depths dark and angry.

Lowering her lashes seductively, Samantha fastened her eyes on his, willing him to come closer, drawing him to her like a fly caught in a web. She held her arms out to him, luring him closer. Her pulse racing, her body eager and willing, she parted her mouth in invitation.

Mesmerized, he left the doorway and weaved across the room toward her. His eyes glazing, he stared into hers.

Samantha's heart leaped. An inspired heat built in her lower region, firing her with longing. Her breasts tingled, waiting for his touch. The rosy, taut nipples peeped from the edge of the lace.

His breath coming rapidly, he stood at the edge of the bed. He bent toward her.

She moistened her lips, her body trembling with desire.

A log in the fireplace popped explosively, throwing a shower of sparks into the room.

Nick blinked. He jerked upright, the spell broken. Giving her a startled look, he uttered a muffled oath and spun away from the bed. His breathing labored, ragged, he lurched toward the desk. He leaned over, gripping the edge, obviously fighting for control. After a moment he bent toward the lamp and blew the room into darkness.

"I'm still waiting for my kiss," she called softly from the firelit bed.

"You've had enough kissin' for one night, *sweetie*," he said. He darted past her and bolted out the door, slamming it shut behind him.

"Damnation! He did it again!" Narrowing her eyes in anger, Samantha sat up and glared at the closed door. She yanked the extra pillow from behind her head and punched it soundly, wishing it were her aggravating husband. She threw it across the room, bouncing it off the offending threshold.

The rain had stopped and the fire burned down to a few glowing coals, but the night stretched into infinity for Samantha. Unable to sleep, she tossed in her bed, her breasts aching, her body longing to know his touch.

The tattletale floorboards in the next room creaked under the weight of restless footsteps as Nick paced from the bed to the window and back again.

"Well, Mister McBride, at least you aren't sleeping either." She turned over on her side and, for the first time that night, closed her eyes. In the darkness, smiling in grim satisfaction, she plotted her revenge.

It was almost dawn when Nick finally climbed into his bed. Weary beyond words, he could feel his strength—and his resolve—growing weaker by the day. He'd tried to remember she was a young girl and probably as innocent as she had first seemed. But it was no use. When he held her in his arms, she was a fiery, passionate woman, a woman who set his senses reeling. She smelled like spring flowers and tasted like warm honey, and if he kept messing around with that honey, he was bound to get stung.

Thank God Jeff barged in when he did. Nick had felt like a rabbit escaping from a snare when his cousin stuck his nosy head through that door. He'd been so hot for her, he'd swear his skin had sizzled when he stepped out into the rain. He stayed there for hours before coming in to dry off.

That's when he'd heard Jeff and her giggling. Nick's eyes narrowed. *Damn him anyway. What the hell was he doing in there for so long?* She'd been half-naked when he'd stuck her back in that bed and let Jeff in. They had been in there—alone—together—in the dark—for hours before he'd stepped back in and sent Jeff to bed.

Jeff sure acted cozy when he'd kissed her good night. *Sweetie! What does he mean talking to my wife like that? And the way she'd kissed him back—why it was downright indecent.* Anger flooded Nick as he remembered how she'd stretched her arms above her head, her nipples poking out of that nightgown like two posies in a field of snow. The way she'd called him Nicky and asked *him* for a kiss, too. "Hellfire!" Nick jerked upright, staring at the wall next to her bedroom. *She'd still been half-naked!* The whole time Jeff'd been in there, *she'd been practically naked!*

The vision of her was stamped on his brain like a hot branding iron on a steer. Her, lying there—*in* my *bed, in* my *room*—her skin, all creamy and soft, shining through that white nightgown—her hair tumbling around her shoulders, smoldering like firelit embers—her body with every curve showing in the glow of the fire—and her eyes. Damn those tempting, lying eyes! Burning with warm, green fire, drawing him to her like a moth to a flame.

Nick groaned, his body aching with his need to possess her. He climbed out of bed, slipped on his pants, and paced barefoot to the window and back. "She plays cozy puss with Jeff all night and then tries to seduce *me* after I send him to bed. Ornery little vixen." He glared at the wall dividing their rooms. "She damn near did it, too." He shook his head. "Shit! I'm the man." Nick jabbed his chest with the end of his finger. "If there's any seducing to be done, I'll be the one to do it."

Outraged, he clenched his fists, then opened his hands and looked at his long, slender fingers. He walked to the wall dividing their rooms and placed his head against the rough plaster. He closed his eyes. Damn, he could almost feel her smooth, soft flesh, and smell the warm, woman smell of her. He moaned, bringing the illusion closer, burying his face in her firm round breasts, taking her pink tender peaks in his mouth, tangling his hands in her long silky hair . . . and *strangling* her with it.

"Hellfire!" He recoiled from the wall, shaking with angry desire. His senses whirled, sending him over the brink of reason. He turned, crossed the floor, and went out of his room and into the hall. His chest rising and falling with ragged breathing, he paused, his hand on her doorknob. Tightening his grip on the handle, he turned it and slowly stepped into the room.

The dim light of a false dawn outlined the sleeping figure on the large Spanish bed. She turned toward him, sighing softly in her sleep.

His lips curved in a wicked half smile, he leaned back against the door and quietly closed it behind him. Reaching down, he unfastened his bulging pants and stepped out of them, leaving them on the floor.

The fire in the fireplace had gone out, and the floor was icy against his bare feet, but he hardly noticed the chill of the room. His mind and his body were consumed in a whirlwind of burning desire.

Like a stalking panther, he moved toward his prey. His heart racing, he reached the edge of the bed. He leaned forward, his hand on the quilt, ready to lift it and take her in his arms.

"Papa?" She sighed in her sleep. She was curled up like a sleeping kitten, her arms wrapped around her pillow, holding it close. Her hair lay in a golden mass of ringlets around her ivory face; long lashes lay innocently against white delicate cheeks; her pink lips turned down at the corners in a childish pout. She looked all of twelve years old.

Shit! Nick slunk back across the floor, feeling like an ornery polecat. His attention on the bed, he climbed into his pants and noticed he had no trouble fastening them. Holding his breath, he eased himself into the hall. He pulled the door shut behind him and sagged against it, weak with relief that she hadn't awakened. He crept back into his room. His legs weak as a newborn's, he closed the door. He crossed the floor and slumped on his bed. Trembling, he buried his face in his hands.

He couldn't go on like this, watching her graceful movements as she went about her household tasks, smelling the sweet rose scent of her that lingered even when she wasn't around, hearing her voice, soft and low, with that husky little catch to it that played with his emotions the way a cat toyed with a cornered mouse.

It was downright unhealthy for her to do what she did to him. He couldn't get any relief and it was getting worse every day. He'd tried staying outside, but damn it, he had to eat. His embarrassment had gotten so bad he'd started carrying his hat around with him. He'd seen Jake and Jeff look at him and his hat, then look at each other and burst into a fit of laughter. He felt like he was drowning in quicksand and nobody would even throw him a rope.

He could go ahead and take her and be damned with the consequences. Hellfire, he knew she wanted him, but he knew he'd never be able to live with the guilt. And when she got her memory back, she'd hate him and she'd leave him—married or not. Right now she could get an annulment and go on with her life.

He knew he hadn't made love to her. He'd been drunk, not dead, up in that cabin. He *knew* he would have remembered that. He also knew if he ever did make love to her, he'd never be able to let her go.

When spring came, he'd have to go on with his search for Billy. He was the man she wanted, the one she'd cried out for more than once in her troubled sleep.

Morning came with a jolt as the object of his thoughts knocked on his door, opened it, and stuck her head inside. Bright green eyes met his. "Good morning, sleepyhead. Did you sleep well?" she asked, smiling.

"Just dandy," he called back, ruefully noticing that she looked fresh as new morning dew.

"See you down at breakfast," she called merrily, shutting the door.

Nick climbed out of bed and staggered to the mirror. "My God," he gasped, shocked to see the red-eyed, bushy-headed, unshaven image staring back at him. Groaning, he shuddered, sensing impending doom, feeling he'd traded his soul for a bottle of whiskey and a hank of red-gold hair.

Winter would come, piling the snow in deep drifts around the house, isolating the ranch from the rest of the world. Outside, it would be freezing cold, with the wind howling and the snow blowing so white you couldn't see. Inside, she'd be in the next room, all soft and warm and sweet smelling.

He picked up his shirt, put it on, and stuffed the tails into his already tight pants. Holding his hat in front of him to hide his embarrassment, he crept down the stairs and out the backdoor. He groaned. By the look of things it *was* going to be a long, cold winter.

CHAPTER

* 13 *

NICK, GRIM-FACED AND SILENT, LIT A THIN CIGAR
and headed toward the bunkhouse. Bathed and clean-
shaven, he'd dressed to fit his mood. From the scarf around
his neck to his silky, pearl-buttoned shirt, cowhide vest, and
whipcord pants tucked into gleaming high-topped boots, he
was dressed completely in black.

A black knife scabbard with a wicked silver blade inside
hung from the matching leather belt encircling his waist. A
black-barreled .44 hung low at his right hip, its walnut
handle shiny from use. His black-gloved hand tugged the
flat-crowned black hat even lower, shading his eyes. He
looked like what he was . . . a very dangerous man.

Nick felt like a cornered wolf with one foot caught in a
trap. He could either struggle against the chain until he was
too weak to escape, or he could chew his foot off and get the
hell out while he could. The alternatives didn't help his
disposition any. He was spoiling for a fight.

He clenched his teeth on the Spanish cigar and pushed
the cookhouse door open. Inside, he picked up a plate and
silverware from a shelf by the door and turned toward the

table. He narrowed his eyes, watching the faces of the cowboys finishing breakfast, daring any one of them to make a comment about why he wasn't eating at the house.

But apparently in response to his mood, all conversation stopped, and with a scuffling of boots, the men found things to occupy them elsewhere and left the building.

Nick helped himself to steak and beans from a large metal platter and topped his plate with a couple of saucer-sized biscuits. He filled a tin cup with coffee strong enough to float a horseshoe. Carrying his breakfast to the rough-hewn table, he sat down on a plank bench.

The cook, a lame ex-wrangler, hobbled over. "Howdy, Nick. Tired of Rosa's cookin'?"

Nick shot him a murderous glare but didn't answer.

"Uh, you go ahead and eat. I think I'll wash the dishes," the cook said, hastily leaving the area.

Nick ate, glancing around. The room contained only the bare necessities, a long pine-board table with matching benches and a hulking black iron cookstove that served to cook the food and warm the building. Next to the stove two sets of shelves held the pots and dishes. The bunkhouse wasn't fancy, but at least here he could eat in peace.

He finished his meal and looked through the window at the main ranch house. He lit another slender cigar, brooding over a second cup of coffee. He felt better now that he was clean and full, but it still didn't help his predicament. He frowned. With Samantha here he wouldn't survive the winter, and he sure couldn't spend all those cold months in town.

He slapped his palm down on the table. *Why didn't I think of it sooner? Hell, I've got a ranch.* He'd move to High

Mesa and stay until spring. He sipped his coffee thought-fully. His dad had built the house when he and Little Fawn were first married. Nick never spent much time there, usually preferring the company of his grandfather and Jeff. He scowled. *That was before Samantha arrived.*

The mesa was pretty. High on a flat bench west of the winter camp of the Cheyenne, it sat at the edge of a grove of pine and aspen trees. On one side large deep-grassed meadows nestled against the foot of a jagged mountain. The other side overlooked the valley. On a clear day he could see the main ranch below. It was a lonely place with deep snows closing the entrance pass in winter. *The snow! I'll have to leave right away if I intend to get through Alta Pass.* He shoved the cup away and got to his feet.

Smiling, his mood lifted, he walked toward the man doing dishes. "Joe Bob, I'm going to High Mesa. Think you could pack enough grub to last me till spring?"

The cook showed a wide snaggletoothed smile. "Shore thing, Nick. I'll do it right now." Wiping his hands on a flour-sack apron, Joe Bob turned and went into the larder.

Knowing the old man would pack enough stuff to last two winters, Nick grinned. He hoped the horse would be strong enough to carry it. Going to the corral, he whistled for Scout, then roped a sturdy gray horse. He saddled the pinto, put a pack saddle on the gray, and tied them both to the hitching post in front of the bunkhouse. That done, he headed toward the house and removed his saddlebags from the storeroom in back of the main dwelling.

He threw them over his shoulder and entered the house by the backdoor. As he crept up the stairs he heard the sound of male voices coming from the dining room. He moved carefully, hoping to make it to his room before he was discovered. Heart hammering, he reached the door. He knocked softly. No answer. He opened it and stuck his head in, relieved that Samantha wasn't there.

Moving quickly through the room, he gathered his heavy coat and whatever else he figured he'd need. He smiled, adding a silk handkerchief containing locks of red-gold hair to the contents of the pack.

He took his carbine down from the wall and added it to the stack, along with two boxes of shells. Finished packing, he closed his eyes, inhaling the faint smell of roses lingering in the air.

"What are you doing, Nick?" Samantha asked from the doorway behind him.

Cornered, he spun around, the trap growing tighter. "I'm leaving for the mountains." *And freedom.*

She looked from him to the bags and coat piled beside the bed. "For how long?" she asked, her eyes wide.

"All winter," he said, watching her face.

"Oh," she whispered. He watched her green eyes fill with tears and saw her effort to blink them back. Her lower lip trembled and she chewed at it with white, even teeth. In spite of her attempts one lone tear escaped and rolled down her flushed cheek.

Damn it, he wished she wouldn't do that. He couldn't stand to see her cry. He thought of the long, dark months when he'd be marooned by the winter storms. Days when he wouldn't see her, or hear her voice. Nights when she wouldn't be near, tempting his sanity the way she had last night after the storm. He sucked in his breath.

Removing his gloves, he strode toward her. Wide pools

of brimming green looked up at him. ''Now I'll take that kiss.'' He reached out and grasped her shoulders, pulling her toward him. His eyes locked on hers, he drew her close and bent his head.

Molding his lips to her soft ones, he forced his tongue between her teeth, bruising her mouth in a fierce kiss. He raised a hand and pulled the tortoiseshell combs from her hair. Like silk, it fell wild and free. When she began to struggle, he wrapped one hand in the tumbling mass, forcing her to be still. The other hand roamed to the front of her blue calico dress. Fumbling with the tiny buttons, he heard one come loose and roll across the wooden floor.

She twisted, beating his chest with her fists, but he paid her no mind, remembering last night when she had held out her arms, calling him to her bed. Smothering her with savage kisses, he slid his hand inside her dress and pulled down the front of her chemise, baring the warm swell of her breasts to his hungry gaze. He cupped his hand around one, rubbing it, feeling it swell beneath his hand. His thumb drew slow circles around the nipple until it grew taut and rosy. He bent his head and took it between his teeth, sucking, lightly biting, teasing it with his tongue.

She moaned and slid her arms around his neck, drawing him still closer.

He moved his mouth to the other breast and slowly aroused her to writhe and twist beneath him. Leaving her breast, his tongue blazed a trail to her mouth. He licked her swollen lips with the tip of his tongue.

Her eyes glazed with desire, she pressed against him.

He plunged his tongue between her teeth, tasting the nectar that for a time was his. He kissed her again and again, his hands roaming her soft, scented flesh. His mouth and teeth nibbled a tender path across her cheek to her ear. "You're mine, kitten, mine." He murmured English and Cheyenne words of love while his mouth and hands made love to her fevered body.

Finally he loosened his grip. She swayed and would have fallen, but he slid his hands beneath her, cupping her firm buttocks. He raised her to him, pressing his hardness against her. He bent and lifted her into his arms.

Her arms went around his neck. Her hands fastened in his hair. She nuzzled his face with soft kisses.

He knew she was his for the taking, and God knows he'd waited long enough. He carried her to the bed. The vision of her half-naked, kissing Jeff, flashed into his mind. Anger made him shake. The little vixen! No, she wouldn't trap *him*. Not yet! He extended his arms and dropped her onto the mattress.

Her mouth opened, and her eyes met his in amazement.

"Now, *sweetie,* you've had your kiss," he said hoarsely. Trembling with emotion, he gathered up his belongings and stalked out of the room. As he savored the sweet taste of revenge his spirits rose higher than they'd been in months. He strolled down the hall, whistling a tune. She might kiss Jeff and love Billy, Nick thought, but by damn she'd never forget him.

After tying his belongings on the horses, Nick paused a minute, then walked back to the storeroom. He lifted a saddle blanket and picked up a bundle of parcels. Slipping back inside the house, he went to Rosa's room and knocked softly. When she opened the door, he stepped inside. "I have some things I want you to put under the tree at Christmas."

"Christmas?" Her plump brow wrinkled in a frown. "I don't understand, Nicky. Why don't you do it yourself?"

He dropped the parcel into a chair and turned to grip her shoulders. "Because I won't be here. I'm going to High Mesa. I'll stay there until spring."

"*Por Dios*. High Mesa? And what of your wife? Will she be going with you?"

"No. I'm going alone," he said. He bent and gave her a quick kiss on the cheek. "Take care of yourself—and take care of her, too." Before she could ask any more questions, he turned and left the room.

"Nick?"

Nick looked up and saw his cousin standing in the entry. "Hello, Jeff. I was just coming to say good-bye."

"I saw your horses. Where are you going?" Jeff asked.

"That's what I'd like to know, too." Jake hobbled out of the dining room and stood beside Jeff.

"To High Mesa to spend the winter," Nick said wearily.

"High Mesa? What the hell are you doin' that for?" Jake boomed out. "And what about Samantha? You just gonna run off and leave her?"

"Don't you think that's the best thing I could do for her?" Nick said.

"That little gal cares for you. Why, I don't know," Jake said, shaking his head. "I've never seen a more muley-headed, ornery cuss than you."

"She deserves better. That's why I have to leave."

"I can see yer mind's made up," Jake said. "But I think it's plumb foolish. Probably freeze to death up there."

"Take care of yourself, old man," Nick said, giving his grandfather's shoulder a squeeze. "I'll see you in the spring.'' He opened the door and stepped out onto the porch with Jeff close behind him.

"Well," Nick said, looking at his cousin. "Spit it out. I can see you're about to bust."

"Nick, I know why you're doin' it, and I think you're a damn fool," Jeff said. "Don't you love her at all?"

"I'll admit I want her, but love?" Nick shook his head. "Hell, I don't even know what love is." He shook Jeff's hand. "Take care of everyone for me." He made a fist and lightly cuffed Jeff on the chin. "And yourself, too. See you in the spring."

Samantha lay on the bed, her eyelids stinging with hot, unshed tears. She blinked them back, rage replacing the hurt. *How dare he treat me like that?* "Damn you, Nick, you'll pay for this," she said to the empty room. Her traitorous body ached for his touch, for the fulfillment he promised but never gave. Clutching her torn dress together, she ran to the window and yanked aside the lace curtain.

Below her, a tall, lean man in black climbed onto a pinto horse. He paused to light a cigar before picking up the rope of the heavily laden pack animal. Heading toward the house, he glanced up, catching sight of her. Clenching the cheroot between white even teeth, he curled his lips in a smile. He lifted his black-gloved hand and swept off his Stetson, giving her a mocking bow. Shoving the hat back on his head, he turned away without a backward glance and urged the horses into a gallop, leaving her and the ranch far behind.

Samantha watched until he had ridden out of sight, her heart aching with frustration and anger. Leaning her head against the windowpane, she felt a curious sense of desertion as she stared down at the empty road. Her lips trembled. No longer able to hold back the flood, she broke into heartrending sobs. She raised her clenched fist. Her voice breathless and choked, she called toward the mountains, ''You'll pay dearly for this, Nick McBride. I swear you'll pay dearly for this.''

CHAPTER

* 14 *

AS NICK LEFT THE VALLEY AND PINE-COVERED foothills far behind, the trail climbed into the rocky crags with the tree line disappearing far below. He glanced at the bleak barren landscape. December, and it hadn't snowed yet. Usually by this time of year snow had closed the trail at this altitude and was piled in deep drifts around the house.

December . . . Christmas. His thoughts drifted ahead, to the big tree smelling up the house and Rosa making her special little cakes. His mouth watered as he thought about them. Damn, he hated to leave before Christmas.

Good thing he'd done his shopping early. He'd wrapped Samantha's presents—the green silk dress, the black stockings, and soft kid slippers. Along with the clothes he'd stuck in small parcels containing all kinds of gewgaws, hair bows, perfume, hairpins—stuff women liked.

His spirits drooped. Now he wouldn't be there to see her open the presents. He sighed, recalling the other times he'd brought her gifts. She'd been like a kid, hugging his neck and planting kisses all over his face, her green eyes shining when she looked over each purchase. He closed his eyes, remembering how sweet she was and how good she felt in his arms.

"Damn it. Get hold of yourself or you'll be turning the horses around and going back," he scolded. He laughed when Scout pricked up his ears. "It's okay, fella, we'll probably be having a lot of conversations before spring."

A gust of stiff wind blew down from the high peaks, cutting through Nick like a sharp knife. Shivering, he turned up the collar on his heavy coat and fastened the bone buttons to keep out the cold. He glanced at the puffy gray clouds overhead. *It's going to snow, and soon.* He urged the horses into a faster gait. He had to get through Alta Pass before the storm hit.

The horses' hooves rang on the granite trail, echoing through the canyon, as did the mournful wail of the biting wind. At Alta Pass sharp particles of ice pelted him. Low clouds hung over the gray cliffs, making them seem even more somber and oppressive.

By the time he reached High Mesa Ranch, fine flakes of snow fell in a thick flurry from the late-afternoon sky. The horses' breath steamed from their nostrils, making puffs in the thin, dry air. They crossed a broad meadow, spooking a browsing doe that bounded away to the cover of the trees.

Nick raised a hand to shield his eyes, barely able to make out the small cabin nestled in a scattered stand of trees. From the edge of the mesa, on a clear day, he could see clear to New Mexico Territory, but today he was lucky to find the house. He guided the animals to the covered front porch and dismounted. After unloading the panniers and the rest of his gear, he carried it inside.

That done, he led the horses to the small barn and put them in stalls. After giving them a ration of feed from the metal-lined bin, he closed the barn door and stepped into the dusk.

Nick's boots crunched through the crust on the frozen ground, disturbing the silence. He looked up at the sky. The wind had stopped. By morning several feet of powder would be on the ground, closing the pass for the winter.

Isolated from the outside world, Nick looked back toward the barn. It was too late to change his mind now . . . even if he wanted to. He sighed, already feeling the loneliness. He had escaped the trap, but like the wolf chewing off his own foot, he'd left a part of himself behind.

The blizzard raged for three days, piling drifts high around the cabin. When the storm was over, Nick stepped out onto the porch. Like a mole coming out of its hole, he blinked against the glare of the sun on the diamond-dusted snow. He fed the horses and puttered about the cabin, carrying in wood and water and eating to pass the time. Chores done, and not knowing what to do with himself, he read and reread the books he'd stuck in his pack.

At the end of a week, already bored and sick of his own company, he saddled Scout and headed for the Cheyenne village.

He smiled, anxious to see his Indian family again. He hated to admit it, but he didn't like being alone. He'd talked to himself and the horses. He'd even tried luring a family of mice out of their home under the cabinet, but he missed the sound of human voices.

He lifted the corner of his mouth in a grin, wondering what Two Feathers and Chief White Eagle, his grandfather, would think about him getting married. Maybe they'd stop trying to marry him off to plump Shy Turtle. White Eagle had been worse than Jake about him getting hitched.

He thought about Two Feathers' son, Little Fox. He was seven now and had probably grown a foot since he'd last seen him. The little scamp was the spitting image of Two Feathers and Nick himself, except for his eyes. Nick thought if he had a son, he'd probably look like that, too.

Jake'd always said Nick and Two Feathers were like two peas in a pod, except Nick was two inches taller, two years younger, and had gray eyes instead of brown.

His grin broadened as he remembered how, when they were boys getting into mischief, they'd taken advantage of their resemblance, knowing from a distance they couldn't be told apart. But they never got away with very much. White Eagle, not knowing which of them was guilty, usually ended up punishing both of them.

He grew sad recalling the flu epidemic six years ago that had claimed Little Fox's mother, Singing Rain. Left with an infant son to raise and torn with grief, Two Feathers vowed never to lose another loved one because of lack of knowledge of the white man's medicine. Angry because Indian remedies hadn't been able to help his wife, Two Feathers became determined to be a doctor.

Jake's friend Dr. Henry Johnson had offered to help. Nick remembered the many long hours the doctor and the Indian spent at the kitchen table at the ranch. One head wise and gray, the other intelligent and black, one teaching, the other learning until the early hours of the morning. When the doctor'd taught him all he could, he'd made arrangements for Two Feathers to study under a colleague in Philadelphia. Four years later John Eagle, as Two Feathers was known among the whites, graduated with honors and returned to help his people.

Nick wrinkled his brow in a frown, wishing Two Feathers had been handy when Samantha was so sick, but he'd gone to a village in the north. Nick trusted Dr. Johnson, but he was anxious to get his uncle's opinion about her loss of memory.

The Cheyenne camp lay in a sheltered valley east of High Mesa. Protected by jagged cliffs, with the only trails in and out guarded, the people were safe from their enemies. Nick waved to a sentry, waiting until he was given the signal to pass. When the lookout returned his wave, he inched Scout down the icy trail to the village.

The lodges, numbering fifty or more, stood in a great circle. Gray columns of smoke rose through the still air, hanging low around the hide-covered dwellings. The camp bustled with activity.

Not even the snow stopped the men and boys from bathing in the stream since they believed the cold water made them healthy and strong and washed away all sickness. Although the women didn't participate, they, too, hurried to and from the river fetching fresh water. The Cheyenne would not drink water that had stood overnight, calling it dead. Other women tended the cooking fires while children and dogs of every description raced about.

Nick, smelling the roasting meat, heard his stomach rumble. Waving to various friends and relatives, he ducked a snowball thrown by a mischievous youngster. He grinned at the impish face of his young cousin peeking out from a mop of long black hair. Living in silence all week, he enjoyed the happy sounds of children and dogs playing in the snow.

Halting Scout, Nick dismounted in front of the largest lodge, that of his grandfather, Chief White Eagle. He called from outside the door, not entering until he was asked to do so. When the chief invited him inside, Nick opened the flap and stepped into the large structure.

The old man got to his feet and placed his hands on Nick's outstretched arms in greeting. "*Haahe,* Fire Arrow," he said, greeting Nick by his Indian name. "*Ne-toneto-mohta-he?* How are you? Come and share my fire and eat. It has been many moons since we have sat together." A broad smile wreathed his weathered face.

Nick walked toward the firepit in the middle of the lodge. It was about a foot deeper than the rest of the ground. A pot of venison stew hanging from a tripod frame simmered over the cooking fire. Its savory smells filled the air, making Nick's mouth water.

The interior of the tipi, a few inches higher than the ground outside to deflect the rain, had thick buffalo robes covering woven, grass mats. More robes lay folded to the side of a backrest. With the arrival of winter, the decorated hides covering the outside of the lodge were pegged tightly to the ground. Additional hides lined the inside bottom perimeter, sealing out the winter cold. Their edges, used as narrow shelves, were lined with weapons, baskets, and clothing.

His grandfather settled himself against the backrest opposite the lodge flap and motioned for Nick to sit down.

Nick lowered himself to the spot beside his grandfather. The flap opened again, and a stout Indian woman, her bright eyes like two brown nuts, entered and fastened her gaze on Nick. *"Haahe, natse,"* she said. "Hello, nephew."

*"Haahe,*Tashina," Nick greeted his great-aunt, the sister of the chief.

Two Feathers, apparently told of Nick's arrival by his young son, called from the doorway. He was asked to enter, and lifting the flap, he stepped inside. *"Heeheoh-ohe, tsehe-heto.* Good morning, my father. *Haahe, natse.* Hello, nephew." He greeted his aunt in a similar fashion and sat down by the fire across from Nick.

Tashina approached the fire and ladled the stew into carved wooden bowls. She served her brother, the chief, first. Beaming at Nick, she dished up an extra-large serving of the savory dish and handed it to him. She also fixed an ample portion for her nephew, Two Feathers. After filling another container, she left the tent to watch over Little Fox while the men ate and talked.

Nick held the bowl to his mouth and sipped at the broth of the stew, finding it deliciously warm and spicy. When the juice was gone, he ate the tender pieces of meat and vegetables that remained. His bowl empty, he looked up, embarrassed to see his grandfather and uncle still eating.

Two Feathers grinned. "Fire Arrow eats like a wolf that has gone too long with an empty belly."

"I've had plenty to eat. I just don't like my own cooking," Nick said, laughing.

"Rosa no longer cooks for you?" his uncle asked.

"She's at the ranch. I moved to High Mesa for the winter," Nick explained.

Two Feathers raised his eyebrows, too polite to ask why.

When they had eaten their fill, Nick handed his grandfather a box of the thin cigars he'd bought in Canyon Springs,

knowing the chief had a secret fondness for them. Two
Feathers generally didn't smoke except at formal ceremo-
nies. They talked and Nick told them of the happenings at
the ranch, and of Jake and Jeff. Then he grinned at them.
"One more thing happened. . . . I got married."

The chief's eyes widened and he choked on the smoke
before regaining his usual stoic composure. He looked at his
grandson, his black eyes dancing with curiosity. "So Fire
Arrow is married. Tell me about your mate."

Nick told them about Samantha, neglecting to mention
the kidnapping, the wedding he didn't remember, the fights
they'd had, and the fact that he had yet to sleep with her. He
also didn't mention her memory loss, saving that for when
he and Two Feathers were alone. They talked until dusk had
fallen and Nick saw his grandfather nod with weariness. He
bid the old chief good night and left the lodge to follow Two
Feathers to his tipi.

When they pushed back the flap and walked inside,
Tashina got to her feet and left for her own dwelling. Nick
saw his small cousin and a mongrel pup curled up asleep on
a bearskin rug a short distance from the fire. His own
bedroll had been removed from Scout and spread on a mat
across from Two Feathers' fur-covered bed.

The Indian sat down and motioned for Nick to do the
same. When they were seated, Two Feathers looked at Nick.
"Now, you can tell me what really happened," he said with
a grin."

After a three-day visit Two Feathers waved good-bye to
his nephew and watched him disappear up the trail toward
High Mesa. Perplexed and frowning, he lifted the flap and
went back inside his lodge.

He and Nick had discussed Samantha's illness at length, and he'd promised Nick he would examine her, even though he respected Dr. Johnson's opinion regarding her condition. He crossed the mat-covered floor and removed a medical volume from his book rack. Vaguely remembering a case he'd studied at the hospital in Philadelphia, he sat cross-legged in front of the fire and searched for his notes. It wasn't just the medical aspect that interested him; he was curious about the woman who could get his nephew in such a state.

He sighed, hoping Nick's judgment of women had improved. He'd met the fair Amanda Blaine and he shared Old Jake's opinion of her. He shuddered, thinking Nick could count himself lucky he hadn't ended up married to her.

Staring into the flames, he pondered Nick's situation. There was more to the strange visit than his nephew had told him, even though he'd said quite a lot.

He shook his head, still finding it hard to believe Nick and Jeff had kidnapped the girl off the stage. He'd bitten his tongue when Nick said he'd been so drunk he didn't remember getting married. He'd known whiskey would get his nephew in trouble, but knew Nick wouldn't appreciate being reminded of the fact.

He frowned, remembering Nick's reaction when he told of her nightmares and the man she'd called out for in her sleep. Nick said come spring he intended to find this man, Billy, deliver the girl to him, and get the marriage annulled.

Two Feathers had known Nick all his life, and even though Nick claimed not to care, he'd seen the pain in his nephew's eyes. He'd also seen the light when Nick had told of her courage and beauty. He narrowed his eyes thoughtfully. Nick never did say why he was at High Mesa instead of at the ranch with his wife. He arched his brow. "Yes, I think there is quite a lot you didn't tell me, Fire Arrow."

After spending the week hunting to supplement their winter meat supply during the morning and studying from his medical books in the afternoon, Two Feathers found himself unable to contain his curiosity any longer. Even though the road through Alta Pass was closed for the winter, he knew he could use the trail of the Old Ones to reach the valley. While he hated to leave Little Fox, the Christmas holiday was not a Cheyenne custom, even though, he knew his son, like all children, would welcome presents no matter what the day. He went to the chief's lodge and told him that he planned to leave for the McBride ranch the next morning.

White Eagle gave him messages for Jake and gifts for the rest of the family. Also curious about the woman his grandson had married, the chief was anxious to hear Two Feathers' opinion of her.

At first light Two Feathers hefted the soft deerskin pack to his shoulders and left his lodge. Even at that early hour the village hummed like a hive of bees.

A group of young warriors riding out in search of game called out as they raced past. Groups of women gossiped and scoured the woods for kindling, while others tended the cookfires. Children, rubbing sleepy eyes, raised the flaps of tipis to see if their playmates were up and about. Dogs of all shapes and colors stretched and sniffed the snow-covered ground searching for tidbits from last night's meal.

Two Feathers wore long, supple deerskin, adorned with porcupine quills and beads woven into intricate designs by his aunt, Tashina. His shirt had a thick fringe of antelope skin along the edges of the sleeves and across the back of his shoulders, while the pants had a thick border of it from waist to ankle along the outside seam. The fringe made a pleasant swishing noise as he made his way through the woods toward the cliff trail.

A warm chinook wind had come up during the night, making the bright day almost balmy. The top surface of the snow melted, running in rivulets down the surface of rocks and stream beds. But Two Feathers knew no matter how warm the day became, the ancient Indian trail down the cliff would still be treacherous. Much of the pathway would have a thick covering of ice under the snow and the bare parts would be wet and slippery, with loose rock underfoot.

Leaving the cover of the trees, he came to the rim of the cliff. He looked over the ledge where a steamy mist rolled up from the depths below. He loved high places, and his heart raced in fierce exhilaration, feeling a kinship with his vision bird, the eagle.

He bent and removed his knee-high deerskin moccasins, tied them together, and looped them around his neck. The climb down the mountain must be made with his feet bare. The moccasins became too slippery when they got wet. He shifted the pack holding the presents and his medical bag to a more comfortable position on his back.

He swung himself off the cliff, clinging by his hands until he'd aligned his body with the ledge below. One mistake and he would either miss the cliff and fall hundreds of feet to the rocks or hit the small shelf just under him and slide down to where there was no way back up to the top. Regardless of the risk, he had to attempt the twenty-foot drop to reach the trail.

Praying his body would fall true, he released his hold. The air rushed past his ears. The ledge came up fast under his feet. He leaned slightly forward, bending his knees to absorb the shock. He landed like a cat, his feet sure and his balance true. He took a deep breath to calm his racing heart. The hard part was over; now all he had to do was avoid patches of ice and loose rocks.

Halfway down the trail, his mind on his nephew's predicament, he failed to notice the rattle of gravel until too late. A steep section of the trail split from the mountain. It slid beneath his feet, threatening to take him with it. He bent and gathered his legs under him. He tensed amid the falling rocks, ready to jump across to safety. A rolling boulder bounced down the hill and crashed into his leg. Agony ripped through his ankle. He staggered, crying out in pain.

Off balance, he crashed to the ground, swiftly sliding after the rocks. He clawed desperately at the ledge of the cliff. The canyon yawned far below. He dug his fingers into a crevasse, slowing enough to grip another with his bare feet. His body trembling with the effort, he stopped his descent. Slowly, painfully, he dragged himself to safety.

Bruised and shaken, he struggled to his feet. The torment in his ankle made him weak and dizzy. He probed the wounded area with his bleeding fingers and found the ankle badly sprained, but not broken. Gritting his teeth, he limped to the bottom of the treacherous incline.

After wrapping his ankle, he slipped the fringed boots back on his feet. He cursed himself for his carelessness. In all the times he'd gone over the cliff, this was the first time he'd gotten hurt. He put his weight on his foot, giving thanks it wasn't worse.

He broke a stout pole, lashed the short piece across the

top of the longer one to form a crutch, and padded it with a moss-stuffed piece of leather he'd cut from the pack. He gathered his belongings and repositioned them on his back. Slipping the crude crutch under his arm, he hobbled down the trail to the main road.

It took him three times longer than usual to reach the ranch. Half-frozen and in severe pain, he limped up onto the porch and knocked at the door. No one answered. Knowing he would be welcome, he opened the door and looked around. Not seeing a soul, he stepped inside and placed his pack on the entry-hall floor.

CHAPTER

* 15 *

HER EMOTIONS IN TURMOIL, SAMANTHA FINISHED
the dishes, determined that no one else would know how
badly she'd been hurt. Her pride wouldn't let them see. She
kept up a cheerful appearance in front of the others, saving
the tears for nights spent alone in her room. Nights when
the memory of Nick's hands upon her body left her weak
and shaking . . . and furious. She clenched her teeth. She
would have her revenge . . . if he ever came back.

She hung up the dish towel and crossed the room to peer
into the small mirror by the backdoor. The sleepless nights
had left telltale signs, haunting her green eyes with deep
shadows. Jake, and Jeff with his antics, tried to keep her
mind occupied while Rosa prepared all sorts of treats to
tempt her palate. But having no appetite, she'd picked at her
food until even her newest gowns hung loosely on her
already slender figure. Turning away from the mirror,
Samantha sighed. Admit it or not, she missed Nick.

Picking up a heavy metal pot, she walked toward the
dining room to put it away. She looked up, catching sight of
a tall figure slipping into the house. *Nick!* Her eyes

narrowed. *Sneaking in like a thief, and dressed in buckskins, for heaven's sake!* Her anger, simmering since the day he'd left, now came to a full boil.

She tiptoed across the floor, watching him peer into the living room. Probably checking to make sure the coast was clear, she thought. *Maybe he's planning to sneak up the stairs and maul me some more.* In spite of her anger her pulse raced at the thought, but the need for revenge was too strong.

We'll just see who manhandles who, sweetie. Clutching the pan by the handle, she crept silently across the floor. Scarcely daring to breathe, she eased up behind Nick. Just as he opened his mouth she brought the pot down squarely on top of his head. He groaned and dropped like a stone. "Take that, Mr. McBride," she said. The pan still grasped in one hand, the other on her hip, she glared down at him.

"What in tarnation is all the racket?" Jake asked, coming through the door from outside. He stopped in his tracks. His eyes wide, he looked at Samantha in amazement. "What the devil happened to Two Feathers?" he said.

"Two Feathers?" Samantha asked weakly. "I thought it was Nick." She bent closer. "Oh, what have I done?" She ran into the dining room and grabbed a water pitcher from the table, rushed back to the entry, and dumped it on the unconscious Indian.

When he didn't move, she fell to her knees beside him. She lifted his head in her arms and rocked him back and forth. "Please wake up," she cried. She looked down. *Damn! It is Nick!* Anger and indignation flooded her. She moved, preparing to drop him back on the floor, but he stirred, opening his eyes.

Samantha's mouth dropped open. Her eyes widened,

staring into dazed . . . brown eyes. It wasn't Nick! "Oh," she gasped, "you aren't him—uh—he isn't you—oh, I don't know what I mean, except I'm sorry."

Two Feathers blinked, looking up at the vision above him. He closed his eyes again, leaning his head back against her soft breasts. He was dizzy, but he suspected only half of it was from the blow she'd given him. He realized she had mistaken him for Nick. He thought since he had taken the punishment for his nephew, he would enjoy the rewards as well. It had been a long time since a woman had held him so, and he intended to enjoy every minute of it. Uttering a pain-filled moan, he snuggled even closer, hearing the beat of her heart against his ear.

She raised a gentle hand and brushed the hair back from his forehead.

Jake cleared his throat noisily.

Two Feathers sighed, knowing Jake was onto his game. Reluctantly he opened his eyes and gazed up at her.

Eyes wet, long lashes spiked with tears, she looked down at him. Her mouth trembled, and she bit her bottom lip.

He smiled gently, feeling guilty for his charade. He raised his dark copper hand to wipe the tears from her ivory cheeks. "Don't cry, pretty one," he said softly. "It takes more than a bump on the head to kill Two Feathers."

"I'm so sorry. I thought you were Nick," she said, then her cheeks flushed with embarrassment.

"So I gathered," he said, grinning at her. He sat up, rubbing his head. "*He* probably deserved it, too."

"Are you two gonna lay around on the floor, or are you gonna sit up on the furniture like decent folk?" Jake asked.

Two Feathers eased himself to his feet, wincing at the pain in his ankle.

"Oh, I am sorry. It hurts, doesn't it?" Samantha cried.

"It's nothing. I sprained my ankle on the way down the cliff," he said, holding out his hand to help her to her feet. She put her hand in his and stood up. It was not until she wiggled her fingers that he realized he was still holding it. Reluctantly he released her. She was the prettiest white woman he had ever seen. The top of her shining head only came to his chin. Graceful as a flower in the wind, she smelled like one, too. Her eyes reminded him of a bottom-less deep green pool—inviting and breathtaking. Regardless of how he got married, his nephew was a lucky man.

"Well, are you gonna stand there gawking all day, or are you gonna show me what you've got in that pack yonder?" Jake asked impatiently.

Two Feathers pulled his eyes away from the girl and started to limp toward the door.

"Let me get it," she said, rushing around him to lift the pack, but she couldn't budge it.

"What have you got in there, rocks?" Jake called.

"No, only books and presents for nosy old men . . . and beautiful ladies," he said, watching a tinge of pink flush her cheeks.

"Two Feathers, this is Samantha, Nick's *wife*," Jake said.

"Nick's wife? Hmm. I'm happy to meet you, Saman-tha." Bowing, he took her hand and brought it to his lips, as he had seen fine gentlemen do in the east. He straightened to see a look of wonder in her eyes. He knew he was making a fool of himself, but he couldn't help it. He didn't know if there was anything wrong with her or not, but in his opinion

Nick was the one who needed to have his head examined. A pounding on the door interrupted his thoughts.

"Hey, somebody, let me in! This blamed thing is heavy."

Samantha rushed to open the front door. Jeff came crashing through, dragging a huge spruce tree.

"Couldn't you find a bigger one?" Jake asked dryly.

"Yeah, but I couldn't carry it," Jeff said, laughing. He tried to stand it up, but even with the twelve-foot ceilings, it was three feet too tall. "I guess it's bigger than I thought," Jeff said. Brushing the snow off his clothes, he grinned at Two Feathers.

"Never mind, Jeff. We can fix it," Two Feathers said, laughing. He helped the young man tug the tree to the hearth and cut off the excess branches, leaving enough for Samantha to decorate the stairway. They nailed a wooden stand to the trunk and heaved the blue spruce to an upright position in the corner. For all its size, the tree was perfectly shaped. Two Feathers thought the custom of indoor trees strange, but had to admit it was an impressive sight.

"Supper's ready," Rosa called from the dining room.

He joined the family for a delicious meal of roasted quail and pinenut dressing with dried apple pie for dessert. Full to bursting, he thanked Samantha and Rosa and followed Jake and Jeff into the living room.

Samantha absently wiped at the dishes, her thoughts preoccupied by the handsome Indian in the front room.

Indian. Nick was twice the savage he was. Two Feathers' gentle kindness and impeccable manners impressed her. He looked so much like Nick it was startling, yet there was a quiet dignity about him that her husband lacked. She thought Two Feathers warm and intelligent, also thoughtful and considerate, with none of the fierce anger Nick had shown.

She felt herself more attracted to the Indian doctor than she cared to admit. But she knew it was because he looked so much like her husband. Her mouth tightened. Some husband. Here it was Christmas and he'd deserted her, running off to some mountain. "I hope he freezes to death," she muttered.

Poor Two Feathers, she'd given him an awful lump, hitting him with that pot the way she had. She narrowed her eyes. Now she owed Nick two, one for herself and one for his uncle. It seemed funny for Nick to call Two Feathers uncle when actually he was only two years older than Nick.

She hung the towel on the kitchen rack and walked back into the living room just as Rosa came from her room with the boxes of Christmas ornaments.

Handing out the decorations, Samantha divided the areas of the tree. Jeff, with the ladder, was given the top part. Jake, with a sturdy chair, was given the next. Two Feathers, because of his injured ankle, had the part just above her head. She and Rosa took the bottom and the staircase. When they were finished, they stood back and admired their handiwork.

Pretty birds Samantha'd cut from colored paper perched on the lush, green limbs. Red-orange berries from the mountain ash she and Jeff had found were strung into a colorful garland. Rosa had sewn the lace-and-calico balls that Jake had stuffed with sweet-smelling grasses. On top of the tree Jeff attached a cloth angel dressed in a flowing satin robe with cornsilk hair and lace wings.

"Isn't it beautiful?" Samantha sighed. "And it smells heavenly."

"I wish Little Fox could be here to see the tree. I know his eyes would pop at the sight," Two Feathers said.

"I'll pack some ornaments for you to take to the village children when you leave," Samantha suggested, smiling.

"Thank you. I am sure they would enjoy them," he said.

With the decorating finished and all the presents placed under the tree, they joined together to sing carols. Two Feathers added his bass to Jeff's tenor while Samantha and Rosa sang the higher notes. Jake bellowed out the old songs in every key, shaking the chimneys on the oil lamps. Then all was quiet as Rosa sang a hymn in soft, melodic Spanish.

They were getting ready to have hot chocolate and eat decorated cakes when Jeff shyly pulled something out of his pocket and handed it to Samantha.

"Mistletoe. Wherever did you find it, Jeff?" she asked, her eyes dancing with delight.

"Off down by the creek aways in the top of that big old oak," he said.

Two Feathers looked at the boy intently, noticing the dreamy way he watched the copper-haired woman. He knew that oak tree; it was a good five miles away! He shook his head.

Samantha tied a piece of red ribbon on the green sprig and handed it to Two Feathers. "Maybe you could hang it there?" She motioned to the dining-room doorway.

Taking the leafed berry branch, Two Feathers secured it with a small, square nail. When it was hung, they took turns seeing who could catch Samantha. Jeff sent her after more cakes, chocolate, or whatever he could dream up. Even old Jake got a kiss. Jeff managed to make it twice.

When the other men were busy with a game of checkers, Two Feathers, seeing his chance, stood by the doorway, waiting for her to come back from the kitchen. "Merry Christmas, Samantha," he said.

She smiled up at him. Her eyes lit with laughter, knowing he'd waited for his turn.

He gripped her shoulders and bent his head, giving her a sisterly kiss on the cheek. He closed his eyes, smelling the sweet rose fragrance of her, feeling her silky hair brush his hand. He fought the urge to kiss her full red lips.

Disgusted, he reminded himself that she was his nephew's wife, and that it was dishonorable for a Cheyenne to entertain such feelings. Yet Nick didn't want her; he had never even made her his own. Two Feathers sighed, letting her go. He might be a disgrace to his race, but his nephew was a fool.

Samantha lay in her bed, thinking of the bronzed man sleeping in the next room. He seemed so lonely. She remembered the sadness in his voice when he told her of his wife, and how he'd beamed with pride when he spoke of the antics of his small son. She smiled. *I'll have to think of something special to send Little Fox.* Happy for the first time in many days, she closed her eyes and went to sleep.

Christmas day dawned bright and cheery. After breakfast they gathered around the tree to open their presents. Jake was delighted with the red shirt and robe from Nick, the new sack of pipe tobacco from Jeff, and the warm slippers from Samantha. The chief sent him one of the hard-shelled squash he loved and a belt made of soft cowhide with quill-and-bead designs.

Samantha had made Jeff a blue silk shirt that brought out the color of his eyes. He opened a penknife from Nick. Jake gave him a new saddle for his horse. Two Feathers brought him small pieces of close-grained wood to carve, saying Nick had told him about the knife.

Samantha looked at Two Feathers thoughtfully. He had seen Nick. *Hmm.* So he'd known who she was after all. She had a feeling that a strong likeness wasn't the only thing he shared with his nephew.

She'd received a box of chocolates from Jake and a bird's nest with small blue-speckled eggs from Jeff. The chief sent her a beautiful doeskin vest, soft as a baby's breath, with delicate, muted beads woven into lovely designs. Two Feathers handed her a pack of tiny bulbs and told her how to plant them to have the first spring flowers.

Samantha saved the gifts from Nick until last. She opened the large package, uncovering the most beautiful green silk dress she'd ever seen and a pair of soft, Moroccan slippers. Tears stinging her eyes, she hugged the shimmering garment close. He had remembered after all. Peeking inside the other package, she'd blushed at finding silky underwear and other things. Being modest, she'd decided to wait until later and open it in her room.

Two Feathers was excited to get a volume of the newest medical knowledge from Jake. Jeff gave him a skinning knife. Samantha gave him a book of poetry, discovering her favorite poet, Percy Bysshe Shelley, was also his.

Little Fox's presents would fill a wagon all by themselves, but except for the smaller things he would have to wait until spring when the buckboard could get through to Mesa Ranch to receive most of them.

Jake, doting on the youngster, had bought him a bright Mexican blanket for his pony. Jeff gave him a penknife like his own and a small telescope. Nick had made him a soft leather bridle with silver conchos for his horse.

Samantha had wrapped a picture book that had caught her eye in town. It'd seemed familiar, and hoping it would trigger memories, she'd bought it. The book of fairy tales had pages full of bright pictures and stories enough to excite any child's imagination.

Rosa had knitted socks for the men out of wool she'd bought in town. She gave Samantha a lovely cream-colored, Spanish mantilla and a tortoiseshell comb for her hair.

While they were opening presents a knock sounded on the front door. Samantha opened it to see a freshly scrubbed, red-faced cowboy holding something behind his back.

"Miz Samantha, ma'am, I saw this little critter and thought you might like to have it," he said bashfully. Blushing furiously, he held out a small basket containing a dainty calico kitten.

Samantha, her eyes filling with tears, took the basket, then leaned forward and kissed the cowboy's cheek. "Thank you, Danny, it's adorable," she said. She lifted the tiny animal from the basket and cuddled it next to her. "Won't you come in and join us?" she asked.

"Uh, no ma'am. I'm on my way into town . . . to church," he said, twisting his hat in his hands.

Samantha smiled. "Thank you, then. Merry Christmas."

When the door closed, Jeff whooped and slapped his knee. "Wonder when Molly started having services."

Samantha placed the basket with the sleeping kitten by the fire. Taking off her apron, she gathered up her presents from Nick and went upstairs to change for dinner.

In her room she sat down on her bed and opened the other parcel from Nick, exclaiming at the multitude of undergarments. She blushed, thinking of Nick picking out the feminine things for her. She was delighted at the assortment of bows, perfume, and other things as well.

She fingered the items, a great sadness settling over her. Every gift had been chosen with care, so why hadn't he stayed to see her open them? Why had he left, preferring to spend the winter on a lonely mountain? What had happened to make their marriage go so wrong?

She lifted the pillow she'd removed from his room and hugged it, inhaling the faint scent of his tobacco. She buried her face in its softness, using it to muffle her sobs, at last facing the realization that he didn't want to be a husband to her. That he never would be a husband to her.

When her tears were spent, she rose from the bed and placed a cold cloth on her eyes to hide the redness. Knowing she had to conceal her sorrow from the others so as not to spoil their holiday, she shook out the folds of the glimmering emerald silk and slipped it over her head. The front, cut in a deep V to her waist, had an insert of delicate cream-colored French lace. It dipped very low, exposing the soft swell of her breasts. The sleeves fit snug to her elbow, then flared with a ruffle of lace. The waist hugged her tightly, leaving the gathered skirt to fall in fluid lines to the floor.

She pulled the front of her hair high on top of her head and fastened it with the tall Spanish comb. She draped the creamy lace shawl over the comb. "Oh, it's so pretty," she said, twirling in front of the mirror. She pulled little ringlets, letting them curl around her face. The rest of her hair fell in long waves to her hips. She pinched her cheeks and bit her lips to give them color and gasped, seeing her reflection. She looked like a Spanish princess.

She opened another present, also from Nick, finding a pair of delightfully sinful black silk stockings. She pulled them on, admiring how they clung to her legs, then slipped the soft shoes onto her feet. Glancing into the mirror, she took a deep breath and swept regally out of the room.

Coming from the bathing room, Two Feathers, freshly washed and his long hair combed smooth, heard a soft rustling noise on the stairs. Raising his head, he stared at the vision above him.

Her eyes met his, haunting, sad, the same shimmering color as her dress. Her slender figure was elegant and graceful; her full, creamy breasts brimmed above provocative lace. Her lips were red as a summer rose. Her hair gleamed, the changing color of fiery embers.

His heart racing, his loins tightening, he stepped forward. "May I escort you to the table?" he said, grateful for once that he'd learned more than medicine at the white man's school.

She gave him a smile. "I'd be delighted, sir." She held out her hand.

He closed his leathery palm over her satiny-smooth skin and led her into the dining room.

Jake and Jeff looked up when they entered. Seeing Samantha, their eyes widened in admiration.

"Honey, you look pretty as a new spring foal," the old man said, a catch in his voice.

Jeff, his mouth open, his eyes worshiping, watched her enter and be seated. "Golly, Nick is a complete idiot," he said softly.

Two Feathers silently agreed with the young man. If she was his, he wouldn't step aside for any Billy, Bobby, or whoever, regardless of what kind of a claim they had to her. If Nick did as he threatened and set her free, there would be any number of others eager to take his place. She was like the princess in a fairy kingdom. His eyes narrowed. Her prince had better beware before he was bounced from his throne.

Dinner finished, they sat around the fire for a while, watching Samantha play with the small kitten until it grew tired and fell asleep. When she'd stood up and said good night, none of them could think of a good reason to stay up any longer, and they each headed for their own rooms.

Two Feathers removed his shirt and soft boots and lay back on the bed. He turned up the lamp and opened the volume of Shelley that Samantha had given him.

A muffled scream came through the wall.

Two Feathers leaped off the bed, grabbed his knife from the scabbard, and raced next door. He entered the room, searching the dark for an invader. Except for the girl on the bed the room was empty.

She's having a nightmare. Placing the knife on the nightstand, he sat down on the bed next to her. His mind clinical, he listened to her ramblings.

"No, Matthew. You're hurting me. I—can't breathe. Katie, help me." Her voice rose and her eyes flew open. She opened her mouth to scream. Recognizing him, she threw herself into his arms.

Two Feathers clasped her close, feeling her body tremble against his. His mind raged at the thought of this Matthew, whoever he was, hurting her. "Shh, it is all right, little one. No one is going to hurt you," he murmured. He raised a hand and gently brushed her unbound hair back from her eyes. It was fiery silk under his fingers.

She raised her hand, her green eyes deep and warm with promise and drew his mouth down to hers.

His touch light, he kissed her lips, her forehead, and her eyelids, feeling the flutter of her long lashes. His heart racing, he drew her to his chest. Through the thin nightgown her skin shown pale as ivory against his coppery arms. The scent and warmth of her intoxicated him, making him yield to foolish thoughts and desires.

"Oh Nick," she whispered.

The shock of hearing her call his nephew's name jolted him back to reality. Trembling, he laid her gently back on the pillow and closed her eyelids with his hand. "It is only a dream. Go back to sleep, little one."

Breathing a soft sigh, she smiled and closed her eyes.

Torn with emotion, he watched until she was in a deep sleep. He bent and placed a soft kiss on the mass of flame-colored hair. "Good-bye, Samantha, my pretty one," he whispered. He picked up his knife and left the room.

Two Feathers knew that in spite of how badly Nick had behaved, she loved him. Determined to see that his nephew hurt her no further, he packed his bag and, without a word to anyone, departed with the first light of dawn.

CHAPTER

* 16 *

NICK STEPPED ONTO THE PORCH OF THE LOG house and gazed longingly at the valley far below. His keen eyes picked out the ranch house, and he imagined he could see Samantha's window. He dreamed he heard her again last night, calling him to come to her. Her voice had been so close, so real. His insides twisted. Damn, he missed her. She'd haunted his memory these lonely days, and the nights had been worse. He'd fall asleep only to dream of her. He'd wake up hard and sick with wanting.

Stuck up here on the mesa, he'd had time to think. He realized he couldn't live the rest of his life without her. He had to know about her past before they could make their marriage work. And in order to do that he had to find Billy.

The bright sun warmed the ground around the house, turning it into a sea of mud from the fast-disappearing snow. Crystal icicles that only days before had hung four feet long from the edge of the roof had melted to the size of peppermint sticks. A warm chinook wind set the sprigs of new grass and golden avalanche lilies dancing in the meadows. Every low spot sparkled, a miniature alpine lake.

It was a picture to delight the eye, but he couldn't wait to leave it. He'd been here since the middle of December, and now it was the third week in April. Four months without seeing Samantha. It had been the loneliest four months of his life.

He'd ridden to the Cheyenne camp once after Christmas and found Two Feathers had been to the JMB. He'd told Nick he'd spent Christmas there and had examined Samantha. He'd said, as a doctor, he knew her loss of memory was caused by the blow to her head, and sometimes people with such injuries never regained their memory. But in Samantha's case there was also something else, something so horrible that maybe subconsciously she didn't want to remember.

Two Feathers told him that the night before he'd left for the village she'd had one of the nightmares. When she'd cried out, he'd gone in and comforted her, and she'd gone back to sleep without even knowing he was there. He said she hadn't mentioned Billy, but she had called out a name—Matthew. She'd been terrified of him.

He felt her nightmares were caused by a horrible experience in her past. He'd also said maybe it was better if she didn't remember, that she might not be able to deal with it if she did.

Nick frowned. Christmas night . . . that was when he'd had the dream the first time. He'd been in bed—but hell, it couldn't have been a dream. He hadn't been asleep. "Nick," she'd called, so close and clear that he'd jumped out of bed and run barefoot into the snow. Of course she hadn't been there. It must have been the wind playing tricks on his mind, but it left him uneasy and he hadn't slept the rest of the night. The feeling had disappeared by morning.

He wondered if that was the night she had had the dream. Nick frowned, remembering how upset his uncle had been. He'd seen the anger in Two Feathers' eyes when he'd asked about Nick's relationship with Samantha. *He'd sure been curious, wanting to know if I'd ever slept with her. He even asked me what I intended to do about the marriage.*

Nick narrowed his eyes, thinking about the conversation. *Curious, hell—he'd been downright nosy.* Nick had a feeling more had happened at the ranch than his uncle was telling. That fact did *not* relieve his mind.

He knew he'd have to wait a couple more days before he could get through the pass, and even then it would be tricky. If it just didn't snow between now and then. He glowered at the gray clouds drifting in overhead. *Damn, I hope they hold off a few more days.* He couldn't stand being up here, not knowing what was happening below.

The thought of seeing Samantha made his pulse race. Would she still be angry at him? Had she liked the green dress? When he asked, Two Feathers said she wore it on Christmas. He'd wanted to hear more, but his uncle had turned over and gone to sleep.

Nick bristled. Come to think of it, every single time he'd asked about Samantha, Two Feathers had avoided his eyes and gone to sleep, or changed the subject. Or if it was daylight, he'd gone hunting. Feeling something twist his middle, he pondered this last fact. *If he'd gone hunting, how come he'd never brought back any game . . . especially since he was the best hunter in the tribe!*

Tormented by jealousy and suspicion, Nick jerked the cigar from his mouth and threw it into the muck. He stared toward the valley. ''Just what the hell's been going on while I've been stuck up here in the snow?''

Nick sighed, glaring at the slush, wishing he had some way to make it melt faster. Having a case of what Jeff called the fidgets, he went back inside the house.

He looked around the room, at the dirty dishes stacked high on the kitchen table, the unmade bed, the floor thick with dirt and mud, and the smoke-blackened windows. He wrinkled his nose in distaste. He should clean house, but he wasn't in the mood. The mice family'd had a new batch of babies. Maybe he could coax them out again. He liked watching the frisky youngsters play. In fact he'd grown quite fond of the little varmints.

Two days later Nick was determined to leave. It had been too cloudy and cold to melt any more snow, but he was desperate. He had to know. Uneasy, he looked at the thick gray clouds overhead. "It had better not snow now, or by damn *I'll* be going over the cliff," he muttered.

He'd tried it once with Two Feathers. He'd misjudged the distance to the ledge and was falling over the cliff when his uncle reached out and pulled him back. By the time he'd reached the bottom, his legs had been like unset jelly, and he never tried the cliff trail again. He didn't know anybody else that had, except Two Feathers.

He packed the bare necessities in the saddlebags and glanced around the cabin. He'd eaten all the food, except what he'd left for the mice. The other things he could do without until later. Carrying the bags, he went to the corral and saddled Scout. He didn't bother to put the pack or a halter on the gray horse. He knew the animal would follow and would be better off finding his own footing. Mounting, he nudged Scout into a gallop, and with the other horse following close behind, he headed for the pass and home.

Alta Pass was worse then he'd figured. Since it was

sheltered by the cliffs, the ice here was thick and slick. He hesitated, wondering if he should wait. Casting a look at the sky, he took a deep breath. "If I don't go now, it'll snow again and I'll have to wait for no telling how long," he said. Samantha's face flashed before him. "It's now or never. Let's go, Scout."

He guided the horse carefully over the ice, dodging falling rocks and sliding snow. The packhorse fell and skinned his knees. Nick dismounted and ran his hands down the horse's legs. The gray wasn't limping, so if he could get him through the pass, he'd be all right. Seeing the trail growing even more treacherous, Nick stayed on foot and led Scout down off the mountain. The gray, slipping and sliding, stayed close behind.

When they reached flat ground, Nick stopped to let the trembling horses rest. Thinking he wasn't in much better shape than they, he lit a cigar to calm his nerves. He glanced back at the thick mist covering the pass. He'd probably been a fool to try it. He could have killed both himself and the horses. He turned his head toward the valley and his spirits soared. Fool or not, he'd made it. He was off the mountain, near home . . . and Samantha.

Nick reached the main fork in the road and pulled the horses to a stop. One direction led to the ranch and the other to Canyon Springs. He hesitated. Although he desperately yearned to see Samantha, how could he? He couldn't waltz in there and say hello and leave again . . . if he could bring himself to leave. And if he couldn't, he knew he'd end up making love to her, and then what would he do? Their situation hadn't changed and wouldn't until he had some answers. Want to or not, he had to find Billy. He closed his eyes, his body filled with longing. Depression settled on him, leaving him sadder and lonelier still. Heaving a resigned sigh, he gave the pack animal a slap on the rump, heading him toward the ranch. He waited until he was sure the gray wouldn't follow him, then turned Scout and headed for Canyon Springs.

Samantha, dressed in a split wool skirt, tall leather boots, and heavy cowhide jacket, tripped gaily down the stairs. Jeff was taking her to town with him for supplies. After being marooned on the ranch for months, even though she loved the place and its people, she was eager to see new sights and new faces. She ran to the front porch and waited impatiently for Jeff to bring the buckboard around. When she saw him coming, she eagerly stepped out into the muddy yard.

"Are you ready, Sammy?" Jeff teased, pulling the team to a stop. He rolled his eyes at the cloudy sky and frowned. "Maybe we shouldn't go. It looks like it might snow again."

Samantha's spirits drooped and she gazed up at the threatening heavens. Her mouth drew into a disappointed pout.

"I'm only teasing, sweetie," Jeff said. "It is gonna snow, but not on us. Looks like the storm is heading for High Mesa." He shook his head. "Nick'll never get down from there."

"Serves him right," she said with a smirk, picturing her tall, savage husband, cold and snowbound. She climbed aboard the wagon and Jeff whipped up the prancing team. She thought the horses seemed as anxious to go as she was.

They were halfway to town when Jeff slowed the horses and turned to her. The smile vanished from his sunny face, leaving it grave, serious. He looked at her intently and chewed on his lower lip.

"What's wrong, Jeff?" she asked, alarmed.

"Do you remember anything about the last wagon ride you took with me?" he asked.

"Why, yes. When you, Jake, Rosa, and I went to town before Christmas," she answered, surprised he asked.

"No, I'm not talking about that time. I meant the time you went on a wagon *alone* with me. Do you remember?"

Samantha peered at him confused. "I don't recall any other wagon ride, Jeff. Should I?"

"Yes—uh—no." He sighed. "It's probably just as well," he muttered. "Well, did you decide what you were going to buy in town?"

"Um, pins, thread, calico, books . . . I really don't know," she said with a laugh.

"We'd better get there then, so you can have time to shop," he said, flicking the reins. "Haa, giddap there."

Curious, she wanted to ask him about the other time he'd mentioned, but the horses lunged forward, sending the wagon careening over mud-filled ruts. Samantha grabbed her hat with one hand; the other clutched the seat.

After they made the trip in record time, she dragged Jeff into every shop. Exhausted from shopping, he took her to Ma Greene's for fried chicken and hot biscuits. After lunch Jeff headed for Molly's to get a beer while Samantha headed back to the dressmaker's to pick up the lace she'd forgotten.

Nick stepped out of the lawyer's office and looked up at the cloudy sky. It was still early enough for him to get a bite to eat and get a head start before dark. He fingered the small box in his vest pocket. He'd bought a gold filigree broach with a carved jade rose in the center surrounded by tiny seed pearls. It was beautiful and delicate, just like Samantha, and the jade green reminded him of her eyes. He couldn't resist it. He hoped Samantha would like it. Now, if he just had some way to get it to her.

His mind on his wife, Nick stepped out onto the sidewalk and crashed into a passing cowboy, almost knocking him down.

Furious, the puncher whirled. "Damn it, why don't—" He stopped. "Nick?"

"Jeff? What the hell are you doing here?"

"I came in to get supplies. What are you doing here? You're supposed to be at High Mesa."

Ignoring the question, Nick asked, "How is she?"

Jeff glared at him. "How do you expect she'd be? She ain't exactly on top of the world, but she's all right. Me and Jake have been lookin' after her."

"Has she remembered anything about us?"

"She's remembered some things, but not about getting married," Jeff said, frowning.

"I have to talk to you. Order the supplies and meet me at Molly's."

"I can't. The wagon's already loaded and she's waiting for me," Jeff said.

Sucking in a breath, Nick grabbed Jeff's arm and pulled him into the alley. "Samantha's here?"

"Yeah, I brought her in with me. She's down the street at the dressmaker's."

Nick closed his eyes, wanting to see her. Wanting to hold her. But he couldn't; if he did, he'd never find the strength to leave.

"Nick, what the heck's the matter with you?" Jeff frowned, his blue eyes dark and angry. "Aren't you even going to talk to her?"

"No. I can't explain now. You'd better go before she comes looking for you. I've got to leave town, and I don't know when I'll be coming back. I'll leave a note at Molly's. If Samantha gets her memory back, give it to her." He reached into his pocket and took out the jewelry box. "Will you give her this for me?"

"How am I going to do that without telling her I saw you?" Jeff asked, plainly peeved.

"You'll think of something." Nick grabbed Jeff's arm and gave him a hug. Then looking down the sidewalk to make sure the coast was clear, he left Jeff and hurried across the street to the saloon.

Samantha paid for her lace and left the shop. Glancing across the street, she saw a tall man going up the sidewalk to Molly's. Intent on meeting Jeff, she spun away, but something nagged at her. She hesitated. Turning back, she raised her hand, shielding her eyes. Something about the man looked familiar.

She blinked and looked again, watching him hurry toward the saloon. She felt the blood drain from her face. She swayed and reached for a post to keep from falling. *Oh, dear Lord.* It couldn't be—but it was. No wonder he looked familiar. The man was Nick . . . her husband.

Nick raised his head and glanced down the street. There on the boardwalk outside the dressmaker's stood a red-headed woman. Stunned, he felt his heart hit his boots. *Oh God, no! . . . Samantha.* Nick lunged through the saloon entrance, hoping she hadn't seen. He went to the bar and ordered a beer.

Samantha. He stared at the foam on the warm brew. He couldn't face her, talk to her only to tell her he had to leave again. He didn't think she had seen him. But what if she had? A sick feeling twisted his middle. Knowing he couldn't leave her like that, Nick spun on his heel and rushed back out. Frantic, he searched both sides of the muddy street. Except for a few old men gathered on a bench and some cowboys, the sidewalks were empty. He closed his eyes in despair. Now he'd never know. Samantha was gone.

Nick's stomach rumbled, reminding him he'd had nothing to eat since yesterday. He raised his eyes, catching sight of Ma Greene's across the street. *Maybe it's for the best.* He couldn't tell Samantha he was leaving without telling her why. If she didn't remember Billy, how could he tell her without telling her all the rest.

He ordered steak and potatoes and strong, black coffee, but when Ma put it on the table, all he could see was Samantha's eyes. Shoving the platter away, he got up from the table and paid for the untouched meal. He found Scout and slid wearily into the saddle. His heart heavy, he rode out of town.

Samantha slumped in the wagon, her mind in a whirl. She stared at the road ahead, but saw nothing except the scene she'd witnessed. It was branded in her mind. At first she hadn't believed her eyes, but it had been Nick. Her lips quivered. He wasn't on any mountain. He'd been in town all winter.

"Sammy, what's wrong?"

"I saw Nick, Jeff. He saw me, too. He looked right at me, but he didn't stop. He kept on going." Her voice caught on a sob. "He practically ran into the saloon to get away from me."

"Damn! I was afraid of that," Jeff said.

Samantha looked at him. "You saw him. You knew?"

"Yeah. I saw him, too."

"Why didn't he talk to me? Why didn't he come home?"

"I don't know, honey. I don't understand either." He reached out and took her hand. "He said he couldn't explain and that he had to leave town. He didn't know when he'd be coming back."

When they pulled into the ranch yard and stopped in front of the porch, she jumped down, not waiting for Jeff's help. Too upset to look into his eyes, she dashed toward the house. Her eyes blurred with tears, she ran inside.

Jake, standing in front of the fireplace, started toward her, his face crinkled with deep concern.

Unable to face him, she rushed up the stairs.

"Samantha, honey, what's wrong?" he called after her. "Gol-durn it, Jeff, what did you do now?" Jake boomed out.

Reaching her bedroom door, she heard Jeff say, "She saw Nick in town. I saw him, too. He wouldn't talk to her, and he ain't coming home. She can't go on like this, Jake. What are we going to do?"

Sobbing, Samantha shut the door, blocking out the rest of the downstairs conversation. Tormented, her heart broken, she gazed around at the place that had been her home. It wasn't her room, it was his. Everything in it belonged to him, even her. She closed her eyes. Hot tears trailed down her cheeks. No, she wasn't his. He didn't want her. After she'd lost her memory, he'd never slept with her. And she didn't even know why.

She drew in a ragged breath, wishing she could get away from here, leave the ranch, but she had nowhere to go. She flung herself onto the bed, sobs racking her body. Samantha cried until she had no more tears left, then she fell into an exhausted sleep.

CHAPTER

* 17 *

RELIEVED TO SEE THE SUN SINK BEHIND A RIDGE
of barren hills, Nick reined his horse off the road and into a
small grove of cottonwood trees. He made a circular motion
with his tired shoulders, trying to loosen some of the kinks.
He groaned. What he wouldn't give to be at home right
now, sitting in the hot-spring bath at the ranch.

Home . . . Samantha. He shook his head. *Damn fool.*
Searching all of Colorado for a man she'd mentioned in a
dream. And when he found that man, Nick knew he'd lose
her. He closed his eyes, seeing Samantha's eyes and
fire-shot hair. *Oh kitten, so warm and soft.* He should have
made love to her. *No;* he shook his head, regretfully. Losing
her would have hurt even worse then.

He wondered if Molly had given Jeff the letter he'd
written before he'd picked up supplies and headed north. If
Samantha had gotten her memory back by the time he
returned, she'd have the annulment. The lawyer he'd seen in
Canyon Springs said it would only take a few days after
she'd filed. Then it would be over. His mouth tightened.
After he found Billy, she was his problem.

Nick threw his leg over the horse and slid from the saddle. Taking the reins, he led Scout to a trickle of water in an almost dry stream bed. Waiting for the pinto to slake his thirst, Nick sighed, noticing the sparse dry patch of grass. "Short rations again tonight, old fellow." He thought Scout was as weary of this business as he was.

He'd searched half of Colorado for a family named Storm. He'd found two dozen Billys, but none of them knew Samantha. It was impossible. He didn't know who he was looking for, or even if they lived in the territory. He was a fool on a fool's errand.

After turning the horse loose to graze, Nick shook out his bedroll and stretched out. He was too tired even to fix something to eat. Not knowing where else to look, he would finish this leg of the journey and then go home, back to the mesa . . . and the Cheyenne.

He sighed, knowing that whenever he looked out over the mesa and saw the ranch below, he'd always see Samantha's face and think of what might have been. Exhausted, he closed his eyes and went to sleep, dreaming of deep, emerald eyes and a sea of red-gold hair.

Nick woke at dawn intending to get an early start, but when he went to saddle Scout, he found the pinto lame. He lifted the horse's hoof and found a small stone wedged under a loose shoe. He took his knife from the scabbard and lifted the pebble out. Holding the weapon by the blade, he used the handle to hammer the nail back, making the shoe tight. "That ought to hold until I get you to a blacksmith's," he said. He led the horse forward and found he still limped. Nick sighed, knowing the mustang was too footsore to travel.

He patted the gelding's neck. "Well, Scout, we could

both use a rest. It's just too bad it couldn't be in a better place.'' He looked at the dry, dusty ground, the big, heat-holding boulders, and the almost dry creek. He gathered up a few mesquite branches, built a small fire, and cooked the last of his hardtack and beans. He finished his skimpy meal with a cup of tea-colored coffee made from grounds he'd used twice before.

His mind drifted back to the day Jeff'd taken Samantha off the stagecoach. Where had she been going? Maybe she didn't have any more people. Jeff'd said she'd been remembering things, like the fact her father was dead. She hadn't recalled anything else about it. What if he couldn't find any folks? What if she never remembered? What the hell would he do then?

He frowned, remembering the trader on Fort Garland and what he'd said about the Storms and trouble. The only trouble Nick'd heard of was the range war in the Yampa Valley. Come tomorrow morning, if Scout was able, that was where he was headed.

He dumped the coffee grounds, took his dishes to the creek, rubbed them with sand, and rinsed them off. Having eaten the last of his food, he stuck them in the saddlebags.

He was tired, but he was also restless . . . and he stank. He looked at the stream bed, wondering if somewhere he could find a puddle big enough to get wet. He walked upstream until he found a small basin of water at the foot of a large boulder. He knelt and filled his canteen, eyeing the puddle. Not enough to take a bath, but at least he could wash his face and hands. He removed his shirt and bathed as much as possible, then rinsed out his shirt, picked up his canteen, and walked back to camp.

The merciless sun baked the hard clay ground until it

radiated heat like an oven. Moving his bedroll to a patch of shade under a scrawny cottonwood tree, he stretched out and put his hat over his eyes. Thinking of the lush green mesa and sparkling small lakes, he drifted off to sleep.

Sometime later, feeling the sun on his bare chest, he lifted his hat. A brilliant sunset set the sky aflame with crimson, gold, and purple. He watched until a slight rustling noise made him turn his head.

Not two feet away a large rattlesnake coiled, ready to strike.

"Hellfire!" Rolling to one side, he grabbed his gun and pulled the trigger. The gun roared, exploding the snake's head in a shower of sand, blood, and flesh.

He slid the .44 back into the holster. Trembling, he sat up and wiped the grit from his face. "I can't believe it. Must be getting old." Shuddering, he got to his feet, recalling a time when an ant couldn't cross the ground without him knowing it was there.

"Good shooting, my friend," a voice said softly.

Startled, Nick wheeled to see a huge, ebony stallion standing in the rocks behind him.

A man in black sat astride a fancy Mexican saddle. The sun glinted off a silver-inlaid gun . . . aimed straight at him. A faint smile, which didn't reach his midnight-blue eyes, crossed the man's face. Like lightning he raised the barrel of the weapon, making it disappear into the holster that rode low on his lean right hip. Without another word he whirled the horse. The dying rays of the sun flashed off the silver-encrusted saddle.

The glare hit Nick's eyes, making him blink. When he looked again, there was only a swirling cloud of dust. The man and the great horse had vanished. Cold sweat dotted Nick's brow. He raised a shaking hand to wipe it away.

What the hell was happening to him? He'd better go home and soon. That hombre had him cold and he hadn't even known he was there. The man's skin had been as dark as his, but without the copper color. He'd been slim, high-cheekboned, his lips thin and cruel. And his eyes— Nick knew he'd never forget those eyes—cold, deep blue, like chips of ice from a high mountain lake. Or the way he'd disappeared . . . a chill crawled up Nick's back. He felt like he'd been examined by the devil and found wanting.

Shaken, he whistled for Scout. He sighed in relief when the pinto galloped toward him. Although the horse wasn't limping, Nick lifted his hoof and examined it. It looked all right, but he'd have the shoe changed first chance he got. He hurriedly saddled the mustang and swung on, glad to leave the camp behind. He reached the main road, and after casting one more uneasy glance behind him, he pointed Scout in the direction of the Yampa Valley.

Early the next morning Nick reached the valley and found the town of Lookinglass buzzing like a hive of angry bees. Men gathered in groups, on benches in front of stores, and on street corners. Frowning, he looked around. *Something's going on,* he thought. If he'd been looking for trouble, it appeared he'd found the right place.

The town had only a half-dozen buildings, scattered on each side of the main street—two saloons, a whorehouse, a mercantile, a café, and a blacksmith shop with a livery. Most looked like a good puff of wind would blow them over.

The townsfolk turned and stared at him. He nodded and

smiled back. Sure wasn't the friendliest town in the world. Still shaken from his visitor of the night before, he decided he'd be smart to play it cautious before asking any questions.

He left Scout at the smithy's to get a new shoe and headed across the street to the café. He opened the door and stepped inside. A hush came over the room. Seeing an empty table in the far corner, he walked toward it and sat down, knowing every eye in the room was on him.

The waitress, a pretty, dark-haired girl about fifteen, came from behind the counter. She smiled back at him. "What'll you have today, mister?"

He smiled back and tried to quiet his rumbling stomach. "Steak and eggs, if you've got them. If you don't, just give me whatever's handy."

She nodded and went back toward the kitchen.

"Hey, you," a gruff voice called.

Nick glanced up to see a burly cowhand coming toward his table. "Are you talking to me?" Damn, he wished they'd waited until he'd ate. He shifted his chair slightly, making sure nothing was between him and his gun. Two more men, younger versions of Burly, got to their feet. Nick narrowed his eyes, not liking the looks of the situation. He was glad the empty seat had been in a corner.

"Are you workin' fer them murderin' sheepmen?" Burly asked.

Nick looked the man straight in the eyes. "I don't work for nobody. I just want my breakfast," he said softly, and he intended to get it even if he had to bury somebody first.

The man swallowed and looked away. "I don't think he's one of them, boys."

Nick, his hand hovering over his gun, stared at the other

two. Seeing the motion, they hastily backed away and found their seats.

The girl came back with the coffee and a tin cup.

"What's going on around here?" Nick asked.

"Range war," she said. "The sheepmen are trying to run the small ranchers out. They've hired gunmen. Clyde thought you were one of them. That's why he and the boys were so touchy."

"Could you sit down a spell?" Nick motioned to the other chair at his table. She seemed to know everybody and she was willing to talk.

"Just for a minute," she said, keeping her eyes on the woman in the kitchen.

Nick guessed the woman was her mother. "I'm looking for somebody. A family by the name of Storm, or a man called Billy. Anybody like that around here?"

Something that looked like fear flashed across the girl's face. "No, I don't know nobody like that." She jumped up and ran to the kitchen.

Nick noticed the room had grown silent again. "I'm looking for a family called Storm, or a man called Billy. Anybody here know them?" he asked. A few men shook their heads, but Nick didn't miss the fact that one of the bunch left and hurried across the street. He tried to see where the cowboy went, but a large, buxom woman stepped between him and the window.

"Here's your breakfast, mister. I suggest you eat it and go," she said. Plopping the plate down in front of him, she turned and went back into the kitchen.

What the hell's goin' on? It had something to do with the Storms . . . or Billy. They all acted like he'd stepped in something, and everybody knew what it was—except him.

Well, he'd feel more like tackling whatever was bothering them on a full stomach.

He picked up his knife and fork and lit into the tender steak and scrambled eggs. He wolfed down the last of the fluffy, golden biscuits topped with fresh butter and blackberry jam and finished his coffee. Then he paid for his meal and left the café.

He stepped to the hitching post, removed his knife, and cut out a sliver. Using it to pick his teeth, he looked down the board sidewalk toward the blacksmith shop.

Nick frowned. The street that had been buzzing with people was almost empty. The hair on the back of his neck started to prickle. He shifted his gun, making sure it was free in the holster. He stepped off the boardwalk, crossing a narrow alley that ran between two buildings.

"Mister?"

Nick turned to see a small ragged boy. "Yeah?"

His eyes big, the child edged toward him. "Dirty sheepman!" he cried. With a quick motion he brought his small hand from behind him, throwing a handful of sand and dust into Nick's eyes.

Unable to see, Nick heard the child dart away. He backed against the building, sensing danger. He tried to wipe the dirt from his eyes with one hand while he groped blindly for his gun with the other. Before his gun cleared the holster, his head exploded with pain. The world spun around him. Falling into a deep black pit, he slumped to the ground.

Nick came to and found himself tied belly down over a galloping horse, his body racked with pain, his head bursting with every hoofbeat. He stuck out his tongue and licked at something sticky near the right side of his mouth.

He recognized the metallic taste. Blood. He tried to open his sore eyes, but they were bound with a rag of some kind. He cocked his head to one side, rubbing it against the side of the saddle. Loosening the cloth enough to see out of one corner, he peered out.

Recognizing the familiar spotted hide as Scout, he breathed a prayer of thanks. He tilted his head. His mouth tightened. Leading the pinto was the man from the café. The one the girl had called Clyde. Nick was sure the other man was his companion. They sure were in a hurry to get him somewhere. Bound across the horse the way he was, even though he was scared, he'd be happy when they did.

The men stopped behind a grove of scrub-oak trees and sat there for several minutes while Clyde checked to make sure they weren't followed. After a muttered conversation the men headed down a trail and into a creek, following it to hide their tracks.

Scout waded through the knee-deep water, splashing the cool liquid on Nick's face and head. Nick licked it off his lips, wishing for enough to ease his thirst. All too soon they were back on dry, rocky ground. He didn't know where they were taking him, and they seemed determined that no one else would know either.

They left the sagebrush and entered a pine-scented forest. The thickly needled trail wound steadily upward around the base of a steep cliff. The horses stopped. Nick saw Clyde dismount and look toward the ridge. He waved his battered brown hat over his head. Slapping the hat back on his head, he climbed back on his horse. He and his companion waited, talking quietly. Nick heard the approach of another horse.

"You got him?" a newcomer asked.

"Yep, that's him," Clyde answered. He jerked Scout's reins, and they moved forward again.

The sun disappeared, and Nick saw they were entering a narrow crevice between two cliffs. He flattened his head against the edge of the saddle to keep from getting his brains knocked out on the rock walls. One of his boots caught on a root, twisting his ankle. He gritted his teeth to keep from crying out.

A shaft of daylight hit his eyes. He tilted his head to see they had entered a broad grassy meadow. The horses' gait quickened into a gallop. Nick, bouncing across the saddle, winced from the pain and silently cursed the men. They stopped at the edge of a dense pine forest. Hearing boot-steps, Nick closed his eyes. He heard a knife sawing the rope and then he was free. He shifted his weight to avoid falling on his head and slid to the ground.

The blood rushed to his limbs, bringing with it a flood of pain. Fighting to stay conscious, Nick felt himself lifted to his feet. A man half carried, half led him to what appeared to be the porch of a building. Reeling across the wide split boards, he was shoved through a doorway. Other hands grabbed him to keep him from falling. The blindfold was jerked off. He blinked, trying to focus his sore eyes in the gloom.

The red tip of a thin cigar glowed from a shadowed corner.

Catching a flash of silver, Nick sucked in his breath, feeling the hair raise on the back of his neck.

"So we meet again, my friend," the chilling voice said softly. "Now, tell me. What do you want with Billy Storm?"

CHAPTER

* 18 *

THE MIDMORNING SUN, LYING LIKE A WARM QUILT on Jeff's shoulders, made him yawn. He'd had little sleep the night before. He'd stayed awake, thinking of what he would say to Samantha. Now that he'd decided to do it, he wondered about the wisdom of his idea. He frowned, considering his options. *There was no other way.*

He remembered Two Feathers' words. "She is wasting away. She doesn't eat, sleeps little, seldom laughs. She tries to act like nothing is wrong, but she is dying inside. Jeff, you have to tell her the truth or be responsible for the consequences."

Jeff stared into his coffee and looked out the dining-room window, seeing Samantha busy doing something by the fence. She worked at an almost frenzied pace, as she had for the past month. Like she was forcing herself to keep busy in order not to think.

He had promised to take her shopping later; maybe he could tell her then. "Damn it, that's just another excuse to put it off and you know it." Setting the cup down, he slowly rose and stepped out onto the porch.

He jumped from the porch and went around the house to find Samantha on her knees, busily working in the dirt. "Hello, Sammy. What in the world are you doing?" he asked. He scratched his head, bewildered at the sight of at least a dozen neat little sticks lining the inside of the fence.

"I'm planting roses. One of the hands brought me some cuttings from town." Getting to her feet, she wiped her hands on the apron covering her green calico dress. "Whew, it's hot. Let's go sit in the shade and have some lemonade. I'll finish this later."

Jeff followed her to a crude log bench in the shade of a pine tree. He sat down beside her and wiped his sweaty forehead with his neckerchief.

She lifted a covered pitcher from beneath the bench and poured a measure into two tin cups and handed him one.

Jeff sipped the lemonade and frowned. He felt uneasy, awkward. He dug his boot toe into the ground. He didn't know what to say. How could he tell her? But damn it, she had a right to know. He took a deep breath and looked up into her puzzled face.

Samantha stared at him, her eyes widening. "What's wrong, Jeff? Is the lemonade too sour?"

Now that she mentioned it, it did give a person a pucker, but he wasn't about to tell her. Especially since he had to confess this other thing. "It's very good, honey," he said soberly.

She clutched his arm. "Is it Nick? Have you heard from him?"

"No. Nothing like that, Sammy. I . . . uh . . ." he stammered, trying to find the right words. He set the cup down and picked up her hand. Looking into her shadowed

228

green eyes, he began: "There's something I think you should know."

"What?" She leaned closer. "Tell me."

"Please, don't talk. Just listen. This is hard enough. I know you don't remember how you and Nick came to be married." He saw her shake her head. "Well"—he paused—"it was all my doing. You see, it all started that morning. . . ."

Samantha listened to Jeff's story in stunned silence. She couldn't believe what she was hearing. All along she'd sensed something was wrong because every time she'd asked about their wedding, Nick had been evasive. Now she knew why. He didn't remember any more about it than she did. He hadn't wanted to get married at all, and probably wouldn't have if he hadn't been drunk.

"The whole thing was my idea," Jeff said. "I was the one that took you off the stagecoach. We thought you were Molly's new saloon singer. You see, Nick was going to pretend to get married because he was mad at Jake." Jeff hesitated, lifted his head to look at her for a moment, then turned his gaze to the ground. "When I found the padre, I couldn't resist getting him married for real."

Samantha narrowed her eyes. It was getting worse by the minute. Outraged, her body trembling with indignation, she listened while Jeff continued.

Jeff finished his horrible tale and sat there in silence. He raised his head slowly, as if ashamed to meet her eyes. "There's one more thing. Nick left a note for you at Molly's before he left town."

Hurt and rage brought Samantha's blood to a boil. Nick hadn't the courage to tell her. The coward left a note. "So he left me a note, did he?'' she asked, hearing her voice shake. ''Well, where is it, and what does it say?''

Jeff hesitantly fished in his pocket and brought out a folded piece of paper. He handed it to her.

Trying to still her trembling hands, she opened the message and began to read.

Dear Samantha,

    I reckon I'll be long gone by the time you get this. I'm sorry for everything that happened. It was all my fault. I guess Jeff told you all about it by now. I talked to a Hershal Martin, a lawyer in Canyon Springs. I signed papers so you can get an annulment.

                —Nick

Her head reeling, Samantha crumpled the note and threw it in the dust. Her hands shaking, she clutched the bench. The paper fluttered along the ground like a wounded thing. Rising in a faint puff of breeze, it caught an updraft and disappeared. Samantha, watching, wished she'd gone with it.

She felt like he'd torn her heart out and stuck it on a stake. An annulment? Her mind flitted back to the times he'd avoided her bed. Now it all made sense at last. That's why he'd never slept with her. He had never consummated the marriage so it could be annulled. He wanted out. Hot tears rushed to her eyes, filling them to overflowing. Nick didn't love her. He had never loved her. Getting married had been a drunken joke, and now he wanted to be rid of her. The tears evaporated. Her body trembled as a burning rage took their place.

"That's all, Samantha," Jeff said, ducking his head. "I'm sorry."

She leaped to her feet. Clenching her fists, she whirled to glare at him. "Sorry? That's all you have to say? You're sorry?" she hissed. "That's supposed to make everything all right?" Jeff winced under her lashing words. His face looked as sorrowful as a kicked pup's, but Samantha felt no pity.

"Damn you!" she cried, remembering another one of his "ideas." She closed her eyes. Heat flushing her face, she recalled the night of the storm. The night she'd tried to tempt Nick into her bed. How he must have laughed at her. And Jeff . . . he'd encouraged her to make Nick jealous. Jealous? The look on Nick's face flashed back through her memory. He hadn't been jealous. He'd been relieved!

She spun back toward Jeff. "Damn you, Jeff. How could you?"

"Why, Sammy, it was all just a mistake."

"How can you sit there and look so innocent? A mistake?" She saw him flinch at the contempt in her voice. "I suppose if I *had* been a saloon girl, it would have been all right? Is that what you're saying?"

"Uh . . . yes, I guess so. No . . ." He threw up his hands. "I don't know."

"And you've let me sit here waiting for him to come back so I could find out what I've done?" Her hands twisted her apron to keep from wringing Jeff's neck. "I can't believe I've been such a fool."

"You're not a fool, Sammy," Jeff said. "You didn't know."

"No, *I* didn't know, but apparently I'm the only one who

didn't.'' She glanced at Jeff. ''Just who else *does* know about this?''

''Just me, and Nick of course, Jake, Rosa, and Two Feathers.''

Samantha's insides wrenched. *Oh no! Not Two Feathers. I thought he was my friend.* Bitterness rose, filling her mouth with a vile taste. Was there no one she could trust? She realized, sadly, that there wasn't. No one . . . except herself.

She lifted her gaze to look around the ranch, seeing the yard she had worked so hard on, weeding, cleaning, planting until it bloomed like an oasis. She blinked back tears, seeing the meadows and woods she had roamed. The days and nights she'd spent dreaming. Dreams . . . that was all they had been. Now they were disappearing, like smoke, into the nightmare of reality.

She raised her hand and bit her fist. Dear God, what would she do now? She couldn't . . . she wouldn't stay here. She couldn't stand seeing the pity in their eyes. And Nick . . . damn him for the coward he was! He'd slunk off like a coyote, not having the courage to tell her the truth.

She shifted her attention to Jeff, who sat on the bench watching her. ''Would you hitch the wagon?''

''Sure.'' He smiled, getting to his feet. ''I'd be glad to.''

She turned away, pain wrenching her heart. He'd be glad to. He, too, couldn't wait to get rid of her. ''I'll just get a few things, then I'll be ready,'' she said quietly. Blinking back bitter tears, she left him and hurried toward the house.

Rosa looked up from her mending when she ran up the porch steps, but Samantha didn't stop. She couldn't.

''Señora?''

Samantha paused, but didn't turn. Swallowing to steady

her voice, she called back to the gray-haired lady, "Rosa, I'm leaving the ranch."

"But leetle one, why?"

The concern in Rosa's voice sliced through Samantha like a sharp knife. Pity. She couldn't stand the idea of anyone pitying her. She took a deep breath, squared her shoulders, and continued upstairs to her room. She went to the closet, yanked out her valise, and threw it onto the bed. She hurried to the wardrobe and took out her riding skirt and blouse and the blue calico. Nick had burned her black dress or she'd have worn it. She looked at the low-cut green silk shimmering at the back of the closet. She gritted her teeth. If she had her way, she'd leave the way she'd arrived . . . naked! She shook her head. *I have to be practical. Besides, Nick owes me something for all he's put me through.*

Right now all she wanted to do was to leave, to get away from all of them. *Leave? But how? I have no money.* She chewed on her lower lip, searching for a solution to her problem. *I'll get a job. That's it. I'll find work in Canyon Springs until I can save enough to buy a ticket on the stage.* She frowned. A ticket to where? She still couldn't remember where she'd been going when they took her off the stage. She stuffed the clothes into the suitcase and snapped it shut. "I'll have plenty of time to worry about that later," she murmured.

"Samantha?" a gruff voice said from her doorway. "What are you doing?"

She turned to Jake, then looked away from the hurt in his eyes. "I'm leaving. Jeff told me the truth, so you know why I can't stay."

"But honey, where will you go? How will you get by?" He put a hand on her shoulder. "Samantha, regardless of how you got that way, honey, you're family. We love you.''

Stifling a sob, she picked up her bag. ''Apparently no one loved me enough to tell me the truth. And rather than be saddled with a wife he didn't want in the first place, Nick left.'' She swallowed. ''I won't stay. Jake, don't you understand? I can't.'' She turned away before he could say anything more and ran down the stairs.

Rosa stood in the entry. ''Señora, I still don't understand why you are leaving.''

''Because now there isn't any reason to stay,'' Samantha whispered to herself as she walked through the front doorway for the last time.

A loud, shrill neigh came from the corral. Red Wind! She'd forgotten about the stallion. Should she turn him loose? No, he'd just follow her. She bit her lip to keep from sobbing. She loved the big sorrel, and couldn't bear the thought of leaving him. But she couldn't afford to board him at the livery stable in town. Eventually she'd have to part with him. At least at the ranch he wouldn't have to suffer because of her.

With her future so uncertain, she had no idea where she'd end up. Anguished tears filled her eyes. She blinked them back, clenching her teeth to keep her lips from quivering. Taking a deep breath, she raised her head and walked proudly toward the waiting wagon.

CHAPTER

∗ 19 ∗

THE SPANISH GUNMAN BLEW A PUFF OF BLUE cigar smoke into the air and pushed away from his slouching position against the wall. The clinking of long cruel spurs cut the silence as he walked slowly across the room. He stopped in front of Nick, his voice cold and menacing. "I'll ask once more. What do you want with Billy Storm?"

The question ringing in his ears, Nick raised his head. He eased upright on the rough bunk. "Are you Billy Storm?"

"No, my friend. I'm not," the Spaniard answered.

"Then why the hell should I tell you?" Nick said.

"Because I will kill you if you don't," he said, narrowing his midnight-blue eyes into slits.

The deadliness of the man's voice sent shivers up Nick's spine. With his hands tied he wasn't in any position to confront the bastard, and the man did know Billy Storm. "I have something I think belongs to him, and I need to talk to him about it."

"What could you possibly have that belongs to Billy?" the man said softly.

"A girl, maybe?" Nick asked, watching the dark face.

"Madre de Dios," the man gasped. His eyes wide, he reached out and grasped the front of Nick's shirt. "What girl?"

"A redhead, named—"

"You have Samantha! Where is she?" The man's eyes glittered with excitement. "Is she all right?" He leaned close and, taking a sharp knife from his scabbard, cut the rope from Nick's wrists.

"You know her?" Nick said, rubbing the circulation back into his arms. He stared uneasily at the tall man. He didn't like this turn of events one bit. No way was he about to turn Samantha over to this dark gunman.

"I've known her since she was born. I've been looking for her. She was on her way here when she disappeared. We were afraid they'd found her and killed her."

"Who wants to kill her?" Nick asked. His heart slammed against his chest. "Is she in danger?"

"Who are you, my friend?" the man said with a frown. "And how did you come to have Samantha?"

"I'm Nick McBride. She's my wife," Nick said softly, staking his claim.

"Your wife?" the man asked amazed. "Samantha isn't married."

"She is now," Nick said. He took a deep breath. *May as well get shot now instead of later.* "I kidnapped her off the stagecoach and married her."

"Caramba!" The gunman turned with an oath and sent the other men from the room. He pulled a chair up next to the bunk and straddled it. He stared at Nick with a look of outrage and amazement. "I think before I shoot you, you have some explaining to do."

"I'm not telling you another damn thing until you tell me who you are," Nick said. "And who is Billy Storm?"

"I'm Miguel Diego Vitorio de Sandoval y Esteban, Samantha's cousin. Billy Storm is her uncle."

Nick's relief sent wings to his heart. Billy was her uncle, not her husband! She had been on her way to her uncle's. Now if he could keep this Miguel character from killing him, he'd try to explain.

A while later Nick eased his hat on over his bandaged head and followed Miguel out of the line shack to the horses waiting outside. They mounted in silence and rode down a narrow path to a gap where the trail wound down the mountain. A shrill whistle rang out through the canyon. Looking up, Nick saw a sentry in the rocks signal to someone at the ranch below.

The Storm ranch lay at the edge of a broad green valley in front of a deep stand of pine trees. Nick noticed that while the place didn't appear to be as large as the JMB, it had the makings of a first-class spread. The meadow they crossed had grass as thick and high as Scout's belly. Off to his left a good-sized stream ran in fast-moving ripples, telling him the ranch had ample water. Fat cattle and long-legged horses grazed in unfenced pastures.

Nick frowned when they neared the buildings. Although the main house appeared intact, the blackened remains of a barn and bunkhouse bore mute testimony to the battle with the sheepmen. Men with rifles stepped from behind their positions to wave at Miguel. Nick thought even a gnat would have a hard time getting through unnoticed.

The Spaniard led the way to a weathered one-story log house and dismounted. A lean cowboy left his position on the long front porch and led the horses away toward a pole corral. Signaling Nick to follow, Miguel walked up the porch steps and called out, "Jack, open up."

A heavyset man with a double-barreled shotgun opened the door a crack and peered out at them. Recognizing Miguel, he stood aside and allowed them to enter.

Nick noticed that although the outside of the house showed the scars of the long Colorado winters, the inside was warm and hospitable. The front door opened into a large room dominated by a rock fireplace on one side and a big window that framed a view of the mountains on the other. Colorful Indian rugs dotted the broad-planked floor. Two leather-covered chairs with a table in the middle faced the window, while a long, long leather couch with an elk hide draped over the back sat in front of the fireplace. The gun rack above the mantel held an old muzzle loader, along with a new Winchester .44 rifle.

"How is he?" the Spaniard asked. He removed his sombrero and tossed it toward a hatrack made of deer horns.

"He must be feeling better," Jack growled. "I know he's cantankerous as hell."

"Miguel, is that you?" a voice yelled from down the long hall. "'Bout time you got back."

"Yes, it's me," Miguel said. Glancing at Nick, he shook his dark head and shrugged his broad shoulders.

Nick couldn't help the faint smile that crossed his face. Billy's disposition sounded a whole lot like Jake's. He hung his hat on the rack next to Miguel's and followed the gunman down the hall. They entered a bedroom where a man with thick blond hair sprinkled with gray lay in bed. His leg was stretched out in front of him, bandaged and propped up on pillows. Another bandage covered most of his wide chest.

"'Bout time you got back," the man repeated irritably. He peered suspiciously at Nick. "Who's that?"

"Billy, I've brought you a new relative," Miguel said. "This is Samantha's husband, Nick McBride."

"Samantha's husband?" Billy frowned. "She's all right?" he asked. When Miguel nodded, he peered up at Nick. "Where in hell did she get a husband?" He looked at the Spaniard, who shrugged. "Thank God she's alive," he said, his green eyes moist. "I'm her uncle Billy," he said, his face wreathing in a broad smile. He held out his hand.

Nick stepped forward and shook Billy's hand. "She's lost her memory. That's the reason I couldn't contact you sooner. Otherwise she's fine," Nick answered.

"Thank the Lord for that," Billy said. "They tried to tell Miguel she was dead, but somehow I knew she was alive. Us Storms don't die that easy." He motioned to a chair beside the bed. "Sit down and tell me about her."

Nick sat down and repeated the tale he had told Miguel. There was a stunned silence when he finished.

Frowning, the elder Storm studied him intently. "Well now, so you kidnapped her and married her. Now that you've got her, what do you intend to do with her?"

Nick hesitated. He'd planned to give her to Billy, but now that the time had come, he couldn't do it. "I married her, so I'll take care of her," Nick said.

"Why?"

"Why? Because I'm responsible for the mess she's in," Nick said. He couldn't tell her kin that she set his blood on fire or that he couldn't look at her without wanting to bed her.

"If what you told me is true, you could get an annulment," Billy said softly.

"No, I can't do that," Nick answered quickly, praying that she hadn't done that very thing. He looked at Billy, noting the frown on his face. He certainly didn't appear pleased. Nick squirmed in his seat. What did the old man want from him?

"Why not?" Billy asked.

Uneasy, and not knowing where the questions were leading, Nick got up from his chair and went to the window. "Because I owe her something," he said, glancing around.

"That ain't good enough," Billy said, narrowing his green eyes. He looked up at the gunman. "Miguel, go back with him and fetch her home here to the ranch."

"No!" Nick spun away from the window. The thought of Samantha leaving tore through his soul. "Damn it, I want her." She was like his life's breath. His days would be empty without her.

"You *want* her?" Billy said softly, his voice filled with scorn.

Nick analyzed his feelings toward Samantha. A sense of amazement swept over him. *Could it be?* He turned toward Billy. "I guess I love her," he said, his voice filled with wonder.

"You guess? Either you do or you don't," Billy growled.

"All right, I love her," Nick said, his voice thick with emotion. "I love her, and I'll never let her go."

"How does she feel about you?"

Nick flopped back down in the chair, remembering her last words. He cradled his head in his hands. "I really don't know."

"Well, knowing my niece, I think you had better find out

before you start making too many plans," Billy said with a chuckle.

Nick listened while Billy told stories of Samantha's unhappy childhood. He heard about how her mother had died and the misery she'd endured at the hands of her stepmother and stepbrother.

"They couldn't break her spirit though," Billy said. "I received a letter from Tillie, her old nurse, saying the girl was in danger, and that she was on a stagecoach on her way here. I sent Miguel to fetch her. I knew he could travel faster than I could. When he got to Fort Garland, he found out she'd never reached there. I guess he put the fear of God into the people around there, but still got no answers."

Nick nodded. That explained the trader's reaction when he'd mentioned the name Storm. After meeting Miguel, he couldn't say he blamed the man for being cautious.

Taking a deep breath, Billy continued. Somebody put a headstone in the cemetery at Storm Haven with Samantha's name on it. They even had a death certificate from the doctor, but her old nurse insisted Samantha wasn't in the grave. She'd had the stable boy dig it up one night to make sure. The coffin was full of rocks. Her mangy polecat of a stepbrother, Matthew, tried to say she was dead so he could get hold of her money. He also claimed he'd married her before she died.

"Matthew?" Nick started. "She's married to Matthew? She has nightmares about him."

Billy shook his head. "She never married him. The ceremony was a fake. Tillie and Katie, her maid, helped her get away after that."

"Caramba," Miguel hissed. "I'll make that bastard wish he'd never been born."

Nick looked at Miguel. "You'll have to stand in line."

"You're both too late, he's already dead. Anyhow," Billy said, glaring at them, impatient at having been interrupted, "Tillie said Samantha bought a ticket on the stage. She only had enough money to get to Fort Garland. We were supposed to fetch her from there, but she disappeared."

That's why she left the stage and went with Jeff, Nick thought. And why she called out for Billy. She was scared and knew she had to reach him.

"I've got some things to tend to, Billy. I'll be back later," Miguel said. He left the room, closing the door behind him.

Billy turned to Nick and continued his story. "Anyhow, about that time all hell broke loose here, and I was shot from the saddle when I was out checking the stock. We forted up at the line shack and waited for Miguel to get back." Billy grinned. "I guess you found out, that boy is hell on wheels when he gets mad. He's been cleaning out them range-stealing sheepmen ever since."

Nick nodded. No wonder Miguel'd been so proddy. It's wonder the gunman hadn't shot him on sight. Nick shivered, thinking of the fate of the sheepmen in the Spaniard's vengeful hands. Not a bad man to have on your side, but you sure didn't want him against you. "He's Samantha's cousin?"

Nodding, Billy explained. "Not by blood, but in every way that really matters. Tom, her papa, and me went to New Mexico to buy horses from old Don Luis. Only when we got there, we found bandits attacking the hacienda. We drove them off, but the old don and his family were dead. About that time Carlos, the majordomo, rode in and found the child hiding in the wine cellar. Carlos told us Miguel was Don Luis's grandson. He said the boy would be murdered if he stayed in New Mexico, so I brought him back with me to Colorado. I raised him as my own son, and I've never been sorry.''

Billy paused and gazed thoughtfully at the door. ''He was only five years old when that happened, but he's never forgotten. Sometimes he's real strange. He spooks people. The Mexicans say he rides with the death wind, whatever the hell that is.''

Nick felt the hair on the back of his neck prickle, remembering the strange whirlwind that had come and gone the first time he'd seen the man in black. Whatever it was, it was sure eerie.

Nick spent a week at the Storm ranch getting acquainted and helping out where he could. He discovered that Billy also had a fifteen-year-old daughter, Sally, who was away at school. He grinned when he saw her picture. Billy said she was a younger version of Samantha, only her hair was darker and she had freckles across her nose. He also met another carrot-topped imp who said she was Samantha's maid, Katie. She and her young husband, a former stable boy, had arrived in Colorado two months ago. She told Nick a tale of madness and murder that made his blood run cold.

At the end of that week Nick, impatient to return home, turned in the saddle and waved good-bye to the man standing on the front porch of the log house.

His leathered face split in a wide smile, Billy Storm lifted a hand from his crutch in a salute.

Miguel followed Nick to his horse, his face somber as

usual. Nick thought the only time he'd seen the Spaniard smile was when he'd found out Samantha was alive.

Miguel tilted his hat back and looked up at Nick. "I'll give you two months from today to make peace with Samantha. If you haven't done so by that time, I will fetch her home to Billy," Miguel said. His cold blue eyes promised he would do what he said.

"Well, it sure isn't going to take me two months, and we'd be proud to have you for a visit," Nick assured him with more certainty than he felt, determined that nobody was about to take her from him. He held out his hand, wanting to leave on a good note.

"*Hasta la vista*. Until later," Miguel said, shaking his hand.

Nick waved his hat at Billy and nudged Scout into a gallop, leaving the ranch yard behind him. A smile creased his face and his spirit sang with joy. He was going home, home to Samantha. And by God, this time he'd stand for no nonsense. He intended to make her his wife in every way possible.

He frowned, hoping she hadn't gotten the annulment yet. The frown disappeared and determination took its place. He intended to have her, whether she had or not. If she got stubborn, he'd kidnap her again and make love to her till she saw things his way. His heart raced at the thought.

He lifted his gaze to the snowcapped peaks ahead of him. By this time next week he should be home. Now all he had to do was get there.

CHAPTER

* 20 *

THE SUN LIT THE RIDGE TOP WITH A GOLDEN glow when Nick trotted Scout through the gates of the JMB Ranch. Trembling with anticipation, he passed the house and looked anxiously toward Samantha's upstairs-bedroom window. His mind whirled with unanswered questions. *Is she here? What will she do when she sees me?*

His heart banged like a hammering woodpecker against his rib cage when he saw the big sorrel racing around the pen. Nick grinned. His spirits soared.

When the stallion sighted Scout, he squealed a challenge. He plunged and bucked around the corral.

Nick shook his head in wonder, still finding it hard to believe Samantha had ridden the big devil. The horse had sure tossed him a time or two. Nick unsaddled Scout, turned him out to pasture, then after giving the sorrel a pat, he hurried toward the house. He raced up the porch steps and inside, then removed his hat and gun and hung them on the deer-horn rack inside the entry. The clatter of dishes and voices drew him toward the dining area.

"It's not a good idea. You don't know what you're doin'," Jake's voice boomed out.

Nick grinned. "Sure is good to be home," he said. He smoothed his hair back with his hand and stepped into the room.

"Nick, you're back," Jeff shouted, a wide grin splitting his sunburned face.

Jake looked him up and down. "Well, it's about time you showed up," he growled. "Things have been in a helluva mess around here." Something that could almost pass for a smile crossed the old man's face. He pulled out a chair and waved to Nick. "Sit down, boy. You're just in time for breakfast."

Nick laughed. "I'll tell Rosa to fix another plate." He stepped into the kitchen, where a plump form was bent over the stove. He peered around the room, but the Mexican woman was alone. Where was Samantha?

"Nicky, welcome home," Rosa said. Her round face beamed up at him.

Nick wrapped his arms around her ample body and whirled her around the room. He gave her a hearty kiss on the cheek before he set her feet back on the floor. "Oh Lord, that smells good." He took another deep breath, inhaling the aroma of fried steak and hot biscuits.

"You look like you've missed my cooking," Rosa said, poking a finger at his ribs.

"You've sure got that right," Nick said, pinching her cheek. "If I wasn't already married, I'd marry you instead," he teased. "By the way, where is Samantha? Is she still asleep."

Rosa's smile vanished. Her eyes filled with tears. "She's not with us anymore."

"What do you mean?" Nick felt the blood drain from his face. "Oh God. Has—has something happened to her?" he asked, afraid to hear the answer.

Rosa grasped his arm, shaking her head. "No, no! Nothing like that. She's fine, but she isn't here. She's left the ranch."

Nick closed his eyes and drew in a deep breath. He clutched at the edge of a cabinet, trying to get his unsteady legs to support him. "Thank God she's all right." He ran a hand through his hair. He couldn't believe it. He was sure she'd be here. Confused, he looked down into Rosa's sympathetic face. "I don't understand. Why did she leave? Where did she go?"

"I think I'd better answer that," Jeff said from the doorway. He took a cup from the kitchen hook, poured it full of coffee, and handed it to Nick. "Come in and sit down. We'll tell you about it."

Nick followed Jeff back into the dining room and sat down in the chair next to Jake. A worried frown creased his grandfather's face.

"I don't understand," Nick said.

"After she saw you in town, she grew quieter and quieter. She wouldn't eat. Two Feathers said she was dying inside. We couldn't let her go on like that."

"We tried everything, but nothing helped. Then I thought if I told her the truth, maybe she'd get better," Jeff added.

"You told her? Well, what happened? What did she say?" Nick held his breath, afraid to hear the answer.

"She cried. . . ." Jeff started.

"She cried?" Nick asked, his guts twisting.

"First she cried, then she got mad. You know how those green eyes of hers can shoot sparks. She gave me a tongue-lashin' that made my ears buzz. After that she asked me to hitch the wagon and take her to town. Well, I was tickled at first. I thought she'd gotten over being mad and wanted to go shopping.'' Jeff shook his head. ''But when she came downstairs, I found out she planned to leave. She'd changed. She didn't act mad anymore. She was just sad and real quiet.''

''You did try to talk her out of it?'' Nick asked.

''Yeah, but she wouldn't stay,'' Jeff said, sighing.

''We tried to reason with her, but she wouldn't listen. She was bound and determined to leave. Said she'd walk if she had to,'' Jake said. ''Jeff finally had to take her to town.''

''She's in Canyon Springs then,'' Nick said, relieved. Hell, that was no problem. He'd just go get her.

''Well—she was, but she ain't now,'' Jeff said. ''I went in yesterday after supplies, and she'd left the hotel. I asked all over town, but nobody's seen her.'' He hesitated, ''I think she must have taken the stage east.''

''East? Where east?'' Nick felt like he'd just been walloped in the midsection.

Lifting her handkerchief to dab at the dewlike film dotting her brow, Samantha found the upstairs room so stuffy she could hardly get a breath. Too nervous and restless to sit still, she got to her feet and paced the floor. She cast a disparaging glance around the tiny room, trying to divert her thoughts from her present circumstances. She eyed the battered dresser with the discolored mirror and the splotches of red roses blooming on the peeling wallpaper. *A coat of white paint would do wonders,* she thought, but hoped she wouldn't be here that long.

She bit her lip. She had to get out of Canyon Springs

before the McBrides found out where she was. She knew Jeff had been asking around town for her. Nick apparently hadn't returned. She shivered, afraid of what his reaction would be. She narrowed her eyes and told herself it was none of his business what she did. Another part of her said that even though she wanted nothing more to do with him, legally she was his wife.

She straightened her shoulders. She had no choice. There were no other jobs. Besides, if he'd left her on the stagecoach, she wouldn't be here. She'd be where she was supposed to be by now. It wasn't like she planned on doing it for the rest of her life, and even though some wouldn't consider it quite respectable, it was honest work.

She had to earn enough to get a stage ticket. The destination didn't matter as long as it was away from Canyon Springs. Anywhere would do, even though she had no idea what she'd do once she got there.

Noticing a slight wrinkle, she walked to the side of the small iron bedstead and drew her hand over the clean, but faded, quilt top. Straightening, she once again scanned the room. Still shabby, but everything was neat and in order—everything but her life, she thought, shaking her head. It was a mess.

She took her turkey-feather fan from the top of the dresser and waved it back and forth in front of her face. Releasing a disgusted sigh, she closed it. The only thing she'd accomplished was to strew feathers across the floor and muss up her hair. Laying the fan down, she glanced at the locked door. *No, if I opened it, they'd think I was taking visitors.* Shuddering at the thought, she eyed the opposite side of the room. She narrowed her eyes thoughtfully. *Maybe.*

She went toward an opening, almost too small to be called a window, and pulled aside a much-mended lace curtain. She tugged at the warped frame, banging it with her fist until it creaked open. A cloud of dirt and grit from a wagon passing below drifted into the room. Waiting until it went by, she fanned her hand, dispersing the last of the dust. She propped her elbows on the windowsill and leaned out. Taking advantage of the slight evening breeze, she gazed down onto Main Street.

The town had settled into its usual nighttime activity, and with the stores closed, only a sprinkling of townspeople remained on the street. Rowdy laughter and the clink of glassware mixed with the tinkling strains of a barroom piano, luring those with a few coins into the saloons. Diagonally across the street, scantily clad girls from the Red Dog perched on the balcony railing and called lewd suggestions to passing male pedestrians.

Her face flaming, Samantha drew her head back inside, fearing she might be taken for one of them. Her gaze drifted to a man lounging in the shadows across the street. She frowned, remembering he'd stood in that same place for several nights now. His hat was pulled low and hid his face, but she'd seen the tip of his cigarette glowing in the darkness. *What is he doing? Has he been watching my window?* She shivered at the thought.

Loud whoops drew her attention to a group of youthful riders racing down the street. The winners pulled their horses to a sliding stop in front of the hitching rail and yelled good-natured insults to the puncher coming in last. They dismounted, slapping dust from their clothing, and disappeared from sight under the covered porch beneath her room. *Cowboys ready for a Saturday night on the town.*

Samantha smiled, thinking of how much they reminded her of Jeff.

She shook her head, thinking she should hate the mischievous boy for all the trouble he'd caused her, but she didn't. Jeff was just being Jeff. He could no more stay out of trouble than birds could quit singing. It was his nature.

She sighed, closing her ears to the noise, and lifted her gaze to the flame-shot sky. She turned toward the mountains and watched the setting sun coat the snow-tipped ridge of Alta Peak with a strawberry-pink glaze. She lowered her lashes, shutting out the world, and imagined herself back at the ranch at the foot of the mountain.

Sitting in her rocker on the front porch, the night breezes clean and cool upon her face, she would be entertained by the chirping of crickets and a multitude of frogs beginning their evening serenade. A doe and twin fawns would creep shyly from the dark woods to graze on the sweet grasses in the broad meadow. A blend of wildflowers, clover, and sharp pine pitch would scent the high mountain air. Her husband would come and sit by her side and together they would enjoy the peace and the serenity. A little one would stir inside her, and she would smile, knowing it was the perfect place to raise a family.

A tear slipped from under her shuttered eyelid and traced a hot path down her cheek. She raised a finger to wipe it away, along with dreams of what would never be. She clutched her hand to her breast when a pain sharp as a Cheyenne arrow pierced her heart. "Damn you, Nick McBride," she cried. She still couldn't believe she'd been such a fool.

A shrill giggle, mixed with a man's gruff laughter, came

from the room next to hers. The sound, echoing through the paper-thin walls, brought her back to the harsh reality of her present. It was fully dark now and almost time. Stifling a sob, she reluctantly turned away from the window and faced the dingy room.

She walked to the oak dresser and stared into the stained glass mirror, eyeing her image with distaste. Twisting a wayward curl around her finger, she coaxed it into submission, letting it fall in a silken spiral to a point just above her left breast.

Nausea rose in a choking wave. Fear crawled with icy fingers up her backbone, setting her body aquiver. She clutched the top of the dresser until her knuckles grew white. She couldn't go through with this . . . but she had no choice. She couldn't—wouldn't go back to the JMB and be dependent on the McBrides. She had to earn enough money to get a stage ticket, and she'd tried everywhere. This was the only job in town.

The owner had been kind and had given her sewing and mending to do. But Samantha knew a lot of it hadn't been necessary. She knew she could have stayed here without doing anything, but her pride wouldn't let her. She had to earn her keep.

Sighing, she tugged at the low-cut, scarlet dress, but it was no use. It wouldn't cover any more of her if she pulled all day. She spun away from the mirror and sat down on the bed, hiding her face in her hands. The frame under the sagging mattress squeaked loudly, protesting her added weight. The one in the room next door joined in, creaking in a steady rhythm to the moans and grunts of its occupants.

Trying to ignore the sounds, she reached out a trembling hand and picked up one of the black net stockings. She gathered it onto her fingers and pulled it over her slender white leg. Holding it in place with one hand, she picked up a black satin garter with a scarlet rosette and slipped it over her foot to her thigh, anchoring the stocking in place. She pulled on the other stocking and garter and slid her feet into the high-heeled black kid slippers.

She stood, brushed a wrinkle from the short skirt, and turned toward the dresser. She caught sight of herself in the looking glass and shame flushed her ashen cheeks. She looked like a brazen hussy, a whore, just like one of the girls at the Red Dog. "What would Tillie say if she could see me now?" Tillie? The image of an old woman flashed through Samantha's memory.

Visions flew into her mind, reflecting her past like pieces of a shattered mirror. A small, gray-haired lady knelt, bandaging a cut on a child's knee. *Tillie!* "Oh, my dear one, how could I ever have forgotten you?" Tillie, her nurse, had cared for her since the day she was born.

Another vision flashed into focus; long-legged colts frolicking on lush, green pastures; low, red-roofed barns; miles of neat, whitewashed fences; and in the middle of it all, a large stone house. It was her home . . . Stoim Haven!

The visions disappeared in a swirl of darkness. Others, bringing a sense of terror, rushed to take their place. Samantha shivered, grabbing the bedpost for support as her past cascaded in to confront her.

She and a girl . . . Katie . . . ran through the darkness. Someone chased them. Fear rose in her throat, choking her. She stumbled—fell. "Katie," she screamed, but Katie had disappeared. Alone, she ran through the trees. Veils of Spanish moss clutched at her from the twisted fingers of ancient oaks. They wound around her, trapping her in a silvery-green cocoon. She twisted, struggled, trying to escape. Behind her a low, mocking laugh rose to an eerie screech. Helpless, she watched a tall figure drift toward her. Samantha strained to see the face . . . but there was no face. Above the body floated a grinning mask of death. Samantha opened her mouth to scream, but could not utter a sound.

A knock on the door jolted her out of the trance. Her heart pounded painfully in her breast. Dizzy, she fought for breath. She blinked. Her eyes slowly focused, bringing her back to her present. The images were gone, vanished into her past. Once again she was alone. Alone in her room— above Molly's Saloon.

Nick climbed onto the wagon seat and picked up the reins. He hesitated before signaling the team and turned toward the ranch porch to reassure his grandfather. "Now don't worry. I'll bring the supplies back, then in the morning I'll head out after her."

The old man sighed, his face crinkling with worry. "I would feel better about it. No tellin' what she's likely to run into out there." Jake shook his head.

Nick clucked to the horses and headed out the ranch yard toward town. He sighed, wondering what else could happen. She had such a head start on him, no telling where she was by now.

But thank God he'd gotten back when he had. He lifted the reins and guided the newest member of the team away from a tempting clump of grass. He gave Jeff a mental tongue-lashing for giving the other horse to the priest, when he could have bought one for half the price at the livery.

Then he smiled. A green team horse was a small price to pay for a wife like Samantha. Frustrated because he hadn't been able to find her, he forced his mind back to the problem.

It was late afternoon when the buckboard clattered over the bridge and entered Canyon Springs. Nick guided the wagon around a sleeping dog and stopped the team in front of the mercantile watering trough, looping the ends of the reins over the hitching post. Going inside the store, he blinked his eyes to accustom them to the dim light. He took the list from his pocket and handed it to the young, freckle-faced clerk.

The boy studied the paper. Frowning, he looked up and shook his head. "I'm sorry, Mr. McBride. We're out of most of this stuff, including the ammunition. The freighter should be in around dark. If you can wait awhile, I'll get your order filled as soon as the stuff gets unloaded."

"Damn." Nick hesitated. "You're sure he'll be here?"

The clerk bobbed his head. "The stage driver passed him earlier. He shouldn't be more than an hour or two," he said.

Nick sighed. He needed the .44 shells. He'd have to wait. "I'll be back later. The wagon's out front. Get it loaded as soon as you can."

"Sure thing. I'll take care of it," the clerk said.

A faint smile lifted the corner of Nick's mouth. He could use this time to try to find out more about Samantha. He walked back into the fading sunlight and headed down the sidewalk to the hotel. He entered the lobby and approached the desk.

The balding, middle-aged clerk looked up from his dinner tray. "What can I do for you, sir?" he asked, wrinkling his nose like a rabbit sniffing the wind.

Nick leaned on the counter and pushed his hat back on his forehead. "A while back you had a guest here—a young redheaded lady—name of Samantha McBride."

The clerk perched a pair of gold-rimmed glasses on his nose and took the register from behind the desk. He opened the book and ran a skinny finger down the pages. He stopped at a name and peered up. "The only young lady we had recently was Samantha Storm. She checked out," he said, slamming the ledger shut before Nick could get a look.

"That's her," Nick said, stifling an urge to yank the man over the counter and take the book away from him. "Do you know where she went?"

The clerk peered over the rims of his glasses. "We don't make a policy of questioning our customers when they leave," he said primly.

Nick scowled down at the persnickety little man. "I thought she might have mentioned it."

"Well, I don't recall her saying." The man sniffed again, left the counter, and went back to his meal.

Nick spun on his heel and went out the door. *He wouldn't tell me if she had.* He tried the door of the Wells Fargo station. *Closed.* Nick sighed. *Where is she?* With the stage depot closed, there wasn't a thing he could do about finding her tonight. His rumbling stomach reminded him it had been a long time since breakfast. "Well, hell," he grumbled, "I can't do nothing else. May as well get something to eat."

He stepped off the boardwalk into the thick dust of the street, sending it swirling about his boots, and headed toward Ma Greene's. Hearing running horses, he glanced up and jumped for the curb to avoid being run down.

A group of young cowboys raced around the corner. With

wild whoops and a cloud of confusion they slid their
animals to a stop in front of Molly's.

"Saturday night," Nick muttered. He stopped to watch
them for a minute, remembering the carefree days when he
and Jeff used to do the same. It all seemed kind of silly now.
He paused for one more look, then opened the door to the
café. He sighed and shook his head. "Lord, I'm gettin'
old."

Nick's middle felt somewhat better after he'd polished
off one of Ma's steaks, but it still hadn't improved his
disposition. He sighed, draining the last of his coffee.
Damn, he had to find Samantha.

After paying for his meal, he left the restaurant and
paused on the porch to draw a cheroot out of his pocket and
light it. He took a puff and glanced up the street, hoping
to see the freight wagon, but the street in front of the
mercantile was empty. In fact that whole end of the town
appeared deserted. It was late and the businesses had closed
for the night and the proprietors had gone to their homes.

Nick leaned back against a post, envisioning a man sitting
down to supper with his family. His wife, a pretty woman in
a crisp apron, serving up platters full of savory food. A
passel of kids, each trying to finish first and get that last
piece of pie. A deep melancholy settled like an unwanted
coat on Nick's shoulders. The evening breeze carried the
tinkling melody from a saloon piano. Nick, grateful for
the distraction, pushed away from the post and crossed the
street to Molly's.

He tossed away the half-smoked cigar and edged his way
through the swinging doors. Grinning, he walked through
the sawdust toward the bar and slipped his arms around the

middle-aged blond woman sitting there. "Hello, beautiful," he said, nuzzling her neck.

"Well, look who's here," Molly said, turning her head to give him a kiss on the cheek. Her blue eyes danced and her wide smile beamed a warm welcome. "Nick, I was beginning to think you'd crawled off and died. Where have you been?"

"You wouldn't believe me if I told you," he said with a sigh.

"Sit down and have a beer." The saloon owner patted the empty stool next to hers and turned to the bartender. "Joe, give Nick one on the house."

"Thanks," Nick said, settling onto the stool. He picked up the foam-topped mug and took a sip, enjoying the slightly bitter taste.

"I heard you've been away for a while," Molly said, frowning. "Did you just now get back?"

"Yeah, this morning," he said. A rumbling noise and the jangling of harnesses drew his attention to the street. He got to his feet and walked to the door in time to see a large wagon pulled by four teams of mules pass by the saloon. It rolled up the street and came to a stop in front of the general store. "The freight wagon," he said, turning back to Molly. "I've been waiting for it to come in."

"It'll take Charley hours to unload it," she said. "Relax."

Taking his place back on the bar stool, Nick gulped another swallow of beer. Peering over the rim of the mug, he saw the blonde wink at the barkeep. Joe grinned back. Nick's eyes narrowed. He had the feeling something was going on. "What have you been up to lately, Molly?"

Looking like a cat caught with its whiskers full of cream,

Molly laughed. "You wouldn't believe it either." The piano boomed out a loud crescendo and the houselights dimmed. "Good. You're just in time to see our new act."

He glanced around the dimly lit room, surprised to see there wasn't an empty seat in the house. "Quite a crowd."

"Yeah, and this is her first night. She's already packing them in," Molly said, grinning.

Nick finished his beer and sat the glass on the bar top. He got to his feet. "Guess I'd better go help Charley unload, or I'll be in town all night." He reached out and gave Molly's arm a squeeze. "Thanks for the beer."

"You're welcome. But Nick?" Molly called.

Halfway through the door, he turned. "What?"

"Aren't you going to stay and hear our new singer?"

Nick winced, recalling the time he mistook Samantha for the saloon girl. "No, Molly," he said, shaking his head. "I've had enough of your singers to last me a lifetime."

The doors closed behind him as a low, throaty voice started to sing.

"I was a good girl until he came along;
  He told me he loved me, you know he done me wrong;
  He wooed me, he won me, he swore we'd never part;
  He laughed, then he left me, alone with a broken heart."

Nick, his mood improved by supper and the beer, strode down the sidewalk toward the mercantile. It'd been good to see Molly again. He grinned. At least she wasn't going broke since he'd quit drinking. In fact it looked like business was better than ever. He walked along, humming the catchy tune the girl'd been singing. Maybe he should have stayed for a while. She did have a nice voice.

Nick's eyes widened. He froze in his tracks. "That voice . . ." He sucked in his breath, straining to hear the music drifting faintly on the night wind. "Naw. It couldn't be," he muttered, shaking his head. But still, there was something. . . . He whirled around. His boot heels thumping loudly on the boardwalk, he stomped back toward the saloon.

CHAPTER

* 21 *

THE SOUND OF THE MUSIC WAFTED AROUND NICK like a silken bond, drawing him toward the voice. His heart pounding like a blacksmith's hammer, he closed his hand over the top of the swinging saloon door. He peered into the smoke-filled room, his grip tightening until his knuckles grew white. He squinted at the raised platform, fastening his gaze on the slender figure. She was about the right size. "Damn it, I still can't tell," he muttered.

"He laughed, then he left me," the girl crooned, dabbing at her eyes with a wisp of black lace.

He entered the room and edged through the crowd, trying to make out her face. Nick's mouth grew dry when he saw every eye riveted on the luscious figure barely contained in the scanty red satin dress. Her creamy breasts, rising and falling with each breath she took, threatened to overflow and spill out at any time, and her scandalously short skirt barely covered her pert bottom. Long shapely legs clad in black stockings swayed across the stage. The room was so quiet you could hear the men breathing. The tension in the hot air grew ugly, thick, and heavy, as if waiting to explode.

"Alone with a broken heart," she sang, her voice catching in a little sob. Finished with the song, the girl appeared nervous. She lowered the handkerchief.

"Hellfire!" Nick's breath left him like he'd been walloped with a fence post. He would have cussed if he could have closed his mouth. He tried to move closer, but his boots seemed glued to the floor.

She brightened, seeming more confident when loud applause and cheers broke the silence in the room. With a saucy smile and a wink she flicked her skirts and tossed the lacy kerchief toward the crowd.

"It is!" Nick's eyes threatened to pop from his head. Standing there, wearing little more than her underwear, was his errant wife. "Samantha!" he gasped. No wonder he couldn't find her. He'd never thought to look in the saloon. He blinked in disbelief. Shocked spitless, he watched her smile and wave to the drunken men. *Damn woman acts like she'd just finished singing in church.* He clenched his hands at his side, fighting the urge to yank her from the stage and fasten them around her ornery neck.

A growl started low in Nick's throat, erupting in a roar. It was lost in the cheer and crash of chairs as the men fought to possess the discarded scrap of lace.

A burly cowboy jumped toward the stage. "C'meer, little gal. I won't leave you." He grabbed Samantha's arm and pulled her toward him.

Samantha screamed. She struggled to get free, pummeling the man's face with her fists.

"No!" Nick snarled, enraged. "Get your hands off her!"

He charged forward and fastened his left hand on the cowboy's shirt. The puncher, surprised at being jerked away from the girl, blinked once before Nick connected with a right hook. The cowboy's eyes rolled back, and he slumped unconscious to the floor.

Nick twisted to find Samantha crouched on her knees on the stage, her face hidden in her hands. Determined to protect her, he raised his boot to step onto the platform. A wrangler grabbed his arm, pulling him backward. Nick crashed to the floor under two battling cowboys. He ducked a thrashing boot and rolled under a table to keep from getting trampled. "Damnation! She's started a brawl."

Nick crawled from his shelter to see two more men fighting to reach the singer. One walloped the man ahead of him with a bottle. Shoving his victim aside, he scrambled onto the stage and grabbed Samantha's wrist.

Nick struggled to his feet. A chair flew by his head with a rush of air and crashed against the wall. Dodging a punch, he caught a glimpse of Samantha, her top half off, struggling in the man's arms. "That's about enough of that!" he roared. Jerking a checkered cloth from a table, he leaped toward the white-faced girl.

Samantha raised a tearstained face. Her eyes widened. "Nick!" she gasped.

"Shut up!" Nick ordered. He reached out and clamped an iron hand on the man's arm, making him release his grip on Samantha. Enraged, the man whirled toward Nick.

Nick put a boot against the cowboy's shoulder and pushed. The move sent the man reeling backward into the crowd. Nick wheeled to find Samantha attempting to cover herself with the remains of the ripped dress. Grabbing her by the arm, he yanked her against him.

"What . . . ?" she began.

"Not a damn word!" he snarled. He opened the cloth and wound it tightly around her, encasing her in a checkered cocoon. Quelling the mutiny in her eye with a single glance, he bent and hoisted her over his left shoulder.

"Oh! Stop it. Put me down this minute!" she cried, squirming to get free.

"Not on your life," he growled. Furious, he raised his right hand and gave her rear a resounding swat.

"Ow! You bully," she screamed.

"I should've done that a long time ago," Nick said.

The men, hearing her cry, stopped their brawling and rushed toward the stage.

Quick as lightning, Nick crouched and pulled his gun. He thumbed the hammer. The .44 roared. The bullet plowed the floor, sending a shower of wood and sawdust on the nearest cowpuncher. "That's far enough," he yelled.

The men milled about, angry and uncertain. "Who gave you the right to run off with her?" a man whined.

Keeping his weapon on the mob, Nick edged sideways toward the door.

"Yeah, what right do you have?" another echoed.

Facing the room, Nick paused halfway through the entry. Seething with anger, he narrowed his eyes, daring any one of them to move. "Every damn right," he said, his voice deadly soft. "She's my wife!"

Stunned silence met his reply. An uneasy stir began and the men began to scatter. One young cowboy stammered, "Hell, m-m-ister. We d-didn't know."

Nick stepped through the door and slid the gun back into his holster. He stomped down the walk toward the hotel, his boots thumping loudly on the gaping boards. Samantha's body, warm and soft, bounced against his shoulder, reviving memories of other times he had held her in his arms. He tightened his grip, wanting to strangle her, spank her, kiss her, and hug her till she was silly. He inhaled the faint scent of roses, and the fear he'd felt in the saloon rushed back to confront him. What would have happened to her if he hadn't been there? The probability left him weak and shaken. Trembling with emotion, he opened the glass door to the hotel lobby and crossed the room to the desk. He banged his hand down on the hotel bell. The shrill sound echoed off the respectable-looking elegant walls.

"Nick McBride, you put me down this minute," Samantha shrieked.

"Here, stop that racket. What's going on?" the rabbit-faced clerk asked in an outraged whisper. Leaving his partially eaten supper, he came toward the desk. He raised a napkin, wiping nervously at bits of food clinging to his upper lip. Recognizing Nick, he sniffed his displeasure at being disturbed. He slid his beady-eyed gaze from Nick to the wiggling girl. He pursed his lips. "We don't—"

"Shut up and give me a room," Nick snarled, daring him to interfere.

The clerk gulped, his Adam's apple bobbing like a bouncing ball. He shifted his eyes as if looking for a hole to hide in. "That'll be two dollars," he squeaked, pushing a key with a numbered metal tag over the counter.

"Later," Nick said, grabbing the latchkey. He strode to staircase and took the steps two at a time to the second floor. Down the hall, finding the room number that matched the tag, he shoved the key into the lock and gave it a turn. The door stuck. He gave it a kick. It careened open, crashing loudly against the wall. A picture rattled and tilted crazily on its hook. Striding inside, he turned, raised his boot, and kicked the door shut.

Samantha wriggled on his shoulder. Her small fists pounded an angry tattoo on his back. "Put me down."

His dander up, Nick raised his hand and gave her squirming rear another swat. "I ought to give you a good spanking," he said, shaking his stinging palm.

"You dirty bastard!" she screamed.

His ears rang with her muffled curses. "Maybe you need your mouth washed out with soap, too," he said, eyeing the cake of soap by the washbasin. Shaking his head, he walked across the room and tossed her on the bed.

Samantha, a green-eyed spitting fury, yanked herself free of the tablecloth and threw it on the satin coverlet. She leaped to her feet, placing the bed between them. "How dare you embarrass me like that?"

"Embarrass you?" Nick bellowed. He couldn't believe she'd said that. Outraged, narrowing his eyes to slits, he raked her up and down. One side of her ripped dress had fallen, showing the pink tip of her breast. He stalked toward her, his throat tightening until he could hardly speak. "How do you think I feel, finding my wife—in a saloon—singin' half-naked to a bunch of drunk cowboys?"

Samantha's eyes widened. She stepped back, smacking against the wall.

Torn with jealousy, he looked her up and down. "Which one of them were you plannin' to take upstairs first?" he hissed. The very idea of another man's hands on her made him crazy. He took another step, glowering at her. "Or maybe you intended to take all of them."

Her eyes narrowed. Edging to the washstand, she curled her fingers around the handle of the china pitcher.

"Samantha," he warned through clenched teeth.

A mutinous glare on her face, she drew the container back and hurled it toward his head.

He raised an arm and ducked. Air brushed his face. The jug whirled past his head and splintered against the wall behind him. "Damn it, woman," he roared.

Samantha gulped, seeing the fury on Nick's face. His gray eyes turned to shards of granite. His lips drew back over his teeth. She gasped. He looked like a snarling wolf. "Oh Lord," she whispered. Frantic, she whirled, searching for something to protect herself. She picked up the china bowl.

Nick leaped at her, knocking the basin from her hands to shatter on the floor. He grabbed her arms and smashed her against him.

"Let me go!" she cried, fighting for breath. She writhed in his iron grip, her heart pounding.

He laughed, but the sound held no mirth. His grasp tightened even more.

How dare he? she fumed. She sagged, pretending to swoon, and felt him relax his hold. Slumping forward, she rested her head on his muscular forearm.

"Samantha?"

Now! She opened her mouth and clamped her teeth into his flesh.

"Ow! You little hellcat!" Nick yanked free and rubbed his arm.

Seeing her chance to escape, Samantha ducked around him and dashed for the door.

"Oh no you don't," he said, his voice determined. He reached out and grabbed the back of her dress.

"Let me go." Incensed, she twisted, hammering his arm with her fists.

"You like bein' half-naked, why not go all the way?" he said softly. He gave the garment a yank.

Samantha reeled backward with the movement. She heard the fabric rip, then she and the dress parted company. "Oh." She peered down. She was wearing nothing but her scanty silk underdrawers and the net stockings. Blushing pink all over, she turned away.

As she tried to cover herself with one hand, her frantic glance fell on the discarded tablecloth. She lunged forward. Before she could reach it, she felt his cold hand against her near-naked bottom. He gave another tug, and except for the stockings she was bare as the day she was born. Stunned and shocked, she whirled to face him. "Have you gone crazy?" she screamed. She raised her eyes to look into his merciless face.

Tall and menacing, a wild look in his eyes, he placed his hands on his lean hips and leered at her. "Maybe."

She swallowed. Her heart hammered erratically. Cautiously, slowly, she backed away. "You have no right to do this."

His eyes bored into hers. "Well, maybe I do and maybe I don't." He took a step closer. "Did you get the annulment?"

"The annulment?" she asked, dumbfounded. "I'm standing here naked, and you're asking about the annulment?" Her brow wrinkled in confusion. *Why would he be asking about that? Unless* . . . Hurt and rage washed any reason away. Fury took the place of fear. "Damn you! You're still trying to get rid of me, aren't you?"

"Did you?" he asked softly, taking another step.

"No, I didn't," she said, drawing her lower lip into a pout. She inched backward. Her leg bumped the edge of the bed. Whirling, she snatched the tablecloth up in front of her.

"Good." A flash of quicksilver lit his eyes before they again became hooded, dark.

Samantha found herself mesmerized by the gaze riveted on hers. Petrified, she saw his hands go to his waist and unbuckle his gunbelt. She jumped, startled, when the weapon crashed to the floor. She felt like a rabbit hypnotized by a deadly snake, terrified, but unable to move.

In a swish of soft leather his vest followed the gun. His movements slow, deliberate, he unbuttoned his shirt. Again smiling that wolfish smile, he shrugged it free of his muscular torso and flipped it away.

She chewed her lower lip, her eyes wary. "Wh-what are you doing?"

He lifted his foot, yanked off a boot, and threw it to one side. He bent, removed the other, and tossed it after its mate. His eyes lit with a quicksilver gleam. "What I should have done a long time ago." A lock of hair black as the devil's heart fell into his eyes.

Her chest heaving, Samantha brought her hand flying to cover her mouth. She slid her gaze down his bare chest and watched the muscles play beneath the dark skin. His hands moved to his waist. The pants he wore like a second skin dropped to the floor. Shocked, she blinked, her eyes wide.

He stood, naked and proud, fully aroused, his dark head held high. He looked like a savage, pagan god.

"Merciful heavens!" she gasped. She clambered over the bed and raced toward the door.

Quick as a panther, Nick loomed in front of her. "Not so fast," he purred. "We aren't finished yet." A wicked half smile twisted his mouth. He reached behind him. The key clicked in the lock.

A flash of metal flew over her head and landed on the bed. *The key. I have to get the key.* Spinning away from him, she dashed forward. She bent over and reached out. Her hand closed tightly over the cold metal. "I've got it," she cried, whirling. She crashed into an unyielding body. She lifted her lashes to meet hooded, obsidian eyes.

He pried the key from her clenched fist and tossed it across the room. "You don't need that." His hand flashed down. "Nor this."

She gasped as a rush of cool air hit her naked body. Horrified, she watched the tablecloth follow the clinking metal.

He slipped his arm around her waist and drew her toward him, crushing her breasts against his dark chest. As he held her in an iron grip with one hand, the other roamed to her hair. Under his fingers her few remaining hairpins tinkled to the floor. Her tresses tumbled down her back, brushing against her hips. "That's better," he said. His hands slid from her waist and cupped her bare bottom.

She leaned her head back and opened her mouth in shocked protest when his heated, naked flesh pressed against hers. "No! Y—" she began.

He bent his head and covered her lips with his, swallowing her words of protest. He rained her face with hot kisses.

She reeled, senseless, under the onslaught. To keep from

falling, she raised her hands and clutched at his shoulders. His skin was smooth and hard, with the muscles moving like twisting snakes beneath her fingertips. She inhaled, fighting the spark flickering to life inside her. She moaned as his tongue invaded her parted lips, delving, probing her innermost crevices. She clutched his hair, pulling him even closer.

Suddenly she remembered his last kiss when she was on fire for him. Laughing, he'd thrown her on the bed and left. She couldn't give in to him. He wanted her, but he didn't love her. He didn't even want to be married to her. She pushed against him, wrenching her mouth away. ''No,'' she sobbed.

He pulled her against his chest and kissed the top of her head. Strong arms wrapped around her and crisp chest hair tickled her cheek. His heart drummed loudly against her ear. Caressing fingers trailed up and down her hips, sending rivers of excitement up her spine. He tilted her head back, and his tongue, soft as a butterfly's wing, licked away her tears. As he dried her face with kisses, his soft Cheyenne words robbed her of reason. His hands roamed her body, igniting it with newly awakened passion.

Slowly, against her protests, she was swept into the maelstrom that whirled about her. Helpless to resist him, she raised her arms and embraced his neck. She fastened her fingers in his crisp dark hair, drawing his head down, wanting more. She closed her eyes and molded her lips to his in a soul-searching kiss.

''My kitten,'' he whispered softly. He slid his arm under her hips and gently lifted her, cradling her against his muscular chest. He carried her a few steps and lowered her onto the slick satin covers. He stretched his long length out beside her, drawing her against him.

She lifted her lashes to see him watching her, his head propped on his palm, a lazy, crooked smile on his face. He chuckled.

Her eyes narrowed. He was laughing at her . . . again. She clenched her fists and pounded furiously at his chest. "Let me go."

"Never," he murmured. He captured her fists and drew them over her head. Holding them with one iron hand, he smiled and eased his body onto hers.

Gritting her teeth, she tried to shift sideways, to squirm away from the weight that pressed her into the mattress. Her movements stopped when hard knees clamped her thighs, holding her into place.

His maleness throbbed, rigid and hot against her stomach. His eyes, hypnotic as a snake's, fastened on hers. Their dark depths, lit by flashes of silver, drained away her will to fight. His lips, soft and warm, lowered to brush persuasively, again and again, against her mouth.

Her breath caught in her throat. She released it in a low, shuddering moan. He kissed her eyes, her hair, and returned to her lips. That special scent, uniquely his, assailed her senses. He drew his thumb in a tickling trail down her cheek and neck to circle her nipple, teasing it into a taut peak. His palm cupped her breast, kneading it, making it tingle and swell to fill his hand.

The spark he'd ignited deep within her crept with insidious intent through her veins. Along with the fire came fear, the fear that once she surrendered, he would leave her. If only he loved her, but he didn't. Torn and tormented by her emotions, she knew she had to stop him before her senses abandoned her. "Nick," she whispered desperately.

"Yes, Samantha?"

"Please don't do this," she said, blinking back tears.

He hesitated. The darkness returned to his eyes. Then taking a deep breath, he leaned forward and breathed soft kisses over her face and neck. His hand again tormented her breast. His knee separated her thighs.

The fire mounted again with sharper intensity. She knew she should pull away, try to run, but her body refused to obey. "Don't," she moaned, when his hand left one breast to tease the other into submission.

"I won't take you until you ask me," he murmured into her ear, nibbling at her lobe.

"I—I'll never ask you," she panted.

Nick lifted his head, gazing at her from under half-shut eyes. "We'll see." He gave her a crooked smile, showing a flash of even white teeth. His hand slipped from her swollen globe to draw small circles on her stomach. From there it blazed a trail of fire down between her legs.

He kissed her eyelids, her nose, her lips until she was giddy. A lock of black hair brushed against her chin. He lowered his head to her breast. His tongue traced the earlier path of his fingers, circling the nipples. When they were hot and tingling, he closed his teeth gently, teasing each rosy peak.

She arched against him, her body wanting more. "Nick?" Hearing her own voice husky with passion, she opened her eyes. Merciful heavens, what was she doing?

Nick raised his head. Arching an eyebrow, he peered into her eyes. "Yes?"

"Nothing." She bit down hard on her lower lip, hoping the pain would cool her fire. But even as she tasted the salty tang of her own blood, she knew she was lost.

Nick's silver eyes washed over her, asking an unspoken question. He bent his head and kissed the blood away from her lip. He nibbled his way across her face to her ear and, after teasing it with his tongue, kissed his way around her neck to her other ear.

Unable to deny her feelings any longer, Samantha sighed. Closing her arms around his neck, she molded her body to his. She sobbed, smothering him with soft kisses. The hint of a beard scraped her face.

He pressed his lips against hers, parting her teeth with his tongue, teasing and retreating until her own sought him out. His hand roamed up and down the inside of her thighs, consuming her in a storm of desire. He parted the silk-covered mound of her womanhood and kneaded it beneath his hand until she arched against him, every part of her body throbbing with her need.

She writhed and groaned beneath him, but still he wouldn't take her. Her hands fastened in his hair and her tongue lashed his in a frenzied mating. She heard him gasp. Giving her one last, long kiss, he pulled away. She reached up to pull him back. "All right," she said, frustration making her weep.

He leaned back and looked at her. "Did you say something, Samantha?"

"All right," she whispered.

"All right, what?" he asked again, pretending innocence.

"All right." Her hands tightened around his neck, pulling him back down to her. "Nick, please make love to me."

She sobbed, knowing whatever it cost, she'd pay the price. At least she'd have this one night to remember.

Nick smiled down at her. "Oh kitten. I thought I'd die before you gave in, but not quite yet."

Dismayed, her lower lip drew into a trembling pout.

He bent his head and kissed it away, then lapped a trail to each swollen breast. When they were rosy with passion, his head ducked lower to her stomach. "Kitten, if you only knew how long I've wanted to do this."

She gasped in shock as his head sank still lower. He parted the gold hair of her womanhood, uncovering the small pink bud of her molten core. His mouth teased, kissed, caressed, driving her insane. She twisted under him, her body straining for a torment so sweet she thought she might die before attaining it. "Nick!" she cried. Reaching the light, she convulsed. Her nectar flowed forth like lava over a molten crater. "Oh," she gasped in wonder as he slid back up to kiss her lips. "I never imagined."

"Hmm, that's not all," he said with a grin.

"Will you teach me more?" she whispered.

He looked at her, his eyes warm and dreamy. He positioned himself above her and, with one downward plunge, parted her maidenhead, entering her at last.

Her lips against his, Samantha soon forgot the sharp stab of pain. Slowly, carefully, he began to move in her, giving her tender, exquisite delight with every stroke. He moved her with him, conquering her fears and inhibitions. She cried out his name, giving her love without hesitation, without remorse, wanting only to be a part of him, even if it was to be only this one time. Her love for him deepened, welcoming every movement of the strong, sensuous body flooding her with passion. In a storm of ecstasy, Nick took her higher and higher until she cried out, her desire ending, exploding on a fiery peak.

As their souls merged into one Nick arched above her and raised his hands toward the heavens. A wild Cheyenne cry of victory tore from his throat when finally he claimed her for his own.

CHAPTER

* 22 *

NICK OPENED HIS EYES AND SMILED, WELCOMING a future bright with promise. He propped himself on one elbow and fixed his gaze, warm with love, on the slumbering girl snuggled at his side. Her long, dark lashes curled against cheeks tanned to a rosy peach by the Colorado sun. A few freckles, like tiny golden coins, sprinkled across the bridge of her nose. Her mouth, red and full, opened slightly to release a soft breath. He leaned forward and kissed the dimple in her small, stubborn chin. His wife, his mate. *Nick McBride, you're a damn lucky man,* he thought.

Cautiously untangling himself from the long threads of fire-laced hair, he wound a silken curl around his finger and brought it to his lips. She reminded him of a spring sunrise, all warm, red, and golden. Being careful not to wake her, he couldn't resist giving her one last kiss. He sighed, feeling his loins tighten, then reluctantly shook his head and eased out of the hotel bed.

He padded across the floor, drawn to the window by the creaking of wagon wheels and the sound of horses. He parted the drapes and took a deep breath, savoring the cooler morning air. The sweet songs of a pair of larks came from the vacant lot across the way. He lifted his gaze to a splash of bright blue sky and the rugged, snowcapped Rockies looming, sentinellike, behind the purple range of the Sangre de Cristos. A wide grin wrinkled his face. It was a beautiful day. He shifted his attention to the street below him, surprised to see the shops busy with activity.

Usually up before dawn, he couldn't remember when he'd slept past daylight, but then he'd never spent a night making love to Samantha. He turned toward the bed and the cause of his tardiness. Exultation swelled his breast.

What a woman, his kitten. He knew if he lived to be one hundred, he'd never be able to get enough of her. He shivered, remembering how close he'd come to losing her. All those times he'd behaved like an idiot, and she said she loved him. He shook his head, finding it hard to believe.

She sighed in her sleep and snuggled deeper into the feather bed. Nick grew hard and sweet temptation beckoned him to sample more of his wife's charms, but he knew after last night she'd be sore and exhausted. Sucking in a ragged breath, he turned away. Carefully avoiding the broken glass, he tiptoed across the room to find his clothes.

He dressed hurriedly, wanting to finish his business and get back before she woke up. Pulling on his boots, he made a mental list of things he had to do: find somebody to take the wagon back to the ranch, get the shells, and get some stuff for Samantha.

He bent and lifted the red dress from the floor, tucking it into a dresser drawer until he could retrieve it. A wide grin split his face as he remembered how cute she looked in it. He'd like for her to wear it again sometime—in private, just for him. In public he wanted her luscious little body covered right up to her dimpled chin.

Picking up the black garter, he kissed it for luck and slipped it over his shirt sleeve. Using the side of his boot, he scraped the larger pieces of the broken pitcher and bowl into a pile. He smiled, shaking his head. What a night! He should be worn-out, but he never felt better in his life.

After buckling on his gun, he picked up the key and blew his sleeping wife a kiss before creeping out the door. He looked up and down the hall, then turned the key in the lock. He didn't want anyone barging in on her before he got back. Reaching the lobby, he strode to the desk and rang the bell.

The clerk peeked cautiously around a corner. Peering over his gold-rimmed spectacles, he shifted his eyes to and fro, scanning the room. Apparently deciding it was safe to come out, he approached the desk. "Can I help you?" he whispered.

"I just wanted to pay for the room," Nick said amiably. "My wife's not up yet, so don't disturb her." He put two dollars down on the counter. "She'll want a bath later, so here's another dollar," he said, adding one more.

The clerk leaned over the counter. "D-d-did you hear anything strange last night?"

Nick frowned. "Strange?"

The man sniffed, his nose quivering, his eyes wide. "Like Indians?" he whispered.

Lifting his hand to his face to hide the grin, Nick raised his eyebrows and peered down. "Why no," he said innocently. "Did you?"

The clerk didn't answer. Seeing Nick was about to leave, the little man scurried back to his hidey-hole.

No longer able to control his whoops of laughter, Nick

hurried toward the door. "Samantha, I guess you'd better civilize me before we spend any more nights in a hotel."

Not even the gloom of the mercantile could dampen Nick's spirits when he went inside to place his order. "'Mornin', Charley."

"'Mornin', Mr. McBride," the young man said, a pained expression on his face. "I loaded the wagon last night. When you didn't show up, I had Tommy take it to the livery. He unhitched and fed the team for you." He leaned closer, eyeing Nick up and down. "What happened anyhow?"

Nick smiled, feeling like a big lazy cat that had gotten at the cream. "Had some unfinished business to tend to."

"I hope it turned out all right," Charley said, his brow wrinkled in concern.

"Um-hum. It sure did," he said. Not about to answer any more questions, Nick diverted the clerk's attention. "I need somebody to drive the supply wagon to the JMB this morning. Could you take care of it for me?"

"Sure thing."

"I'll also need those forty-four cartridges, a bedroll, and some clothes."

"I think this will fit you," the young man said, holding up a blue chambray shirt.

"I'll take it, but it's not what I had in mind," Nick said. "I want breeches, about so big, and a shirt to match. Oh, and a pair of boots about this long." Nick held out his hands, estimating Samantha's size. "I guess I'll need some ladies' underwear, too, also a comb and a hat."

The clerk raised his eyebrows. His eyes bright with curiosity, he filled the order. He wrapped the clothing in paper and tied it with string. "Anything else?"

"I'll need provisions for a couple of days and a couple of pans. Those will do." Nick pointed to a stack of battered pots the mercantile kept on hand for prospectors and such. "I'll pick them and the other stuff up in a while." Tucking the bundle under his arm, he left the mercantile and headed down the boardwalk to the stable. After making arrangements for horses for him and Samantha, he returned to the hotel.

Deep in thought, he climbed the stairs. He'd decided this morning to take a few days away from the ranch. He grinned. At long last he planned to take that honeymoon he'd been postponing for so long. And he didn't intend to have Jake or Jeff sticking their noses in every time he started making love to his wife.

Samantha sighed and inched over in the bed, seeking the comforting warmth she'd cuddled up to all night. Not finding it, she reached out her hand. The spot was cold—and empty. Alarmed, she opened sleep-filled eyes and peered around the room. "Nick?" She sat up, bewildered. A pile of glass littered the floor, but Nick and all his belongings were gone.

Confusion and hurt brought a rush of tears to her eyes. He couldn't have left her. Not after last night. Not after she'd told him how much she loved him. A nagging fear crept into her mind. He had never mentioned loving her, only wanting her. She pushed the thought away. He'd acted like he loved her. She raised her hand and brushed her hair back from her eyes. "Then why didn't he say it? And why isn't he here?"

She slipped from the bed, noticing the faint red stain on her legs. She flushed, remembering the passion they'd shared. The wild cry he'd uttered when he'd taken her virginity and made her his wife. Wrapping the sheet around her, she carefully avoided the slivers of glass on the floor and made her way to the window. Before she could reach it, a slight noise in the hall made her shift directions.

Seeing the knob slowly turn, she took a step toward the entry. "Nick?" she called. Her heart pounding, she waited. No answer.

Something bumped the door—once—twice—as if a heavy body was trying to force it open.

She eased closer, straining to hear. Was it Nick? She stopped. What if it wasn't? She sucked in her breath. The terror of the saloon rushed back to confront her. Again she felt the horrible groping of strange men's hands on her body.

Boots thudded heavily as the intruder hurried away.

Sighing with relief, she reached out to check the latch. Dismayed, she heard other footsteps approaching and jerked her hand back. When a key clicked in the lock, she flattened herself against the wall.

The door opened, shielding her from the view of the intruder. "Samantha?"

Nick. She released a quivering sigh. "I'm here."

He closed the door and peered at her with puzzled silver eyes. "What are you doing hiding behind the door? I thought you'd still be asleep."

"I woke up and you were gone. Someone tried to force the door." She tried to stifle a sob. "I was afraid."

Nick dropped the bundle he carried on the floor and gathered her into his arms. "Honey, I'm sorry you were scared. It was probably some cowboy had the wrong room." He lifted her and carried her to the bed. He sat on the edge of the mattress and cradled her on his lap, brushing her hair back with his hand.

Samantha clung to him, drawing courage from the strong arms wrapped around her. Tears of relief and joy trickled from her eyes. "I thought you'd left me again."

He tilted her head and kissed away her tears. "Samantha, you are my wife, my love, my life. Don't you know I couldn't leave you, ever?"

"You love me?" she whispered. "You never said so."

An amazed look crossed his face. "You didn't know?"

"How could I? You avoided me. When you did kiss me, you were so angry. You moved to High Mesa to get away from me." Her voice broke on a sob. "You even left town to avoid talking to me."

He squeezed her tighter. "Kitten, I loved you so much, and I wanted you so bad I ached. You were driving me crazy. When you called out for Billy, I was afraid you loved him and were engaged or married and you couldn't remember."

Samantha frowned, puzzled. "Who's Billy?"

"In your dreams you cried out his name," he said, kissing the top of her head. "When I left, that's where I went. I had to find out the truth. I knew I had to find him so you could be happy."

"Did you?" Samantha whispered, afraid of the answer.

"Yes, I did." Nick smiled, sensing her fear. He kissed her again. "He's your uncle."

"My uncle?" Samantha said, feeling a weight lift off her shoulders. Excitement filled her. "Tell me."

"I searched half of Colorado, but finally found Billy Storm, and his daughter, who is your cousin Sally, and your adopted cousin Miguel.'' He grinned. ''I also met a carrot-topped imp named Katie, who said she was your maid.''

''I remembered Katie and Tillie, my old nurse. I even remembered my home, Storm Haven.'' She shook her head. ''Other things are so confused and hazy, I don't know if they were real or not. So much of my past is still a mystery,'' she said with a sigh.

Nick gave her a reassuring kiss. ''You were on your way to Billy's ranch when Jeff took you off the stage. Apparently you thought he had come from the ranch to get you.'' He hesitated, wondering how to tell her the rest. ''You know the nightmares that you couldn't remember?''

A frightened look in her eyes, she nodded.

''Billy explained everything to me. After your father died, you asked too many questions. Lucinda, your stepmother, and her son, your stepbrother, killed him. Afraid you would sic the law on them, they drugged you and held you prisoner.''

She sighed. ''Maybe that's why things seem so confused.''

Nick gave her a gentle smile. ''Your father had lost all his money after the war. Apparently Lucinda and her son decided to get the inheritance coming to you from your mother. But you couldn't touch the funds until you were twenty years old, or married. That's where Matthew came in.''

''Matthew?'' She shivered.

''Do you remember anything about him?'' When she shook her head, he held her close. He couldn't bear the fear and pain in her eyes, but she had to know the truth in order to be free of her nightmarish past.

''You had a bad dream about him, too. He was your

stepbrother. The way Billy pieced things together, Matthew planned to marry you and take control of your money. Tillie, your old nurse, and Katie helped you escape.'' His arms tightened around her. ''That's when Jeff came in.'' He lifted her chin and kissed her lips.

''What happened to the ones who killed my father?''

''They're dead,'' Nick said. ''They died in the fire.''

''What fire?'' she interrupted.

''Listen and I'll tell you. After you left, apparently Katie got worried about Tillie and went back to Storm Haven. She told your Uncle Billy that she hid so they couldn't find her. One night she heard screams coming from the big house and went to see what was happening. She peered through a window and saw Matthew choking your stepmother. The housekeeper—Maugre?—was screaming, trying to stop him, but it was too late. The woman picked up an oil lamp and threw it at him. Katie said the windows were open and the wind fanned the blaze. Before she knew it, the room exploded and the whole house burst into flames.'' He paused, watching her. ''The next day the sheriff found nothing left but ashes.''

Matthew, Lucinda, and Maugre, all dead? Even though she didn't remember them, she felt a strange sadness, tinged with relief. Somehow she felt Storm Haven had wrought its own justice on the three. Suddenly afraid, she looked up. ''Katie? Tillie?'' she asked. ''Were they hurt?''

Nick shook his head. ''They're just fine. Once Katie knew Tillie would be all right, she headed out to find you. She and your stable boy are at Billy's. He's her husband now. They were married a couple of months ago. If you like, we can go up and visit all of them sometime.''

She nodded. ''I'd like that.'' She snuggled closer. ''I

don't care if I ever remember the rest of my past. I just want to put it behind me.'' She smiled up at him. ''It's the present I'm interested in now.''

He lifted her chin, giving her a kiss on the lips. ''Speaking of the present, come here, wife,'' he growled.

Heat flushed her cheeks under his teasing gaze. ''Where did you go this morning?''

''I went to get you some clothes. Fetching as you are in that sheet, I couldn't take you out of here like that, and we have a honeymoon of our own to take.''

A knock sounded, drawing Samantha's attention to the door. She looked questioningly up at her husband.

''Your bath has arrived, kitten.'' He tucked the covers around her up to her chin and opened the door, ushering in a man carrying a tub and a broom and another with buckets of hot water. When her bath was full and the glass removed, Nick dismissed the men. He closed and locked the door. Turning with a wicked grin, he prowled toward the bed.

Samantha, rosy and clean, stepped from the tub into her husband's arms. She giggled, slipping on the suds-splashed floor. ''Looks like we caused a flood. I don't think they designed that tub for two,'' she said. ''But I'd like to have one just like it.''

Nick hugged her to his soap-sheened chest. He leered down at her, fondling her breast with his bronzed hand. ''Hmm, but that was half the fun.'' He scooped her up and carried her toward the bundle he'd opened on the bed. ''Now, would you like to see what I bought you?''

Her passion building, Samantha wrapped her arms around his neck. She drew his mouth down to cover hers. ''Not just yet, my love,'' she whispered.

"Mrs. McBride, you are insatiable," he teased.

"Are you complaining, Mr. McBride?" she asked.

"Never," he whispered.

Pulling him down beside her, she stroked his strong body with her fingertips, giving him a seductive smile when his body hardened under her touch. "Do you still want me to examine my presents?" she asked, arching a brow.

"Later," he growled. He gathered her into his arms and covered her body with his own.

Once again, Samantha, her heart full of love, surrendered to her savage-warrior husband.

CHAPTER

23

DEEP IN THOUGHT, THE BLOND-HAIRED MAN propped his booted heel against the weathered false front of the stage station and leaned back. He fumbled in the pocket of his checkered shirt, took out a cigarette, and lit it. Scowling, he blew a trail of smoke into the air. *What the hell am I going to do now? If only that damned breed hadn't turned up.* He frowned, cursing his run of bad luck.

Voices approaching made him raise his head. Recognizing the man and woman crossing the street toward him, he tugged the brim of his battered cowboy hat even lower over his eyes. Slouching against the building, he cupped his hands over his cigarette, pretending to light it. He held his breath, hoping his lazy pose hid his agitation, but the couple, apparently engrossed in each other, passed on by.

Fastening hate-filled eyes on the pair, he watched them mount their horses and head out of town. He pushed away from the wall and walked toward his bay gelding. Tossing away the half-smoked cigarette, he curled his lips in a thin smile and swung into the saddle. Nudging the bay into a trot, he followed.

Shaken by his close call, he chided himself for not being more careful. He'd been lucky. He had to keep a low profile. His plan depended on it. From what he'd seen of Nick McBride, he couldn't afford to be careless or he'd wind up dead. Noticing the pair just ahead, he pulled the bay to the edge of the road to lengthen the distance between them.

He sighed. Being careful didn't solve his problem. He could bushwhack the breed, but if he didn't kill McBride with the first shot, he'd be a dead man. He had to do something before they reached the ranch, but what?

He eased the gelding out of the brush and trailed from a safer distance. Puzzled, he saw them leave the main road and head north. Why would McBride go that way?

Whatever the reason, it certainly made his job easier. Maybe his luck was changing. He smiled. Staying out of sight, he followed the couple to a spot high in the hills, watching them enter a sheltered draw and make preparations for the night. His smile widened. "I couldn't have planned it better myself." He turned toward a rock bluff and set up a camp of his own.

After they'd disposed of a quick supper of bacon and beans topped off with a tin of peaches, Samantha hurriedly washed the dishes. Stacking them neatly on a rock, she stood, marveling at the high desert scenery around her.

Their camp nestled in a cluster of rust-colored boulders, hidden from the view of any passerby while allowing them to see and hear anyone who approached. Off to one side, edged by a fringe of willows, a snow-fed stream rushed at the foot of a pink-ridged slope. The end of the ravine provided enough grazing for the animals and still the walls were steep enough that they wouldn't stray.

How beautiful and how different it was from the grassy valley below, she thought. She knelt and cupped her hands, lifting the icy liquid to her lips. Drops clinging to her face and lashes, she raised her head, inhaling the faint scent of sage and mesquite from the campfire mixed with the musty odor of wet moss and sand. She'd grown to love this Colorado country with its alpine peaks and high desert, the exhilarating air and broad open spaces. Wild and free, it reminded her of Nick. She couldn't imagine being away from either of them very long.

Just thinking of her husband made her heart skip a beat. She looked around, wondering where he was. She carried the dishes back to camp and sat them by the firepit. Glancing at the stack of wood he'd gathered for the morning, she smiled. He couldn't be too far away.

She paused, watching the fiery sun light the sky with bands of purple, orange, and gold before it sank from sight behind a row of hazy, purple hills. With the twilight came the sounds of the night. Chirping crickets and the deep bass of frogs added their chorus to the singing ripples rushing over rocks in the small, swift torrent. A pack of coyotes yipped in the distance.

Spying Nick in a grove of creekside willows, she strolled toward him. "Hello, handsome. Want some company?"

The bronzed, shirtless man turned and flashed her a smile. "I'd love it, but I'm all done, kitten." He tossed one last limb on a nearby pile, folded his knife, and slipped it in his pants pocket. He gathered the branches and carried them to a spot he'd cleared of rocks and twigs. After arranging the greenery in a neat rectangle, he shook out the blankets and placed them on top. Motioning to his handiwork, he grinned. "Your bed, my love."

"If that's my bed, where's yours?" Samantha teased, leaning over to inspect the mattress.

"Right here." Laughing, he grabbed her and pulled her down with him on top of the covers.

She wound her arms around his neck. "Comfortable, but I don't think we need such a big bed."

"Umm, I think you're right," he agreed.

She nestled her head on his sweat-sheened chest and gave him a kiss. "You taste salty," she said, licking her lips.

"And I smell," Nick added. He sat her to one side and tugged off his boots. "Take your clothes off, kitten." He got to his feet and removed his pants.

Smiling, Samantha unbuttoned her blouse and slipped it from her shoulders.

"I'll help," he said, easing the chemise over her head. He slid his hands down her stomach, unbuttoned her pants, and slipped them down to her knees, leaving her standing in her lace-trimmed bloomers. "Sit, and I'll pull your boots off."

She sat on the blanket and held up her foot, feasting her eyes on the sight of him. Watching the flickering firelight play over his dark skin, she longed to trace its path with her fingers.

He removed her boots, tossing them to the side of the bed. He followed them with her underwear.

Samantha smiled and held up her arms, waiting for him to join her, but he shook his head.

Stepping back, he bowed gallantly. "Care to join me in my bath, my lady?"

She blinked. "Bath? Where?"

His mouth twisted in a mischievous grin. "I'll show you," he said. Scooping her up in his arms, he turned and trotted toward the stream.

Samantha gasped, realizing his intent. "Nick! No! You can't be serious. It's freezing."

"Good. I'll have more fun warming you up." Despite her shrieks of protest, he carried her into the thigh-deep, icy stream and submerged both of them with a shallow dive. After the initial plunge they left the frigid deeper water for the only slightly warmer shallows.

Sitting waist-deep in the water, Samantha soon forgot the cold when she caught Nick, his eyes black as the approaching night, watching her. "Warming up, are you?" Giving him a wicked grin, she scooped up the icy water and smoothed it over his hot flesh. Reveling in the feel of the muscles rippling beneath her fingers, she bathed him gently, but thoroughly, teasing him with her fingertips. He let her have her way until, with a quick intake of breath, a shudder shook his whole body. "Vixen," he growled.

Samantha giggled when he reached out and pulled her down in the water in front of him, drawing her back against his chest. He lifted his hands and slowly, deliberately, spread the water over her skin, starting at her neck. His hands moved lazily down her arms, to her middle. She felt the calluses on his palms as he washed first one breast, then the other. When he had her whole body aquiver with his touch, he slid his hands down, massaging her stomach. She moaned as his fingers slipped even lower, stroking the soft flesh of her inner thigh. "Oh Nick." She sighed. He delved down deeper, and she thought she would burst into flame.

Ablaze with her desire, wanting him, needing him, she turned in his arms. "Devil," she whispered. His eyes burned into hers. She faced him, straddling his hips, and ran her hands along the inside of his muscular thighs, smiling when he groaned low in his throat. His manhood throbbing hard and hot against her legs set her on fire with hunger. "Nick, love me," she pleaded.

He gave her a roguish grin and lifted her to him, filling her very core with pulsating heat. Wet skin rubbed against wet skin, creating a sensation both slippery and thrilling. She fused her lips to his, lost in a world of passion. Warmed by her husband's love, she no longer felt the chill of the water swirling around them. She whispered his name, sobbing with joy as wave after wave of exquisite pleasure joined them into one.

Later, her skin dotted with gooseflesh, she nuzzled his neck as he carried her back to the blankets.

He lowered her gently, as if she were something very fragile and precious, and stretched his long length beside her. His eyes gleaming like molten silver in the light of the fire, he drew her close to him. "*Ne-mehotatse,* Samantha. I love you," he said.

Her heart singing, she whispered, "*Ne-mehotatse,* my husband." They kissed each other's skin free of the tiny droplets, and Samantha worshiped her handsome husband's body, learning new ways to pleasure him. Under a diamond-studded canopy, their loving sighs joined other sounds of the night in a song old as time.

Satiated and exhausted, but too happy to sleep, Samantha turned on her side and bent her elbow, propping her chin on her palm. She plucked a willow leaf from the bed and drew lazy circles on her husband's stomach. "Nick?"

He raised ebony lashes to gaze warmly at her. "Hmm?"

"Would you mind if we got married?" she asked softly.

He quirked an eyebrow. "We're already married, remember?"

"No. That's just it. I don't remember. Do you?"

"No, not really," he said, laughing.

"Could we do it again?" she asked, leaning over to plant a kiss on his shoulder.

"Gladly." Grinning lecherously, he pulled her closer.

She pushed him away. "Not that. I mean get married."

"You really want to?"

"Yes, I do." She nodded, snuggling beside him.

He crossed his arms behind his head and stared at the night sky. "It might be a good idea at that. We only have Jeff's word and that paper. I would like to make sure we're legally wed before our son is born."

She jolted upright. "Our son? You're not serious."

"Oh, but I am. I knew the minute it happened. I'm an Indian, I sense these things," he said solemnly, placing a hand on her flat stomach.

Not that she believed him, but still there was a chance. She hugged her husband's chest. Her head on his heart, she throbbed with its strong beat. "Our child."

"Our son," he insisted, holding her close.

"When?" she asked.

"As soon as possible," he teased.

"Not the wedding," she said. Sometimes he was infuriating. "I mean when did it happen?"

"That night in the hotel."

"But that was the first time," she said dubiously.

"With a Cheyenne warrior, once is all it takes."

"Ha!"

"Woman, don't laugh at me," he said severely.

She trailed a finger down his bare chest. "I'm sorry, my handsome, arrogant savage, but you're half-white, too."

"Not the half that counts." He gave her a wicked grin.

She let out a whoop.

"But since you doubt me, would you be happier if we made sure?" he growled, nibbling at her ear.

"Um-hum," she sighed.

"Well, it's really not necessary,"—he sighed—"but if you insist." For a moment he hovered over her, then his hands and lips began their special magic, carrying her again on a journey to the stars.

CHAPTER

* 24 *

NICK PULLED HIS WIFE INTO HIS ARMS AND GAVE her a hug. "I won't be gone long, honey. I want to see if I can bag one of those pronghorns we saw yesterday." He grinned at her. "Even lovers need something besides beans and jerky."

"But why can't I go?" she asked.

He lifted her chin and kissed the pout from her lips. "After last night, Mrs. McBride, you must be worn-out. I want you to rest today." Even though she tried to hide it, he saw the exhaustion in her eyes. "I'll be back early, then maybe we can take another swim," he teased.

She grinned back at him. "Nick McBride, you are a fiend." She wrapped her arms around him, "But I do love you so." Her brow wrinkled into a frown. "Do you really think you can get an antelope? I am getting a little tired of beans."

"Don't worry, I won't let you starve." He raised his hand and mussed her hair. "I'll be back after a while and then I'll fix you the best steak you've ever eaten."

She clutched his shirt sleeve, her green eyes big and concerned. "Please be careful. I don't want to lose you."

He smiled, holding her close. "Nothing's going to happen to me." He frowned down at her. "You'll do what I told you and keep a sharp eye out for strangers?" Uneasy, he remembered the man he'd seen yesterday. For a while he thought they were being followed, but the man disappeared. Probably just a drifter, but in this country you never knew.

"I won't forget," she promised. After giving her husband one more kiss, she watched until he was out of sight. She sighed, already missing him, but had to admit she was tired. She yawned and stretched her arms over her head. Smiling, she closed her eyes, and the memory of their passionate lovemaking the night before returned, bringing with it a warm glow.

She patted her middle, imagining she could feel the new life stirring there. If she hadn't been pregnant before, he'd drawn her to such heights last night that she certainly could be now. She laughed, recalling his declaration. He'd been so funny. Half-Cheyenne, indeed! But thinking back, she wondered how she could have doubted him. Her heart raced, thinking of the raw sexuality lurking beneath his calm surface. She felt a wondrous sense of peace and contentment wrap around her, knowing that along with his seed, the tall, savage man had given her his heart.

She left the neck of the draw and walked back to the safety of the site among the rocks. They'd been here three days and hadn't seen another living soul. It was as if they had the whole country all to themselves.

She hummed to herself, musing on that thought. Picking up her pack, she walked to the stream and washed her face and hands. She combed the tangles from her hair and arranged it into a thick long braid, securing the end of it with a rawhide thong. Now that she'd finished her toilette, she glanced around. Maybe if she kept busy, she wouldn't miss him so much.

She shook out the blankets and rolled them tightly to guard against any small intruders, then she pushed up the sleeves of her blue cotton shirt and did the dishes in the creek. Finishing, she carted them back to the firepit and sat them on a rock. Sighing, she put her hands on her hips and looked around. The chores were done and the camp tidy. *Now, how can I pass the time?* she wondered.

Hearing the coffeepot hiss and sputter at the edge of the fire, she poured the last of it into her cup. Bringing it to her lips, she grimaced and tossed it out. It smelled scorched and looked thick enough to float a horseshoe. She took the pot to a clump of sage and dumped the grounds.

A sudden chill sent icy fingers up her spine. She shivered. A premonition so strong it shook her very being washed over her. Tense, she turned, slowly scrutinizing every bush, every inch of ground, but saw nothing to cause her unease.

The camp lay calm under the bright early-morning sunlight. Except for her horse and a chattering Steller's jay, she didn't see a thing. She shook her head. "You're being silly, Samantha," she scolded.

She walked to the stream, rinsed the pot, and filled it full of fresh water. She carried it back to camp and sat it on the ledge of the smoldering embers. Even though the morning was quite pleasant, she held out her hands to quell the rising gooseflesh on her arms.

"What is the matter with me? I'm jumpier than a flea in a henhouse." Releasing a deep sigh, she attempted to shrug off the feeling by gathering more wood for the fire. Nothing helped. Her unease persisted. Along with it came a terrible fear for Nick.

Unable to suppress her feelings, she climbed a small hill. Sitting motionless, she scanned the sagebrush and piñon pines dotting the red-earthed landscape. *Nothing but a jackrabbit and a couple of quail.* She shook her head, sighing with disgust. *Probably not a soul in fifty miles.*

But still, she crouched on the ground, unwilling to return to camp until the heat of the sun on her bare head reminded her of the hat she'd left on top of the bedroll. She brought her hand to her mouth. "The pistol!" Under the hat lay the gun Nick'd told her to carry. Guilt-ridden, she scrambled down the hill and hurried to the bed. She shoved the hat onto her head and buckled the weapon around her waist. Awkward and heavy, it did little to comfort her.

Maybe I'm just tired, she thought. She eyed the willow bed, but finding it in the sun, she walked to the creek and picked a spot under the trees. Lowering herself to a patch of sand, she leaned back against a boulder and watched the dappled shade from the leaves play on the water. The soft soughing of the branches and the rippling stream played an irresistible melody. Unable to resist their lullaby, she closed her eyes and drifted off to sleep.

Leaving Samantha, Nick discovered fresh horse tracks. Shaken because they were so close to his camp, he turned and followed them up a rocky trail to the top of a nearby ridge. He approached cautiously, alert to any movement. Easing his gun from the holster, he peered around for any place of concealment, but the area was deserted. He frowned, thinking the hilltop an odd place to camp, especially when water and grass were so close by.

Spotting a ring of rocks against the edge of a bluff, he dismounted and knelt, picking up a piece of charcoal. The ash-covered wood was still warm. Whoever was here had left not long ago. But what were they doing up here? He frowned, uneasy. A fresh boot track in the dirt made him pause. He stepped into it. Almost the same size. He followed the prints to an overlook and found a pile of cigarette butts. He glanced down over the rim. A chill shook him when he realized that with glasses the man could see right into his camp.

"Samantha!" Filled with concern, he shielded his eyes, letting out a relieved sigh when he spotted her small figure busy at the stream. Cursing himself for putting her in danger, he scanned the area. From his position he could see for miles. He scrutinized every inch of ground. "Not a soul in sight," he muttered. He watched Samantha for a few more minutes, hoping she'd remembered to wear the gun.

Uneasy for her safety, he mounted his roan and nudged it into a trot, following the tracks down off the mountain. He let out a sigh of relief when they turned north. Whoever had been there had ridden on. Eager to get an antelope and return to camp, he kicked the horse into a gallop and headed for the ravine where he's spotted a herd the day before.

When he drew near the canyon, he raised his hand to shield his eyes from the glare and peered into the distance. A slight breeze lifted swirls of red dust into giant columns. The heat wavered in ripples, giving an unreal look to the landscape, but there was no sign of the pronghorns.

The sides of the gulch blocked the wind, making it like an oven. Sweat gathered under the rim of his hat and ran in salty streaks down his forehead, stinging his eyes. He guided his horse into the shade of a gambel oak and dismounted. After removing his kerchief, he dampened it with water from his canteen and wiped his face. He took a long drink, then poured water into his hat and gave it to the horse. When the roan had finished, Nick slapped the wet hat back on his head and swung into the saddle. The only thing he'd seen so far was a jackrabbit, but the antelope tracks were fresh. The animals were in there.

He eased the horse forward, then paused beside a thicket. Narrowing his eyes against the glare, every sense alert, he carefully scanned the brush for a telltale white rump. A slight flash caught his attention. ''Damn!'' He ducked to one side.

The bullet whined. Parting the air close to his shoulder, it grazed the horse on the hip. The terrified animal bucked and reared.

Nick fought the roan, trying to bring it under control. Another shot cracked, echoing off the rocks. A brand of fire exploded in Nick's skull. He reeled backward and crashed to the ground, plummeting into a whirlwind of darkness.

The hot sun on her body woke Samantha from her nap. Kneeling by the creek, she splashed water on her face and hands. Brushing a lock of hair out of her eyes, she glanced up at the sun, judging the time the way Nick'd taught her. She frowned. If she'd done it right, it would be about four o'clock. The horrible unease she'd felt earlier returned, stronger than ever. He should have been back by now. She bit her lip. Where was he?

Her heart pounding, she started toward her mare, then remembering her promise to stay in camp, she stopped. Chewing her lip, she raised her eyes to the distant hills. But what if something had happened? The idea sent her heart slamming against her ribs, taking her breath. Her mouth grew dry and tinny tasting.

She walked back to the firepit, wondering what she should do. *He'll be back anytime,* she told herself. She raised her head, listening. A horse running. ''Nick.'' She ran to the edge of the rocks and peeked over the rim.

Nick's roan stretched low, raising a long trail of dust.

''Thank goodness,'' she said, holding her hand over her pounding heart. A welcoming smile on her face, she left the rocks and ran out the neck of the draw to meet him.

The animal raced toward her, closing the gap. The rider bent low over its dark neck.

Samantha frowned, slowing her pace. It wasn't like Nick to mistreat a horse. *I wonder why he's in such a hurry?* She narrowed her eyes, jolting to a stop. *Something's not right.* The pair grew nearer. Her eyes widened. She clamped her hand over her mouth, stifling a scream. *The horseman isn't Nick!*

CHAPTER

* 25 *

SAMANTHA WHIRLED AWAY FROM THE HORSE-
man and dashed toward the safety of the rocks.

The horse thundered alongside. Turning in front of her,
the man slid it to a stop, blocking her retreat.

Fear rose in her throat, choking her. Trapped, she raised
her lashes and stared at the rider. Any hope for escape
disappeared under the cold, malignant stare. "Who are you?
Where's my husband?" Swallowing, she shrank back.

Not answering, he swung from the saddle and swaggered
toward her. "What, no kiss, Samantha?"

She reeled backward, crashing to a stop against a large
boulder. The blood drained from her face and congealed in
her veins. "Who are you?" she whispered.

He removed his hat and leaned toward her. "I'm your
husband. Remember?" Below a thatch of pale blond hair, a
horrible scar twisted his smile into a hideous grimace. His
pale blue eyes glittered with an unholy light. "Recognize
me now?" he rasped.

"Matthew!" The ground under her feet tilted. A sinister
darkness claimed her, dragging her back to the horror. . . .

---

* * *

Samantha, dizzy and weak from the effect of the drugs, eased slowly off the edge of the mattress. She glanced down at the hated white dress. She had to get out of here before he came back. She tightened her fingers on the post of the cherry-wood bed, praying her trembling legs would be strong enough to climb down the trellis. "I'm ready, Katie," she told the small freckle-faced maid.

"Then we best be a-gettin'." Her eyes wide and uneasy, Katie clutched her hand. Raising her gaze, her mouth opened. Gasping, she dropped the satchel. Her hand shaking, she pointed toward the entry. "Oh God. It's him!"

The hair rose on the back of Samantha's neck. Fearful, she twisted toward the door. There, weaving unsteadily in the faint light of the lamp, stood her worst nightmare—Matthew! "Run, Katie!" she cried. Terror lending her strength, she lurched toward the window.

"You're not going anywhere, Samantha." Matthew reeled forward. Clamping his cruel hand on her shoulder, he jerked her to a stop.

"Let me go!" she cried, wincing away from the pain.

"Never!" Matthew snarled. Curling his fingers into a fist, he drew back his arm.

Samantha flinched away from his grasp. She raised her hands to protect her face. "No! Don—"

His blow slammed into her jaw, whipping her head to one side. Agony splintered the side of her face. She sagged to the floor. Her ears rang with his curses. She shook her head and licked her split lip, tasting blood.

He reached for her, fastening his hands in her hair. "Slut. Did you think I'd ever let you leave me?" He jerked her to her feet. He loomed over her, an insane light glittering in his ice-blue eyes. "You're mine. You belong to me." He dug talonlike fingers into the soft flesh of her neck. "I'd kill you before I'd let you go."

Pain scalded Samantha's throat. "No!" Desperately she raised her hands. She raked his face with her nails, felt them rip his flesh.

He smiled like a demon through the blood-filled slashes. He bent her backward, forcing her hands away. His blood dripped, splattering like red tears on the front of the white lace dress.

Excruciating pain tore through her. It disappeared as she welcomed the velvet-shrouded darkness.

"Missy!" Katie cried for Samantha. "Help m—"

The scream reached into her subconscious, dragging her back to the awful torment. She gasped, choking, battling the burning agony for a life-giving breath. She raised a trembling hand and rubbed her injured throat. She opened her eyes, blinking to focus.

Across the room Matthew yanked Katie from his back and slammed her to the floor. He pummeled her with his fists.

He'll kill her. I've got to stop him. Reaching out with blood-covered hands, she dragged herself across the rug to the fireplace. On her knees she grabbed the mantel and pulled herself to her feet.

Laughing, Matthew drew back his arm to hit Katie again.

"No!" Samantha croaked. She groped behind her, closing her hand over the poker. Strengthened by rage and pain, she lurched forward, raising the tool. "No!" she cried again.

A surprised look on his face, Matthew turned toward her.

She brought the poker down. Her arms vibrated from the force of the blow. The weapon slid from her fingers and rolled to a stop beside his body. Shuddering, she stepped around him and reeled across the room. She helped Katie to her feet.

Bloody from her battering, the maid stared past her to Matthew. "Oh, dear Lord. Missy, you kilt him."

Samantha turned slowly, forcing herself to look. There was blood—so much blood. Someone screamed. The room swam, disappearing into a scarlet-rimmed darkness.

Hot pain riveted Samantha's cheek.

"Shut up!" a voice said impatiently. He slapped her again.

Trembling, afraid of what she would see, she raised her gaze to the man looming over her. Her past came crashing back. "Oh, God help me." The nightmare had come true. "Matthew!"

Her hands tied together, Samantha closed her eyes, fighting the exhaustion and pain from the jarring motion of the horse. It had to be a horrible dream. She raised her lashes, knowing it wasn't. Matthew was still here. And Nick . . . ? The breath left her body, leaving her weak. *Dear Lord, what has he done to Nick?* She swallowed. "Matthew?"

He turned, smiling. "Good, my sweet. You're awake. You're feeling better." He brought his horse alongside hers and reached out, placing his palm over her hands.

"Matthew, where is Nick?" Fear made her voice tremble.

"Who?" He frowned. "Oh. You mean that half-breed." He caressed her cheek with the back of his hand. "It's all right, my dear. He won't bother you anymore."

Her heart pounded. Bile rose in her throat. Fear left a bitter taste in her mouth. "Matthew, what have you done to my husband."

He stared at her, his scar growing an angry red. "I'm your husband. He tried to take you from me, just like all the rest." His face brightened. "But now they can't. No one will ever take you away from me again."

"You can't mean—" Her voice broke. "What have you done to him?"

He patted her rawhide-wrapped wrists. "Just what any husband would do when someone steals his wife. I killed him."

"No! No!" Her voice broke on a sob. "Please, say you didn't."

He raised his brows. "All right, I didn't."

She stared at him. An icy fist squeezed her heart. "Where is he?"

He waved his hand, motioning to a distant rise of hills. "Over there, somewhere."

"You said you killed him? How?" She had to know.

He frowned. "I thought you wanted me to say I didn't." He sighed. "This game is growing tiresome, Samantha."

"Will you show me, Matt?"

He shook his head. "No. We don't need to worry about him. I have you now. You're safe again."

"Oh no!" she cried. "Please, take me to him."

"No!" He edged his horse ahead of hers.

Fear for Nick tore her apart. Spasms shook her, erupting, flooding her with tears. "Please, Matthew. I'll go anywhere with you, do anything you say. Please. I'm begging you, take me to Nick."

He turned in the saddle, his eyes like chips of pale blue

ice. "No! I forbid you to say such things. Now stop that noise. I find it quite irritating." He kicked the roan into a gallop, silencing any further pleas.

She twisted in the saddle, fixing her gaze in the direction he had pointed. Horror widened her eyes. "No! Nick . . ." Her words ended in a sob. Above the rugged ridge of hills, dark wings hovered, circling on the airborne currents. "Vultures!"

She didn't know where Matthew was taking her, or what he would do to her after she got there, but somehow it didn't matter. Now nothing mattered. Nick was dead and every part of her that felt and breathed had died with him.

Sometime later, reaching the crest of a hill, Matthew pulled the laboring horses to a stop. Dismounting, he came back to stand beside her. "Let me help you down, my sweet. We have to rest the animals." He drew a small knife and sliced the rawhide thongs binding her wrists. He closed his hands around her waist and dragged her from the saddle. Holding her fast, he raised a hand and pushed a strand of hair out of her eyes. "There, that's better." He cupped her chin. "Oh, my pretty one is tired."

Flinching away from his touch, Samantha trembled. Her legs threatened to give out beneath her. She let out a sigh when he left her and walked to the horses. Her relief was short-lived when he returned a few moments later with a blanket. The very one on which she and Nick had lain and made love. She wanted to shriek at him, claw him, tear his defiling hands away from the cover. But instead, like a wooden doll, she allowed him to guide her toward the shade of a scrub-oak tree.

When he spread the blanket and pushed her down on it,

she made no protest. It was as if she had ceased to exist. Whatever she was, whatever she had been had died with Nick and now nothing remained but an empty shell. Something pushed its way between her teeth and a lukewarm liquid trickled into her mouth. Water. She swallowed.

"There, my dear. Now lie back and rest." Recorking the canteen, he stepped to the horse and hung it over the saddle horn. He walked back down the trail and brushed their hoof prints from the thick dust with a piece of greasewood.

Samantha frowned. He was hiding their tracks. *Why?* There would be no reason, unless he was afraid of being followed. But who would follow? Nobody knew she was out here, except Nick. Her heart leaped. Maybe he wasn't dead. Hope flowed back into her body.

If by some miracle he was alive, he had to be badly hurt. If he wasn't, he would be here. She had to get to him. But first she had to get away from Matthew.

Fixing her gaze on Matthew, she eased herself to her feet and slipped toward the horses. Yanking the reins free of the bush where they were tied, she reached a trembling hand toward the gray mare. The horse sidestepped, bumping the roan. He snorted and nipped the mare's flank, making her squeal.

A shock of fear sent Samantha's heart racing. Blood roared into her ears. She twisted to see Matthew running toward her. She scrambled into the saddle. She wheeled the mare and kicked her into a gallop.

"Samantha! Stop!"

She glanced back to see Matthew drawing a rifle from the gelding's scabbard. A bullet whined, kicking up the dust beside her. She leaned low over the gray's neck. Another round cracked, burning the heel of her boot. She felt the horse falter, then it fell to its knees. She flew over its head and crashed into the dirt, the breath knocked from her body. Stunned, unable to move, she saw Matthew's horse thunder up beside her.

A few feet away the mare thrashed in agony, throwing sand and dirt. The rifle boomed and the gray lay still.

Matthew jerked Samantha to her feet. "You shouldn't have done that." His iron fingers dug into her arm.

She winced, trying not to cry out as he dragged her back to the blanket.

"Stay here," he ordered. He walked away and retied the roan.

Swallowing back her fear, she rubbed her bruised flesh. She'd failed and now there was no telling what he would do.

Coming back to her side, he shook his head. "I told you to rest. Now you are all dirty." He reached out and brushed the dust from the front of her shirt. He ran his hand over her breast again, his pale eyes lighting with a strange excitement.

Her mouth dry with fear, Samantha stepped back. Before she could run, he grabbed at her, yanking her toward him.

Gripping her shirtfront, he shook her. "Stand still. Don't fight me, Samantha. You're mine. I can do anything I want, and you can't stop me." He shook her again. A button ripped from its mooring and plopped into the dirt.

"Now look what you've done." His finger flicked her shirtfront. He gave her a slow smile.

Her heart pounding, she looked down. The front of her shirt gaped open, exposing the tops of her heaving breasts above her lacy chemise. She clutched the torn section, holding it together.

"No!" He grabbed her hand, ripping the shirt apart. He panted for breath. A slow smile spread across his face.

A chill crept over her as she realized the truth in his words. She was no match for his superior strength.

His hands closed over her shoulders and tightened, pushing her to her knees. He forced her backward onto the blanket. "I'm your husband. Don't be afraid of me." He threw his leg over her, straddling her. He gripped her throat with one hand, the other hand stroking her exposed flesh. His eyes narrowed. "You're trembling like a frightened bird. Stop it!" He slowly untied the ribbons of her chemise and drew it open. He closed his hand over her breast. "So soft. So white. I missed you, Samantha. Remember how you loved for me to do this?" His thumb circled her nipple.

"No!" she cried. Nausea rose in her middle. Hot tears welled behind her lashes. She squirmed, trying to push his hands away.

Anger flashed in his eyes. "No! Be still." He gathered her wrists in his hand and held them over her head. Clamping his legs tight against her, he held her immobile. His hand again caressed her breast. "See, you like it."

To her horror and shame she felt it grow rigid. She tried to take her mind away from what he was doing. She concentrated on his words. He acted like he'd done this before, but he'd never touched her. Not that he hadn't tried. He'd attempted to rape her when she was twelve. The stable master heard her screams and rescued her. The old man had died a few days later, apparently kicked by a horse.

Matthew's hand left that breast to torment the other, taunting it into firmness. His breath grew ragged and heavy. His eyes glittered with excitement. He bent his head.

Samantha closed her eyes, willing herself away from the

hot mouth suckling greedily at her nipple. Through his pants she felt a hardness rise to press against her legs.

Her mouth thinned in anger. She was determined not to let him defile her. Filled with loathing, she turned her head, riveting her gaze on a good-sized rock. She attempted to wriggle toward it.

He raised his head. "I know you are anxious, too, my love, but don't be impatient. We can't do it yet. Not here. Everything has to be right, perfect. Just like it was before." He raised himself off of her and pulled her to her feet. He rubbed his swollen front. "I want it, too." His hand closed over hers. Drawing her to him, he forced her palm down over the swelling. "See." He kissed her cheek. "But now it's time to go."

Samantha shuddered with relief when he released her and folded the blanket. She closed her eyes, telling herself not to fight him. No matter what happened, she had to endure it. She had to stay alive. It was the only way she could help Nick.

Matthew kept saying they were married. Told her she'd lain with him. She knew she hadn't. So many things in her past were hazy, probably because of the laudanum Matthew and his mother had forced down her, but one thing she was sure of. She had been a virgin until Nick had claimed her, made her his wife.

Nick. She glanced at the sky. She had to get away while it was still light enough to see, otherwise she'd never be able to find him. She eyed the horse. *No.* He'd tied it so securely this time she wouldn't be able to free it before he caught her. She switched her gaze to the rock, inching toward it. His back was turned; maybe . . . She reached out. Before she had it in her grasp, a hand fastened in her hair.

He jerked her to him, his eyes cold and merciless. "Don't make me angry, my sweet. You wouldn't like that. You wouldn't like that at all." He pushed her toward the horse, making her wait until he secured the blanket. He lifted her into the saddle then slid in behind her, forcing her close to him. He ran his palms over her, stroking her exposed flesh. He laughed when she winced away, knowing she was powerless to stop him. One hand fondling her breast, the other on the reins, he nudged the horse into an easy gallop.

Samantha, numb with fear and exhaustion, watched the late-afternoon sky grow crimson. All too soon the sun would slink from sight and disappear behind the ebony treetops, taking with it her last chance for escape.

She shivered under his taunting fingers, knowing darkness would find her alone with a madman.

CHAPTER

* 26 *

NICK CLENCHED HIS HANDS IN THE THICK DUST. A thousand demons ripped at his skull. He moaned, fighting the red tide of agony burning his senses. A whirring, dry rustling sound reached into the dimness and dragged him screaming back to consciousness. He fought to open his eyes.

The flapping came again. A heavy weight pressed restlessly on his ankle. A sharp pain tore at his calf.

He blinked, focusing on a large black buzzard perched on his leg. Stretching its raw red neck, it turned its repulsive head toward him.

"Awgh!" he cried, jerking back in horror. He raised his other leg and kicked.

The bird lifted its wings and hopped to one side, remaining a short distance away.

Shuddering, Nick rolled out of reach. *Damn stink birds.* He groped for his pistol. It was gone. His stomach lurched. He brought his hand up to cover his eyes. Something warm and sticky covered his palm. He raised his hand, staring at a dark red stain. *Blood. What the hell?* He touched his head, feeling the oozing groove. *I've been shot!* Confusion and darkness lapped at him again. He lay still, fighting it away. He frowned, trying to recall what had happened.

He'd seen the sun flash off a rifle barrel. He'd ducked, but the shot had seared the horse's hip. He'd tried to turn it when another shot rang out. *That must be when I got hit.*

A rush of air made him blink. He turned to see another buzzard join the first on the ground. Gritting his teeth, he grabbed a rock and threw it in their direction.

They hopped in the air, avoiding the stone, and settled again to watch and wait. Their red necks leaned toward him.

Nick shivered and raised his hand. He traced the bloody trail running the length of his scalp. Deep and bleeding like hell, but his skull seemed to be intact. "Whew! Good thing I've got such a hard head." He rolled over and gingerly eased himself to a sitting position. He looked around. Spying his hat, he reached out and picked it up. He brushed the dirt off and set it on his throbbing head.

A wave of nausea and dizziness hit him again, draining his strength. Gritting his teeth, he closed his eyes and waited for the sickness to pass. He glanced up at the sky. More sets of black wings circled, dipping and soaring on the upper winds. He had to get out of here. If he passed out again, he would be done for.

A horse nickered softly.

Nick tensed and rolled onto his stomach. He flattened himself on the ground and crawled toward the cover of a mesquite bush. Had the bastard come back to finish the job? He inched up on his elbows and peered over a slight rise.

A horse. Not the roan he'd been riding, but a strange bay gelding stood head down in a nearby clump of buffalo grass. The animal, clearly exhausted, had been ridden hard. Rings of dried sweat circled its chest. Still saddled, it grazed, reins trailing.

Nick eased to a sitting position and looked around for the rider. But he and the gelding were alone. Apparently the man who shot him had taken his roan and left the bay. He frowned, thinking he must have been in a hurry not to have even unsaddled the animal. Probably thought it was done for, too. Nick whistled then called softly in Cheyenne.

The bay lifted its head. Dragging its feet in the soft sand, it edged toward him. It nudged him and sniffed, shying away when it caught the scent of blood.

Clenching his teeth against the pain, Nick reached out, forcing his hands to grab the dragging bridle. He crooned softly, holding the animal steady with one hand while he gripped the stirrup with the other. He'd only have one chance. If he failed, the horse would bolt.

Gathering his strength, he took a breath and heaved himself upright. Waves of pain sent his head spinning. He lifted his foot. It seemed heavy as a blacksmith's anvil. He shoved it into the stirrup, praying the horse didn't move. He took a deep breath and hoisted himself up, collapsing onto the saddle.

Clutching the saddle horn with both hands, he closed his eyes, afraid to let go for fear he'd black out. When he was able, he opened his lashes and scanned the ground. He stopped and shook his head, wondering what he was looking for. Then he remembered: his gun. Another wave sent his head spinning. His mouth tightened. He couldn't find the weapon. He didn't even know why he was looking. He couldn't get off the horse, even if he did see it.

He found it hard to think and knew he was in bad shape. He'd have to get back to camp and let . . . "Oh God!

Samantha!'' He looked at the sky. Almost dark. He'd been shot about noon. A chill shook his body. The man knew where she was. He also knew she was alone. Nick closed his eyes and prayed she was safe, but a sick gut feeling told him different.

Who had shot him? It wasn't that he didn't have any enemies. He couldn't count the men who hated him. But why would they pick now, unless . . . Cursing, he remembered the scene in the saloon. *Could one of those men be after Samantha?*

He clenched and unclenched his fingers on the reins, resisting the urge to kick the horse into a faster pace. He sighed. He was lucky the bay had lasted this long. When the horse stumbled, Nick patted its neck and called out encouragement. He prayed it had enough stamina to make it to camp. He knew he'd never reach it on foot.

When Nick rounded the last bend and rode into the campsite, it was full dark. An egg-shaped moon bathed the land in a pale light, casting eerie shadows on the clearing. He eased the horse forward. He didn't see any signs of life. Maybe she was hiding in the rocks. "Samantha," he called. He scanned the area, fear gripping his heart with a cold fist. The fire was out, the site deserted. She was gone. "No!" he cried.

The bay, feet spread wide, shuddered beneath him.

Nick slid from the horse, knowing the animal had given its last. He grabbed a handful of mane, holding himself upright while he unbuckled the saddle. Allowing it to fall into the dirt, he fumbled with the bridle and managed to slip it over the gelding's head. "Go on, boy," he said.

The horse, relieved of its burden, stumbled into the

darkness. He'd done all he could for the animal, but he doubted the beast would live until morning.

His head reeling, Nick searched for Samantha's saddle gear and found it gone. Did she hear the shots and ride out to look for him? His throat tightened. He'd lain there for hours and she hadn't found him—and he hadn't passed her on the way back. He closed his eyes, praying that she was lost and not in the hands of the man that shot him. Either way she was in terrible trouble.

"Oh kitten," he cried, fighting off visions of Samantha alone in the dark at the mercy of some stranger. The moonlit landscape swam before him. He fought to stay conscious. He had to find her.

He looked around for signs of a struggle. The pots and pans sat neatly on a rock by the firepit. His gaze roamed the willow bed, seeing only a pile of clothing. The blankets were gone, so was her pack and the guns. *Kitten, where are you?* Using the last of his waning strength, he struggled to his feet and called out again, "Samantha."

The sound echoed mournfully, dying on the night wind.

"Oh God, help me," he cried. He staggered, his knees buckling. He crashed to the ground.

Darkness had settled like a mantle, bringing a sharp chill to the land. The moon tangled in the treetops, gilding the surroundings with an eerie, pearllike sheen. An owl called "who-whoo-oo" from a shadowy clump of brush. Fragrant sage and mesquite mixed with pine pitch, spicing the high mountain air. Matthew had ridden long and hard through narrow hidden canyons and tortuous mountain trails. Samantha, clinging to the saddle horn, drooped with weariness.

When Matthew halted the horse, she raised her head and looked about her. The dark walls of a narrow canyon loomed in front of them. A cold gust of wind moaned through the crevice, cutting her thin shirt like an icy knife.

She shivered, wondering why he'd picked this place to stop. Rocky and windy, it didn't look like a camp site. The thought of spending the night alone with him filled her with dread. Her nerves drawn taut as a bowstring, she jumped when his sharp whistle broke the silence.

When a whistle from the rim answered, Matthew eased the horse forward.

She tensed in the saddle, realizing their destination was near. At least she wouldn't be alone with him, she thought. She trembled, finding very little comfort in that fact. Her heart hammering in her chest, she peered into the darkness. Ahead, a light gleamed from the window of a small shack. A chill crept up her spine. They'd reached the end of their journey.

"Wake up! Shut up that racket," a voice yelled.

Samantha opened her eyes, awakening from a nightmare. A bright sun streamed through the cracks in the door of a rustic cabin. Remembering, she sobbed, finding the nightmare of reality worse than the dream. By now Nick must be dead. And Matthew was her husband.

Filled with pain, she found she couldn't move her tortured limbs. Under the blanket rawhide bound her wrists and ankles where he had tied her to the bed. Her boots were gone. He hadn't taken her last night. After they'd reached the cabin, he hadn't touched her, except to tie her shirttails together, covering her front. For some reason he must be waiting. Her mouth twisted bitterly, knowing that whatever he decided to do, she would not be strong enough to stop him.

She shifted her gaze across the room, where Matthew and another man were engrossed in a game of cards.

Matthew grinned and placed his cards one by one on the table. "Four deuces. Guess I win again." He reached out and raked the pile of money into his hat and set it aside.

Curses filled the air as the stranger, a dirty smallish man, threw down his cards. "I'm out," he said. He screeched his chair backward and rose from the table.

"Where are the things I told you to get?" Matthew asked.

"I stacked everything in that corner with the rest of your stuff." The man pointed to a pile of bundles.

"Excellent," Matthew said with an evil laugh. The scar down the side of his face turned his smile into a grimace.

The small man turned his weasel face toward her. "When can I have her?"

"You are referring to my wife, Weeks." Matthew gave him a chilling look. "No one but me touches her and lives."

Samantha struggled against her ties. She swallowed her fear and tried not to think of the fate looming before her.

"When are we leavin'?" the man asked, standing in the open door.

"In the morning. Unless you can steal more horses."

"Naw. These'll have to do until we reach Salida. I'll see if I kin scare up somethin' fer us to eat." Raking Samantha with his hot eyes, the little man picked up his rifle and slithered out the door, leaving it open behind him.

Samantha took a deep breath, welcoming air not filled with smoke and the smell of whiskey. She watched the cowhand. Would he help her? He might, but the cost would be too dear.

She couldn't stand the thought of another man's hands on her, not after being loved by Nick. They'd had so little time together. She closed her eyes, imagining she was safe in his arms, feeling his strength, his passion, his love.

Tears welled behind her eyelids and overflowed to trail down her cheeks. She thought of all the months they'd wasted. Now he was gone. She couldn't help but wish she'd died with him.

Her stomach rumbled in hunger. She looked at her middle. How could she have forgotten? Nick had been sure his child was already growing in her. What if he was right? Love for the tiny being, a part of Nick, overwhelmed her. A scraping sound drew her attention to the man at the table. Matthew rose and walked toward her. As she felt his strange eyes on her a shiver crawled up her spine.

She looked longingly toward the open doorway. She'd been allowed to go to the outhouse only once since she'd arrived, and now her bladder threatened to burst. "Please, I need to go outside," she asked.

"Of course, my dear." He bent and removed the blanket. He untied the thongs holding her wrists, then removed the bottom ropes from the bed, fastening them like hobbles around her ankles. "If I could trust you, this wouldn't be necessary."

She brought her hands up, wincing at the pain shooting through her. She lifted her hands and rubbed her arms, trying to restore the circulation. She tried to get up but couldn't stand. She felt like she had no feet.

He watched her for a moment, then bent and lifted her into his arms. The movement sent a thousand needles into her skin. She bit her lip to keep from sobbing aloud, but the tears welled over and ran down her cheeks.

Reaching the outhouse, he opened the door and shoved her inside. Filthy and swarming with flies, the place made her stomach roll. Holding her breath against the stench, she finished her business and adjusted her clothing. She opened the door and hobbled outside.

With her balance unsteady and the sharp rocks piercing her bare feet, she made her way to a nearby pine tree. She leaned against the trunk, savoring the short spell of relief from the lusting glances and the smoke-filled air. Soft footsteps crunched on the pine-needled ground. She took a deep breath, watching Matthew's approach. Maybe if she was nice to him, he wouldn't retie her. She had to take the chance. "Thank you," she said.

He narrowed his eyes, giving her a suspicious look. "Ready?" he asked.

"Could I have just a few more minutes?" she begged. Anything would be better than going back inside.

"I guess," he said. He seemed jumpy, uneasy. He glanced toward the shack.

She lifted a shaking hand and placed it on his arm, feeling him tense under her fingers. "Matthew, you told me I am your wife. It came as a shock. I don't remember."

"You are my wife." He ran a finger down her cheek. "You were sick, that's probably why you don't remember. But we are married." He reached into his pocket and took out a paper. He unfolded it and waved it before her eyes. "See."

Samantha's heart thudded dully in her chest. It was a marriage license and it had her name on it.

"Now let's go back. I need to get some sleep. I want to be well rested for tonight," he said.

"Tonight?"

He pulled her into his arms, his eyes lighting with excitement. "It will be beautiful, just like it was before." He ran his hand down her body. "We've waited so long, but after tonight we'll be together forever. I won't have to worry about anyone else ever taking you away." He pulled her to him, lifting her to his lips. His mouth plundered hers in a savage kiss. His whiskeyed tongue crept between her teeth, lashing hers with a tormented movement. He hardened against her stomach. His hands cupped her bottom, bringing her still closer.

Samantha's eyes widened. What if he didn't wait until tonight? She twisted her head away from his and pushed against his chest. "No, not here. You have to rest first," she reminded him. "That way it will be better."

He shuddered, holding her for a moment, then he slid his hands from her buttocks to grip her arms. His breathing rapid, he hesitated, glancing toward the shack.

Samantha's heart pounded. She raised a trembling hand and touched his cheek. "Wait, you'll see."

Matthew stared at her, his eyes wild and strange. "Tonight," he said, his breath rasping. He drew his knife and cut the bonds around her ankles. "Tonight," he muttered, pushing her ahead of him toward the shack.

CHAPTER

* 27 *

EXHAUSTED, SAMANTHA SAT ON THE NARROW bed and hugged the blanket tighter around her, grateful to be alone in the cabin. After eating their supper, the men had gone out to smoke and care for the horses. Her own meal, an untouched bowl of rabbit stew, sat by the side of the bed swimming in a mass of congealed grease. She stared longingly at the open door, but the sound of Matthew's voice told her he sat just out of view. Freedom, so close and yet so impossibly far.

Her mouth grew dry and tinny-tasting with fear as she watched the moon rise and climb high into the trees. Through the cabin door came a soft who-who-who of an owl. It seemed so peaceful. Yet she shuddered, knowing the dreaded ''tonight'' Matthew promised was at hand.

Closing her eyes, she willed Nick's image before her, imagining herself safe in his arms, away from the nightmare about to unfold in the shack. She choked on a sob. This time the vision wouldn't come. For the first time she was forced to face his death. Nick was gone. She was totally, helplessly alone.

Footsteps sounded on the porch and a tall shadow crossed the threshold. Samantha's heart lurched. Bile rose in her throat when Matthew, smiling, entered the room.

He closed the door and went to check a pot of water steaming on the stove. Lifting the kettle, he poured the liquid into a tin basin. He tested it with his finger and nodded. Gathering up a towel and cloth, he carried the basin toward her and sat it on an upturned box. He put a finger under her chin and tilted her head. "It will be so beautiful. Just like before." He pried her fingers loose from the blanket and tossed it away.

"No!" she screamed, cringing away from his touch.

He jerked his hand away. A hurt look came over his face, making him look vulnerable for a moment. "Samantha, I'm disappointed in you." His expression hardened. He shook his head. "Oh well. Have it your way."

Sighing, he crossed the room and removed a bottle from one of the bundles. Popping the cork, he took it to the table and added a measure of dark liquid to a tall glass of water. He stirred it with a spoon and carried it to the bed.

She shrank away from him, staring at the amber-colored glass. *Laudanum!* He was going to drug her. "No! Please, Matthew." She couldn't let him do it, no matter what she had to endure. "I will be good," she whispered.

"We'll see," he said, eyeing her dubiously. He drew her to her feet and untied the shirt. Caressing her, he slipped it off her shoulders. He undid her pants and undergarments and slid them down her legs. Lifting one of her feet, then the other, he removed the clothing until she stood naked before him.

She closed her eyes. Tears of shame and humiliation overflowed and trailed down her cheeks. He dipped the cloth into the water and rubbed it with the cake of rose-scented soap, then washed the tears away. Screaming inside, she forced herself to endure his touch as he stroked and washed every inch of her body. She knew if she survived this night, she would never again be able to stomach the scent of roses.

He finished bathing her and dried her with the towel. "Isn't that better?"

Numb, Samantha nodded. She watched him set the soap aside and toss the water out the door.

He stepped back to her. He sniffed. "Excellent. Now you smell just like you did then." Opening one of the bundles, he removed some lacy underthings and came back toward her. He had her step into the underdrawers and fastened them. He slipped the chemise over her head, rubbing his cold hands over her breasts as he did so. Tying the ribbons, he frowned. "You've gained weight, darling."

She looked down at the tiny hearts embroidered on the lace. Her heart turned to an icy lump of fear. She gasped. The clothes were hers. He'd brought them from Storm Haven. An uncontrollable tremor shook her body, but he appeared not to notice.

He brushed her hair, removing the tangles. He left it loose, hanging to her waist. "Now, my darling, one more thing and I will finish the surprise." He lifted a silk cloth and wrapped it around her eyes, then led her across the room. He pushed her into a chair and tied her hands behind her.

Hearing him bustle about, she tried to will herself to be calm. He hadn't hurt her . . . not yet. But as she faced the unknown, terror clutched her with frozen fingers. Her heart fluttered like a trapped bird beneath her breast. Blood roared in her ears, making her light-headed, luring her toward an uncaring darkness. She fought it away. *I have to stay conscious, no matter what. It's the only chance I have.*

A strange smell filled the room. She sniffed. Candle wax. And something else, something sweet and musky. The smell wrapped around her, making her dizzy.

The door crashed open. Footsteps stomped into the room, stopping beside her.

"Damn you, Redford. You won back all you paid me. I know you cheated. I been watchin' through the window. Forget the money. I'm takin' some of this."

A rough hand closed over her breast and squeezed. Samantha gasped and shrank away.

"Don't touch her," Matthew screamed, running toward her. "Get out! I'll give you what's coming to you."

Hearing them leave the shack, she struggled against her bonds. But it was no use, she couldn't get free. Hot tears dampened the blindfold. A gun roared outside. "Matthew!" she cried.

"I'm right here, darling." She heard the door close and the bolt sliding shut. He ran his hand down her breast as if trying to remove the other man's touch. "He won't bother you anymore. Now, where was I?"

She swallowed, knowing he'd killed the man. She heard a bumping sound like he was moving something heavy. His footsteps hurried around the room, accompanied by the soft rustle of paper and cloth. All too soon he returned to her side. He unfastened the ropes and drew her to her feet. She lifted her arms, intending to take the binding from her eyes.

He slapped her hands. "No! Not yet." He pulled her to him and nuzzled the hollow of her throat, tasting her with his tongue. "Patience, love."

She cried out, frightened when he drew a stiff garment over her head. He fumbled with the back, apparently fastening a multitude of tiny buttons.

"Now, are you ready?" Not waiting for an answer, he pulled the blindfold from her eyes. Dressed in fine, black linen and a silky white shirt, he smiled down at her. "See. Just like it was." He waved his hand around the room.

Samantha blinked, accustoming her eyes to the dim light. Her terrified gaze focused on the bed he'd moved from the wall and placed in the center of the room. The rough blankets that had covered it were gone. In their place lay a white satin brocade spread, turned back to expose snowy-white sheets. She sucked in a ragged breath. Her sheets, her spread—from her bedroom at Storm Haven!

Around the room a multitude of candles and dishes containing a smoldering powder filled the room with light trails of smoke and flickering shadows. A champagne bottle and two crystal glasses glittered beside the glass of laudanum on the now lace-covered table.

Her heart fluttering in her throat, she looked down at her dress. Her eyes widened in horror. A trail of icy fear ran up her back, leaving her a shivering mass of terror. Rust-colored blood-stains spotted the creamy front of the lace wedding gown. "Nooo!" She pulled at it, trying to rip it off. But the fabric was too strong. It encased her body like a satin cocoon.

She raised her gaze to the man smiling down at her. For some terrifying reason Matthew had re-created the nightmare that had haunted her dreams. She opened her mouth to scream, but only a sliver of air escaped her lips. She swayed, her legs buckling beneath her.

"I knew you'd be overcome, my precious." His pale

eyes filled with passion, Matthew slid an arm around her, supporting her. Leading her to the table, he lifted the glass of amber fluid. Forcing the glass between her lips, he poured the liquid into her mouth. "There. Drink."

She struggled, trying to turn away. To keep from strangling, she swallowed. When she'd downed a little of the laudanum, he released her. Quickly, the potion took effect. A soothing languor crept through her veins, robbing her of her will to resist. A light, drifting sensation washed over her, divorcing her from her body, making her feel as though it belonged to someone else.

A slow, satisfied smile crossed his face. "Now, isn't that better?"

She smiled and nodded, trying to remember why she had struggled. Somehow, it didn't seem to matter now.

He popped another cork, filling her glass and another with a sparkling clear liquid. "There. This will take away the taste." He held it to her lips.

She obediently took a swallow, washing the bitterness from her mouth. She took another sip, enjoying the tiny fizzing bubbles. When she'd finished, he set the glass on the table.

Lifting his own, he raised it toward her. "To us, my love. Till death do us part," he whispered. He downed his glass and poured himself another. He refilled hers and held it to her lips, forcing her to drink.

She choked, gasping for air. As she sucked in a deep breath her head swam from the effects of the drugs and the drink. The room shimmered, becoming a wild and beautiful kaleidoscope of spinning colors. An erotic happiness rushed through her veins, heating her blood. She gazed up in fascination at the tall blond man holding her in his arms.

He drew a caressing finger down her cheek. "Breathe deeply, my sweet." As he met her stare a slow, strange smile spread across his face. "Isn't it beautiful? You will soon become a slave to its pleasures. Pleasures only I can provide." He bent his head, plundering her mouth with a sensuous kiss while massaging her tingling body with his hands. He raised his head, allowing her to gulp the sweet exotic air. "And now, my darling enchantress, I will teach you of other raptures, of passions too long denied." Sweeping her up in his arms, he carried her across the room. Molding his body to hers, he lowered her to the bed.

Racing the exhausted bay through the darkness, Nick felt the horse falter then stumble. His heart sank. Kicking himself free of the stirrups, he leaped to safety as the gelding fell, his great heart bursting. Moisture filling his eyes, Nick drew his knife and put the horse out of its misery. He'd never ridden an animal into the ground before and never would have if the stakes weren't Samantha's life.

He knew she was still alive. He'd felt her cries, her terror. They had guided him this far, but now the pleas had faded. The voice had grown faint.

From far off the crack of a pistol sounded. A quiet just as deadly followed. "No!" A coldness closed around his heart. He couldn't feel her anymore. Only an aching emptiness. *Oh God, it might already be too late!*

Like an avenging shadow he slipped swiftly through the darkness, his hunting knife clutched in his hand. Attuned to the sounds of the night, he heard the soft beat of the wings of an owl beginning its nocturnal hunt.

He lifted his head and sniffed the air. Catching a faint whiff of woodsmoke, he ran toward the smell. The pale glow coming from a distant cabin window made his heart leap with hope. "Samantha!" On winged feet he raced toward the light. Gasping, his lungs burning, he faltered. A dizzying blackness washed over him. He fought it away and forced his quivering legs to go on. He had to reach her.

Sick with dread, he saw a small, motionless shape lying in the yard. He knelt by the body. Reaching out a trembling hand, he turned it over. A man, a stranger. Not Samantha. He staggered to his feet. Filled with silent rage, he turned toward the cabin. "Samantha!" he cried.

Leaping onto the porch, he kicked aside a pile of blankets and pushed against the door. Solid and locked tight. His heart sank. He'd never be able to get in. He ran to the small window and ripped away the remainder of the thin, translucent hide covering it. His heart pounding, he peered through the opening. An anguished cry tore from his lips. "Oh God, no! Samantha!"

A voice penetrated the haze, dragging her back from the exotic dream. A vision of a tall, dark man flashed into her mind. "Nick." A rush of love, clean and pure, washed away the dark, heated blood pulsing in her veins. She struggled against the heavy weight pressing her backward into the mattress. She raised her lashes, looking at the man hovering over her. "Matthew!" She raised her hands and shoved at him.

His hands like iron bands, he forced her back. "No! You're mine. I'll never let you go!" He shed the black jacket and tossed it aside. He jerked his shirt open. "See what I suffered? I did it for you. I killed them, all of them—the old man in the stable, your bastard father, even my own mother. All for you, Samantha,'' he cried, his voice agonized.

Helpless, frozen by his words and her horror, she stared at his chest. It was grotesque, reddened and puckered with angry burn scars. Shivering with revulsion, she shrank away.

''No! You are mine!'' His cold hand closed on her throat, pressing her back into the bed, holding her immobile. He lowered himself onto her, his weight making it difficult for her to breathe. His hand left her throat to grip her hair. His mouth ground against hers. His tongue lashed her clenched teeth with torturing insistence.

Sobbing, she twisted her head away. A sudden rush of heat made her scream with terror. His discarded jacket had ignited in a burst of flame. The fire, fed by the packing paper, spread rapidly across the wooden floor. Samantha watched, stunned, as the flames danced closer and closer.

Desperate to reach her, Nick battered the entry again and again with a long, thick chunk of firewood. Finally the door splintered and crashed inward. A thick haze of musky, sweet smoke filled his eyes and his lungs, making him feel strange and dizzy. He coughed, remembering the smell from a Chinese mining camp. Opium!

Fed by the outside air, a solid wall of heat and fire roared to life, driving him back onto the porch. ''Samantha!'' he screamed.

''Nick!'' her faint voice called.

Remembering the blankets he'd kicked aside, he snatched them up. Tossing them over his head, he charged through the blazing heat. He stumbled into a large object in his path.

He threw back the blanket. It was the bed, but Samantha wasn't in it. "Samantha, where are you?"

"Here!" she cried.

He turned, searching the smoke-filled room. He found her. The breath left his body.

The man had one arm wrapped around her waist, holding her body against him. His other hand clutched a flaming candle. "She's mine. I'll never let her go."

"No, Matthew! Please!" she screamed.

Matthew! In spite of the heat, Nick grew cold with fear. Before he could reach Samantha, the man touched the candle to her long white dress.

"Till death do us part," Matthew screamed. Dropping the waxen torch on the floor, he bent her backward, covering her mouth with his own. The flames roared up around them.

"No!" Nick leaped forward, battling his way through the fire.

Samantha sagged in the man's arms. She had fainted.

Nick pulled at Matthew's arms, trying to free Samantha from his insane strength. Horrified, he saw the tiny flames creeping, rising up her skirt. *She's running out of time.* Nick drew his knife and plunged it through the blond man's chest into his heart.

Matthew sank to the floor, carrying Samantha with him.

Prying her free of the man's clutch, Nick slashed at her dress, cutting the flaming fabric from her body. He lifted her in his arms and dashed to the bed. He snatched up a blanket and wrapped it around her to shield her from the flames. Draping the other cover over his head, he picked her up and ran from the building.

Nick staggered a safe distance away and fell to his knees

beside a pine tree. Gasping for breath, his lungs burning, he gently placed Samantha on the ground and smothered the rest of the glowing embers on her clothing. After tearing off his own smoldering shirt, he gathered her into his arms and held her close. He brushed her singed hair back from her forehead. "Oh kitten, thank God I was able to reach you." Sobs shook his body. Unashamed tears flowed from his eyes and dripped onto her smoke-blackened cheeks. He trembled, horrified at how close he'd come to losing her.

The cabin collapsed inward with an brilliant shower of sparks and flame. From inside came an eerie wail, rising on the fire-swept wind to drift around them. "Samanthaaa—"

Nick shivered, telling himself it had to be a trick of the wind. He'd killed Matthew with the knife. Still he drew Samantha closer, grateful that she remained unconscious.

Filled with an uneasy sense of urgency, he carried her to where the horses were picketed and laid her on the ground. He quickly saddled the animals. Bending to pick her up, Nick kissed her cheek. Her skin was ice cold, as was a pocket of air surrounding her.

"Sa-man-tha," a voice sighed.

His skin crawling with fear, Nick scooped her up and ran for the roan. He mounted, cradling Samantha before him. Leading the other horse, he raced away from the area. When they were some distance away, Samantha jerked in his arms, then the cold presence disappeared.

In spite of himself Nick shivered. He'd never believed in ghosts, yet there was no other explanation. With his insane obsession Matthew had tried to claim Samantha even from the grave.

* * *

Back in their campsite, Nick gently removed and burned Samantha's torn and bloodstained clothing, then bathed the smoke and soot from her body. He'd found her legs reddened from the fire, but not burned. Her mental state was what troubled him. She had regained consciousness, but she still hadn't spoken. Although he could feel her terror, she seemed unaware of everything around her.

Having nothing else, he'd clothed her in his extra shirt and wrapped her in a blanket. She lay on the willow bed, her white face gleaming in the firelight. Fear shone in the wide eyes she'd fastened on his.

"It's all right, kitten." His movements slow, he knelt beside her, knowing that in her fragile state any further shock might send her over the edge. He held a cup of coffee to her lips. "Take a sip. It'll help," he urged. He managed to get a small amount into her mouth.

She swallowed and pushed the cup away. She shuddered and looked up, recognition at last dawning in her eyes. "Nick?" She raised a shaking hand to touch his face.

He clasped her hand, bringing it to his lips. "It's me, love."

"But Matthew said you were dead," she cried.

"I was only wounded," he said softly. "I'm here, and I'll never leave you again." He leaned forward and drew her slowly into his arms.

She stiffened, drawing away from him. "The cabin. Matthew. I felt so strange. Oh Nick." Her frightened eyes searched the darkness. "Where is he?"

Nick hesitated then told her, hoping it might ease her fear. "He's dead. He intended to kill you. I killed him instead."

She tucked her head. "He made me drink laudanum. He

burned something—something that made me want to do awful things,'' she said with a sob.

"It was opium. He knew that was the only way he could keep you.'' He tilted her chin. "Samantha, no matter what happened—no matter what he made you do, you're my wife. I love you. I'll never stop loving you.'' He reached out and brought her against his chest, smoothing her hair, comforting her as he would a child.

She stiffened, then sagged against him as the tension left her body. She convulsed against him, choking back a sob.

"Cry, love. It'll help,'' he whispered.

A shiver shook her body, the motion setting free a torrent of emotion. Her tortured sobs ripped through his soul. His own tears fell unheeded on her head. He felt sick, knowing what she'd been forced to endure.

His chest was wet with her tears when finally the weeping stopped. He lifted her head and gently kissed her tear-spiked lashes. "Are you all right now?'' he whispered.

Her eyes shining, she nodded. "Nick,'' she began. "He didn't. I'm not—''

He drew her head back against his breast, his heart breaking. "It doesn't matter, sweetheart. It's over.''

She pulled away. "No. You don't understand. I'm all right. You saved me.''

Nick's pulse pounded. His heart leaped, slamming against his chest. His gaze locked on hers. "He didn't—hurt you?''

"He was waiting until tonight. He wanted to make everything just like it was when I left him. He brought my clothes, my bedding—even the wedding dress—from Storm Haven. . . .'' Her voice trailed off. "He said he was my husband.''

"Samantha, he wasn't. And even if he did force you to marry him, the ceremony couldn't have been legal."

She shivered. "He said he loved me. He killed people to get me—my father, the stable master, the man at the cabin. He even killed his own mother."

Nick felt a chill slide up his spine. "He was insane. His love was obsession. But he can't hurt you anymore. Wrapping his arms around her, he drew her close. He knew she'd been through a terrible ordeal, and it would take time for her to get over it, but thank God he'd reached her in time. Matthew hadn't raped her.

"Nick?" she said.

"What, Samantha?"

"Do—do you still love me?" she whispered.

Amazed that she could ask such a thing, he grasped her shoulders, losing himself in her eyes. "Of course. How could you doubt it?"

"Will you show me?" she whispered, her voice warm and soft.

His pulse racing, Nick shed the remainder of his clothing. He spread the blanket and lifted his wife carefully, tenderly onto the cover. Worshiping her body with his healing love, he showed her just how much.

Dear Reader,

I do hope you enjoyed reading this tale of mayhem and romance as much as I did writing it. Since this is my first book I would appreciate a note telling me whether or not you liked it. Feel free to write to me in care of Berkley Books, or send your letters directly to me:

> Mary Lou Rich
> P. O. Box 101,
> Murphy, Oregon 97533.

A flyer telling of future books and an autographed bookmark is yours upon request and with a self-addressed stamped envelope. Please print your name and address clearly. If you enjoyed this book, tell a friend.

Good reading,

Mary Lou Rich